HARES IN THE HEDGEROW

THE GARDENING GUIDEBOOKS TRILOGY
BOOK 2

JESSICA MCHUGH

Ghoulish Books
an imprint of Perpetual Motion Machine Publishing
Cibolo, Texas

Hares in the Hedgerow
Copyright © 2022 Jessica McHugh

All Rights Reserved

ISBN: 978-1-943720-76-7

www.GhoulishBooks.com
www.PerpetualPublishing.com

Cover by Don Noble

ALSO BY JESSICA MCHUGH

The Green Kangaroos
Nightly Owl, Fatal Raven
The Train Derails in Boston
A Complex Accident of Life
Strange Nests
Rabbits in the Garden

PRAISE FOR HARES IN THE HEDGEROW

"*Hares in the Hedgerow* is as beautiful, compelling and seductive as a haze of lethal perfume. McHugh writes with a level of assurance that makes me utterly breathless."

—Gemma Amor,
Bram Stoker Award nominated author of
Dear Laura and *Full Immersion*

"Expands the fascinating world of *Rabbits* into an inescapable spiderweb of grisly generational trauma. Against a backdrop of cult obsession, McHugh deftly weaves varied timelines and desires into a murderous familial saga."

—Hailey Piper,
Bram Stoker Award-winning author of
Queen of Teeth and *The Worm and His Kings*

"Jessica McHugh's writing, and *Hares in the Hedgerow* in particular, is like a silken noose around your neck— beautiful and horrifying, the softness of the writing lulls you even as it draws you further and further into the darkness, snapping you with a blast of pathos that leaves you broken afterwards."

—Paul Michael Anderson,
author of *Everything Will Be All Right in the End*
and *Standalone*

"*Hares in the Hedgerow* doesn't just pull you in and much as it lures you in and refuses to let you leave. This is part of McHugh's biggest asset; characters that grab you tightly and refuse to let you go. This is Jessica McHugh at the top of her game. Beautiful and haunting."

—Nelson W Pyles,
author, voice actor and creator

For Joni, laughing it all away . . .

PART ONE
1975

PART ONE

1975

CHAPTER ONE

THE CEILING FLOWERED and released wilted wet blossoms that tasted like blood and the boy. Sophie opened wide and swallowed the petals, afraid but unable to stop. There were twinges of the same fear before all this started, back when Liam unzipped his jeans and she lay beneath him on the rock-and-roll camper bed in his sea-blue Volkswagen Kombi. Her mind prickled and perspired over taking such a big step, but anxiety was no match for Liam's lips, his fingers, his tongue and breath repeating, "You're the one, Sophie Francis."

The scene was set for romance that sweltering November night. Splayed out on the conversion bed, jeweled with anticipation, Sophie and Liam shared a joint, a bottle of lukewarm cold duck, and a few hazy philosophies as Joni Mitchell purred from the radio. The wine had its own methods of persuasion, but Sophie's decision to go all the way with Liam LaSalle had more to do with the music. *Court and Spark* was released the previous year and instantly became one of Sophie's favorite albums, so when Joni Mitchell's dulcet voice reminded her of how Liam seemed to read her mind and quell her deepest worries, her choice was simple. Like Joni, she would clear and sacrifice her blues. She would complete Liam. She would complete herself.

He lulled her into a place of writhing worship, and she longed to stay there, safe in his poetic calm for as long as possible, but dread rose again like a clammy corpse from the earth. As Liam worked himself inside, the creature climbed out into the moonlight, every loathsome lump and gouge on display as it howled for freedom.

She was naive to think intimacy wouldn't unearth her secrets. But maybe it wasn't such a tragedy. She couldn't hide the truth forever, not from the man who loved her.

"Oh, he doesn't," the corpse hissed. "This is a fluke. This relationship, this leap into womanhood—it's all a lie. You'll never be anything but a lonely little girl."

Sophie's abdomen constricted so tight against the first thrust she couldn't breathe. The echoing pressure glazed her eyes with spotty film, and once he was buried deep, his body an aching annex of hers, Liam disappeared into the graveyard haze.

She was alone then, paralyzed by the ceiling's strange undulating blooms. The stench of copper and worm-dirt replaced the thick marijuana air, and her brain fogged with gruesome imagery that made her wrinkled mouth tremble in confusion. She cried out and tried to roll away from the molten garden, but no one helped her, no one heard her. Her brain throbbed, her lungs collapsed, and her flesh mawed open to catch the ceiling's sopping jewels.

"You're perfect," he said. "You're everything I've been waiting for."

When the Kombi shed its last petal, and love's pressure was a phantom, Liam's angelic face appeared above Sophie again. She embraced him, shivering, and the bus's rosy glow tapered to a secret place in her mind, a swollen bud throbbing in time with the pain between her legs.

It didn't hurt as much as Dionne said it might, but Liam still looked at her with a guilty pout like he'd introduced her to the concept of pain. Warming with pride, he kissed her cheeks and neck and chest and pulled her into a bear hug.

In the sticky aftermath, wet flora clung to the edges of her mind, and Joni's words turned to sludge. Liam couldn't possibly quell her deepest worries if he didn't know them, and no amount of intimacy could complete her as long as she hid such vile and lovely things from him. She wanted to tell him everything right then, but he wore a hopeful expression like a kid on Christmas morning—the way they did in movies, at least. As the Francises were too poor for lavish holidays, Sophie doubted the look ever graced her face. She envied its ease, its untroubled buoyancy. Liam's beauty was too rare to destroy, and the truth would do just that.

Tilting back her head, she gazed out the skylight window at her apartment down the street. The taupe cube was identical to so many in that part of Concord. It didn't look like much from the outside, but inside, the box of apartments on Mohr Lane felt like a clenched steel fist in desperate need of oil. The cramped walls groaned, and the floors creaked, even while the tenants slumbered. Sophie had trouble joining them once the ghosts in the attic got going. She'd stare up at her ceiling for hours, where remnants of mashed glow-in-the-dark stars glowed faintly in the ravines between stucco like stiff meringue. She had to shine a flashlight at the ceiling for ages to activate the hidden chunks, but it was worth it. The room was pitch dark with her curtains closed and electronics unplugged, and the malformed stars appeared to hover independent of the ceiling, dissecting it with greenish halos. The halos shivered like footsteps in the attic's groaning, but it wasn't from the ghosts who walked the floors. It was Sophie, a different Sophie, every night in the gummy places between waking and sleep.

Her mother told her the attic had been converted into an efficiency apartment that remained unoccupied all these years. Sometimes she attributed the noise to the landlord, whom Sophie didn't recall meeting, and other times she claimed it was just the wind or the wood or her daughter's wild imagination. But there was nothing wild about it. The noises came at mundane times too. While she listened to records, ate dinner, or did schoolwork, a phantom tenant thumped around the crown of the cube.

As for official tenants, there were only the Francis women, Dionne Hamilton and her mother Jackie, and a quiet old man named Mr. Mio who occupied the first floor. It was a drab little cube Sophie loathed calling "home," but tonight she envisioned every inch illuminated by an idyllic Christmas tree in the living room window. She pictured her mother too, hanging brass bells from the curtain rod and singing a holiday song.

Sophie's brain throbbed as she tried to remember if her mother had a nice singing voice—Sophie must've gotten her gift from *someone*—but she couldn't recall the last time her mom sang. Maybe it was another luxury Ava Francis decided she couldn't afford.

This Thanksgiving would be different. Despite budget concerns, Ava promised Sophie a real feast befitting the holiday. Food, music, dumb turkey and cornucopia decorations—the whole shebang.

Sophie hadn't confessed any excitement about the event, but she'd been counting down in secret for over a month. She was afraid if she told her mom how much she looked forward to the day, she'd also confess how much she wanted Liam to be there too. There was no point in asking. Ava would never allow it, and considering she'd follow it up with a mess of flack over her daughter's choice of boyfriend, Sophie decided to avoid the conversation entirely.

Her mom's disapproval was inconsequential anyway. She'd forgotten what love looked and felt like ages ago, along with fun, freedom, and joy. Romance was an even colder cavern in the woman's heart—or so it seemed to a girl whose heart was newly set aflame. She hadn't been in a relationship since Sophie's father, who'd died less than a year after his daughter's birth. Sophie never thought to question the story when she was little, but dark nights under scraped-up stars eventually gave way to speculation, doubt, and fear. The story was no story at all—just a generic tragedy, love gone wrong and left to wither. She knew more about characters in Kris Kristofferson songs than she did about her own father.

It could've been her mother's unwillingness to relive the heartbreak, or it could've been a lie. Despite numerous grand declarations about Ava's first and only love, Sophie wouldn't have been surprised if this "Paul Dillon" was just some guy who drifted in and out of her mother's life.

Sophie's best friend and twenty-two-year-old neighbor, Dionne Hamilton, agreed with her.

"Lots of haystacks in Ohio," she'd said, winking. "Lots of rolling around with farm boys."

It didn't sound like her mom, but people changed, got duller. And if her father wasn't the great love Ava claimed, Sophie felt sorry for her. How awful it must have been to grow up all alone in Nowhere, Ohio only to move to the dreariest part of the Bay Area.

Liam LaSalle was no farm boy, that was for sure. His ride was no haystack, and their love wasn't "just some" anything. The imagined Christmas colors were fading, and beams of orange light shone from the window, stabbing her eyes through swaying vertical blinds. The pain was a reminder—and a warning. Although Sophie had more haunts than her mother had as a child, she'd seen them all. The drive-ins, the old cement factory, and every inch of Sunvalley Shopping Center. After sixteen years, more than half of which she'd been homeschooled, her favorite places looked like haystacks too. They were itchy and arid, and she lost herself all too easily in their heaps, praying she'd be more than another piece of straw. All that time her mother hid her away, was she ever the needle in someone's desperate search? Did anyone hope to raise her to the light and stitch of her something golden and grand?

No. That was an inside job. Like Patti Smith before her, like Joan Baez and David Bowie, she had to craft an artistic life on her own. Every night another song, another sad story to tell. Every night, she lay on her bed, the AC unit sputtering just enough to hold the beads of sweat to her forehead, and dreamed as she sang with her favorites. Her gaze traveled over posters and lyrics she'd pasted over rips in the yellowed wallpaper, and she prayed for an existence with fewer stains and more poetry.

She accepted that art would carve an isolating pit into her life, a catchall for raw emotions and their contagious rhythms, but those excavating muses would never close their fingers around her heart while she was too lonely and ignorant to feel them.

As a child she looked to her mother to rescue her from such thoughts of inadequacy, but either Ava wasn't there, or she was so preoccupied by her own troubling thoughts that she couldn't be bothered to notice her daughter's pain. When it came down to it, Sophie learned more from her former tutor, Moira Shunn, than she ever would from Ava Francis.

She was surprised by how much she missed Moira. She never warmed to the crone—she was dull as dirt and clingy as all get-out—but something about the way she disappeared never sat right with Sophie. Or maybe it was guilt over the way she treated the widow who'd come out of retirement to teach her about civics and division and how knees work. With her mom working nonstop, meeting new people and having new experiences, Sophie took her anger out on Mrs. Shunn. She was cold for weeks after Moira started schooling her out of the Francis home, but as was usually the case, Sophie's standoffish attitude became fiery and confrontational. She threw tantrums and marched around the apartment singing Helen Reddy's "Ruby Red Dress" at the top of her lungs while Moira was trying to explain the Electoral College and other aspects of government policy when she knew damn well Sophie didn't want to hear about a government she couldn't respect. But Moira didn't want to discuss how politicians ensnared young men and sent them off to die. She didn't want to answer for the hypocrisy and prejudices of lawmen or indulge Sophie's assertions that peace couldn't be bought with blood and ruin.

She resented Moira's bland optimism, and how she always took Sophie's cold stares and rude noises with grace and irritating poise before launching into a lesson built around an Emily Dickinson poem that would live in Sophie's bones forever. She didn't know it at the time, of course, because although she remembered liking the poem at the first reading, she didn't give it due credit until Moira Shunn disappeared.

She thought of it all the time now, and she wondered if the funeral she felt in her brain was not only Moira's, but a punishment for Sophie's mistreatment of the missing woman.

Ava blamed music for her daughter's dark and disagreeable moods, and Sophie would of course have to defend every accusation against Jefferson Airplane and Pink Floyd. But deep down, she knew her mom's claims were partly true. Music twisted Sophie's insides into a devious little knot she longed for some slick tongue to untie. In every guitar lick, she imagined a savior's approach, slow and suspenseful like a scary movie that had her scrunched up and trembling, but she knew she'd let him devour her, muscle and bone and brilliance all, wringing hidden joy from her soul until she was left limp and wet and numb to the emptiness she usually felt.

Liam's eyes glistened in the moonlight, and Sophie's heart ached.

She was wrong. She had both music and savior now, and the emptiness remained.

His smile shone with adoration and trust, but she felt neither—only the guilt in having tricked him into believing she deserved both. He kissed her shoulder, her breasts, her belly. His breath was both hot and cold against her damp skin as he whispered, "Was it everything you expected?"

She gritted her teeth. Maybe Liam could handle the truth. He was four years older than her, after all, and a man of the world—a man of Southern California, at the very least, and that was farther than Sophie was allowed to take the BART train. Concord Pavilion was the farthest she'd gone in sixteen years, and it took weeks of begging for Ava to let her see the newly formed Jerry Garcia Band. She suspected her mother would regret the decision the moment she revealed she'd met Liam LaSalle at that show.

Tossing herself into a raucous sea of Deadheads was a hell of a way to celebrate her first concert. Her body vibrated with terror and bliss as Dionne led her across the grounds by the hand, which Sophie didn't release until they reached the front of the lengthy bathroom line. Dionne was stoned and on her fourth bottle of Bud when she said she'd wait outside the restrooms, but Sophie still believed her friend would honor the drunken vow.

She didn't.

The sun was sinking, and ruddy darkness laid claim to the star-speckled sky when Sophie emerged alone. The pavilion teemed with unfamiliar faces, and terror prickled her flesh inside and out.

But then came the music. "I'll Take a Melody" sailed like skate blades across the butter-smooth ice of the rink in Sunvalley Mall. The rhythm pulled her into the crowd until all she could see were bodies like candles, tipped with swaying Zippo flames. Nikki Hopkins merrily meandered across the keys while Captain Trips himself instructed the candles to shine on, and everyone in the audience obeyed.

Except for the tall, lovely boy staring at Sophie Francis.

The young man had lost his lighter flame to the wind, but he ignored Jerry's directive. The wick exhaled its last smoky breath when he flipped the Zippo closed, and Sophie tracked it into the sky where it disappeared in the veil of stars. His face was warm with worship as he broke from the candelabra audience and strode toward her.

Liam LaSalle was a musician and a poet. As they stood on the edge of the crowd, he told her of his artistic pursuits, of his spirituality, and how he'd spent his life searching for something he couldn't define—until Sophie introduced herself, he said.

It was cheesy, but she didn't care. Age didn't matter to him. Experience didn't matter to him. He'd followed a saintly fate to the concert that night, and it led him to her. Everything he said was simple and clean, in calm and honest tones, without a second's faltering. He was steady even now, waiting too long for his lover to answer such a crucial question.

"Yes," Sophie said. "It was everything I expected."

He laid beside her with a shuddering sigh like the keynote of his climax had been waiting for those words. Their fingers intertwined, and he kissed her fist. She mimicked him because she figured he needed it. Lying beside her, Liam sculpted his body to hers, both still glazed in cooling perspiration. He kissed her shoulder, then lay his cheek upon it. The casual intimacy felt like love, and love felt so grown-up.

Liam's fingers danced up her belly like he'd played this game before but never won it until now. The celebratory waltz stopped at her breastbone, however, and he tapped the brass ring on the copper chain.

"What's this thing, babe?"

Sophie pinched the ring and flipped it between her fingers. "It's from a carousel in Ohio, one with a brass ring game. My mom could never win one herself, so my dad bought it for her. On her twelfth birthday, I think."

"Wow. Your parents have been together a long time."

Sophie held the ring to her mouth. It was like an icicle in the balmy car. She couldn't help puckering her lips against it, a quick ghostly kiss before resting it in the notch between her clavicles.

"He died when I was a baby. I never knew him. Never even seen a picture of him."

"Oh, Soph. I'm sorry." He exhaled slowly and traced the ring, round and round, with his fingertip. "I didn't have a father either. Not really. He was there, but I spent a hell of a lot of time pretending he wasn't. He was always angry, always telling me I was wrong in this way and that. He wasn't a good guy, if that makes you feel any better."

She furrowed her brow and sat up on her elbows. "That sounds awful. Why would that make me feel better?"

With a chuckle, he eased her back down and pegged his chin to her chest, gazing up at her with doleful puppy dog eyes. "It's like we were suffering together. Like the only thing that's gotten us through all this shit was our hearts, shielding each other from afar, absorbing one another's pain. Like sacrificial lambs."

She curled her lip and stuck out the tip of her tongue. "I don't know about that."

"But I do. Our pain led us here, to each other, for a divine purpose."

"Divine?"

"Of course," he said. "We're in love. Can you think of anything godlier than love?"

"I can't say I know much about godliness."

His face brightened with a toothy smile. "I'll teach you. I'll help you erase the past like I have."

"Well, I don't want to erase *everything*."

"Yes, you do, and you will, in time." He caressed her face as he whispered, "Your past is important, but only as a means to wrangle the rhythm. The melody, the harmony, the words: they belong to the here and now. When it comes to who you are, you won't find your future on a flimsy chain. You'll find it here, with me." He pushed the ring aside and kissed her chest. "Let me be your choir, Sophie. Let me sing your praises."

Liam LaSalle was easy to love. He stared into her eyes so deeply she thought he might fall in, and she hoped he would. He could paddle around in her, stir up the waters of her subconscious and maybe, just maybe, tame the troubled tides of her mind. But even so, he could only calm the surface. He would still have to contend with the riotous depths Sophie fought tooth and nail to conceal.

She'd done a fair job so far, tricking him into believing she deserved his love, but she couldn't keep it up forever. Someday she'd tell Liam how much his music soothed the savage chaos in her soul, and how safe he'd made her feel that night. She'd tell him she believed he was her savior and that their union would inspire her, even teach her what it meant to be human.

Yes. Someday she would be honest with him about the first time they made love. Someday she would tell him she didn't remember any of it.

CHAPTER TWO

"IT'S YOUR SOUL *that sings. Forget practicing scales. Forget that music can be confined to paper. Forget trying to figure out how to stoke that starmaker machinery. You must first find the harmony within yourself. The melody in your movements, the muscled drum of breath. Without that, instruments are useless."*

Dionne stared blankly, silent as Sophie shredded blades of grass behind Pleasant Valley Motor Movies.

"I guess it sounded better when Liam said it," Sophie added with a shrug. "Anyway, that's why I'm not going to stress about the technical stuff right now. I'll focus on the poetry, the inspiration. Experience instead of expertise."

Dionne tilted her head, incredulous as she twisted a finger around a fat lock of hair. "You don't say."

Sophie tossed the grass into the air like confetti. "Give me a break, okay? Being with him . . . it's like nothing I've ever felt. It's magical. When we're together, the world's more peaceful, more honest. I think . . . " She exhaled slowly, her hands balled at her chest. "I think I love him."

"Of course you love him. You're sixteen."

She grunted. "It's not like that. What Liam and I have is about inspiration and enlightenment. It's about ascending to a higher plane of understanding."

Dionne snorted and patted Sophie's back pityingly. "No, honey, I'm pretty sure it's about fucking."

"Ha ha. Joke's on you. He said all that nice stuff *after* we—" Sophie caught herself and quickly turned her attention to the golden retriever chasing the skateboarders across the back lot of the drive-in. "Come here, Nilsson! Here, boy!"

Dionne howled with laughter and poked Sophie's side. "No way, girl. You're not getting off that easy."

The golden retriever pranced over, and Sophie scratched him behind his scabby left ear until he yipped in satisfaction. The stray had been hanging around their various haunts since he was a pup, and despite Ava's repeated rebuffing of her daughter's adoption requests, Sophie felt like Nilsson was already hers. She'd named him, and she sang him "The Puppy Song" most nights before bed. He followed her home a lot—or used to before Liam started driving her—and greeted her in the morning. She'd even dreamed of him on a few occasions, but not in ways she cared to share aloud. Those cameos belonged with the ceiling gore and the fragility of Mrs. Shunn's skull when Sophie attacked the woman in her dreams. More than a year after Moira's disappearance, she still had those dreams and worse, and she still woke sweat-drenched in abysmal guilt she couldn't understand.

Dionne tugged her arm, and Sophie smacked the ground with such a loud huff, Nilsson bounded away to chase the boys again.

"Fine! Okay! We did it! Are you happy now?"

"Hell no," Dionne said, crossing her arms over her chest. "You bust your cherry with a hot hippie boy, wait an entire night to tell me, and all I get is attitude and 'we did it?' I thought I was your best friend."

Sophie didn't want to make a big deal out of it. She wanted to believe it was just sex—two people connecting on the most natural and primal level—and though she loved Liam and believed their union was more significant than a random lay at a Dead show, it wasn't the most important thing in the world. Besides, beneath the delicious curd of lovemaking sloshed a mysterious whey Sophie didn't want to leak into her life. If she'd seen

Dionne last night, lost in aphotic contemplation about blacking out, she feared she wouldn't be able to hold it in. So she didn't knock on the Hamiltons' door. She instead slunk up the stairs to Unit C, through the dark to her bedroom, where she listened to the ghost in the attic until she fell asleep.

Dionne heard the creaks and thumps too, though not nearly as often. She and her mother Jackie had jobs at Sunvalley Mall that kept them away almost as much as Ava Francis. Sometimes Sophie felt like the only living thing in the cube on Mohr Lane. Even all those years Moira craned over her shoulder like a gargoyle clinging to a slippery moss ledge, Sophie felt like the ghost in the attic. Alone and trapped.

She had more freedom now, of course. After years of homeschooling, Ygnacio Valley High was a dream come true. For about a day. All at once Sophie's clothes had hidden value and told stories about her home life. Her thoughts on the Vietnam War spoke volumes about her patriotism—or lack thereof—and conversations about her favorite singers and bands turned her insides out, revealing secret organs she didn't know were there, pulsating fists of flesh pushing her to some hideous end. She couldn't see it, but everyone else could. If they couldn't, they would soon. Just like Moira Shunn.

The heft of the woman's memory made it difficult to shrug at Dionne. "It was too late to knock. I thought about catching you this morning, but I didn't want to barge into the Robin Hood while you were working with my mom."

"That's fair." Uncoiling the hair from her finger, she crinkled her nose. "But you *know* I would've told *you* if *I* had a new man in my life. Though I guess I'd have to find one first." She shouted at the boys kick-flipping over a line of dented cans. "Ya hear that, Addy? I'm gonna find me a new man!"

Adam and Trey skidded to a halt and swiveled at Dionne's comment. Adam kicked up his banana board and tucked it under his arm as he strode to her, his shades sliding down his nose with each step.

"Hey, no badmouthing me while I'm trying to show off," he said, readjusting his sunglasses.

She waved her hands in surrender. "Sorry, man. The last thing I wanna do is throw off your flow while you're getting cozy with this fool."

Adam scrunched his nose in disgust, but the insinuation didn't register with Trey.

He said, "That's mighty groovy of you," and smacked Adam's ass with his board.

Adam playfully shoved his friend away before whipping out his own board, leaping onto it in mid-air, and grinding a nearby bike rack for a few seconds before wobbling off.

Adam and Trey were junior high dropouts, which meant they had an educational edge on Sophie. Despite her mother's assertions that kids like them were below her, they'd forgotten more about American history than she'd ever learned. Or maybe she'd just missed those lessons from Mrs. Shunn because her attention was elsewhere, out the window, ripping up the soil of the aching earth to see the wrinkled red flesh beneath.

Mr. Rivers popped out of the dilapidated Motor Movies snack shack, his jowls waving like mud flaps as he shouted for the kids to scram.

Sophie sighed. Rivers was right on schedule. His tirade pushed them from their spot behind the weathered movie screen to the smokestack beyond The Crossings and the old Cowell Cement Plant. They could've gone to the pond after that, or to Bancroft to hang out under the BART rails. The afternoons were theirs, but the kids of Concord resigned their evenings to voices on the wind: mothers and fathers calling them home, sometimes pimply older brothers home from college who wanted company cruising for baby groupies at the Iggy Pop show.

But Ava Francis wasn't a typical part of the choir that

raised its voices at night, and Sophie wasn't likely to hear it for most of the evenings during Thanksgiving break. Her mom frequently picked up shifts at both JCPenney and the Robin Hood bar in the mall, keeping her either away from home or too exhausted to do anything when she did return to the apartment. Sophie spent years trying to convince herself that her mother's long hours had more to do with money than a secret distaste for her daughter's presence, but she wasn't as successful as she pretended in front of Dionne or Liam—sometimes even to herself. She thought about it too much, all the loose knots, all the little threads, frayed and fluttering on her life's perimeter, and try as she might, she couldn't push the poisonous notions from her mind. She was sure her mother could see them, like tumors roiling just below the surface. The kids at Ygnacio Valley, too. She tried harder there; mostly by keeping to herself, watching the other kids and mimicking their behavior while trying not to get worked up.

That was easier said than done, apparently. Public school was tougher than she'd expected. The homework alone was dizzying, and long hours without the numerous breaks granted by Mrs. Shunn left her incapable of patience or pretense. When her head ached, she gripped it with both hands. When her knees weakened, she sat on the floor. And when her mind clouded like the slow diffusion of octopus ink in a tank, she ran away. The girls bathroom proved a good hiding spot to wait through the spells, but she'd nearly been discovered a few weeks ago when a janitor found her passed out on the floor of a stall.

She hadn't done anything bad during her blackout that time. Or maybe, she pondered in sweaty terror, she'd learned to cover all her tracks.

It had happened before. She assumed it would happen again.

But her mother didn't and couldn't be allowed to find out. If she learned Sophie was still having blackouts, she'd rip her out of school without a second thought. High school was disappointing for the most part, but after so many years of begging and blaming her mother for isolation, Sophie couldn't bear to admit she was wrong.

Maybe she just needed more time. Being around kids her age had to be healthier than being confined to the quadrangular prison on Mohr Lane. As much as she loved having Dionne as a friend, her job and their six-year age difference kept them at an inexorable distance. Her mom Jackie was nice too, but attending night school and working a full-time job kept Mrs. Hamilton away almost as much as her own mother.

The other tenant probably wouldn't have socialized with Sophie even if they were the same age. Mr. Mio rarely made a peep from his bottom floor apartment, and since his curtains remained closed most of the time, Sophie usually only spotted the man when he was working a shift at Sunvalley Cinema. Even there, Mio seldom regarded her with more than a nod. It wasn't a "how do you do" nod either. More of an "I'll thank you not to contaminate my day with false respect or wonder, take your popcorn and go" sort of nod.

This dismissive bob was common in her day-to-day. Maybe it was a grown-up thing, or a lonely person thing. Or maybe it was just her: a weird combination of pheromones sending out signals to anyone who approached that treating Sophie Francis with kindness simply wasn't worth the trouble.

Then there was Liam, who'd been inside her and wanted to go deeper.

More kindness, more trouble.

His love allowed her to be objective when it seemed all the world's expressions slumped because of her. He reminded her that there were greater forces at work. Despite her habit of taking on blame like a sinking ship takes on water, Sophie wasn't oblivious to the reasons why frustration commanded the muscles in her mother's face when they were together. How could Sophie downplay the difficulty in single motherhood, especially for a then-eighteen-year-old middle-American farm girl living alone on the west coast?

It was admirable, really. After Sophie's father died, Ava could've buckled. She could've given up her baby, scraped together what remained of her teenage years and started over—a free woman at the start of the swinging sixties. Maybe she would've been happier. Maybe she would've been a better mother to the next kid.

Sophie massaged her temples as her crew and their faithful hound crossed onto the loose gravel surrounding the smokestack of the old Cowell cement factory. It hadn't been active since the forties, unless to house passing artists, vagrants, and stoners, but the place still stunk of smoke. It came from the throats of her fellow artist-vagrant-stoners, yes, but there was something scorched and still searing in the smokestack's shadow, and it cast a cinderous net about Sophie Francis. It singed her nostrils, though worse from a distance. Up close, in the heart of the fire, the scent was sumptuous as freshly baked bread. Homey. Enticing.

She searched for a patch of shade as Nilsson barked joyfully in pursuit, but the best places were taken. Seniors from Ygnacio had the prime spot, under the darkest blotch in the heavens where they could survey the pockets of kids stationed around the gulch. They passed a joint and cackled. A few swayed and snapped their fingers while a girl with a platinum Bardot cut sang a passable rendition of "Tangled Up in Blue".

She and Dionne chose a spot on the sunny side of the stack. Leaning against the concrete, Sophie heard people inside the old chimney—hanging out on couches and beanbags, if the rumors were true. She hoped one day to confirm them, but the notion of embarrassing herself in front of the cool kids kept her outside. As she lay her jacket beside the pillar of Americana, Nilsson barked and whipped his slobbery tongue across her cheek. She

20

laughed, wiping away the compliment and scratching him behind the ear before he bounded away to chase the boys.

Dionne sighed as she watched them, and Sophie rested her head on her friend's shoulder.

"What's the fuss, Gus?"

"Oh." She exhaled heavily. "Life. Thanksgiving. You know."

Sophie often obsessed about the fussy frustrations of life, but for the first time in years she wasn't dreading Thanksgiving. Remembering her mom's promise accelerated her heart and curled one side of her mouth.

"I wish you worked at the mall," Dionne said. "Crazy barfly season has officially begun at the Robin Hood, and I don't know if I can take another year. Thanksgiving really messes with those weirdos' heads. With some of the shit they say, sometimes I think I'm gonna lose it, throw drinks in their faces and smack 'em silly."

"I doubt you're alone in that. I've heard some horror stories from my mom."

"I wish I had her patience," Dionne said. "She never loses it; hardly even complains. That woman's a damn saint."

Sophie tossed a clod of dirt across the lot. "I wouldn't go that far."

"I would. No fooling. I've seen her yelled at, swung at. I even saw some jackass toss his vodka tonic at her. All that, and she hasn't broken once. Keeps on smiling, hardly even raises her voice. Whatever zen shit she's smoking, you gotta get me some."

Sophie scoffed. "My mom doesn't even drink. I doubt she's toking up in Sunvalley Mall."

"Could be pills," Dionne said, bobbing her head.

"Doubtful."

"Maybe she got herself a man," she said, winking. "It sure calmed your ass down."

A frenzy of appalled shivers overtook Sophie's body, and she shook her head. "You've *met* my mom, right? I don't think she even notices men anymore."

Trey skated over on a cloud of pungent smoke. "I still notice *her*," he said with a braying laugh. "Your mom's foxy as hell."

Sophie gagged. Though she supposed her mother was objectively attractive, she didn't want anyone thinking of her like that.

Like Sophie, Ava Francis had an athletic physique, and despite her slender frame, ropy muscles ran up her legs and upper arms. Her jet-black shoulder-length hair glistened with sporadic silver strands that framed her square face, and though her lips were paler than her daughter's, they were fuller and lived beautifully in their baby pink pout. So there was nothing aesthetically *unappealing* about Ava, but she was missing something that kept her from reaching the heights of "foxy." She was missing a spark—the kind that welcomed opportunity with open arms, or pulled someone into a crowd lit like candle flame.

Or maybe Sophie just didn't see it. Maybe her mom had the spark with other people, away from the cage on Mohr Lane and her freakish daughter. But why? If her mother threw out smiles willy-nilly for the mean old drunks at the Robin Hood, why couldn't she save one for her daughter?

Then again, Sophie hadn't exactly been generous with genuine smiles either. Very few meant more than: "I see you still exist. I guess that's a good thing."

Their interactions were more civilized following Sophie's return to public school, but a palpable tension remained, like the feeling of her throat tightening to hold back a sob. It was no wonder she couldn't write a decent song. Her soul was stifled, devoid of the faith and glory required to weave the kind of lyrics that changed lives, if only for a day.

Liam had that magic. He had the power to take her far past the last BART stop, out of Concord and into a world populated by artists and dreamers like her, people who felt passion to the marrow and strove to kindle those fires in others. She wanted that, *needed it*, and Liam was the only one who could teach her.

Adam howled, "Oh shit! Get it, Nilsson!" He whooped and pointed at the dog chasing an animal across the asphalt.

Nilsson barked at his prey, drool swinging like rope ladders from his chops. The animal was several feet ahead and blurred by speed, but when it slowed to turn about, Sophie saw the desert hare clearly, its black-tipped ears shuddering and claws skidding through the gravel in evasion. Blood pumped from a wound on its left hind leg, which it shook frantically as Nilsson closed the distance between them.

The hare screamed, the dog's jaws snapped, and tufts of red fur took flight. Adam and Trey cheered for Nilsson, then groaned in disappointment when the hare wriggled free. But its speed diminished, and the trail of blood thickened. The underside of its tail flashed white warnings, but Nilsson wasn't daunted. He nipped at the hare's hind leg, barely missing it before the jackrabbit launched itself into a patch of desert scrub. Dirt billowed as it burrowed, and the dog snorted as he stuck his nose into the brush.

Nilsson backed away suddenly, whimpering and pawing his face. Blood stained his snout, and he was squeezing his left eye shut, but he wasn't giving up. He dug at the bushes again, growling in hunger, until Sophie shoved him aside. She pushed herself between him and the hare, and he whined as she held him at arm's length and peered into the brush.

The hare sat half-buried in dirt. Its ears were flattened to its back, and its eyes whirled like frantic marbles as it twitched its pointy snout at the girl.

"Easy, friend. I'm not going to hurt you." Sophie reached out, and the hare's body jolted as if electrified.

Its lips peeled back from its chapped incisors, and it issued a wet hiss.

Sophie knew it was coming. She'd been here before. She moved slowly, spoke calmly, her fingers outstretched. "I'm not going to hurt you," she repeated, but it felt less truthful that time.

When Nilsson barked, Sophie and the jackrabbit nearly jumped out of their skins. The hare tore out of the brush and Nilsson lunged after, but Sophie latched onto the dog's neck. Its fur slid sinfully easy over the bone as he struggled to escape her grasp, but the more he tugged, the tighter her fingers closed on his throat.

He whined and twisted his body, but instead of giving him freedom, the position allowed Sophie to grab onto his hind leg.

Her mouth went dry. It was difficult to swallow, and the arid wasteland on her tongue spread down her throat, thickening and hardening her windpipe. A scant whistle of breath was all she could manage. It wasn't enough.

Her head swam with onyx dots that rippled outward into a pooling oblivion. But it didn't frighten her. It was her salvation. She could breathe there. She just needed to get closer.

She yanked Nilsson's leg with everything she had, and the bone skipped the socket. The femoral head dragged beneath, then through the flesh along his hip, down his thigh, impossibly gruesome as muscle poured out of his leg like tangled wet shoestring. Nilsson screamed in agony, but Sophie couldn't hear him. She was submerged in the onyx lake, smiling and breathing deep.

"Hey, baby."

Liam kissed Sophie's neck, and she jolted back to reality, the darkness draining from her brain in cool droplets of sweat that spangled her forehead. The hare was gone, leaving dotted crisscrossed tracks of blood across the landscape. Nilsson yipped and licked Sophie's face, replacing salt with drool and violent glee with disorientation.

Liam crouched in front of her and pressed his palm to her brow. "Are you okay, Soph? You look pale."

"That mangy dog nearly mauled an innocent little jackrabbit," Dionne said. "Don't get me wrong, I dig the mutt, but I don't need that nasty stuff in my brain."

"Me neither," Sophie whispered.

Nilsson's tongue flopped out the side of his massive grin and he snuffled his muzzle against Sophie's palm. Her hands trembled as she scratched him beneath the chin, which worsened when she noticed the blood in his whiskers, in his fur, and now on her fingertips, like red hash marks calculating and compounding her fear.

"Hey there, Romeo," Dionne said, playfully punching Liam's shoulder. "Heard you gave my girl her first big O."

Liam's eyebrows jumped halfway up his forehead, and his mouth shrank to a pale point as Sophie growled, "Dionne, shut up."

"I'm not trying to embarrass you or anything," her friend said, hands raised chest-high in supplication. "I'm just impressed is all. The way Sophie's been talking, I'm starting to wish I'd found you first."

"That's awfully nice of you," he said, "but even if I'd met you first, you and every other girl would always be second to this one."

Dionne shook her hand as if scalded by his reply. "Damn, kid, you don't fool around."

"I certainly don't," Liam said, giving Sophie a little squeeze as he added, "My mother raised me better than that."

"Speaking of which, I should get going." Sophie wiped her bloody hand on the grass and chirped, "Drive me home?"

CHAPTER THREE

NOVEMBER 1975 FELT like the hottest month of Sophie's life. The Francises suffered the heat for weeks before Ava caved to her daughter's pleas to switch on their ancient AC unit. For two full days, the apartment felt like heaven. By the third day, the window unit had burned out, again, and the taupe box on Mohr Lane returned to feeling like hell on earth. With her mother's hectic working schedule Sophie hoped they could get another window unit soon. Maybe even a better apartment, something closer to Liam's house in Petaluma.

Sophie exhaled, leaning against Liam as she passed the smoldering joint. "Do you live in a nice neighborhood?"

The smoke thinned Liam's voice when he replied, "No neighborhood. There's not much around us at all, actually. Farms, mostly. Our house is probably the biggest in the area."

"Do you have a big family?"

"You could say that."

Sophie played with the fringe on her secondhand blouse, which smelled faintly of mothballs. Liam knew she wasn't the richest or even most middle-class girl in town, and she doubted the scent would diminish his affection, but that didn't stop her from worrying about it every other minute. When he leaned close, she threw herself into any conversation that might distract him from her bargain basement smell.

"I'd love to meet your family sometime."

"Me too." He cradled her face and kissed her, but uneasiness hunkered down on his expression. "There's something you should know first, though. Something important."

He passed her the joint, and she took a long drag that went straight to her eyes. They filled with water and burned as she blinked out the tears. He handed her a tissue, and she thanked him as she dabbed them dry. "What is it?"

"You know I'm a spiritual person, right? I believe in God."

"So do I," she said. Draping her hand over his, she shrugged. "At least, I *want* to."

"You have no idea how happy that makes me. I want more than anything for you and I to believe in the same things, but . . . Sophie, my family isn't like everyone else's, and neither is our faith. We live together, we pray together. We sing and serve and nurture our beliefs with every atom and space between."

"That's one of the things I love most about you." She pulled his hand into her lap. "When I was being homeschooled, I had nothing to do but think about all the things I wanted, but there were too many. They'd get all jumbled up in my head until I couldn't focus on anything except the wanting itself, the ache of it. But I don't feel that way with you. When I look at you, I can see all those things distinctly, and I finally feel like I can grab onto them. Even *hold* onto them. Spirituality, faith—whatever that light you have inside you is, I want it too. I want to glow like you." She pressed Liam's fingers to her lips. They were rougher than hers, his nails dirtier, but she gratefully inhaled the scent of soil and marijuana resin as she chuckled. "Unless the glow actually comes from a special skin cream or something. That might be easier than finding religion."

The smile dropped from his face, and he withdrew his hand. "It's not about ease, Sophie, and it's not a joke. My faith is the most important thing in my life."

"I know. I'm sorry."

"She saved me. She saved everyone in my family."

"She?"

"Mother Agnes. I was lost for so long, searching for happiness or a cure or, hell, just a place to call 'home,' and she was there for me, for everyone in the Choir of the Lamb. She welcomed us into her flock without judgment. I haven't known one day of loneliness since I welcomed the Lamb into my life, and the same goes for my brothers and sisters."

"How many brothers and sisters?"

"Dozens," he said. "And not just in California. Our Choir sings as one from all over the country."

Sophie wiped her sweaty palms on her legs. "I think I'm a little confused."

Liam smiled. "I'd be surprised if you weren't confused *and* suspicious. That's healthy. It's even healthier to ask questions. Truth can't bloom in blind obedience, Soph. You must till and tend your own fate, turning over new soils and digging out roots, even the ones you value, for the greater good, for the possibility that everything you've been taught is a grand and debilitating deception. Question everything. Trust no one."

"Even you?"

"I was hoping I'd earned your trust by now, but yes, you should be suspicious of me too. You're too special to give anyone the gift of your trust without proving their worth. That's part of the sacrifice required for a blessed crop. You must fall in love with the constant tending of your soul. You must fall in love with discovery."

She hit the joint and exhaled the smoke at the closed window. It struck and pitched off the glass, rolling slowly over her dewy face. "As long as I can still fall in love with you."

He wrapped his arms around her neck, and she closed her eyes to savor the moment leading to his kiss, but in the darkness, she saw the hare from earlier, screaming in agony. Its incisors were wide and its tongue wriggling like a spastic mouse trying to pull free of a trap. Then there was Nilsson, his musculature exposed and weeping, begging for an exhibition of bone. She wanted to dig in her fingers and help it along.

She tasted blood when he kissed her, and it was beautiful. More intoxicating than wine, and more soothing than a glass of warm milk when such visions kept her awake.

She drank a lot of warm milk.

Sophie grunted and pulled away, her eyes quickly filling with tears as she stared at Liam. "What if Dionne's right?" she asked. "What if this isn't love? What if I'm just sixteen and stupid? These feelings, having sex—what if it's my body's blind obedience after all those years of being alone?"

His head was in her lap then, his breath like hot swells between her legs. "You've got it backwards, babe. Love can be blinding, but sex never is. It exposes its blood and guts at the get-go. It turns you inside out till you're pink with perfect honesty. Faith can be like that, too. It encourages you to catch fire, to burn so bright that God sees you before all others. And to spread the flame. To stand like torches lighting the way to chastity and salvation."

Pleasure rippled through Sophie's body, and she raked her hand through his downy hair. "Sex leads to chastity?" She giggled through panting breaths. "I don't think I ever read that in the Bible."

He lifted his head, his face glistening but expressionless. "No, but you will find incest there. And rape."

Sophie bristled and slowly closed her legs, causing Liam to sit up.

"I'm sorry," he said, touching her knee. "That was incredibly rude and insensitive of me. It's just that I don't believe in the Bible as written. It's biased, and frankly, a sloppy read."

Back in the driver's seat, he closed his hands on the steering wheel. The moon gave his blond ringlets a bluish aura. Even his eyelashes appeared to glow. He was so angelic, so good. He brought to mind the poetry of David Bowie, George Harrison, Paul Simon and Art Garfunkel, which she realized was unrealistic and over-romanticized, but still . . . those men were real enough. They were all over the world, so why not here, why not for her? Why couldn't she find everything she was looking for between rows G and H of Concord Pavilion?

But could she really be with someone with so much faith? Her mother didn't oppose discussions of God and theology, but she shied away from articulating her personal beliefs. After looking up her mother's hometown, Bucyrus, Ohio at the library, Sophie learned it existed in something called the 'Bible Belt,' yet she'd never seen Ava pray. She didn't make her daughter say grace before eating takeout like Mrs. Hamilton did. She assumed even the reclusive Mr. Mio worshiped something—maybe even the ghosts in the attic. That, and so many other thoughts unnerved her late at night when the moon stretched the shadows in her room, and the cool, disemboweling earth turned ordinary structural groans to dying shrieks.

Most of all, she worried about her soul. If she even had one. Maybe the soul was a seed that only blossomed when nourished by faith, and her spells were a side-effect of the seed's slow rotting.

Then why was her mother immune? Was Sophie really the only one walking a frayed mental tightrope without a spiritual safety net?

Sophie's hand fit so well against Liam's cheek. Her thumb fell just below his cheekbone, in the last soft groove before blonde stubble dominated his face. She glided the edge of her thumb over that first patch of roughness and exhaled a breath that fluttered his pale-yellow lashes.

"You're going to teach me, aren't you," she whispered. "Everything? The good and the bad?"

His eyes sparkled when he smiled. It could have been the moonlight, or a trick of her own rose-tinted gaze. Or maybe it was the fresh curtain of tears in his eyes when he replied softly. "Yes. And I'm ashamed to admit this, but I'm glad your mother kept you hidden away. I'm glad she saved you for me."

Sophie's jaw dropped. "I think that's the most sexist thing I've ever heard you say, Liam LaSalle."

"I'm sorry, but I can't apologize for wanting you all to myself. How can I, especially when I believe you're the key to every door I've longed to open." He cupped her face and kissed her. "Yes, I'll teach you, but I need you to teach me too. Sophie, I love you, and my family's going to love you."

She crinkled her nose and smirked. "Are you saying you want me to meet your mother?"

He bounced his head back and forth. "Meeting Mother might take some time, but my parents are already dying to meet you."

"Your parents . . . ?" Sophie furrowed her brow, then gasped. "Oh, I'm sorry. I didn't realize you were adopted."

His gaze floated to the misty moonlight sky. "I guess I am. That's another thing about my family, Soph. Most of us aren't related by blood. A few people have been born into the Choir, but not in the California house. Soon though. Paleo's due very soon."

"That sounds like an interesting family."

He pinched her chin and pulled her face so close his words heated her lips. "It is. It's the kind of family you need. People who believe in you and support you. People you can love. People better than your mom." When her focus fell, Liam released her chin, and her head drooped.

"I don't hate my mom, you know. She's doing her best. The jobs, the homeschooling—it's because she wants my life to be better than hers was. But . . . " She twisted the brass ring on her chain and inhaled the warm metallic scent that served as a security blanket since she was a baby. "She had Paul. My father. They were best friends according

31

to her. She had someone to share secrets and jokes with, to play games with. I guess they still share them in some way, but only with each other. She keeps that part of her life from me. She'd rather spend time with a ghost than her daughter. And why not? I'm a freak."

"You and Dionne are close though, aren't you?"

Sophie's voice caught in her throat, sounding like a leaky tire when she said, "You have to know it's not the same."

He brushed a tendril from her face and nodded. "I do now."

She blinked, her lips perched on the edge of a dozen questions, but he stopped her before any slipped out. His hand fit perfectly on *her* face too, fingertips unfolding into the lair of damp hair between her loose French braid and her neck.

"You don't need all the answers now, babe. We'll find them together. Or hell, we'll make our own. What you call a freak, I call blessed, and I want nothing more in this life than to make myself a man worthy of your magic."

Sophie and Liam crashed into an embrace that deliciously bristled her flesh. The more she kissed him, the more she hungered, and her pulse quickened to a chant that urged her hands to his belt.

She wanted him again, but this time she wouldn't let the darkness steal her away. She squeezed her eyes once more to crush the horrible imagery already pervading her brain, then opened them as wide as they'd go. Tears instantly filled them, and though she was sure she looked monstrous, his gaze treated her like a goddess. While she lived, she refused to lose another moment of his adoration to her nightmarish thoughts. She was about to dive into a healthier fantasy when someone knocked on the passenger side window.

The lovers froze. Then, Liam peeked over Sophie's head, winced, and waved at the person standing beside his bus.

The woman peered through the steam, her brow knitted as Sophie rolled down the window. Squeezing out a smile, she said, "Hi, Mom. Be there in a sec, okay?"

Ava Francis didn't move. She tightened her grip on the grease-spotted paper bag at her waist, each blink as urgent as a check engine light.

Sophie flapped her lips, swung her purse from the floor to her hip, and pinched Liam's thigh. "See you tomorrow."

"Count on it."

"Sophie . . . " Ava Francis's voice was soft but commanding. The paper bag swung in one hand while her other fingers flicked her palm with increasing agitation.

Sophie's kiss was brief, barely a breath of contact, but when she scooted from Liam's car and gave her mother a clear view of her lover, Sophie might as well have stained Liam with head-to-toe slobber.

CHAPTER FOUR

T HE BUILDING SMELLED strongly of patchouli and faintly of pot, which meant Dionne was home.

Sophie wished she were spending the night there instead of with her mom, who wasn't even supposed to be off work for another three hours. Sophie dug her key out and thrust it in the lock before her mother finished ascending the foyer steps to their second-floor apartment. She whipped off her purse, flung it onto a kitchen chair, kicked her shoes into the corner beside their avocado Frigidaire, and strode to her room.

What followed was the characteristic crackle of take-out food being unloaded, uncovered, and crisscrossed with utensils, which Sophie heard over the roiling start to Pink Floyd's *Dark Side of the Moon*. She plugged her headphones into the stereo, freeing her of the meager attempt to court her into a real family meal. Real families didn't eat nightly meals of open-faced turkey made by a lumpy man in a red hair net. Real families didn't dance around discussions about a child's fainting spells or a parent's secrecy about their past. If it was all the same to her, Sophie would rather skip the production and go to bed hungry.

Sinking into her pillow, she stared up at the clumped stars on the ceiling. Her gaze rolled down the walls, over the rustling pictures and posters, but when light from the living room pierced the gloom, her focus flew to the window, away from her mother.

"I got us some food," Ava said, scraping a patch of uneven paint on the door frame.

"Not hungry. Thanks anyway."

"Don't you want to know why I'm home early?"

"Not really."

Ava entered, and Sophie grunted as she turned her back to her mom.

"Curtis got blitzed again," she said. "Broke a window, punched a wall, chased a whole bunch of people out the bar."

Sophie's shoulders were hitched to her ears, her arms folded over her chest as if wearing a permanent shrug.

"He left us all a heck of a tip, though. I brought something special home."

Sophie opened one eye. "Right. It's almost Thanksgiving, so the open-faced turkey has a cranberry sauce garnish?"

"Wrong again, Miss Smarty Pants. No cranberry sauce or turkey. But if you're not in the mood for yellowtail sashimi, I guess I can toss it out."

Sophie craned to see colorful rows of sushi lining the circumference of the kitchen table. She scuttled out of her room and squatted in front of a collection of shiny pink slabs bound to bricks of white rice with what looked like electrical tape. She gave the oddities a prolonged, closed-eyed sniff. The sushi didn't smell like much, but the nearby plate of ginger and wasabi nipped her nostrils.

Sophie wasn't good at apologies. She had little occasion to practice penitence over the years, unless to pacify dolls with loose buttons or stuffed bunnies with ripped stitches. With all the time the captive princess spent in her bedroom cell, she wasted none making apologies sound sincere for her captor. But she didn't have to strain for sincerity. When her mother smiled and said, "Surprise," Sophie said she was sorry, and she meant it.

Ava pulled out a chair, and Sophie sat. Crossing her ankles, she unfolded a napkin on her lap and lifted a pair of white plastic chopsticks adorned with delicate pink and white cherry blossoms. She struggled with the utensils more than anticipated. They flopped wildly between her fingers, and when she finally pinched a piece of pink sashimi, the sticks crossed and chopped the slab of rice from the fish.

Ava laughed and Sophie sneered, but it turned playful when she said, "Think you can do any better?"

Her mother crinkled her nose, summoning the crow's feet that framed her eyes. She twiddled chopsticks decorated with blue flowers and vines, then thrust them at a tuna roll with the intensity of a crocodile snapping at a shorebird. The chopsticks squeezed the expertly rolled sushi until pale tuna squished out of the flattened rice jacket. Ava popped it in her mouth while her daughter chuckled.

Sophie poked at the mountain of wasabi with cautious curiosity. She had a basic understanding of the green gunk but felt it needed closer examination, so she dug out a chunk with the tip of her chopstick and held it to her nose. The aroma stung her nostrils, surged to her sinuses, and summoned a curtain of tears, but it didn't deter her. She cautiously stuck out her tongue and touched the pale emerald pill to the tip for the tiniest of tastes. The wasabi suddenly dislodged from the chopstick and fell onto her tongue. Not wanting it to tumble down her throat, she snapped her tongue to the roof of her mouth, squishing the wasabi into the ridges of her upper palate. Seconds later, a stinging deluge poured from her eyes. She fanned her face and howled as she panted through rising pain.

Ava leapt from her chair and poured her daughter a glass of milk. Sophie gulped until it was gone, tears rolling down her cheeks.

"Are you okay, sweetie?"

Sophie wiped the milk from her upper lip and nodded, cooling the burn with a long inhalation. She scooped up more wasabi with her chopstick, stabbed a sesame salmon roll, and closed her grin around the sushi shish kebab.

Ava rarely caught her daughter looking so joyful. She wished she could take a photo to remind herself on the bad days that Sophie could still be as delightful as she was when she was a baby. Even as a toddler, mired in the terrible twos, smiles were as common as diaper changes and games of peekaboo, as frequent as her warbling attempts at saying, "I love you, Mommy." Ava couldn't remember the last time her daughter uttered anything close, and she resisted trying to coax it out now. She hugged her instead, squeezing until Sophie whined and muttered something Ava pretended to be those three massive words cabooshing a train of complaints.

Sophie popped a slice of ginger into her mouth and scrunched her nose as her mother returned to her seat. "So what's the occasion?" she asked.

Ava's lips promptly dropped to a frown. She dabbed her mouth with a napkin and flattened it in her lap. "Can't I do something nice?"

"You can. It just usually doesn't work out that way."

"I'm sure kids at school have the same complaints about their parents."

Sophie hummed and speared a piece of sashimi.

"You are getting along with the kids at school, aren't you?"

She stopped chewing and locked eyes with her mother. "Sure I am. Why? Did someone say something?"

Ava bit into a crab roll, and cream cheese squished out. Sophie snickered as it fell to the table, and her mom's cheeks reddened. "No, nothing like that. I just figured I'd see more of your classmates around here by now. You begged to meet new people, but I keep seeing you with the same kids. The dropouts and Dionne—"

"Dionne is my best friend."

"I know, honey."

"I thought you liked her."

"Of course I do. Dionne and her mom are lovely people. They've been excellent neighbors all these years, but—" Ava

37

raked her teeth over her top lip. "Dionne's older than you, sweetie. You don't have that much in common. She's been through school. She's been out in the world—"

"Yeah, and I haven't. So who's fault is that?" Sophie snapped.

Her mother's chin dimpled, trembling slightly when she said, "Mine. It's my fault. I have no problem admitting that."

Sophie grumbled. "Nope, but you've obviously got a huge problem regretting it. *And* making up for it. You're not home enough for that."

"What do you call this?" Ava displayed the sushi-laden table like a spokesmodel on *The Price is Right*, all teeth and flair, but her daughter scowled. "What do you want from me, Soph?"

"Quit one of your jobs." She punctuated the statement by popping a sushi roll onto her tongue and gesticulated with her chopsticks as she munched. "We'd have more time together if you only had one job."

"How do you expect me to pay the rent? How will we afford clothes and school supplies?"

"With *my* contributions, of course," Sophie said, her chopstick stabbing air.

"Ah . . . I see your game, young lady, and my answer is no."

"But I want to help."

"I don't need your help."

"Yes, you do. If you didn't work so much, I wouldn't have assumed dinner was leftover Robin Hood sludge."

"That's what makes it special. It's different."

"Letting me get a job would be different too."

Ava's lips inched up one side of her cheek, and she drummed the tabletop in pensive silence.

"Maybe it would be good for me," Sophie continued. "You see how well I've done since I started at Ygnacio. Not a single spell."

Her eyes narrowed in doubt. "Not one?"

Sophie bobbed her head. "Some dizziness once or twice in the hallway before class, but it's so loud in there, and there are so many people, it's overwhelming for everyone. But I don't let it get the best of me. I breathe deep, the dizziness goes away, and I'm fine."

"What about the boy?"

She gulped. "The boy?"

"The boy in the car, Sophie. That was my not-so-subtle way of asking about the boy in the car. Does he go to school with you?"

Sophie's stomach flipped like the planes of a gyroscope. "His name's Liam LaSalle," she answered stiffly.

"And he goes to Ygnacio?"

The gyroscope's clearance diminished. Her gut stiffened and collided into a mess of broken machinery. "No."

"Because he's older than you?"

"Not as old as Dionne."

"That's not relevant." Ava chomped a piece of white and purple sashimi in half and smirked as she chewed. "Besides, I don't think I'd be as worried to find you making out with Dionne."

Sophie exploded with squeals of rosy embarrassment, and her mother chuckled.

"You know I only want what's best for you. That's all I've ever wanted. It's hard to watch you grow up, and even harder to watch you slip away."

A pain that Sophie loathed wrenched her heart. After all the years, all the sacrifices and restrictions, she didn't think it would have strength left to twist her rage to sympathy, but Ava had a way of kickstarting it. As much as she wanted to leave the sad woman in her swamp of negligence, her mother's voice wasn't something one could simply abandon. Unless, maybe, by death. And maybe that's why Ava was the last of her family left alive. Sophie considered using it to wound her mother on angry days, but she never worked up the nerve. Her mom always found a look or sigh that pushed the vitriolic urges to the back of Sophie's mind, where they burrowed and itched like secret spiders. But as the ungoliant thoughts rose up from their webbing, she surrendered to the velvet tones of Ava's voice.

"I'm glad you're back in school," she continued. "Seeing how well you've adjusted, I admit I wish I'd listened to you sooner. I wouldn't have fought it so hard if I'd known you'd be safe. But I was so afraid for you, about your spells . . . "

Sophie wished they could divine a better name for her weird symptoms. It was either something cute like "spells" or something closer like "madness," and she didn't like either.

"What if you made them worse?" Sophie whispered, catching her mom's gaze. "Keeping me out of school so long, away from other kids, refusing to take me to a doctor. What if you made the spells worse in the long run?"

Ava pressed her fists to her forehead in anguish. "That's my greatest fear. I pray to God I didn't do that, Sophie."

"You pray?"

Her hands popped apart and she sighed loudly. "It's an expression."

"No, it's a real thing, Mom."

"You know what I mean."

"So you *don't* pray."

"I . . . I guess not."

"Do you believe in God? Or Heaven? Do you believe in Hell?"

She pushed around grains of rice with her chopstick like halfheartedly assembling a neighborhood of Mohr Lane condos. "I'm not sure. Do you?"

Sophie pouted. "Maybe."

"Does Liam?"

"Yes."

Ava's focus jumped from her plate to Sophie's face. "You've discussed religion with him?"

"Yes. It's an important part of his life, and I want it to be an important part of mine."

Ava set down her chopsticks. "I didn't know it interested you so much. Would—" She cleared her throat and averted her eyes. "Would it interest you this much if it weren't for Liam?"

Sophie was still rosy but not embarrassed. "I've been interested ever since I realized you'd never bring it up."

Ava blinked rapidly, like she was trying to turn back time with her eyelids. She stared at her daughter in disbelief but made no attempt to argue the point. She stuffed a piece of sushi in her mouth and exhaled heavily through her nose as she chewed.

"Look, I'm not trying to mess with your happiness, but I need to know that you're being safe with this boy. I need to know he's not going to hurt you, or get you in any trouble."

Sophie didn't want her emotions to register on her face, but tension rose like acid, souring and tightening her expression. "Trouble? You mean like the kind you had with my father?"

"Your father and I loved each other."

"But once I showed up and he left the picture, your life was over," Sophie said. "I get it, I do, and I sure as shit don't intend on copying it."

"It wasn't like that."

"Come on, Mom. I remind you of shitty times. Why else would you pretend I don't exist?"

Ava tented her fingers and leaned forward, eyes fixed and gleaming. "I'm sorry I'm not everything you want me to be. I wasn't given a guidebook for this, and I didn't expect to be doing it alone. Part of me is still shocked I've been able to do it at all."

"What's that mean?"

Ava's fingers crossed out of the tent and clasped to a fist she pressed to her lips. "With everything you think I've denied you, honey, you still have more opportunities than

41

I did. When I was your age, I could barely *have* good dreams let alone live them."

"Growing up on a farm is really that bad?"

Ava licked her lips and winced at the leftover wasabi. "It could be, especially with a family like mine. Sometimes I didn't know who I could trust, myself included. I was alone—or felt like it—a lot of the time."

"Except for Dad." Sophie looked up optimistically, and her mother edged her shoulders to her ears.

"Yes. Except for Paul." She exhaled a thin stream of breath to relieve the pressure of grief from her belly. "But after he died, I learned quickly it was better to disappear than to stand out. Especially since I had you to protect. You became the most important thing in my life. The only thing, really. As long as you were safe, I didn't care about my dreams anymore. I didn't need to."

Sophie's face crumpled to a red fist of outrage. "See? It's my fault you're miserable!"

"You know I didn't mean it that way."

"Don't tell me what I know," Sophie said with a snarl. "It's like you had to suffer a bunch of bullshit, and now I have to suffer it too. Like it's genetic or something."

"Our suffering isn't the same." Frowning, she laid her hand upon her daughter's. "I was trapped on that farm, honey."

Sophie jumped to her feet, knocking the fiberglass chair to the floor as she screeched. "And I'm not trapped here?"

"How are you trapped? You're going to school just like you wanted."

With her eyes squeezed shut, Sophie screamed at the top of her lungs: "After a hundred years with lame old Moira!"

The echo was so powerful Sophie was certain Dionne and her mom heard it across the hall. She envisioned Mr. Mio tilting his face to the ceiling in curiosity and Nilsson's ears perking in his junkyard canopy behind the drive-in, and with each imagined response, the nauseating flavor of battery acid swelled in her brain. Exhaling slowly, she righted her chair and sank into it. "I'm sorry."

"You're sorry for shouting, or for . . . "

Sophie lifted her chin, her eyes as wide and wet as the first time Ava saw them, gazing up from Paul's arms at her sister's funeral.

"For what, Mom?"

Her voice caught in her throat. "Do you miss Moira?"

Sophie shrugged. "Sure. She was an annoying old coot most of the time, but I didn't want her to leave the way she did." Sophie flapped her lips and slammed her palms on the table. "You're changing the subject! Going to school doesn't make me any less of a prisoner. You still wig out whenever I go out with my friends. You won't let me have a job or learn to drive. You won't even let me have a pet!" Sophie threw her hands in the air. "Forget it. I'm tired of talking about this."

She leapt up and stomped to her bedroom, but her mother followed. When Sophie swung the door closed, Ava stopped it with her foot.

Pain registered as flushed cheeks and a grimace that tightened Ava's face, even as Sophie apologized.

"Look, I actually had an okay day," she said, sighing, "and I'm not in the mood to ruin it with a fight. None of this matters anyway."

She snatched her new Joni Mitchell album from the floor and flopped onto her bed to read the lyrics while her mother stood motionless. She tried to focus on the words, but her focus eventually drifted back to Ava, still hunched in the doorway.

A rough sneeze could've blown her off her feet, but when she said, "Of course it matters," her voice commanded the room and all its broken stars. "Sophie, you have the potential to do something amazing with your life. You have more talent than anyone I've ever known."

"Yeah? How many people have you known?"

Her mother wasn't even confident enough to lie like a normal person. She clammed up and bowed her head.

Sophie flipped onto her side, rolled off the bed, and stood seething at her bookcase. "Read my poetry and tell me it's good. Tell me I'm the next Joan Baez or Nina Simone if you want, but I hope you do a better job lying about that than you have pretending to love me."

Ava stumbled backward, holding her chest. "What do you mean? God, Sophie, I love you more than anything."

Sophie threw herself onto the bed and back into the lyrics for "The Hissing Summer Lawns". Frowning, Ava sat beside her.

"I've read your poetry. I've heard your songs. I'm not lying when I say they're good."

"They're shallow."

"You're sixteen.'

Sophie popped up like a jack-in-the-box. "What's that supposed to mean?"

"You know what it means," Ava said with an exhausted huff. "Those people you mentioned are my age or older. They've lived a thousand lives more than you. I'm sure their work was shallow at sixteen too."

Sophie grumbled from behind the open album cover. "At least they have something deep to inspire them. They have things to love about the people and places they come from. Even things to hate. Heritage and history. Things to celebrate and things to suffer. It's what makes their music so powerful."

"You want to write songs about suffering?"

Sophie set aside the album and looked her mother dead in the eyes. "For a start."

Ava gestured at the brass ring around her daughter's neck, and her cheeks twitched with the ghost of a smile. "What about that? It's a family heirloom."

"From a guy I know nothing about. Bitchin'." Sophie tucked the ring under her shirt as her mother's face sagged in misery.

"If you knew what I've done to help you, you'd be kinder to me," she said. "If you knew what I've sacrificed, you'd thank me."

"But I don't know, Mom. I don't know anything about you, and you don't know anything about me. And maybe that's the way it should be. It's obvious you only care about yourself. Oh, and a one-time lay who died to get away from you."

Ava smacked Sophie's cheek, then withered into herself as she gripped her hand. "Oh my god, honey, I'm so sorry."

Sophie glared as she clutched her face. It felt as though Ava's hand was still there, digging in, like she was trying to wrench a turnip from frozen soil.

"Sweetie, please forgive me. For all of it. I just want you to appreciate what you can do. You're so talented—"

"Stop saying that!" Sophie barked. "Stop pretending there's anything special about me. There's nothing. Just lukewarm bullshit. And I'm sorry if this hurts your feelings, Mom, but it's because of you."

Ava's expression rang with Sophie's cruelty, but she didn't let it stop her.

"Liam's part of a spiritual community. A family, really. The way he talks about them, the look on his face—he has so much pride, so much love. You never told me I could have love like that. Why didn't you raise me with any kind of faith?"

Ava's eye twitched, and she rubbed her forehead. "I grew up in a family like that, hon. My mother, especially. Faith can be a beautiful thing, but I've seen it go bad too. Anyway, I figured if you wanted it you'd go after it."

"So it's my fault?" Sophie slapped her knees in exasperation. "Yes, of course it is. It's my fault I was born. It's my fault you have a shitty life. It's my fault I'm stupid and lonely and God doesn't give a damn about me."

Ava patted her shoulder, but it felt like a dying fish falling cold on her bones before flopping away.

"Honey, please calm down."

"Why? Are you scared I'll have a spell?" She laughed spitefully. "Sure you are. That's the only special thing about me. It's your favorite thing about me."

"That's not true."

"Then why won't you take me to a doctor?"

Ava groaned, and Sophie didn't need to listen anymore. Her mother would simply launch into her usual bluster about her distrust of doctors and hospitals, how medical professionals can be as clueless as their patients and even worsen the situation. She nodded thoughtlessly until Ava said, "They don't know how to deal with your affliction."

"How do you know? Have you taken me before? Has it happened to you? Or to my dad?"

"No, Paul was . . . " Ava's focus floated away, glistening with bittersweet memory. "No. Paul was wonderful."

"What about my grandparents? My aunts and uncles?"

"I'm an only child," Ava said, gaze still distant. "It wouldn't change anything. We'd still be here. You'd still hate me." Ava's voice cracked in the final phrase, and her eyes drained of light. They remained dull and lidded as she sighed. "There's a job opening at the ice-skating rink. The movie theater too. I don't know if they hire kids your age, but I can put in a good word for you if that's what you really want."

Sophie sat up on her knees with an excited squeal, but suspicion soon clouded her eyes. "Wait a minute. Why the change of heart?"

"I guess I wanted to give you something special for the holiday break."

"But we're still doing Thanksgiving on Thursday, right?"

Ava fidgeted, digging at her cuticles until her nail beds were inflamed.

"Mom?"

She deflated in her chair. "I'm sorry, Sophie. I have to work."

46

"On *Thanksgiving*?"

"The mall's staying open and the bar's shorthanded."

"But you promised!"

"I said I would try, and I did, I really did. But I have off on Wednesday, so we can celebrate then."

"So while every other family is being thankful for each other on the real holiday, we'll have gone right back to . . . whatever this is." She heaved a frustrated sigh. "I'd like to be alone now."

"Are you sure?"

"Yup."

"Do you still want to go to the mall tomorrow?"

"Fine."

When her mom didn't budge, she slid off the bed with a huff and stared her out of the room. The moment Ava was in the hall, Sophie locked her out and returned to bed. But as much as she tried to focus on other things, she couldn't stop herself from glancing at the spectral shadow that remained for hours on the other side of her door.

CHAPTER FIVE

SUNVALLEY SHOPPING CENTER glowed mustard yellow in the flush of morning. As the largest indoor mall in the country, Sunvalley's proximity to the Francis home provided Sophie with her only illusion of wealth. Extravagant department stores anchored the two-story shopping center, but Sunvalley's true grandeur lay in the ice skating rink on the first floor and the aviary mews of rare birds on the second. Classic cars were frequently on display, beside the elevators this week, with soft leather seats that tempted Sophie whenever she walked the mall with her mom. Could she slip away and curl up in one of those cars without Ava noticing? How long would it take her to realize her daughter was gone? How many stores would she pass, how many polite nods would she bestow on strangers and associates while Ava hid in a Rolls-Royce?

She'd witnessed the mall's awakening dozens of times, but never as a prospective employee. She hadn't watched the fatigued croaking of clerks so closely before, silently questioning the choices that deposited them there. It chilled Sophie's bones outside of JCPenney, where she waited for her mother to roll up the gate. They hadn't spoken a word to each other since the night before, but the lifting gate revealed a smile like rumpled wallpaper on Ava Francis's face.

"Harry from the rink should be in the booth by eleven, but the theater opens in a few minutes. I can go with you after I finish opening. Until then, you can help me dress the mannequins."

Sophie's face scrunched like she'd bitten into a bad apple. Dressing the mannequins amused her when she was a kid, but it disturbed her now. For one, the fleet of snowy faces didn't represent the neighborhood at all, so the dead smiles and blank blue eyes made her shiver like she was being watched. They looked especially creepy that morning, like the night crew had had a bit of fun with them. Stripped nude, with their nippleless breasts and smooth mounds for sex organs, the mannequins were positioned one on top of the other and bent over, like short-distance runners with no chance to place.

Rocking from heel to toe, she said, "I'd rather go on my own, thanks."

"Okay. Just wait a sec."

As her mom dashed back inside, Sophie's gaze waterfalled down the orange walls and crawled across the tile toward the entrance to the World's Faire Food Court. As gates rolled up and lights sporadically illuminated the second floor, music squawked, then oozed from the speakers. A saxophone solo like soft cheese curled Sophie's top lip in aversion as the world below awakened. She crept to the escalator and peered over, learning the birds' morning feeding was louder and more irritating than the mall's Camembert jazz.

Jogging back, Ava flapped an application for a JCPenney salesclerk in the buzzing amber light. Sophie skimmed it, her face scrunching at each blank space.

"I don't think I'm ready for sales," she said.

"No one ever is," Ava replied. "Anyway, this is just an example of what you'll have to fill out and the kinds of questions they might ask you during the interview."

Sophie gulped. "Interview?" She scanned the application with its bold type and daunting caverns of solicitation. The harder she stared, the less the words kept their places. They swam in and out of the spaces until she questioned the spelling of her own name.

What *was* her name? Sophie. So-fee. Was Sophie short

49

for something? Was she named after someone? Someone from her father's family, maybe? The questions cavorted from the page until all of Sunvalley was a bleach-burnt family tree. The world went white, the exotic birds screamed, and Sophie tilted drunkenly onto her heels.

As the application fluttered over the railing and sailed to the first floor, the questions fell away. Her mother's fingernails dented her skin, and her voice broke through the aviary din.

"What just happened?" Ava said. "Are you okay?"

Sophie dug her knuckle into the base of her skull and stretched her neck. "It was nothing. I didn't sleep much last night. Too excited, I guess."

The excitement was true, but it's not why she didn't sleep. Strange visions scurried through her brain like strangled hares desperate for air. But they didn't scare her. They elated her, and the elation followed her like a waking nightmare into the sun.

Ava's face softened with sympathy, and she kissed her daughter's forehead. "Things can only improve from here, right?"

"I guess."

"Good luck, honey."

"Thanks."

The escalator carried Sophie down to meet the Penney's application. The visible side of the paper requested the names and numbers of people who could vouch for her as a worker and a person, but family members were excluded. Who, then, could Sophie use? Dionne? Dionne's mom? Liam?

For a moment, she tasted cold duck and hot blood, and her breath thinned. She looked to the second floor, afraid her mom would still be there.

All around her clerks were opening their stores, arranging window displays, and nodding heavily at her. They were already wearing fake smiles, which barely clung to the bags of sallow porridge below their weary eyes. They looked miserable, and the day had just begun. As much as Sophie wanted to work at the mall, those faces reeled back her conviction like a desperate fisherman. The back of her head ached, and she massaged it with her thumb.

The cinema marquee was dark, but the glass cases comprising the snack counter were illuminated, bathing the Jujubes and Skittles with abrasive white light. Sophie crept in, her palms clammy and skull pinched by pliers of pain. She knuckled the back of her head again, massaging it with circular motions until relief radiated down the knots along her shoulders.

Sophie peeked over the snack counter and around the popcorn machines but saw no employees. A light flickered in her periphery, and the box office buzzed to life seconds before a person popped up behind the counter. She approached slowly, cringing, and standing on her tiptoes, she cleared her throat and greeted a woman in a maroon vest spotted with oil. She imagined trading her loose floral blouse for the cinched costume, or working for more than ten minutes in the stench of stale popcorn and disinfectant. Dark gray slabs of gum and candy were crushed into the carpet, and every surface looked greasy. It was as if the Sunvalley Cinema had a secret slimy side she hadn't noticed in all her years attending their movies.

"Can I help you, young lady?"

Sophie licked her lips nervously. "Um, I heard you were hiring?"

"That's true. Do you want an application?"

"No."

The woman blinked at the terse response, and so did Sophie. She hadn't expected it to leap out like that. She fumbled for an explanation that wouldn't make her face burn even hotter.

"My friend is looking," she said. "She was wondering what kind of stuff she'd have to do."

"Well, the job has several responsibilities. Mostly, we need another person on the snack bar—it goes wild before shows—and we need theater checkers to make sure kids aren't sneaking in and people aren't being disruptive. There'd be some stocking and cleaning duties too. If your friend does a good job—sorry, what did you say her name was?"

Sophie's throat tightened, and she coughed up the first name that sprang to mind. "Dionne."

"Ah. If Dionne does a good job, she could eventually move up to the box office." The woman squinted one eye. "Your friend isn't Dionne Hamilton by any chance, is it?"

Sophie gritted her teeth as she nodded.

"She's leaving the Robin Hood?"

The popcorn smell was dizzying, and Sophie's stomach flip-flopped as she backed away.

"Where are you going? Doesn't Dionne want an application?"

Sophie called "No, thank you" over her shoulder, but she didn't slip away as discreetly as intended. Facing forward, she slammed into a mall patron and fell to the floor. The person laughed, apologized, and helped her to her feet all before Sophie realized it was Liam LaSalle.

"I knew you couldn't keep your hands off me," he said with a wink.

Sophie brushed her hair out of her eyes and punched him in the chest. "You scared the shit out of me!"

"Hey, you ran into *me*, babe."

"What are you doing here anyway?"

"I've been stalking you to find out what kind of Sunvalley gift certificate to get you for your birthday."

She bobbed her head like an incredulous peacock. "My birthday isn't until July."

"And I'm not really stalking you. I'm on official family business," he said, gesturing to the second-floor post office with a stack of letters. "I never miss an opportunity to serve St. Agnes."

Sophie twisted her sneaker on the floor until it squeaked. "Is St. Agnes the same as Mother Agnes?"

"Not exactly."

"Oh. Sorry."

Liam ran his hand down her arm with a calming hum. "You don't have to be sorry."

Sophie was still holding the Penney's application, but she'd crumpled and refolded it so many times the paper was soft with translucent creases, and her perspiration had smudged an "s" from the word "skills."

Liam wrapped his arm around her waist and pulled her into his arms. "What are your plans today, little lady?"

Sophie balled up the application and lobbed it into a trashcan.

"Oh, I was hoping some nice handsome dude would teach me about St. Agnes. Do you know where I could find one?"

Liam's smile crinkled his nose as he answered. "I think I can scare one up."

CHAPTER SIX

S OPHIE DOZED OFF during the hour drive from Concord to Petaluma, waking drowsily when the Kombi rattled to a halt. She rubbed the sleep from her eyes, thinking she had to be seeing things wrong. Liam had mentioned the house was off the beaten path, but the plot belonging to the Choir of the Lamb didn't have a neighbor for miles. There was only the white wooden farmhouse, a collection of VW buses in various shades and styles, and a massive garden the house wore like a fine mink stole. A tall picket fence surrounded the vegetation, but several shapes moved between the posts, hard at work on an autumn harvest.

Two young women and a teen boy bounded down the porch stairs, swinging off the spindled posts while a little girl with a dirty but cherubic face stumbled awkwardly after them. One of the teens held a cluster of carrots, the vegetables still wet with rich brown soil. Her clothes were tracked with dirt too, but it didn't faze her—not like Sophie was by her own damp pits and frizzy hair as she exited the bus. The kids' beaming faces shone through the grime as they rushed to Liam and enfolded him in jubilant embraces. One of the girls bopped him on the nose with a carrot, and he chomped off the tip with a happy growl. He gave them a thumbs up, humming as he chewed.

"Lee-lee!" The little girl squealed, and Liam scooped her into his arms while Sophie stared on in idolatry. He shone even brighter there, and everything in his radius caught a bit of his golden glow.

Two adults appeared on the porch, watching adoringly. The woman, whose blonde hair nearly reached her pregnant belly, cocked her head with a smile. The man beside her had a shaggy beard, long hair, and his bare muscular chest twinkled with sweat. He looked like he could tear a phone book in half, but he held the woman's hand delicately as she descended a step ahead of him. In her sheer white gown, the woman appeared to float, angelic and effulgent, her freckled face slightly sunburnt. Cradling her belly with one hand, she embraced Sophie with the other.

"Welcome to our home, darling. We've heard so much about you." She spoke in a voice as fragile as Janis Ian's in "At Seventeen", but it acquired a devilish lilt when she added, "Liam hasn't stopped raving about you for a minute."

He blushed and clapped a hand over his eyes. "Paleo, please."

"Oh shush. Your song is clear and true, Liam, and you shouldn't be ashamed of it. Love is the most courageous music man can make." She smiled at Sophie. "Speaking of which, I hear you like to write songs, my dear. I hear you have a lovely voice."

She shrugged. "I have my moments, I guess."

The bearded man wagged a finger at her. "Don't be so modest. I can hear it when you speak. There's confidence and whimsy there. There's soul."

She clenched her jaw, but her cheeks lifted anyway, and she whispered a thank you.

"Peter and Paleo Light," Liam began, "this is Sophie Francis. Sophie, these are my parents."

She extended her hand, which was quickly folded up in their joyous embrace. When released, Paleo introduced her to the others. A girl named London waved a carrot at her while the other teens, Gaya, Melody, and Ash sang out a happy greeting.

Paleo laughed and closed her hands in prayer. "What

a glorious day this is! Agnes has truly blessed us: mothers and martyrs and miscreants all."

Sophie followed the upturned gaze of the Choir to the sky, where the fluffy clouds scrunched and stretched like cats waking from a nap.

The little girl pointed a chubby finger at the winking sun and giggled as she squealed. "Mama Aggie!"

Paleo lightly bopped the child on the nose. "That's right, Sunny. Mother Agnes is always watching." Then, with her smile tossed like a net around the Choir, she took Sophie's arm and led her up the stairs. "Would you like some iced tea, dear? Junipero's recipe is to die for."

⋇

The Choir of the Lamb's west coast headquarters was frantically neat. Cots and pillows were piled on the perimeters, sometimes with a child still sleeping on the topmost cushion like an untroubled princess, and hot plates and camp stoves were tucked into the corners, but most of these things—even the child—were partially covered with dark velvet curtains, allowing the Choir plenty of space for study, meditation, and prayer. Footprints and shoe scuffs stained the white staircase, and several patches along the walls were unevenly layered in white paint, like hasty canvases for art yet conceived. But there were plenty of paintings behind the curtains, bizarre and raw as the farmhouse's strong, tangy odor. It was overwhelming at first, but Sophie couldn't imagine it was easy keeping a house filled with so many people smelling fresh. The candles helped, and the marijuana that circulated during prayer sessions. Maybe that was why the house wasn't as noisy as she'd expected. Except for some buoyant guitar playing upstairs and the occasional sound of laughter, people were quiet, contemplative, and content.

A pair of teenagers skipped past Sophie into the kitchen and toward the back door. She stretched her neck to follow them before realizing Peter and Paleo Light were leading her in that direction, through the dining room, to the thin grinning woman at the stove.

She waved a wooden spoon at the kids and warbled. "Hey you harebrains! Get your little tails back here!"

They popped back inside and apologized to Junipero, who playfully tapped their heads with the spoon. She gave a large jug a quick stir and reached out to the row of hanging mugs that ran nearly all the way around the room. The first mug, labeled "Kerry," was near the stove, but "Bianca" was further away, paled by sunlight. The children held their mugs eagerly, bouncing on their toes as Junipero poured in a slosh of burgundy liquid.

Bianca and Kerry smiled as they drank, finishing with a dramatic sigh of refreshment. By the time they'd washed their mugs, there were three more people in the kitchen, carrying gardening tools. They'd ascended from the basement singing a song that echoed up the steps until Junipero closed the heavy steel door behind them.

"Your gardening stuff must be really important to you," Sophie said as the trio headed out back to join the harvest.

"Have you ever grown something?" Liam asked. "Even a mung bean?"

She raised her eyebrows. "I guess not."

"We're creating life out there, Soph. Just like you create life with your poetry and songs." When she scrunched her face, he chuckled. "You might not believe it, but you do. And you protect that stuff pretty fiercely, don't you? You *should* anyway. Not everyone can create like we can. Gardening, music, art, faith: these are the channels through which all humans can be mothers."

Sophie snorted. "You want to be a mother, Liam?"

Junipero laughed. Her loose twists of hair bounced as she threw her arms around the girl. "Well, aren't you the little ball of firelight?"

"Sorry?"

She tried to wriggle back, but the woman cupped her face and exhaled breath like fresh vanilla. "Fire requires no forgiveness. Only respect. Whether it cooks or consumes, whether it lights or licks too close, it was doing the job you begged of it. A flame is only as deadly as its kindling."

Liam and his parents hummed in agreement, so Sophie did too, despite her confusion.

Her eyes crossed briefly, and her mouth felt dirty and dry from sleeping in the car. When she braced herself on the wall and exhaled swirling tension from her gut, Liam jumped to her side and wrapped his arm around her.

"Are you okay? You look pale."

"Yes, sorry. I didn't have a good breakfast this morning."

"That's a shame," Peter said. "Your parents work mornings, I assume."

Liam cleared his throat. "Sophie's father passed away. Her mother's raising her—if you can call it that."

The temperature in the room changed in a millisecond. It was a sauna now, the air thick with hot pity. Peter offered Sophie his arm with a slow blink. "I'm so sorry to hear that, Sophie. Let's get you somewhere to relax and Junipero will bring along some palm tea and fresh fruit." He led her slowly from the kitchen to the stairs with Liam and Paleo close behind, his voice soft as a dove's call. "Why isn't your mother feeding you, dear?"

"Oh, it's not like that. She's just really busy. She works two jobs."

Paleo poked her head between them, matching her husband's coo. "But parenting is the most important job of all."

At the top of the staircase, Sophie broke free and moved to Liam's side. She didn't know why she felt the need to defend her mom, but as the Choir of the Lamb closed in, her words thundered out following their lightning quick accusations.

"She does the best she can, okay?"

Liam's parents gaped at her with amalgamations of shock and shame, but Liam looked angry, even offended, at her outburst. His arm was around her but not touching her as he frowned.

"You don't have to pretend here, Soph. We accept you. We love you."

"Maybe *you* do," she whispered. "But these people don't even know me."

Peter and Paleo backed away while Liam led her to the railing overlooking the first floor. Standing behind her, his body molded itself to hers, and his words pelted the back of her neck like sporadic bursts from a faulty radiator.

"Some people spend all their lives as bombastic and brazen creatures. They spout their opinions left and right, but for every effort, their true selves are never known, even by those who claim to love them. You aren't one of those people, Soph. You're like us. Your passion, your grace: I saw them without a word when we met."

"I can't speak for my husband," Paleo said, "but I saw it the moment you arrived."

Peter nodded. "I did too. You shine from the inside, my dear. Only a selfish or corrupt person wouldn't be able to see it."

As the Lights spoke, people populated the area below the balcony. They gazed up at her, their faces bright and hopeful as the first day of spring. Though there were a few older folks and adults that looked to be around her mother's age, a great number of the Choir members didn't look much older than Sophie. The young men and women were tan and fit, and though the former wore smiles it seemed no pain could strip away, they'd obviously experienced their fair share in the past, their faces and bodies scarred, and even confining one man who looked barely old enough to drink to a wheelchair. She couldn't imagine fighting in an honest to God war, but if she'd sacrificed blood, limb, and heart to the battlefield and lived to tell, she'd probably lock herself away in a big secluded house too.

The Choir's lips moved, but Sophie couldn't hear them.

It didn't look like they were saying the same things at first, but their lips eventually found an identical rhythm. Still, with everyone chanting in unison, she couldn't hear anything above a spiritual susurrus.

"They sure are quiet for a choir," she whispered over her shoulder.

"Sometimes we have to shout our throats bloody to be heard," Liam said. "But sometimes the occasion calls for silence, especially when ignorance and blasphemy roar. Let the cynics be loud as lions and empty barrels. And the faithful, in all our quiet strength, will be the blessed and patient Lamb."

The Choir agreed with a hushed "Amen" as they executed what Sophie perceived to be their sign of the cross. Together, the members lightly touched one hand to their throats and the other to their hearts. Then, while the men moved both hands to their hearts, the women moved both hands to their bellies—one hand flat, one a fist.

Sophie shakily mimicked the movement, and the Choir cheered softly as Liam wrapped his arms around her.

"Your soul was crying out for this," he said. "Now it's singing."

She faced him, searching his eyes for the secret to invalidate it all. If it was there, it was buried too deeply to see. She was so tired, so thirsty. She leaned against Liam's chest and exhaled as much doubt as possible. Her chest felt looser, but her belly felt emptier.

"Come on, babe," he said. "Let's get some food."

Together, Paleo and Peter Light knocked on the black door at the end of the hall, and the steady stream of guitar music stopped.

A man cheerfully shouted, "Entre!" and resumed strumming an enthusiastic flamenco melody. In the room known as the "black chapel," Choir members shimmied and clapped along to the music. Some swayed in place while others danced with wild abandon. One such woman whose plaited silver hair almost perfectly matched the guitarist's, pulled Sophie from Liam's arms with a whoop and twirled her through the room. Though the children and adults whirling around prickled her anxiety, it was a kinder, more diluted anxiety than she felt at Ygnacio. There, teenage faces blended into identical caps of ivory foam in the scholastic sea, salty and suffocating, but the Choir of the Lamb was coral, vibrant with life and florescence. It was a swell of rosy shells stirred up by a dolphin pod. No one was identical, and no one disappeared. Each face wore a unique curve of worship and delight.

The guitarist strummed the final chord, waited for it to die on the crowd, then patted his guitar as if the song filled its belly past the brim. Setting it aside, he stood and joined hands with a clean-shaven man who had an infinity symbol tattooed on his forearm. The same symbol was on the guitarist's arm, which he noticed Sophie staring at as he approached.

He said, "Who is this angelic creature?" but it felt like everyone in the room had asked. They tittered with anticipation and inched forward, but when she said, "My name's Sophie," the room seemed to freeze with a collective gasp.

"What did I say?" she asked Liam, who chuckled and crinkled his nose.

"I guess I did mention your name once or twice."

The more enthusiastic the Choir, the pinker Liam's face—and the deeper Sophie fell in love.

"If you don't mind, Yanosh, we'd like to borrow the chapel," Paleo said to the guitarist, and he bowed his head.

Gesturing to the dancers, he said, "Collect your mugs on the way out, and don't forget to sign up for next week's community service assignments."

A zaftig woman with a harelip raised her hand. "I thought we were taking the week off for Mother's visit."

"That's an option," Paleo started, "and yes, there will be plenty of opportunity to collect CI during the

Thanksgiving banquet, but that doesn't mean you close your eyes or heart to the world around you. There's no holiday from one's faith, Irina. Wouldn't you agree?"

The woman seemed alone in the room for a few moments. Her fellow members remained close, but their body language changed in an instant. It stiffened, even cooled, until Irina said, "Yes, of course. I want as much CI as I can get. I want to make my mothers proud."

Paleo floated to Irina and cradled her face. Her thumb grazed the deformity as she pulled the woman closer and lay a gentle but unifying kiss on her lips. "You already have, darling. You all have." Turning back to Sophie, she added, "You all will."

As the Choir members exited on a wave of rollicking chatter, a thin freckled girl bounded up to Sophie. "Hi, I'm Bella! I'm new too!"

"Nice to meet you, Bella. Where are you from?"

Irina returned to the room and put her arm around Bella. "Come on, sweetheart. You don't want to be late."

The little girl waved goodbye and Sophie waved back. "Talk to you later, Bella!"

Liam unstacked a chair from the perimeter and set it in the center of the room. "Sophie?" He patted the seat, and she shuffled to him.

"Sorry, I was just meeting some of the members."

"Actually . . . " Peter's lips pulled to one side of his face as he wrung his hands. " . . . we'd prefer you didn't just yet."

"Oh. I thought this was supposed to be like a family."

"It is," Paleo said, "and you're going to be a big part of it. But there's a certain protocol to these things—for their protection and for yours."

Liam kissed both of her hands and eased her into the chair, where she surveyed her surroundings. The so-called "black chapel" was like no chapel she'd ever seen. It was the color of the Pacific on a clear summer day, and the carpet was nearly the same shade of robin's egg blue, their differences only perceptible where they joined. It dizzied her for a few seconds; all the blue made her feel like the chair was floating.

She looked away, to the black curtain rod running the perimeter of the room and the ebony curtains pulled tight into the corners. The cinched draperies looked like caves flanking the meagerly adorned walls. There were no altars, no candles, no stained-glass saints, but iron and porcelain muzzles peeked out from behind the curtains and clutter, granting Sophie a glimpse of secret and surveying statues of sheep.

Junipero appeared beside her with a plate of diced melon, a pitcher of iced tea, and a blank white mug. She poured Sophie a cup and bowed her head before leaving the pitcher with Paleo. Sophie looked up at the pregnant woman as she drank, only then noticing the tattoo on the underside of her milky chin. A thick black line ran down the middle, flanked by small blue dots.

Paleo noticed her staring and slid her finger along the design. "Pretty groovy, huh?"

She nodded. "I don't think I've seen someone with a tattoo there before."

"Well, now you've seen two." Peter chuckled, then lifted his chin, proudly stroking a design identical to his wife's.

The melting ice diluted Sophie's tea, but it was still a bit heavy for her taste. It had a cloying cherry flavor that blanketed her tongue, but the more she drank, the cleaner and more refreshing it became. She swished her tongue around her mouth as she tossed her focus to Liam.

"Do *you* have a tattoo?"

The apples of his cheeks flamed, and a smile twitched onto his lips. "Not yet." He refilled her tea, set the pitcher aside, and joined his parents in transforming the room into a place befitting its name. As Sophie imbibed, the trio released and spread the black velvet curtains. The lamb statues pinned them over the perimeter clutter, but sky-blue slivers flashed in the openings until Peter dimmed the overhead lights and disappeared the color into the gloom.

In less than five minutes, the room became a midnight mass. Sophie sat her empty glass beside the chair and watched as the Lights assumed spots in the front corners while Liam crouched at the record player between them. Like a holy relic, he slid a record from its sleeve and placed it on the spindle. The LP hit the turntable with a sacred pop, and the room crackled for several seconds. Then, a single violin pierced the atmosphere. More strings and keys joined the mix, but the original violin lorded the cobalt dark for a solid minute before another instrument dared to sound a louder voice.

Sophie thought it was an oboe at first, but following a prolonged note, the sound dipped sharply and shifted into a human singing: *"How luminescent is our worship. Raising voices in the night and choices in the day."*

The singing then blended with the music so exquisitely it became indistinguishable from the instruments, except for lyrical bursts like *"tend the faith"* and *"burn, burn, burn."* It enraptured her so completely she didn't notice Liam approach until he was directly in front of her.

"Sophie, my parents are going to talk to you now," he said soberly. "Is that okay?"

Her eyelids were heavy, and color flooded her mind when she squeezed them shut. "We're already talking."

Peter clamped a hand to Liam's shoulder, and the trio shared a poignant look. They turned their focus to the ceiling in apparent gratitude, their mouths moving soundlessly.

Sophie wondered if she was supposed to be listening to them, but the voice on the record rose again, filling their lips with the singer's words: *"Rise, little lamb, and feast at the altar of shame."*

Liam shrank into the background and sank to the floor. He leaned against the rump of a bronze sheep while his parents gazed down at Sophie like mythical titans peeking through the haze of unreality to grant her a sliver of truth.

"Before we begin," Paleo said, "you must understand

the sanctity of what we're about to tell you. Any fool can interpret our history to her liking. Any skeptic can denounce us with brash and insulting headlines—and they do—but what you hear today and for the rest of your time with us are holy maxims. Gospels. This isn't a game to us, Sophie. This is what all life should be."

"It isn't a game to me either," Sophie said, spitting up the words like lumps of clay.

The Lights moved like sluggish phantoms around her. Everything did but the lamb statues. They bleated at her with tongues outstretched as their spirits pranced and pronked through the room.

Paleo dabbed sweat from Sophie's brow and gave her another sip of tea. It wasn't cold anymore, but it still felt good rushing down her throat, like it awakened vessels and nerves that had long lain dormant. It was normal for the Choir to care for people like they did, to welcome everyone with the same embrace and celebrate whatever twisted magic brought them to the garden.

The singer on the record agreed. She crooned about "*flower children*" and embracing "*the fires that bore them.*"

But there was another creature baying in the chapel, hazier than the rest. It was a female, that much she could see, but there was such darkness and mist ensconcing her, gender was just a dumb word given as a gift that became a burden. Warmth wafted from her shadowy body like a promise, which Sophie wanted to doubt but couldn't. The love of the dark figure ribboned toward her in waves of color and textured light. When she reached for it, the color washed over her arms and crashed misty against her chest, billowing over the rest of her and leaving droplets like candy dots on her skin.

The figure stood, and the world pulsed with the rising song. "*Live with the lamb on your tongue. The green buds are cracking. Live with Agnes in bloom.*"

Sophie whispered, "Agnes," and the chapel flashed crimson.

This wasn't normal. But what *was* normal these days? The violence that devastated Vietnam? How about the monsters that assassinated Martin Luther King Jr. when Sophie was ten, or the bastards that murdered his mother six years later? She'd rather find normality with the hazy girl-creature bathed in blood-light. At least she felt love there, like a vine digging its way up through miles of sedimentary fear.

"Mother Agnes is within you," Paleo said, "as is our patron saint, Agnes of Rome."

Sophie licked her lips, and her head lolled on her shoulders. "Who is she?"

"She was just a kid," Liam said, voice clipped by sorrow. "A young girl who wanted nothing more than to live a good and chaste life, and to worship God and Mother Mary's holy children, regardless of station." His chin trembled, and he clenched his jaw. "They hated her purity. They hated her faith and everything it stood for. They wouldn't let her live in peace."

Sophie had seen Liam in daylight and dusklight, in blanching florescence and a bonfire's glow, but he looked like a new man in the dim chapel. She gripped the seat of her chair as he advanced, his pupils preternaturally sharp in the shadow. He begged her focus, but as the music ascended to a steady throb, Sophie fell into the color and rhythm, and her lips moved in time with the soprano screeching, "*Burn, burn, burn.*"

Touching Sophie's back, Paleo delivered her voice straight into the girl's bones. It filled her eyes too, but it drained when the figure in the corner assumed a shape not unlike her own.

"Agnes the virgin-martyr was born of Roman nobility," Paleo said as the beautiful girl lifted her eyes to Sophie. "She was a buoyant symbol of God's love, and men couldn't help but desire her—or want to destroy her."

"Someone killed her?"

"Many tried," she replied. "After Agnes chose a holy

union with her creator over every prospective suitor, the resentful men submitted her name to the authorities and exposed her as a Christian. As punishment for her crime, they stripped her clothes and dragged her through the streets to a brothel—the intended site of her public deflowering."

The sight unfolded before Sophie in such horrific detail she thought it might be one of her spells, but a sharp turn in the melody flooded the black chapel with pristine starlight.

Paleo kicked off her shoes as the music livened to a plucky waltz, and Agnes of Rome grinned at Sophie as her sandy hair grew long enough to cover her exposed body.

"Like enchanted vines," Peter said fondly. "Agnes's hair shielded her from the gaze of her oppressors."

"But that didn't stop them," Liam said.

The stars went dark like a single delicate flame snuffed by breath, and he continued softly. "Overcome by rage and jealousy, some of the men tried to defile her right there under the watchful eye of her Christian god, but those who attempted to rape her were struck blind by a mysterious force."

Agnes tilted her head to Sophie, and luminosity shone from every pore as the music proclaimed: "*Again our mother is saved.*"

A violin announced its presence with squealing marcato that bristled Sophie's arms. Just as the gooseflesh was melting back into her skin, a faint, singular voice came in a minor key. "*But all is not well in the garden.*"

"There were brawls in the streets," Paleo said. "The attempted violation of Agnes spurred so much violence that the son of the prefect who sentenced her to the brothel was killed in the skirmish. Many rejoiced at this, but not sweet, godly Agnes. She did not see his death as vengeance for the wrongs against her, rather a needless death in her name. So she knelt beside him and prayed for his life to be restored."

"I can take you many places. I can show you many things."

The corpse at Agnes's feet twitched, then rolled onto its side. She touched his face, and slowly, sure as the sunrise, his eyelids lifted and he looked into the soul of the child who saved him.

Sophie gasped. "Her prayers saved his life."

"Yes," Liam said. "And the prefect was so grateful he refused to participate in Agnes's persecution."

"They let her go?"

Sophie's question was answered quickly, first by the teary eyes of the young girl who knelt, still praying, her body entwined in hair, and then by the trio standing before her, heads bowed in sorrow.

Sophie shook her head as faceless men stormed from the shadows and grabbed Agnes by the arms. They spat on her and yanked her hair, but nothing could dim the holy light radiating from her skin.

Sophie jumped out of her seat. "This isn't fair! She saved his life, and they're going to kill her! Fight back!" she screamed at the figment being dragged into the shadows.

Liam coaxed her into the chair and held her hands as she whimpered.

"She has to fight. Or God does. Why did He bring that man back to life and refuse to help Agnes?"

"You're asking the wrong question, my love. It isn't our place to know why God and the great mothers needed to take Agnes from this earth, but the more we work to find her magic within ourselves through worship and service, the more we become worthy of such devotions. Until that time, we have an earthly guide to our patron saint's holiness. One who serves as mother to us all, one who shares our patron's name."

"Mother Agnes," Sophie whispered.

Liam's hands were damp, dripping down her cheeks, but her brain felt like it was spinning in her skull when she pulled away. Each new piece of theology felt like a mallet pounding a metal peg into porridge.

Her stomach growled, and she gulped more tea.

"Burn, burn, burn."

The lyrical fire kindled her throat and made her thirstier. It danced over her tongue and out into the black chapel like the vines of hair shielding St. Agnes. Red and orange flames lit the room and licked the velvet curtains to holey shrouds. Sophie squinted through the firelight at the limp girl on the floor, and her heart ached for the virgin-martyr. Her body was swollen and stretched, and the loosened skin glistened with scarlet stains. The fire devoured her hair until only a helmet of oily matted veins remained sizzling on her scalp.

"She's hurt," Sophie whispered. "They're burning her alive."

The Lights glanced at each other, and Liam stroked Sophie's cheek.

"How did you know that?'

"I can see her." Sophie squeezed her eyes shut, and bold colors swam through her brain. She opened them to quell the building nausea and apologized. "No, it can't be. I don't know what I see."

"The truth," Liam said. "They did try to burn Agnes alive. They tied her to a stake and stoked the wood at her feet."

"The world is a garden . . . burn, burn, burn."

"But the kindling wouldn't catch," he continued, nearly singing. "They even set their torches to her body, but the flames wouldn't harm her. Young as she was, Agnes was a whetstone of a woman, born to sharpen all she touched . . . and never burn. They had to behead her to kill her, and they never perverted her chastity. Even as her blessed blood flooded the stadium floor and the mourners soaked it up with lambswool, she remained pure."

The frolicsome statues in Sophie's periphery returned to their plaintive bleating—except for one. An impish lamb resembling something from a Mother Goose rhyme spoke in a voice that turned her stomach, and with pink lips peeled back from its milk teeth, the creature hissed, " . . . *it must be tended . . . burn, burn, burn.*"

Her face glazed in sweat, she reached for her tea, but Liam whisked it away.

"You need something colder."

She nodded woozily, and a bead of sweat dislodged from her brow. It rolled into her eye, and she grunted at the stinging. She blinked, and the room was clad in massive ribbons of scarlet. With another blink, it flipped back to midnight blue.

Music twirled around her like falling stardust, and an oboe moaned with the singer: "*We are your hair, your flesh, your womb.*"

The room flashed with light when Peter returned with a glass of ice water. Liam fished out a cube and popped it in Sophie's mouth. It melted almost instantly, filling her head with a cool fog that billowed as she exhaled. There, a face bloomed, but it was pale, parched, and unwelcome. She wasn't a saintly martyr like Agnes, though her mutilated image was no less jarring. Her hair was long too, often shaggy and shaking like an itchy veil in Sophie's face when she leaned over to point out homework errors. Tilting her head back, the woman's throat opened like a sloppy mouth that wheezed and whistled and called another beast into the room.

He was bigger than normal, and his golden body bulged with tumorous sores. Nilsson growled at Sophie's former tutor, Moira Shunn, his monstrous jaws slick with hunger.

Sophie screamed, but Nilsson wouldn't listen. He sunk his teeth into the woman's mangled neck, and laughter bubbled from the fresh wounds. Sophie covered her ears, but Moira's voice was on the record now, singing louder and louder.

"*What in the soil spoils first? Why do rotten seeds take root?*"

"Stop it!"

HARES IN THE HEDGEROW

"It's the maggots in your mind, child. It's the blood on your hands."

"Why are you doing this to me?"

Nilsson ripped the vocal cords from Moira's throat, and she cackled from between his teeth. *"Why did you kill me, Sophie Francis?"*

CHAPTER SEVEN

RIGID WATER ROLLED down the bridge of Sophie's nose, and a gust of mentholated breath plucked a curtain of tears from her eyes. When she blinked them away, Liam crouched in front of her, his hand dripping and face flushed like a kid at a magic show.

"Where did she take you?" he asked.

The chapel's black skin was peeled back, and the room was a calm blue ocean again, but Sophie's stomach tightened in terror when Liam's parents looked on her adoringly, clutching mugs of tea.

The tea. There was something in it, some kind of hallucinogen. Sophie jumped to her feet, but her legs were rubbery and sore. Her hips ached too, like she'd been sitting in the same spot for hours. Dizziness struck her like a mallet, and she sank to the floor. When Liam tried to help her, she slapped him as hard as she could, and he backed away, pouting.

"What's in that tea?"

"Sophie, just calm down and let me explain."

She shook her head. "You did something to me. You drugged me." Scrambling to her feet, she flew toward the door, but it was locked from the outside. "Why are you doing this? What did you give me?"

"A test," said Paleo firmly. "And you passed with flying colors."

"A test?"

"Some of us have deeper blessings than others, a more

72

natural connection to the holy mothers," Paleo said, approaching cautiously. "Agnes of Rome had the purest connection to her maker, and we have to accept that a lot of us will never come close to that, but we can still graze the magic that bridges Agnes and God. Some are born with it. Others have to work for it. No one starts on an equal footing. Such is life."

"But we can all reach higher levels of enlightenment," Liam said. "We can mimic Agnes's gifts. Her visions, for instance—the ability to communicate with God as intimately as mother and child."

Sophie massaged her aching head. "What does that have to do with the test?"

Liam stood beside her, and she let him. He stroked her hand and kissed her knee and spoke in a comforting purr. "I'm sorry, Sophie. We needed to see how easily you can communicate with Agnes. The palm tea helps. It's special."

Her nostrils flared. "Special. You mean drugged."

"You can think of it as medicine if you like. Or vitamins," Peter offered.

"Fuck you. You violated me." Sophie smacked the door and shouted for someone to let her out.

"Sophie, please," Liam whispered. "If you take a breath and look at it objectively, you'll realize this is a big misunderstanding."

"You drugged me."

"And I would do it again if it meant liberating the soul in your song." He leaned his chin on her shoulder, and she quieted. "That's what you want, isn't it?"

She exhaled heavily as he drew so close his words warmed her earlobe. Her legs throbbed with wobbly pain as she turned and pressed her back against the door.

"The Lamb will awaken and replenish your heart," Liam said. "She will be your eternal muse. She will never forsake or deny you, and from this time on, you will hear only truth. Can your mom say that? Has a day passed that she hasn't lied to you?"

"I don't know."

The Lights were behind her now too, all the world's regret in their voices as they hazarded an embrace.

"It won't happen again, we promise," Peter told her. "It's a requirement, I'm afraid. All first timers do it, the three of us included. But it was nothing like that."

"What do you mean?"

"What you saw today—this wasn't the first time, was it? You see things without the tea."

She averted her eyes. There was no blood on her hands, but her fingers felt tacked together like two scabs grown into one. "What kind of things?"

"God?" Paleo asked, then added evenly, "Death?"

"Those are two different things."

"Are they?" Peter said. "Tell us, dear. What did you see?"

She clenched and unclenched her hands, searching for a way to say "the tutor I think I killed" without actually saying it. In the end, all that came out was, "Someone I used to know."

"Your father?"

"No, I never knew him."

"If you don't mind me asking," Paleo started softly, "how did he die?"

She squinted. "A boat wreck. I don't know the details. My mom—" She stopped in a wave of grief. "It hurts my mom too much to talk about it."

Paleo glided closer, her head at a sympathetic slant. "Does it hurt you, dear?"

Sophie's hand flew to her chest where the brass ring hung beneath her shirt. She'd been hiding it all day—she didn't know from who—and only now felt its weight like an albatross around her neck.

"How could it? I never met him, or don't remember anyway."

"You've never met the devil," Peter said, "but that fella hurts us all every damn day."

"Maybe I *have* met him. Maybe the devil's the one giving me visions."

When Sophie crossed her arms over her chest, the Lights laughed and patted her like a dumb puppy.

"Oh my child, you burn too brightly for the devil to touch," Paleo said fondly. "I know it's hard to understand, but you're what we all aspire to be."

"I can't imagine having gifts like yours. I doubt I'll ever be that strong," Liam said, and Paleo rubbed his back.

"Of course you will be, dear. Just keep your CI up, and Agnes will reward you for your service."

"What's CI?" Sophie asked.

"Chastity Intelligence," Liam said. "It's how we measure our level of enlightenment. I'm a four."

"Is four . . . low?"

"No one is low," Peter answered quickly. "All levels are blessed."

"But some are more blessed than others, it seems," Sophie muttered. "And you get CI by doing community service?"

A grin lifted Liam's ears, and he kissed Sophie's hands. "I knew you'd catch on."

"Is that what *I* am? Community service?"

Liam shook his head so hard it looked like he might fling off his skin. "Of course not! How can you ask me that?"

"So you didn't get CI for bringing me here?"

He exchanged pensive glances with the Lights, then bowed his head. "Yes, recruitment is rewarded, but that's not *why* I brought you here. I want to share everything with you. Sophie, I love you."

Tears spilled down her cheeks. Her stomach ached, and the throb in the back of her neck felt like fat vines constricting her spinal cord.

"You shouldn't love me," she said, and pushed through the trio to the bronze sheep statue lowing at the velvet cave. The lamb's head was cool, but the metallic tongue protruding from the bleating rictus was as warm and moist as a hard-boiled egg. Sophie recoiled, then spotted something odd on the wall: a green streak under the cinched curtain. Pulling back the black drapery, she exposed a garden flourishing in secret paint. Among the tall and swaying flowers, birds flitted and swooped, and hares poked their pointed snouts up through the vegetation.

When she pressed her hand to the wall, damp roots grew thick from the painting and entwined her wrist. "There's something wrong with me," she hissed. "Spells. My mom calls them *spells*."

"Your mom doesn't understand you," Liam said, drawing closer. "As long as she insists on lying to you, it's impossible." He spun her around, breaking the roots and squeezing fresh tears from her eyes. "It's not good for you being with her, and you know it. There's no home for you there."

"There's no home for me anywhere," she whined.

Liam lifted her chin and smiled as he dried her cheeks. "Oh Soph, you have no idea how wrong you are."

"What do you mean?"

Closing his hands around hers, he said, "It's time to see your place in the garden."

 ❧

Liam and the Lights led Sophie through the golden gullet of a dining room. Its appearance had changed significantly in the last couple hours. A large red rug sat below the extended table like an eager tongue, and swaying paper lanterns textured the palate of the room. Choir members of all ages zoomed in and out, experimenting with table settings and china patterns.

"Things aren't usually so hectic," Liam said. "With the holiday coming up, we're working hard to make sure everything goes to plan."

"Thanksgiving is a big deal for you guys, huh?"

"This year's different," Paleo said. "Mother Agnes is coming, and she's invited some very special guests. Michael Wooden from channel six. Gorman Best from channel eight, and Janet Evey from the *Chronicle*. A few politicians too."

"Leftwing loudmouths," Peter grumbled.

His wife frowned. "Forgiveness, my love. And faith. Some people find those qualities hard to swallow—thick and bitter, like strange medicine—so we must show them the elixir of our ways. We shall drink deeper than ever before, and when the Lamb comes, in all its goodness and glory, they won't have any choice but to believe." Paleo smiled at Sophie, pinching a lock of her hair as they entered the kitchen. "But I'm sure they'll come around the minute they meet Mother Agnes. They won't need to fear us or write those horrible things about our community. Calling it a cult." She coughed up the word like the last acidic glob of a vomiting jag, her stomach fiercely cradled like the poisonous word could hurt her unborn child.

"You'll be here to meet her, won't you?" Peter asked Sophie. "Or I suppose you have plans with your mother."

Sophie's skin still buzzed from the tea, sometimes in elation, sometimes in dread, but when Peter reminded her of the broken Thanksgiving promise, every pore felt like a nauseated gut.

"No." Her voice cracked, and she cleared her throat. "No plans."

"Then it's settled. You'll spend the day with us." Liam hooted and wrapped his arms around her. "I can't wait for Mother Agnes to meet you. She's going to flip out."

Sophie scoffed as they reached the back door. "She really likes weirdoes, huh?"

"You betcha. Weirdoes like Agnes of Rome," Liam said. "And like Saint Agnes she also embodies chastity, femininity, guidance . . . " He opened the back door, revealing the vibrant yard. " . . . and gardens."

Outside, more than a dozen members of the Choir of

the Lamb waved to Sophie. The air was cool but cloying, almost oily, and she had to brace herself on Liam to breathe it all in. He led her down the stairs to the garden where the stone walkway cut through a rich grid of plants and flowers. They walked through sun-streaked patches of vegetation, carrots and cabbage and dew-speckled peppers, and into a lush plot of pink and purple chrysanthemums. Beside the flowers, the bordering hedgerow grew thick as a child's fear at night. Choir kids giggled, a few answered the passing birds with a whistle, and there was always the sound of trowels and rakes, punctuated by the occasional ding of tools dragging up stones.

Hand in hand with Liam, Sophie gazed down at a tiny spot of tilled earth disappearing under the hedgerow. "We tend the entire garden," he said, "but every member gets their own plot. This is mine," he said, gesturing to a rich patch of peppers and mushrooms. "And the one beside it will be yours."

The tea and its resulting rage still coursed her veins, it wasn't as frenetic as before. It simmered and shrank with every sunny welcoming face that appeared to watch Sophie find her place.

Kneeling at the empty plot, she pushed her fingers into the soil and felt for the writhing wet things she saw in her dreams. They were there; they had to be. After years of slimy vines knotting up the backs of her eyes and dropping her sanity like rotten fruit, she'd finally come to meet them in the Choir's garden.

But there was nothing under the surface. Just Sophie and the empty earth. Her fingers and her fear.

And the tiny claw marks flanking a tunnel under the hedgerow.

"Sorry about that," Petal said from her tomato patch. "A hare dug its way in a few days ago, ate up everything in that spot. I can fill it in for you."

"No," Sophie said, her fingers walking deep into the burrow. "No, I can do it."

She stood too fast, and dizziness whipped through her like a flu chill. But it wasn't as scary as before. It was purer, more swoon than spell. Even when her belly clenched with sudden nausea, she couldn't focus on anything but the encircling Choir. She'd never seen so many smiles in one place or felt such generosity, like a flood of adoration, a whirling dervish of support.

But it was all too much. The tea, the garden, the Lamb in all its goodness and glory—wanting *her*.

Sophie's vision doubled, her knees buckled, and Liam helped her wilt to the ground. He cradled her as the Choir closed in, gazing upon her clammy face like a doting family around a newborn's crib. Pain radiated to her toes, and a quick bit of math made her flush with humiliation. She'd never been great at tracking her menstrual cycle, but she'd never slipped up this bad.

Tears stung her eyes as she stood shakily, and then fell fast when she saw the severity of her flow. Blood soaked her pants and stained Liam's, and even though he didn't look disgusted or angry, Sophie couldn't imagine he was anything but. She wished she were home in bed, ringed by poetry and mushy stars, where only the vinyl voices of her idols could cool her embarrassment.

But Liam wouldn't let her run. He closed his arms around her and whispered a prayer against her shoulder. The Choir bowed their heads in uniform worship, except for the little girl named Sunny, who pushed her way to the front of the crowd and pointed at Sophie.

"Lee-Lee," she squealed. "Lee-lee, she's bleeding!"

"Yes, she is," he whispered against her throat. "She's the one."

CHAPTER EIGHT

NIGHT WAS FALLING when Sophie yawned and opened her eyes to the rushing road. She rolled her head over her aching shoulders and swished her tongue around her mouth.

"Good morning, sunshine," Liam said playfully, shifting his eyes from the road to blow her a kiss. "Feeling any better?"

Her cramps echoed all the way to her toes, which she flexed inside her shoes. She rustled the plastic bag containing her blood-stained clothes on the Kombi floor and scowled. She doubted they were salvageable, and the loose gown Paleo lent her was more comfortable anyway. She could wear a muumuu for the rest of her life and be perfectly content.

Liam passed over a thermos, which Sophie gave a suspicious squint, and he chuckled. "It's plain water, I promise. No more tea unless you want it."

She took the thermos and grumbled as she unscrewed the lid. "I wish I'd had the choice the first time."

"I know, and I'm sorry. But it worked, Soph, just like Mother Agnes said it would. It proved you're one of us." He patted her thigh, and she gingerly laid her hand on top of his, prompting his fingers to sink into her skin. "You don't have to go back to Concord, you know. The Choir will take care of you."

"I know."

"If you're worried about your music, we have a good collection too. We can replace anything you left at your mom's."

"I know, but . . . " Sophie sighed and rested her chin on her hand. She thought back on the farmhouse as they'd driven away, its facade studded with seeming angels. The Choir of the Lamb was tangled up in one another, leaning and lounging and waving goodbye to the bloody girl. Children chased after Liam's bus, singing Sophie's name as they shrank in the mirror on the long, bare road. A large part of Sophie had wanted to stay. Doubt over their rituals roiled her guts, but she couldn't deny their kindness and unwavering faith. No one had ever made her feel so welcome—or so normal.

But eager as she was to cloister herself in a new house with a new family and start a new life with Liam, she couldn't leave without tying up the loose ends of the old one. She felt like that was something her mother would do, and Sophie refused to make the same mistakes. Like St. Agnes, she would confront Ava, forgive her, and move on.

"There are things I need to do first," she said. "You understand, don't you?"

"Of course," he said, but revved the engine slightly. "It's just that I couldn't wait to get away from my old family, and I know our situations are different, but I see similarities and patterns in yours. Mother Agnes teaches us to recognize souls in pain. It's easier with people like me, a kid who'd rather live on the street than at home with monsters, spending every moment of my life praying for a miracle. I didn't want to hide my loneliness or heartbreak. I just wanted to be safe. But you're still lying to yourself. You're still pretending you're safe when you're not. You're alone on an island, lost in the dark, like I was. And being misunderstood by people who are supposed to love you—I know how painful that is."

Being misunderstood did hurt, but as Liam looked at her, Sophie knew the anguish of being *understood* too. He saw the real her like she saw the writhing wet things climbing out of the earth.

Except those things weren't real, and Sophie was. *She*

was the writhing thing. She was the worm stuck in the dirt, and she knew it, loved it, wanted him to get down in the bloody soil with her.

"You're too special for your mother to understand. That's why she hides things from you."

Sophie recoiled. "I don't know for sure she's hiding anything."

"Like I said, the Choir teaches us to read people, especially those in pain. Your mom—I can see it—she's hiding something and whatever it is, it's big." He hooked his finger under her necklace chain and pulled out the brass ring. "You said this was a gift from your dad."

She held the ring in her fist, her forehead crinkled as she tucked it under her shirt. "It was a gift from my dad to my mom on her twelfth birthday."

"When she lived in Ohio?"

"Yup."

He wiggled his nose like a butterfly had landed on the tip. "Under the name 'Francis?'"

"Liam, spit it out."

"Look, I don't want to accuse your mom of anything serious, but I've learned that people are capable of concealing all manner of sins. My dad had a second family I didn't know about until the Choir took me in. They helped me understand why I am the way I am, and where to put the anger I'd been holding inside for so long on the street. It's just—" He ran his hand through his hair and shifted his focus to his lap. "I don't like what you've told me about her. And I don't like what you *haven't* told me about her. Basic stuff."

Sophie didn't know what to say because she'd been asking herself the same questions all her life. She scooped out her brass ring and pressed it to her lips. It was hot, the scent strong. It had comforted her all her life, this scent she came to think of as her father's. It was all she had of him, and doubting it felt like insects infesting her veins. Still, she removed it and shoved it in the bag of bloody clothes.

"Take me home."

"To the Choir?"

She snapped her head to him. "No. Home-home."

He sighed in resignation as he glued his eyes to the road, and they didn't speak for the rest of the drive.

The lights were off in her apartment, a small mercy that allowed Sophie the opportunity to take her first full breath since she woke on the road. She didn't feel like subjecting her mother to an inquisition any night, but especially not a night when her insides felt like a Jell-O mold spiked with rotten fruit.

She thanked Liam for the ride and started away, but his pleading whisper stopped her.

"Ask her," he said. "Please. However bad the truth is, it's not as toxic as a lie."

She couldn't bear to look at him directly, but she nodded and said, "Talk to you later." As she marched away, she felt like her muscles were bundles of frayed wire crisscrossing her chest, poking her, tearing at her, making it feel like she barely had lungs left when she reached the top of the stairs.

The ghost in the attic stomped and scuffled—then jiggled the doorknob in the vestibule. She'd never seen it jiggle before, never seen anyone go in or out, and she squealed as she gasped for air.

When Mr. Mio exited, they both yelped and clutched their respective belongings—her bag of clothes and his stack of papers—and he stared at the girl like her hair was engulfed in blue flame. As if annoyed by polite society, he forced a stiff nod of recognition and hurried down the stairs.

Once his door was closed, she tried the knob. Locked. So, Mr. Mio had a key to the attic apartment? Was he the ghost all these years? Did her mother have a key too?

Despite the safety the darkness gave her like a secret kiss, a sliver of Sophie feared her mother would be somewhere nearby, waiting in the cold, angry dark to judge her.

Relief washed over her when she entered the empty apartment. There was a note on the table, but by the time she'd showered and slumped down in the easy chair at the front window, she'd forgotten all about it. She sat in the dim room, silent, turning over the brass ring in her fingers and wondering how many fake worlds had been built to protect such a tiny thing. Was it all the things Ava said it was, or was it just some silly toy to which she'd lashed the memory of an absent man? Heavier than before, she set the brass ring on the windowsill, tilting back her head as the pain in her uterus bowed to the anguish in her heart.

She woke to the blast of a car horn. Popping up, she spotted her mother from the window and rushed from the living room. Sometimes it disturbed her how well she'd gotten at hitting her bedroom light and burying herself in blankets before her mother's key turned in the lock, but not tonight.

Sophie's bedroom door opened, and Ava's shadow oozed over her. She didn't speak, barely even moved for nearly a minute. Then she sniffled and walked into the living room, where she loudly collected the brass ring from the windowsill.

CHAPTER NINE

SOPHIE SLEPT PAST NOON, and she still felt like shit. The brass ring was on her bedside table when she woke, and as much as her mom leaving it there annoyed her, a strange relief washed over her.

Hanging it over her heart again, she trudged to the kitchen where a new note sat atop the one she hadn't read. No need, really. What connection could her mother possibly make with her through a hasty note that she hadn't already done in years of cold, distant parenting?

But like the brass ring, maybe she'd feel better after a little more distance. She pocketed both notes, swigged some milk, and headed over to Dionne's where her friend looked like she was going to rip her head off.

"Did you tell someone at the theater I was looking for a new job?" she screeched.

Sophie winced. "Whoops. Yeah. Sorry. I never should've said your name."

"Mrs. Casavettes thought I was quitting and asked me all kinds of dumb questions. It was a huge pain in the ass. What the hell were you thinking?"

"I was going to apply for a job at the theater, but I changed my mind. I don't know why I said your name. I panicked. I didn't mean to make trouble."

Dionne pegged a fist to her hip and pursed her lips. "Well, you did."

She was still wearing her Robin Hood uniform from the breakfast shift, the brown button down shirt spotted with grease and Tabasco. She must've just gotten home because the apartment only smelled like one variety of stale smoke. Plus, she hadn't noticed the mustard on her right cheek yet. She waved Sophie inside and unknotted the bandanna at the nape of her neck, freeing her massive mane of curls. Digging her nails into her scalp, she sighed and strutted to her bedroom, where she liberated a joint from the false bottom of her music box. The smoke floated up, making it look like her Jimi Hendrix poster was exhaling through puckered lips. Most of her bedroom was draped in colorful tapestries and an intimidating concert poster collection featuring musicians like Jimi and Jefferson Airplane at Bill Graham's Fillmore East, as well as a picture of herself with a replacement bass player from The Quick, who she'd fooled around with at the Starwood earlier that year.

Sophie heard the story of her quickie with The Quick's bassist at least a dozen times since, and it got filthier each time Dionne told it. As much as she loved Jerry Garcia's music, one of the many reasons Sophie fought so hard to attend the JGB concert was to meet a bass player of her very own.

Sitting on Dionne's bed, the friends smoked and Sophie talked. She told Dionne about the Choir of the Lamb, Agnes of Rome, and the hallucinogenic tea, but not that the Choir dosed her, or the horrible things she saw while tripping.

"That's when we went to the garden," she said, "and right there, in front of Liam's whole family, I got the heaviest period of my life. Like, murder scene heavy."

Dionne snorted, and plumes of smoke shot out of her nostrils. She made a quacking sound as she caught her breath and pounded her chest.

"Sorry. Whew, so how'd they take that?"

"Surprisingly well. They acted like it was some big important sign."

"A sign for what? That you should be minding your tampon instead of tripping with hippies?" She headed to the kitchen for water, and Sophie followed. Leaning against the counter as Dionne gulped half the glass, she gnawed on the inside of her cheek.

"They think it means I belong there," she said.

Dionne raised her eyebrows and wiped water from her chin. "Well, that's the weirdest damn cult initiation I've ever heard of."

"It's not a cult!"

"Whatever you say. I know better than to pick a fight with you while you're ragging." She refilled her glass and took another sip. "But come on, Soph, you're not seriously considering joining this thing, are you? Living in that house with all those people?"

"I don't know. That's why I need your help." Taking Dionne by the shoulders, Sophie whined and shook her friend until she laughed.

"Okay, okay! But you owe me one. And if you *do* leave me behind, you better expect a ton of late-night phone calls. I'm kinda fond of you, kid." She knocked against Sophie's shoulder, and Sophie knocked back.

They playfully shoved and smacked each other until Sophie called for a truce. Ripping out a piece of notebook paper, she scrawled Liam's phone number and threw it at her friend.

"Pleasure doing business with you," Dionne said cheekily, spun on her toe and strutted out of her bedroom, hips swinging like wrecking balls as Sophie called after.

"Is this the right time to mention you have mustard on your face?"

Dionne gasped and popped into the pale pink bathroom, her eyes like saucers as she groaned at the dried goo. She scrubbed her face and returned to the bedroom, stripping off her reeking Robin Hood uniform. Once her sweater was tucked and her hair tamed, she dabbed a thin layer of homemade black gloss on her lips. After a vivacious pop, she slid a cigarette out of the pack on the sink and struck a match while Sophie stared on, silent.

"Okay," she said. "How can I help?"

"Break into the attic with me."

Dionne pulled a green glass ashtray out from under her bed and tapped her lipstick-stained cigarette on the edge. "I'm intrigued. Explain."

"I've heard noises through the ceiling for years. Haven't you?"

"Run-of-the-mill ghosts. Or mice." She shrugged. "Or ghost mice."

"Or Mr. Mio," Sophie said. "I saw him coming out of there last night with a bunch of stuff." She sat across from Dionne, their knees forming a diamond beneath the rising smoke rings. "If he has stuff up there, maybe our moms have stuff up there too."

Dionne plucked a piece of tobacco from her lip and flicked it into the ashtray. "What's that got to do with this Choir thing?"

"Liam thinks my mom is hiding something from me, and as much as I want to ignore it, I can't. I've thought about it too much myself, way before he said anything. I've searched our place before and there's nothing from her childhood. Just this stupid ring. I have to know if she has stuff up there."

"And if it's just an attic?"

Sophie's lips parted, but she didn't answer. She extended two fingers, and Dionne passed over the last of her cigarette. Sophie closed her mouth on her friend's glossy lip print and took a consumptive drag. Exhaling, she stood in front of the mirror, then spread the dots of ebony gloss over her lips.

"How much do you know about your mom, Dionne? Or your dad?"

"A little," she said, rising. She pulled an eye shadow kit from her rickety vanity drawer and gestured for Sophie to sit. Dionne squatted and swiped Sophie's eyelids with midnight blue powder. She blew the excess from her friend's face and smiled. "My mom was a preacher's daughter in Alabama. She lost a toe in a thresher when she ran away from home once. She trusted the wrong stranger, got in way over her head, but it was better than home, apparently. Open your eyes."

Sophie complied, and Dionne analyzed the symmetry of her work.

With a nod, she put the eye shadow away and pulled out a handful of tiny elastic bands. "Her mama died having her," she continued as she separated a chunk of hair on Sophie's left side and began braiding. "And her daddy beat her. Not as bad as her grandmama though. The old bitch went after her with a switch if she didn't eat her vegetables." She tied off both braids and massaged the ravine between the plaits with a dab of coconut oil. "My dad was a glorified spunkrag, but if you really want to know how many times he disappointed my mom over the years, I could rattle off the shit-list."

"That's way more than I know about *my* mom."

"It's more than I wanted to know, frankly," Dionne muttered. With a sigh, she spun Sophie to face the mirror.

Gazing at her friend's handiwork, her scowl slowly shifted to a smile. She batted her eyes at Dionne.

"Are you sure you want to do this?" her friend asked.

Sophie shook her head. "No. But I need to."

"Then let's not keep the ghost mice waiting."

➤⦁◀

Sophie's library card made short work of Unit A's lock, though not without sustaining damage. The door popped open with a chirp of warped wood, and Dionne searched for a working lamp while Sophie bemoaned her scratched card.

The attic wasn't well furnished, but it was larger than Sophie thought. The kitchen and living room were adjoined, neither anything to brag about. No tables or electronics, and not a stick of decor on the bare sunflower walls separating the small, empty bedrooms. Sophie was reaching out for a doorknob when Dionne called to her from another room.

Crouched in the closet beside an Andronico's box filled with photographs, she flapped a black and white picture at Sophie. "Looks like you were right about Mio."

Sophie and Dionne inspected the photo of Mio as a young man standing beside a petite woman and a young boy missing his two front teeth. Their pose was familial yet stiff, almost cautious, as if the pine building with the tar paper roof behind them would collapse at any moment.

Flanking the family and peppered in the unfocused background, men, women, and children of Japanese descent milled between white soldiers in the shadow of the Sierra mountains.

"Man-za-nar."

"What?"

Dionne held up another photo. The gaze of the young boy sitting on Mio's bare shoulders was distant but firmly rooted in the moment of the flash, though his hands were blurred from fidgeting with the numbered tag on his shirt.

"Manzanar. It's written on the back," she said. "I learned about it in high school. It was a Japanese internment camp in the 40s. There was a big riot there, and they shut it down."

Sophie's eyes fluttered. "Shit. Where do you think the rest of his family is?"

The question hung in the air like the names of dead men drafted by lottery. Sophie dug into another box, finding more photos, letters written in Japanese, even a tiny box wrapped in Christmas paper.

At that, Dionne smacked the dust from her hands and threw them in the air. "That's enough for me."

"But we haven't found my mom's stuff yet."

"You don't even know if your mom has stuff up here, and if it's anything like this shit, maybe you're better off not knowing. I need a nap before my date tonight anyway. Can we hang tomorrow? I think we need to talk more about this Choir thing." Her tone suggested it wouldn't be an encouraging conversation, but Sophie agreed with a tight smile and wished her luck on her date.

Once she was gone, Sophie sat stock-still, listening for the ghosts that thudded through the tattered stars on her ceiling. But there was only her and the photos falling through her fingers. With a huff, she boxed up Mio's belongings and closed the door.

The second room was mustier, and dust coated nearly every surface. Her cheeks flushed with glory as she entered to pillars of boxes like conquered kingdoms to her left and right. She opened the blinds and light streamed in, illuminating the wafting dust. The ceiling sloped, and she had to stoop to investigate her treasures, but it felt right, like a Wonderland discovery. A smaller stack of shoe boxes had less dust, so with a mischievous smile, she aimed for those. She flicked the lid off the topmost, which incited a brief sneezing fit as she waved away the stale cloud of grime. Catching her breath, she peered at the letter staring up at her from the shoe box. One page, two sentences, and no date.

Dear Paul, it said.

Do you remember how you used to chase me? Did you know you still do?

She set the letter aside and reached for the next. It was longer, with the ink significantly smudged. Hovering her fingers over the blots and wrinkles as she squinted at the blurry words, she read aloud.

Dear Paul,

I'm starting to think these letters are a bad idea. I thought they'd help me say goodbye, but it's obvious I can't. I don't want to say goodbye to you. I was never ready. Not in the hospital, not on the boat, and not here. Maybe I'll never be ready.

Or free.

There are times I think I'm still in Taunton. I wake up freezing. I'm awake when I think I'm sleeping. And I burn. Even when I'm freezing, I burn and burn, and that's when I can't remember why you loved me—or if you even did. After all this time, I'd be lying if I said I believe every memory.

Except the really bad ones. They feel true.

There are so many horrible, gut-wrenching things I've learned since you left, and I want to tear them out of my brain until I'm as stupid as I was at twelve. But you know that, don't you? You're in the same miserable place, with all the poor souls I left in Taunton. And my dear Natalie.

Sophie scrunched her nose and mouthed the name. *Natalie.*

Are you happy when I can't see you? she continued. *Do you and Natalie take comfort in each other? Is 'comfort' a thing Death allows?*

I let in as much as I can, but I don't think I deserve it. Not comfort, not love, not forgiveness. Even if she gave it willingly, I'm afraid I'd never feel deserving of it.

Julian says it's possible, and I want to believe him, but it's so hard. I spent years believing I was innocent, fighting anyone who called me guilty because I thought I was a good person. I really did.

We know how wrong I was now. No point in beating a dead rabbit.

Jesus Christ. I feel worse than I did when I started. This might be the last letter.

Sophie lowered the note and looked to a scrap of paper, brown, thinned, and wearing the fewest words of all. The name "*Antonia Archer*" was written in sloppy capital letters that looked different from the rest—shakier, less deliberate—and the only of its kind. The others were written in a script too similar to the hurried notes in Sophie's pocket to be anything but her mother's handwriting. But why was her mom writing to a dead person like he was alive? Who was Natalie? And Julian? And what the hell was Taunton?

Sophie set the letters aside and flipped the lid on the other shoe box. A sunbeam illuminated the photograph on top, and as she gingerly lifted and tilted it to the light, a thumbprint glimmered on the face of the young girl.

She was smiling, standing next to a boy with ghostly pale eyes directed at the little girl mugging for the camera. The greasy fingerprint distorted her face, but Sophie instantly recognized her mother in the smile and oil-black bangs. It was Ava as a child, and beside her, Sophie's father Paul stood like a dutiful soldier in love. She was compelled to kiss the photo or hug it to her heart, but something in the background distracted her. Pulling it closer, she squinted at the out-of-focus sign reading "The Flying Horses, America's Oldest Carousel."

A door slammed closed below Sophie, and she hurriedly stacked the letters, but when she tucked the photo back in its box, a newspaper clipping snagged her focus like a fishhook.

"Child Murderess Avery Norton Still at Large" was a heart attack of a headline, and words like "massacre" and "arson" dropped icicles from the awnings of her veins. The door slammed again, and she replaced the shoe box lids before closing up the memories in the dark.

Sophie exited the attic apartment in a cloud of confusion, and she ran dizzily down the stairs. Outside, her bristled flesh warmed by the afternoon sun, she took large rejuvenating breaths. When Nilsson spotted her from across the street, he bounded over with his tongue flapping out the side of his massive grin. She sat with her head bowed, and he jogged over to lick her ears and face and rub his cold nose on her calves while she giggled.

But with laughter came tears, like someone was wringing out her heart, and she could do nothing but let the sadness have her. It settled into a knot at the nape of her neck that made her feel wound up so tight only putting her fist through a wall would release it. She removed her necklace to massage her upper back and realized the area felt better without it. As the pain dulled, she sat up straight, and dangled the brass ring in front of her. Nilsson sniffed it enthusiastically, sneezed, and panted through a goofy smile.

"Do you like it?"

Nilsson yipped and bounded in circles as she adjusted the chain. Hanging it around his neck, Sophie kissed his nose, and said, "I don't need it anymore."

For the rest of the evening, Sophie imagined she was a bad memory closed up in the box on Mohr Lane. Staring at her broken stars, she pined for ghosts the way she'd imagined them: vaporous, almost elegant in their imprisoning sorrow—or like mountains of molting gore, leaving slimy trails as they shambled. There was nothing romantic or revolting about the dusty dry shoe boxes stacked with pain and more questions than answers. They filled her up like a water balloon, her skin stretching and sagging with the weight of disorderly rationale.

She tried to distract herself by flipping through nearly every *CREEM* magazine on her shelf, but her thoughts kept snapping back to the letters and the nagging suspicion that Paul Dillon might still be alive.

Sophie's throat went drier than the Mojave. What if Paul Dillon wasn't even her father? Then again, she'd never seen a picture of herself as a baby with Ava either, so maybe neither of them were her parents.

No, she thought. Her life was entrenched in deception, but she couldn't start doubting every slab of concrete in her foundation. She had to have faith in something, or she was no better than her mother.

Gliding her fingers over the buttery pages of *Rolling Stone*, she reread the section where interviewer Cameron Crowe asked Jimmy Page how much he believed in himself, reciting the guitar god's words like scripture.

"I may not believe in myself," he said, "but I believe in what I'm doing. I know where I'm going musically. I can see my pattern and I'm going much slower than I thought I'd be going. I can tell how far I ought to be going, I know how to get there, all I've got to do is keep playing. That might sound a bit weird because of all the John McLaughlins who sound like they're in outer space or something. Maybe it's the tortoise and the hare."

Sophie lifted her eyes from the article, pensive. She agreed with creating art slowly—as thoughtful a tortoise as Jimmy—but as she pondered real life races, she thought Aesop was wrong to depict the hare as the fool. Yes, it was a cocky creature, but it was a survivor. She'd seen Nilsson chase a dozen jackrabbits in her life, but she'd never witnessed him catching one. Turtles, however, he could catch easily. If it came down to the two of them, by the end of every race, it would not be the hare flipped over, scooped out, and eaten from its own dish.

Nor would it be Sophie Francis. Seeing the scuffed library card on her bedside table, she sat up. She refused to wait around for the truth to gut her. She would be both hare and hunger, dashing from danger but still flashing warnings to all who pursued that she, a future member of the Choir of the Lamb, would be ignorant no longer. Gazing out the window of her boxy prison, her mind possessed by a grisly headline, a picture of a carousel, and the name "Avery Norton," Sophie knew where to start.

CHAPTER TEN

"I'M GLAD YOU called," Liam said.

Sophie smiled, squeezing his hand as they stood outside Concord Public Library. "I'm sorry for the way I acted. I was tired and achy and just plain wrong."

"No, you were right. Your relationship with your mom is none of my business. Sometimes I think my biggest flaw is caring too much."

She rolled her eyes so hard she fell against him. "What a line!"

He laughed. "Hey, I never claimed I wasn't cheesy! I've always been upfront and honest about my total lack of machismo."

"I like this kind of machismo," she said, grabbing his shirt and pulling him into a kiss.

"But I am still worried about you."

"It turns out we were both right to be worried. Now we just need to find out what all those little worries add up to."

"But—"

"Liam LaSalle, if you say '*but*' again, you'll never see this *ass* again." She chuckled as she smacked her rear end, and he resigned himself to her reassuring kisses as he wrapped himself around her.

The one-story, caramel-colored building on Salvio Street wore a banner like a beauty queen's sash, though its words were slightly headier, inviting library patrons to "turn on your mind, tune in to words, and check out books."

Sophie groaned at the bastardized quote, but her aggravation melted away when the library's sweet musty air pelted her face. She was granted only a few moments of peace, however; it was slashed in half when she saw the cardboard turkey in a pilgrim hat grinning from behind the circulation desk.

Ava had left early that morning to pick up items for the fake Thanksgiving Sophie had no intention of attending that evening, so although they'd existed around each other, orbiting the rooms of their home like silent planets, she hadn't seen or spoken to her for almost two days. Maybe she never would again.

The realization made her tear up a bit, but she dabbed her eyes with her sleeve before Liam noticed, and she strode, head held high, into the library.

She spent innumerable hours there during her childhood, sometimes alone, sometimes with Moira, and always as the jovial shadow to the librarian, Ms. Gambrill. When she was little, the friendly woman plucked books from high shelves and helped her look up unfamiliar words. She played multiple parts when Sophie was reading a stage version of *James & the Giant Peach,* and made a patient audience member when the girl stumbled her way through her first Shakespearean soliloquy.

She was there for the breakdowns too. Tantrums were more frequent with her tutor present, but when she lost herself to tears in the children's section, Ms. Gambrill was there in a flash to tell her jokes and distract her from the devastation in *Where the Red Fern Grows* and *Bridge to Terabithia*. She gave her the strength of Fern Arable throwing herself between her best friend and her father's ax in *Charlotte's Web*.

Sophie had felt like she'd never known love like Fern and Wilbur, and though she didn't explain her tears to the librarian—she usually didn't understand them herself until she was beneath her broken stars—Ms. Gambrill would sit with her and pet her hair and say, "Don't cry, little one."

It was simple but effective. Her fists and jaw would unclench, and the librarian would put a happier book on her lap. They'd recite poems by Shel Silverstein or pretend to be monsters from *Where the Wild Things Are*. But as reassuring as the cocooning library shelves were in the past, they couldn't protect her today.

By the time she reached the card catalog, fear had unfurled another slick red petal in her brain. Her heart raced and her hands were clammy as she closed her fingers around the drawer labeled "Ni-Nu." It glided out of the cabinet's abdomen, and Sophie searched the cards pensively. Reaching the "No" section and actually seeing the name she was looking for filled her with a sort of horrified relief.

Trembling, she plucked the card from the drawer and whispered, "Norton comma Avery. See also: Martha's Vineyard Massacre."

Breath vacated her lungs like an unwelcome party guest, all bluster and revulsion, and knocked the strength from her legs. She collapsed into a wooden cube chair nearby, and Liam squatted beside her with a whimper.

Slipping the card from her shaky hand, he squinted at the name. "Sophie, what's happening? What's this all about?"

She couldn't answer. Her throat was tight as a fist, and she had to drop her head between her knees to get a breath. "I'll be fine," she finally wheezed. "Keep looking around, will you?"

Liam vanished from her side, but someone lurked close by. Someone looked over her shoulder. Someone smelled like microwaved death. And Sophie was afraid to confirm the source. She was still folded over, her hands clamped over her nose when Liam returned with a stack of papers he'd printed off the microform.

The top article had the same breed of eye-snagging headline as the newspaper in her mother's things, except "murderess" was bolder, and it described an incident of arson that reduced Taunton Hospital in Massachusetts to smoldering rubble. In July 1959, a handful of patients and felons escaped during the blaze, including eighteen-year-old Avery Norton, convicted serial killer and resident of the asylum for six years, and who many believed to have started the hospital fire. The word "allegedly" was sprinkled through the article, but it felt shoehorned into the sentences, spread messily among the facts like boogers stuck to pages in a schoolbook.

The next article, released the previous year, commemorated the fifteenth anniversary of the fire by interviewing former Taunton patient, Pamela Mason. A current San Francisco resident, she described the incident as "gruesome" and "the work of a true madwoman."

"Pamela Mason . . . " Sophie read aloud, " . . . spent five years in the same juvenile ward as Avery Norton and admitted she was frightened of her. 'She attacked me the first day,' Miss Mason stated. 'Nearly broke my nose.' She went on to describe Avery Norton's behavior as 'erratic' and 'prone to bouts of violence and amnesia.'"

Liam grabbed the next article written by Howard Leonard of the Vineyard Gazette. "In July 1954, the bodies of seventeen people were found on the peaceful resort island of Martha's Vineyard. Authorities are withholding the victims' identities, but Police Chief Marvin Blake described several as 'troubled youngsters' that the department originally considered runaways. He has confirmed, however, that one of the first victims was Dr. Jason Norton, a prominent physician at Martha's Vineyard General and father of the accused. Sources revealed Dr. Norton was presumed to have deserted his wife and children on the island years before."

Liam switched pages and gasped. "Wow. It looks like they charged Avery's mother, Faye, too. Obstruction of justice and accessory to murder. She hid the people her daughter killed. Her own husband." He made the sign of the Lamb and wrung his hand on the arm of her chair.

"Why would your mom keep an article about something so awful?"

"I have no idea."

Sophie's hands felt as dry as sandpaper, like she was wearing gloves of attic dust when she massaged her temples.

"Sophie Francis? Is that you?" Ms. Gambrill pouted as she peeked around a shelf. The woman smelled suffering like dogs smelled disease. She embraced Sophie without a word, but instead of her usual comfort, her hug felt more like the desperate leechings of a lonely shrew. Why was she so solicitous of Sophie's needs? What did she get out of handling the girl's emotions like this?

Sophie clenched her teeth. That's what she'd been doing all this time, hadn't she? *Handling her.* Did her mom suggest it the first time she carried Sophie into Concord Library—for Miss Gambrill to keep an eye on her when her mother couldn't? Or was it Moira who'd broached the idea? Had she seen something of herself in the girl? A shared emptiness and feeling of displacement? Or was she just lonely?

Sophie's skin shriveled on her bones when the wheezing and whistling began. It wasn't the librarian giving her the creeps. It was the woman over her shoulder, the one reeking of sundrenched roadkill, whose malevolent presence poisoned Sophie's mind against the kindly librarian approaching in her periphery.

The corpse of Moira Shunn was like a Wacky Packages prism sticker that revealed more color and dimension with Sophie's shifting gaze—though not as whimsically. Her gaping throat was sludge black, and her once attentive eyes were sunken deep in a spongy, green-gray skull. She couldn't smile for the scabbing, but her sloppy neck wound flexed with wet kisses.

Sophie tried to focus on paging through the stacks, but her hands trembled uncontrollably, and she was unable to turn the page. Frustration colonized her expression and her eyes glimmered with a rising curtain of tears.

When Ms. Gambrill said, "Don't cry, little one," and left to fetch the girl a cup of water, Sophie's dead tutor laughed.

"So dutiful. So pathetic," she hissed at Sophie.

"You're not Moira," she replied, eyes to the paper. "She was shitty, but she wasn't mean."

The ghost leaned forward, her knees cracking and hands sliding through the sloughing skin of her thighs. "Then why is guilt pouring off of you in sheets?"

"I don't have anything to feel guilty about."

Moira threw back her head with a chortle that vibrated every wound in her rotten body. "Lie, lie, lie. Die, die, die," she said. "Say . . . what if this is all fate? What if you're following in Mommy's footsteps?"

"What does that mean?"

"Come on, Sophie, you're smarter than this. *Avery, Ava*. It's pretty similar. Plus they have the same handwriting."

"No, I can't believe that."

"You already do."

Ms. Gambrill returned, but Sophie didn't accept the water. "Can I get you something else, dear?"

"She's okay," Liam said. "She just needs space."

"That's the last thing you need," Moira wheezed. "You need people close. You need them to hold you together, or you might just . . . " When she gestured, her left hand fell off at the wrist like a dollop of melted ice cream. Her right bicep slid away next, followed by the slow and squelchy unscrewing of her right eye. " . . . well, you know. Let's face it," she said, as her cheek slipped down the bone, "something's horribly wrong with you, Sophie. Your mom will call it spells, Liam will call it a blessing, and the librarian will call it—lord knows, artistic tendencies? But it's none of that, you know. Whatever goodness could've come from your wrongness was spoiled the day you killed me."

"I didn't kill you." Sophie stood slowly, and the corpse reclined on the cube chair opposite hers.

"You don't look sure. But you're not sure about anything, are you? What a trustworthy person you are. What a valuable member of society."

"Shut up."

"Why are you even here?" Moira continued. "Say your mother *is* Avery Norton and perpetrated this notorious Martha's Vineyard Massacre. What right do you have to judge her? You're two peas in a pod."

"No."

"That's why the Choir wants you. They see the evil in you as clearly as I did that afternoon on your birthday. They see what you're capable of, and they want to lock you away before you can do to them what you did to me."

"I said shut up!" With a ferocious growl, Sophie dove at the corpse of Moira Shunn.

Except there was no corpse. There was only Ms. Gambrill, whom Sophie propelled backward in screeching rage. The librarian smacked her spine on the cube chair's sharp wooden arm and fell to the orange carpet, moaning. But as clearly as it all transpired, as much as Ms. Gambrill's voice penetrated the malodorous fog in her mind, she only saw Moira twitching on the floor.

Patrons and employees gathered around the periodicals, whispering and pointing, but Sophie ignored them. Willowed over the librarian, she hissed. "Is she my mother? Is Avery Norton my mother?"

Ms. Gambrill cringed and sobbed for help.

"Did she kill those people?"

"I don't know what you're talking about," she cried. "My back—help, help me, please!"

Liam hooked his arm around Sophie and urged her away as the crowd closed around the wailing librarian. Neither spoke as he towed her to the exit, nor once they were in the bus, on the road—any road—away from Concord Library.

Sophie's head was down, hands clamped and brain pounding, and she didn't unclench a single muscle until they stopped on Parkside Drive. Windows down and Joni Mitchell crooning faint consolations, she felt better, but her gaze remained glued to the floor.

"Are you going to tell me what happened back there?"

She licked her lips, trying to figure out a good way to phrase it. But there was no "good way." Only the truth.

"I saw something. Someone I knew. Someone who . . . who . . . shouldn't be here. Someone I thought was dead."

"You saw a dead person?"

She bit her lip and nodded tearfully.

"I thought this might happen," he said, wringing the steering wheel. "Sophie, it's the Lamb."

"The Lamb?"

"It's inside you. It's making you see things."

"What? No, it can't be . . . " At last, she lifted her head and looked at him. "Can it?"

He wasn't exactly smiling, but shades of triumph colored his expression as he caressed her face. "Whatever you saw back there, it wasn't real. But," he continued cautiously, "the librarian *was* real, and she got what she deserved."

"No, Ms. Gambrill's nice. She didn't deserve that." Sophie's hands flew to her face. "Oh my God. *I* did that. I *hurt* her. We need to go back."

"If she didn't deserve it, the Lamb wouldn't have made you do it. The Lamb allows you to see people for who they really are—their shadow selves—just like Mother Agnes. It's a gift, and it's invaluable to the Choir's cause. You can see people in pain, the ugliness of it, the rot. You can see the truth."

Her brain felt like old mashed potatoes: an oxygenated crust protecting mealy innards and the rock-hard lumps of ideas beginning to ferment. As pain pounded her temples, she closed her eyes and pictured the road ahead. There was a bus stop, the BART station, a police station—plenty of places for her to launch an escape from the growing mold—but it all disappeared when Liam pulled a piece of paper from his pocket.

"I know I shouldn't have taken it, but I want to help you. I'm sorry I was impatient before, but I'm here for you now. You need to know where you came from, and I think I know how to find out." He passed over the newspaper interview with Pamela Mason. "She lives in San Francisco, and I think we should talk to her."

"And if she says my mother's a murderer?"

"We'll burn that bridge when we get to it." He speckled Sophie's hand with kisses, but she was too numb to feel them.

CHAPTER ELEVEN

THE FORMER PATIENT of Taunton Asylum lived in a block of kitsch-encrusted rooms for which she and her twelve companions paid the Lanai Motel weekly. Room twenty-one, or "the brain" as Pamela Mason called it, stunk of pot and greasy leftovers from Sambo's Restaurant in front of the motel on Lombard Street.

Locating Pamela took some work, but after following a few dead ends, Sophie and Liam stood face-to-face with the woman who claimed to know Avery Norton. Ashtrays and beer bottles littered nearly every surface in the motel room, and less than a foot of blank wall space peeked out between sheets of butcher paper decorated in scribblings and schematics. The drawings were elementary at best, but the circles and targets over specific locations suggested these people weren't playing around.

Pamela Mason leaned against a dresser, her stained teeth clenching a cigarette that nearly singed her wild gray hair every time she moved.

Sophie tried her best not to make eye contact with any of the occupants, but her fearful avoidance beckoned them like hungry wolves. A shirtless man in a black beret and a double-wrapped rosary perfectly cradled by his mahogany chest curled himself around Pam's shoulder and grinned at the guests.

"I don't want to take up too much of your time," Sophie said in a hurried whisper. "I just have a few questions."

The man pulled his sunglasses down the ridge of his

nose and stared over the rims, his fat pupils glazed with wonder. "You got devils swimmin' in them eyes, baby. Back and forth, inside and out. Whatchu on?"

"Nothing," she said.

"Nothing?" The man chuckled. "Yeah, I believe that. Nothin' is the strongest shit they make. Fucks you all up in here." He pointed to his head, then to his heart. "In here, too."

"Who's *they*?" Liam asked.

"The man," he said, drawing out the last word like a death rattle. "That's where the nothin' comes from, you know. Ain't no god can hook you as good as *they* can. They got the kinda shit that fills you with snakes and strawberries. The kind of shit that hunts you down, kisses ya, and makes you run away. Again and again, all over creation until your runnin's spent. That's when the devils start showing themselves. That's when the nothin's got you for good."

Sophie opened and closed her fists, silent. She wanted to call the stranger crazy, but after what she'd seen—corpse, shadow-self, brain-fever, whatever—she didn't have the right to accuse anyone of mental instability.

Pamela and her cohorts were privy to the punchline of a joke Sophie and Liam weren't, and the more the squatters laughed, the more Sophie and Liam shrank back from the door.

"Don't worry, kids. I'll answer your questions." Waving to her friends, Pam stepped out of the room and closed the door behind her. "Let's get you some privacy, huh?"

She called room eighteen "the quiet place," which was odd considering the amount of audio and visual equipment piled in the corners. It reminded Sophie a bit of the Choir's house with their cots and chairs, but Liam scoffed at the comparison when she whispered it in his ear.

"Do me a favor and don't tell my parents that," he said.

"Speaking of which," Pamela started, sitting on one of the cigarette-burned beds, "Did you kids get Mommy and Daddy's permission before you chose to slum it?"

"I'm not a kid," Liam said.

Pam smirked. "The one with the devil eyes is, though. This chick can't be older than fifteen."

"I guess the devils make me look younger than I am," Sophie said blankly.

It was a joke, but it ripped the playful smile from Pamela Mason's face. She lit a cigarette, took a drag, and exhaled a series of smoke rings. "I bet they do," she said. "Take a seat, baby devil."

They sat on the other bed, though Sophie couldn't bear to put her entire weight on it, like hovering just a bit would save her from whatever diseases hid within the cheap fabric.

"You said on the phone you had questions about Taunton Hospital. Something for school?"

"It's due after the holiday break, and I've been putting it off. I'll get in big trouble if I flunk another assignment."

Pam blew smoke out her flared nostrils as she squinted at Liam. "How 'bout you? You got the same assignment?"

"I'm her boyfriend."

Pam bounced her eyebrows. "Figures. Young girl, big city, rough people all around. Makes sense she'd bring her muscle."

Grabbing Pam's attention with a bob of her head, Sophie said, "*I'm* the muscle."

Pamela's tongue slid over her teeth as she inspected Sophie up and down. Extinguishing her cigarette, she pulled open the top drawer of the end table and removed the King James Bible. She set it down and opened it gingerly, like the fables might escape, but when she revealed the hollowed out section containing a mirror and several vials of cocaine, her piety made sense. She tapped out a line and used a creased prayer card to thin it out. She snorted, threw her head back with a guffaw, and massaged her left nostril as she nudged the mirror toward Sophie.

"No thanks. But you go ahead," Sophie said. "It can't be easy talking about those years."

The woman was unkempt, rough around every edge, but her free-spirited attitude smoothed the lines and buffed the scars, if only for a few moments. She looked her age again, maybe even older, after she hocked and swallowed the bitter cocaine drip. Wrinkles like ancient ravines branched from the corners of her eyes and down her cheeks, nearly meeting the parenthesis framing her pale lips.

Her cigarette was a dead stump between her fingers, but she took another drag anyway, and a tiny orange dot appeared in the ash, reviving the last of the tobacco. Once it died for real, she dropped it in the ashtray, snorted another line, and lit up again. It was a routine the woman didn't realize had become so, and though Sophie wasn't a big cigarette smoker, the constant sucking and exhaling triggered her craving. When she outstretched her fingers, Pam handed over a smoke she lit with a grin that turned the parenthesis to hyphens, temporarily interrupting the gloom accumulating in the woman's brain.

"I was on the run for a while," Pam finally said. "I spent years hitching, hooking, doing whatever I could to stay outta places like Taunton." She tapped off a cube of ash, and rising smoke haloed her brow. "The saddest thing about that place was that *my* screws were tighter than most. Some of the girls were orphans and castaways like me, but chicks like Flint and Brianne, and that little wretch Avery Norton, were mad as March hares." She picked a sliver of tobacco from her lip and flicked it at the floor. "And they were my best friends."

"Friends? You said Avery attacked you," Liam said.

"Oh, she did, and she's lucky I didn't kick her teeth in."

"Do you believe she was innocent?"

Pam's shoulders danced through a shrug. "I didn't buy her mom's story about Avery killing people when she was really young, and I never believed she killed her father, but that chick was by no means innocent. I guarantee she killed some of those people. And then there was the fire . . . "

Liam squinted. "But you still considered her a friend?"

Pam smashed her cigarette into the ashtray and ran tar-stained fingers through a stack of mail on the bed, revealing a shriveled used condom between an overdue bill and an envelope without a return address. "Taunton was a deep and rushing river lined with banks of shit, kids. If you didn't grab onto something, it would pull you under and bash out your brain in no time flat. Sick as it is, you paddled like mad to grab those shit banks. It would get under your nails and in your mouth, but you didn't care because eating shit is better than what happens when institutionalization sets in. When that happens, you don't even try to breathe anymore. I'd cling to anyone I could to keep myself from drowning in it, even Avery Norton."

Sophie ashed her cigarette and shook her head. "I thought hospitals were supposed to help people."

"The basis—and the basest—of Taunton's intentions. Avery came in when I was sixteen, right in the big rush of therapy changes. The days of ice baths and lobotomies were going out, and the drugs were coming in, but the man liked to mix it up—a little ice, a little Vitamin T." Pam dropped her face to the mirror and snorted another line. She grunted and dug at her nostril with her eyes squeezed shut. "That shit did us all more harm than good, but the meds hit Avery especially hard. I feel like they made her blackouts last longer, and let me tell ya, those blackouts were no joke."

Sophie bristled, and a small squeak escaped her lips. She cleared her throat to play it off, but her coloring gave her away. Her hands had drained of blood, almost bluish in their paleness, and though a piece of hair hung in her left eye, nagging her eyelashes, her hands trembled too much to risk raising them. She clasped them on her lap and whispered steadily as possible. "Tell me more about the blackouts."

Pam squinted as if trying to peer into her memory. She flicked her cigarette, but the ash missed the tray and became one of many stains on the carpet.

"Sometimes you didn't know they were happening," she said. "She'd seem totally lucid—but then she'd see things or talk to people that weren't there. Other times she was out of it completely, in a world of her own, and she hated being there. She got angry. She got violent. It wasn't nothing the nurses couldn't handle, but it was scary as shit." Pam rubbed the back of her neck and exhaled. "And sometimes she'd just talk. She'd tell us about the bad water, about the rabbits and how she punished them, but she rarely remembered telling us, or she thought the conversations were dreams." Pam dug at something stuck between her two front teeth, her pronunciation muffled as she continued. "Like most of us, the girl was born with something wonky in the works, but her mom and the doctors didn't help matters. They stuffed her with drugs and forbade the rest of the patients from telling her about the blackouts . . . or whatever they were."

"Spells," Sophie said softly.

"If you wanna be weird about it," Pam said, shooting smoke out her nose. "Anyway, the staff was obsessed with getting patients to accept and solve their own issues through therapy, without interference from other patients."

"But they had no problem with drugs interfering?" Liam asked.

"That's right. No problem with shock therapy either. See, I think she just didn't fix up fast enough for them. They had to show that rushing an alleged child murderess through the system without a real confession was worth it. They wanted that confession. Well, after they shocked the shit out of her, she confessed to a whole hell of a lot. She might've confessed to murdering Napoleon if they'd asked. Either way, she said enough to convince the doctors she was a danger to herself and others. A bunch of this happened after I turned eighteen, mind you, but I heard it from Flint. And when Avery got bumped up to the women's ward before her eighteenth birthday, I knew something horrible was going to happen." She crushed her cigarette with a phlegmy sigh. "I was right, as usual. That crazy bitch and Flint started cooking up their master plan the moment she moved over to the women's ward, and everything went to hell."

"Who's Flint?" Sophie asked.

"Francine." Pam said the name like it was a trite line in an otherwise expertly-crafted song. "She was a pyromaniac and Avery's best friend in the joint. It was no surprise they went out the way they did: Flint into the fire and Avery out the front door."

Liam slapped his hand to his mouth as if catching a geyser of vomit. "Holy Mother on Earth, she killed her best friend?"

Pam discovered some powder on the back of her hand and massaged it into her gums. "I figured Flint tossed herself in, and if you ask me—which you are . . . " She tapped out her second to last cigarette and lit it. " . . . Avery probably did all she could to get Flint out alive. She needed her. Flint was the only one who believed her." She coughed up a wet laugh. "Except for that dumb boyfriend of hers."

Sophie's breath caught in her throat. With everything she'd seen and learned about Avery Norton, she was still hoping it was all a coincidence, that her mother Ava Francis was a normal woman harboring a secret fascination with the Martha's Vineyard murderess, but there could be no more dispute if the boyfriend's name was . . .

Sophie's stomach alternated between iron and gelatin as she struggled to cough up his name.

"Paul?"

Pam lifted her head.

"Was it Paul Dillon?"

Her lips twitched into something between amusement and suspicion. "You did your homework."

Sophie buried her face in her hands, and her fingernails sunk into the flesh along her hairline. She wanted to scream, but she couldn't. Sorrow and rage compounded into something that dammed her windpipe.

As Liam consoled Sophie, Pamela Mason leaned

forward on a smooth outward breath. "You're not writing a paper on Avery Norton, are you?"

Sophie raised her eyes, teeth gritted. "No."

"What are you? A junior associate? Undercover fuzz? Maybe you're some kind of baby groupie for the mentally unhinged?"

"I'm her daughter."

Pam's lips popped open, and smoke swelled out. Leaning back on the bed, a smile slid up her weathered cheek, and she gestured at Sophie with the cigarette as if trying to burn holes in her from a distance.

"That's a gas. Little Avery Norton had a kid? What poor sap did she dupe into that?"

"You already know," Liam said.

"Do I? Sorry, kid, I haven't exactly kept in touch with the old gang. I didn't even know Avery was still alive and kicking."

"Paul Dillon," Sophie said matter-of-factly. "He's my father."

Pam's brow furrowed, and ash tumbled from the end of her cigarette. "No, that can't be right." She closed one eye and pointed at her. "How old are you—sorry, I've forgotten your names."

"Liam," he said, patting his chest, "and this is Sophie."

Pam's eyebrows arched, and she set her cigarette on the edge of the ashtray. "And I bet you've gotta be sixteen, huh?" Rubbing her face with both hands, she groaned. "Jesus fucking Christ, Avery."

"What is it?" Sophie asked.

"Avery Norton ain't your mother, kid. She's your aunt."

Sophie's voice cracked dryly when a nervous laugh claimed her words. Clearing her throat, she said, "I think I misheard you. How can she be my aunt? She doesn't have any brothers or sisters."

Pam whirled her fingers whimsically through the air as if painting a picture with the cigarette smoke. "Well, not anymore, no."

Liam jumped to his feet and looked down on the woman with a menacing sneer. "This is ridiculous. You obviously don't know what you're talking about. You're just some sad old extremist looking to stir up whatever shit you can before 'the man' drags you back to the nuthouse."

Without meeting his gaze, Pam replied. "Not entirely false. But in this case, I'm just answering your questions to the best of my ability. If you're Sophie Dillon—*the* Sophie Dillon—your mother was Avery's older sister, Natalie."

Natalie. The letter in the attic: "*Are you happy when I can't see you? Do you and Natalie take comfort in each other?*"

"So Paul Dillon—"

"—was married to Natalie Norton, yes. But she died in a fire not long after. How *curious.*" Pamela crushed out her cigarette and slithered past Liam. She spat in the sink outside the tiny bathroom—adding another brown loogie to the collection—and undid her pants. They were loose around her knees when she shuffled into the bathroom and hunkered down on the toilet, leaving the door open and staring dead ahead at the mirror on the opposite wall.

Liam shielded his eyes with a snarl, but Sophie didn't flinch. She glared right back into the woman's reflected eyes and crinkled her nose as Pam urinated.

"Are you saying Avery killed her sister?" Sophie asked.

"I'm saying it's curious. Same with how Paul died. Another fire, I believe, though that one was at sea." The stream slowed to a drip, and she wadded up some toilet paper. "I was on the run then, so I paid close attention to the papers while I was still on the east coast. They said Avery ran off with Paul after Taunton came down. With Paul and . . . " She wiped herself and winked. " . . . with you, babydoll."

Pam pulled up her pants and left the toilet unflushed, her focus on the ashtray of partially smoked cigarettes. Finding a good one, she blew off the excess ash and clenched it in her teeth. "After the boat blew, Avery escaped from the hospital on the island, and you went to your grandmother." The cigarette was nearly gone already, but she'd lined up sizable butts to take its place. "I didn't hear about her for a while after that, and I was pretty fucking glad. Then I heard something about Avery's mother turning up dead at Taunton, and you were gone." Pam lit another cigarette from the dying cherry. "Say, if that woman you call 'Mom' really is Avery Norton, the pigs'll wanna know. A serial killer right under their noses. Maybe there's a reward. Even if there isn't, they're extra itchy to bust some heads after the strike. She'd be the perfect target. The perfect distraction."

As Sophie rose, so did the bile. She gulped it back with teeth clenched and fists balled, and though she felt her skin might catch fire, Pam looked at her like a petulant child.

"Oh sweetie, don't act like that. If this woman really is Avery Norton, you're better off without her. She's dangerous."

A ratty laugh rollercoastered through the room, but only Sophie heard it. She shrugged her shoulders down her back, her stomach flip-flopping as she focused on the figure behind Liam. Moira Shunn sat on the bed, rigid as a pole except for her rotting chartreuse skull. It lolled on her shoulders, back and forth to accommodate the wheezing black wound in her throat.

"But Sophie," Moira said, "you're dangerous too."

Her left eyeball was stuck in its socket, refusing to budge when she shifted her gaze to a nearby pile of papers, ashes, food, and silverware. She didn't need to speak for Sophie to know her mind—or to act on it.

Sophie grabbed one of the forks and thrust it at Pam, causing the woman to stumble backward against the sink.

"What the fuck do you think you're doing, kid?"

"You can't—" Sophie said, trembling. "I won't let you turn her in. She's still my mother."

"She kidnapped you," Pam said.

Sophie shook her head like the truth would glance off

her skull instead of sinking in. But it was already there—had been there—nestled in the dim broken stars.

Liam touched her arm, coaxed the fork from her fingers, and her energy went with it. Once her hand was empty, Sophie felt like she could melt to the nasty motel carpet and fall into a sticky sleep.

Pam laughed. "What a gas. After all this time, I can't believe Avery Norton's gonna solve all our problems."

Liam glowered and gestured at her with the fork. "I suggest you stop talking."

"Oh, I'm gonna do a lot more than that. This is fate, kiddies. For me, for you, and for that bitch who got away with murder. She's gonna help us get our message heard, and then she's gonna get what she deserves."

"The Lamb will judge her, not you," Liam said. "If she's found guilty, she will be punished in the proper way."

"The Lamb?" Pam's face crinkled, then stretched with a derisive chuckle. She pushed past the pair and sat on a chair in the corner, where she found a crumpled cigarette on the floor. "Oh you poor stupid girl, what have you gotten yourself into?" She lit it and exhaled with a flick of her hand. "Forget it. I don't care. Just get out while you can."

Moira's corpse crawled rigidly from the bed and stood beside Pamela Mason with one eye trailing the rising smoke. At the same time, Liam strode forward, his voice a church bell ringing clear compared to Moira's, as she spoke in scratchy unison.

"Don't threaten us," they said. "We are the Lamb, the blessed children of Agnes and the Virgin Mother. You have no idea what we're capable of."

Pam shook with uproarious laughter that made Sophie feel like dozens of little fingers were twisting lumps of meat from her guts. The sensation intensified when Moira tilted back her head and opened her black wound wide. Pam's voice barreled from the corpse's throat too, whistling through shredded flesh, sticking to the jelly, and causing the fingers tied up in Sophie's sinew to tug her forward.

The corpse watched in grotesque glee as Sophie charged at the woman, ramming her shoulder into Pam's chest and launching her backward.

Pam's head hit the floor with a wet crack. She gurgled and moaned, and blood dripped down her neck when she tried to sit up. Surrendering to pain and gravity, she reclined again and squeezed her eyes shut.

Sophie's heart sped as Liam enfolded her, the edge of the fork pressing into her back. Moira's corpse had vanished, but a tangy memory remained, a whiff of death between stale cigarettes and moldy room service roast beef.

Staring up at the pair, Pam sneered. "What the hell do you want from me?"

Liam squeezed Sophie's hand, then squatted beside the woman. "We can't allow you to tell anyone what you discovered today. It's not your place to shine a light on this Avery Norton business. If the Lamb decides she deserves to be penalized, St. Agnes will let it be known. Just as she let us know about you."

"Me? What did *I* do?"

"Nothing. You knew Avery was going to set that fire in the hospital, and you did nothing. Nothing," Liam said, "might be your biggest crime, Ms. Mason. Would you like to find out if you deserve forgiveness?"

"Okay, I've had enough of this shit." She tried to sit up again, but Liam pushed her back down so forcibly the impact sounded like a sloppy kiss when her head hit the marshy rug. As she struggled to focus, he began.

"You wake up on an island, naked and afraid. To your right is a low field at midnight, and to your left, a lush garden in Spring. Just before you are two women and three men clothed in one-piece tunics. Whom do you ask for clothes?"

"I'm not doing this. You can't make me do this."

Liam smiled then stuck the fork to her throat. "Whom," he repeated calmly, "do you ask for clothes?"

Pam gritted her teeth, and her nostrils flickered with rage. "One of the women."

"Thank you. One of the women agrees, for she doesn't mind walking free and unfettered in the eyes of the Lamb, but once you're clothed in her garments, the rest of your party decides that it's shameful to be naked. Why else would you have been so quick to cover yourself?"

"What? That's not what I meant. You asked me—"

"They shun the woman who gave up her clothes. Now *she* is naked and afraid. Because of you."

"What the fuck? This is bullshit!"

"Your party banishes her to the field while they make their way to the garden. Where do you go?"

Pam growled. "I don't know. The garden, I guess."

"Interesting. And it's nice for you, because the others found a bounty of fruits and vegetables in the garden. But the longer you're there, the more uncomfortable your tunic becomes. One day, you find a sheep among the trees and realize you can skin it to make some new clothes. Do you do it?"

Pam's lips stretched to reveal brown eye-teeth. "Ah ha. I see the game you're playing at, boy. Do you think doctors didn't try shit like this on me? Or priests? Or my parents?" She snorted. "I do use the sheep's wool to make clothes, but not for myself. I give the wool to the woman in the field."

Sophie stared at Liam, studying his face as it warmed with a vicious smile.

"Oh, I'm afraid it's much too late for her. She froze to death long ago, alone, in the dark. And now, that lamb gave its life for nothing."

She scoffed. "Sheep don't die from being sheared."

"I didn't say 'sheared.' I said 'skinned.' Your disregard for detail and foolish desire to win what you perceive to be a game has now taken two innocent lives." He scraped the fork across her neck. "But it's not a game, Pamela. How you fair in this hypothetical situation mirrors the decisions you make in your real life. And how you've suffered." Lowering the fork, he whispered, "You've been lonely, haven't you?"

Her chin dimpled. "Yes."

"It doesn't matter how many people are around you, or how hard you try to change into someone who won't be brushed aside, you will always be alone. Because of the choices you've made, like standing by while others inflict harm, every scrap of tenderness people offer you will wither at your touch. Every bit of friendship will turn cold. Real life will distort itself until, yes, it all does look like a game you can never win. Because you don't deserve to." Liam stood and said, "You can get up now," but Pam didn't move.

Her hands hovered in front of her chest, nicotine-stained fingers bent, almost apish, and her face wrinkled in shifting shades of rage and anguish. Slowly, she sat up and crawled to the wall. Planting her spine against it and panting through the pain, she raised her watery gaze to Liam and whispered. "Give me another chance. I can figure it out."

Liam extended his hand to Sophie, who squeezed it tenderly as he began again. "You wake up on an island, naked and afraid. To your right is a low field at midnight, and to your left, a lush garden in Spring. Just before you are two other women and three men clothed in one-piece tunics. Whom do you ask for clothes?"

"I walk naked and free in the eyes of the Lord—" Pam twitched her lips. "Or the Lamb, or whatever."

"An excellent decision. Two of the men wish to go to the field. The other women and the last man want to go to the garden. Which do you choose?"

"Well, I haven't left anyone naked, so if they freeze in the field it's their own fault, right?" When Liam didn't answer, she sighed. "The garden again."

"The moment you enter the garden, the flowers and plants wilt. A sheep enters and informs your group that you may only select one type of vegetation to survive: strawberries or cabbage."

"What the hell? It wasn't like that the first time!"

"Yes, but you also made the wrong decision the first time. Did you think you got a clean slate because you had to start over?"

She grunted. "Fine. Strawberry fields forever."

"You're starving, so the four of you eat as many strawberries as possible. They satisfy you, and there are plenty more to be had, but as time passes, the satisfaction fades. The strawberries taste of ash—"

"Fish!" Sophie interjected. Figuring Pamela's mouth was mostly ash by this point anyway, she thought a fishy taste would affect her more.

When the woman's face screwed up in disgust, Liam mouthed "thank you" to Sophie, his face illuminated with idolatry.

"Yes, the strawberries taste of fish," he said. "You try to eat them, but you can't. You can hardly stand to look at them. The man suggests eating what's left of the rotten food. The women suggest asking the lamb what to do."

"I ask the lamb, obviously."

"*Obviously*," he said, crinkling his nose. "The lamb informs you that St. Agnes can restore the garden to its former health, but she requires a sacrifice."

Pam slowly pushed herself up from the floor, a smile crawling up one side of her face. "Well, I don't know who this St. Agnes person is, but I see where this is going now."

"Do you? How fortunate."

They stared at each other, silent for a few moments, until Pam threw open her arms.

"Well? Don't I get any options?"

"I thought you saw where this was going," Sophie said snidely.

Pam grunted, and her head drooped—from frustration or blood loss, Sophie couldn't tell.

"Fine," she said, deliberating. "I got in trouble for sacrificing the lamb last time, so I can't do that. But I can't sacrifice any of the people either, can I?" Her furrowed face suddenly flickered like a kernel of corn bursting open. "One of the men in the field! All this time has passed; they've got to be frozen to death by now. Can I sacrifice one of them?"

"You can," Liam said. "You abandon the forest for the field and find it warm and pleasant. The men have cultivated crops and built the equipment necessary to farm it. They are healthy and thriving."

"But you said—"

Liam raised his eyebrows, and Pamela growled in annoyance.

"Whatever. At least I don't have to sacrifice anyone now."

"Who said that?" Sophie asked.

"He did!" she said, pointing. "He said they have food. And they'll share it with the garden people, won't they?"

Liam hummed. "Yes, they will."

"So I won."

"He already told you this isn't a game."

"Even if it were," said Liam, "you definitely didn't win."

"But if the field people are sharing with the garden people, everyone gets fed."

"Not *you*. You don't live in the garden anymore. You left them so you could murder someone from the field. The garden needed to be restored, not its people temporarily fed. The people in the garden hate you for abandoning them, and the people in the field hate you for wanting them dead."

"But that's not fair!"

The room grew hot, and the stains on the walls appeared to sweat as Sophie watched the exchange, her heart fluttering against her breastbone. Her head ached, but there was a strange pleasure in its throbbing, like that of massaging a muscle deeply knotted.

"The lamb said I needed to kill someone," Pam insisted shrilly. "It said I needed a sacrifice."

"*You* are the sacrifice, Pamela Mason, because you were too foolish to see that you could've lived happily in the garden—with the others, with the strawberries. But you let boredom turn you into a killer."

She narrowed her eyes at Liam, and her lips peeled back from her stained teeth. "You set me up."

"No, your sins did that. All your transgressions, all your greed and deception—they set you on this path."

"This is bullshit," she said, lips glazed in brown foam. "You didn't tell me there were secret choices."

"No one tells you in life either. Like the night you fled Taunton. You speak of the screams, the horrors, but you didn't try to stop it. You admitted you thought the plan was crazy, but you let Avery and her friend carry it out. You didn't warn anyone. You didn't rescue anyone from the blaze. You didn't stop Avery Norton when you saw her or alert the police to her whereabouts. You ran, like a coward, like living sin." Liam drew closer, his voice low and dangerous as he backed her against the wall. "You, Pamela Mason, stared into the fires of Hell, where innocent people begged for help, and you ran as fast as you could."

Pam's expression cracked to quivering leather, and her shoulders hitched forward as if she'd been socked in the gut. When Liam stepped back she doubled over, her hand clamped to her mouth as if blocking a sudden upsurge of vomit. Apologies poured out of her instead, over and over, as she sank to the floor.

He lay his hand upon her head in a saintly way, and his voice was lovely and devastating as a waterfall when he spoke again. "You can come with us, Pamela. The Choir of the Lamb can save you. We can show you the Lamb's power and how to recognize it in others. We can teach you about conversion, ascension, castigation. We can bring you to Agnes's glory, and in time, the mothers of God may love you again. All you need to do is say, 'Yes.'"

She lifted her face from her palms. It was wet, rosy, and wrinkled, and it shifted from grief to confusion as she scrutinized the pair. "You're joshing me, right? I'm not going anywhere with you nutjobs."

"We're giving you the opportunity to save your soul and to be part of a greater community, a new and better way of life."

Pamela snorted back dripping snot and dried her eyes with her coat sleeve. "I don't give a fuck about your community. I regret leaving the hospital the way I did, I admit that, and I spent a lot of time mourning the people who lost their lives in that blaze, but I didn't light it, I didn't condone it, and I sure as fuck won't atone for it. That's on Avery—maybe on her whole family," she said, squinting at Sophie. "Putting their deaths on me won't bring them back any more than blaming thousands of lawmen will bring back all those boys who died for a country that never loved them, anyone in 'Nam, in the wrong place at the wrong time, all those babies who died for jack shit. You can call me and my friends extremists, but we're greater patriots than any woman's son reduced to a number and thrown into a war they couldn't understand, let alone support." She gulped hard and tried to stand, but a sudden dizzy spell nearly toppled her.

Liam offered her his arm, and she took it, releasing the moment she had balance enough to reach the bed. "I'm sure you feel superior to me—it's hardly a novel achievement—but I'm not ashamed of what comes next."

Sophie felt like the back of her head was as wet as Pam's, dripping hot blood between her shoulder blades, but she was too dry for it to be real, too dusty and attic-entombed. She stood between the beds, holding the woman's focus as Liam slithered up behind her.

"I won't mourn the annihilation of evil men, even if it makes me an evil woman," Pam continued. "And if I should die for my country, I won't be a sheep like the wretches in Saigon or the people in Taunton. I won't die for nothing."

"You're right," Liam said. "You will die for the Lamb, Pamela Mason."

"Why do you keep saying my name like that?"

He spun the fork in his fist and said, "So the Lamb of God knows who to devour."

His arm moved like a bolt of lightning, so swift Sophie didn't realize what was happening until blood pearled from four holes in Pamela's throat. The rivers ran independent until they reached her collarbone, then united in one crimson deluge. She collapsed on the bed and grasped at her neck to stop the bleeding, but her fingers slipped from her carotid artery and, within minutes, relaxed against her chest. Though her eyes continued to roll and shift in her skull, there was no light in her gaze.

"Liam, my God . . . "

He turned to Sophie, smiling. He was so beautiful, lit in holy pride, and he pocketed the fork like a precious gem. He tried to touch her, but she shrank back, suddenly afraid.

The exhilaration of watching Liam castigate the woman morphed to shame, and the knowledge she'd imparted returned to Sophie's mind in ferocious waves. She tried not to look at Pamela Mason, but the blood kept calling her back. The sheer amount of it darkening her body created a sort of black hole that sucked every ounce of energy out of Sophie.

Her knees weakened, and she collapsed to the floor. "Oh my god. What did you do, Liam? What did you do?"

He knelt opposite her and forcibly closed his blood-soaked hands over hers.

"Don't worry, my love. I'll tell Mother we did it together."

CHAPTER TWELVE

S HE'D NEVER SEEN so many people smile at a fork. The Choir celebrated the flailing utensil in hungry awe for the entirety of the evening prayer. For a while, Sophie thought they might put the makeshift weapon into a glass case for daily worship, but it was soon passed off to a barrel-chested man named Marco and a purple-haired woman named Bet. They dropped the utensil into a plastic bag and shoved it in a knapsack stuffed with coveralls, fireplace matches, and a stack of papers emblazoned with crudely-drawn American flags. After a quick private prayer with Paleo and Peter, they made the sign of the Lamb to their brethren and dashed out of the house.

"I want to congratulate and thank everyone who collected CI today," Paleo sang to the Choir. "Big or small, conversion or castigation, the Lamb values every stone unearthed to widen the passageway to our mother's love. You are the future, my children. You are sentries of goodness and chastity. People out there can be the fruit on the Tree of Life, but we all know what happens to that fruit, don't we?"

The Choir murmured in agreement, and Sophie nodded, though she wasn't sure why. When all was said and done and she was walking back to Liam's bus with her bloody hands in her pockets, the things she'd worried about for sixteen years seemed so tiny. On Mohr Lane she had no control and hated it, but the more she considered the possibility that some mother-god really did want her and Liam to help create a better world, the more she wanted to give into it. Terrified as she was in the motel room, sitting in Liam's passenger seat with the window open and a joint casting a ballooning net behind them, Sophie felt calmer than she ever had in her life.

She wanted to believe it was the Lamb's doing. She wanted to believe it was a reward.

While Junipero and a merry crew cooked dinner, the Lights led Sophie and Liam to the basement to take the official report on Pamela Mason's castigation.

Sophie expected the basement of the old farmhouse would have a story to tell, but she never would've guessed that the Choir of the Lamb would have a large amorphous swimming pool deep set in the masonry. She gasped at the area studded with lanterns, black curtains, and lamb statues until Liam said her name.

"This way, Soph."

He beckoned her from the pool to the bare gray hall leading to another chain of rooms. They were as empty as the condo's attic apartment, with only sporadic chairs positioned over large drains. The room Sophie was led into, however, had a large orange oval rug at its center.

Liam and Sophie sat on cold folding chairs in front of an ebony podium where Peter and Paleo received their testimonies. Sophie's eyes were down while Liam explained his reasons for killing Pamela Mason in St. Agnes's name, but each time he neared the revelation about Avery Norton, Sophie's head bobbed, and her shoulders hitched to her ears.

"But what were you doing there in the first place?" Peter asked.

"It's my fault," Sophie said. "Liam was helping me do research." When the Lights' gaze shifted in sad curiosity, she sighed heavily and buried her face in her hands.

"Sophie," Paleo said softly, "is there something you'd like to confess?"

Liam looked to her with eyebrows raised, and she

clenched her jaw. Holding her hand, he said, "Just be honest, babe. No one's going to hurt you. No one's going to judge you."

The way he was talking, the way they stared at her, Sophie felt like the one who'd punched four perfect holes in a human being's throat. Her mind was still such a frenzy of rumor and doubt, she didn't know what to say. Was Ava Francis really Avery Norton? Was Avery Norton really the monster Pam Mason claimed? And did she kill Sophie's biological parents: her own sister and the man she'd claimed to love?

She didn't want the answers. Admitting the woman she'd spent the last sixteen years with was a kidnapper and a killer made her feel stupid and weak. She cleared her throat and tightened her muscles so she wouldn't sound stupid and weak too, but her voice came out soft and trembling when she said, "My mom's not my mom."

With simultaneous hums of sympathy, the Lights sat on the floor in front of her; Liam slid from the chair beside her and joined them in listening to her story as if he hadn't heard these truths before . . . if they *were* truths . . .

She retained her composure for as long as possible as she relayed the things she'd learned about Avery Norton, Taunton Asylum, and herself: the only child of Natalie and Paul Dillon. But like boiling water blowing off a pot lid, her emotions eventually exploded out of her. She blubbered like a baby one second, and she punched the air the next, but neither Liam, nor his parents consoled her. Not one sympathetic smile, not one nod or embrace. They stared at her like she was rattling off a grocery store receipt of bad deals and day-old donuts.

When she finished, Peter slapped his hands on his thighs and sat up.

"So, this woman pretending to be your mother," he said, "she's at worst a murderer and at best a compulsive liar. Is that right?"

Liam urged her to agree, but she shook her head. "I don't know. It's possible."

"And how do you feel about that?"

"I haven't really processed it."

It was Paleo's turn to pop up to her knees. "And the murders? How do you feel knowing that the woman who tucked you in every night killed dozens of people?"

"She didn't tuck me in every night."

Liam sat up too, though he leaned into her and rested his hand on her knee. "Baby, you know that's not what's important."

She did know. Still, she envisioned a fictitious montage of Ava making sure she was safe and snug in bed instead of a hospital engulfed in flames.

A hollowing terror struck her then, like someone had hammered a frozen railroad spike into her chest. She clapped her hands to her heart like it would stop the pain from climbing her throat, but it shot up her gullet anyway and stuck there, lodged in the roof of her mouth like a stone causing nonstop pressure. She thought Ava kept her in solitude to prevent her from hurting people with her spells, but maybe it was to keep her from venturing far enough to discover her so-called mother's secrets.

She didn't realize Liam had scooted closer to hug her until he whispered in her ear: "No one will hurt you. Not even you."

Comfort rolled over her like a warm morning tide, but the longer Liam held her and told her he'd keep her safe, the more his bones seemed to calcify, constrict, and squeeze the pain in her palate to the rest of her body.

"He's a murderer too," Paleo said.

His wrists locked behind her back, and she squeaked in discomfort, but he didn't loosen his grip. He looked straight into her eyes, which he'd done plenty of times before, but there was nothing of the man she cherished, only the cold stiff stare of the lamb statues sprinkled around the house.

"That's how some people would classify what he did today," Paleo continued. "And what *you* did today."

"I didn't—"

There was no point in finishing the thought. No one in the room would believe it, especially not Sophie. Her heart and mind were just slowing down from the day's events. Despite the horrors she'd witnessed, she hadn't put much thought into the fact that the man she loved killed someone an hour before—or that she'd encouraged him.

"Pam Mason wasn't a good person," Sophie muttered. "And she was going to hurt people. It had to be done."

Liam finally released her. Backing away, his face blazed with worship. "So you really do understand what we're trying to do here. What the Choir stands for."

"I'm doing my best."

Paleo cradled her belly with one hand and touched Sophie's face with the other. "You're doing wonderfully, sweetheart. But that's no surprise for someone like you."

"What do you mean 'someone like me?' I'm no one."

"Oh my dear, that's just not true," Paleo said. "There are people in this world who live apart from it, and they think that means they don't matter, or that they're not special, but it's quite the opposite."

"She's right, Soph. You're special. And . . . " He blinked as if suddenly struck by a breeze laced with pulverized glass. "You know I love you, right?"

"Yes, of course."

"And I want to spend the rest of my life with you."

She giggled, but his face remained tense, almost wounded by her response, and her smiled dropped. "Sorry," she said. "I hope you know I feel the same way."

He stood up, and the Lights went quiet. Kneeling dramatically, he took Sophie's hand in his and gazed at her with such quivering desperation that his tear-filled eyes inspired a fluttery sort of fright in her chest.

"Marry me, Sophie Francis. Make me happy. Make me immortal. Make me yours."

She laughed again, this time like a scoff through flared nostrils, and again Liam's expression didn't break. "You can't be serious." She lowered her voice and drew closer. "Liam, we've only known each other a month."

His words came out gummy as moist bread when he spoke next, remorseful. "I'm sorry, but that's not actually true." He swallowed hard. "I've known you much longer."

Peter Light said Liam's name like a warning, but Liam didn't falter. He tightened his grip on Sophie's hand and seized every centimeter of her gaze. "She deserves to know who she is, Peter. That's all she wants. After everything she saw today, after everything she's seen living in the same house as a murderer, she needs peace. We can give her that peace."

Sophie squinted. "Liam, what are you talking about?"

"He's been watching you," Paleo said matter-of-factly. "We all have."

Sophie's eyes widened, and Liam lifted his hands in submission.

"You don't have to be scared."

She pulled free and shoved the chair between herself and the Choir. "That's easy for you to say," she said, eyeing the exit.

"You're right. And it would be much easier for you to give in to fear right now, but I'm begging you to hear me out and trust that what I'm telling you comes from the heart. Can you do that?"

"It depends. How long have you been watching me?"

Paleo stepped forward, serene yet beaming. "Maybe it's best if we start at the beginning, when Mother Agnes had her first vision. She was around your age when St. Agnes appeared and told her, 'One day, I will be reborn.' With the heart of the Lamb, she said a human would emerge from the shadows to save the sick, punish the wicked, and enrich the souls of all who seek the majesty of the great mothers. According to the prophecy, this living embodiment of God's grace would have visions that allowed them to communicate with our patron saint. Just like Mother Agnes. And like you, Sophie."

She gripped the chair, her hands wet with anxiety. "Wait a minute. You're not saying what I think you're saying."

Liam stood, his eyes to the floor. "I lied to you, Sophie, and I'm sorry for that, but it was for the greater good. When I said you were the one, I meant it. Intimately, yes, I meant you're the person for me. But . . . " He at last looked at her again, and though a tinge of remorse creased his brow, the corners of his mouth were upturned, almost prideful.

"But?"

"You're the one for *all* of us. The one we've been waiting for. You . . . " he whispered, " . . . are Agnes of Rome."

Her hands slipped on the chair back and she nearly pitched forward. Liam jumped to help her, but she picked up the chair and thrust it at him like a lion tamer.

"Mother Agnes gave us all the information years ago," Liam said, hands up in surrender. "You have the right eye color. You're the right age. July 1958, right?"

"I never told you that," she said, tears threatening to spill.

"You didn't have to. It was obvious the moment I learned your name. She knew that, too."

They came at her as one, and she swung the chair at them as hard as she could. She hit Liam's hand, and pain crinkled his face, but it didn't stop him. He latched onto one of the legs and tossed the chair aside.

Sophie spat. "You've been following me! You've been lying to me! You're just like my mother!"

"But she's not your mother, dear," Paleo said. "She's your kidnapper."

Sophie's heart sank in her like a hot stone, and gripping her now hollow chest, she backed against the wall and slid, weeping, to the floor. "This is crazy. I'm going crazy."

"No, Soph."

"You think I'm a saint! You think I have magical powers! If I'm not crazy, if this isn't a delusion, it means I fell in love with a religious nutbar."

Liam's face reddened, and cradling his injured hand to his heart, he dropped his gaze with a somber nod. "I don't blame you for feeling that way. But I promise you, this is very real."

"It can't be. I'm not who you think I am."

Paleo bent to her, serene as ever. "But you are, my dear. Accept it or not, it'll still be true. Refusing will only bring you pain. Refusing means you lose us, you lose Liam. All you'll have left is that lying snake. And your spells. And your misery. You will still be lonely and songless."

"You'll still have visions of hurting people too," Peter said. "And you'll still hurt them for real."

Sophie's breath stuck in her throat like glass wool. "How—who—"

"Don't make her relive it," Liam said. "She doesn't always remember. She doesn't know what we know."

"What do you mean?" she demanded, frothing. "What did I do? Was it her? Was it Moira?"

"You see, Peter, she feels guilty enough."

"No! I didn't kill her! I couldn't have! I didn't hurt anyone!"

Liam eased her to the ground. Kneeling with her, his voice faint with pity, he brushed back a loose lock of hair. "You don't have to talk about those things ever again. It wasn't you. It was the Lamb working through you."

"This isn't real. I didn't do anything!" Sophie collapsed into Liam's arms and wailed. "Why is this happening? I don't deserve this."

He hummed in sympathy. "Agnes of Rome thought the same thing. The blessed are often tested, and sometimes they're destroyed, but for all their sacrifices, they're granted a blissful eternity in realms beyond our greatest dreams. And they are deeply loved, with such unbridled devotion—the way I love you—in ways no song has

131

captured before. But you *will* capture it. God speaks in the heartbeats of unfinished songs, and when He speaks of the great mothers' devotion to you, I'm telling you, Soph, the universe makes the most glorious music. He is more joyful in the mere notion of you than any fully realized creature in existence."

When she shrank away from his gaze and curled into a small quiet thing shuddering on the edge of darkness, he released the kind of sigh that made her feel even smaller for having frustrated him. But then he backed away, held up his hand in half surrender-half worship, and slowly tilted until his forehead rested on the floor.

It was stupid; she wanted to tell him to stop, but Peter followed suit. And when Paleo awkwardly bowed to the floor, Sophie's smallness had no choice but to inflate. It wasn't that she felt bigger or stronger because of their gesture. She instead felt like someone thrust up in the air by a mob, lifted but not elevated. A fearful rage still charged through her like bulls through the streets of Pamplona, but it didn't motivate her to do anything but cry.

They sat up on their knees and tilted their heads to their sad god.

"I know you don't believe me," Liam said, and Sophie tearfully met his eyes, "but I didn't know who you were when I met you. Yes, the Choir assigned me to look for the girl who would be Agnes of Rome, but I never expected to find her, period, let alone fall in love with her that night under the stars."

Paleo rested her hand on Liam's shoulder and smiled at Sophie as if basking in a low but holy fire. "We all want you to be part of this family, but we won't force you. There's no point. You have a spectacular natural magic, but it can't possibly do the Lamb's work without your full cooperation."

"This was fate," Liam said. "Even your resistance. Even your fear and distrust. And I wasn't sure I even believed in fate until I met you." He stood, and his parents stood beside him, their hands linked as they stepped toward her in unison. "But I have to believe in it now, because it's made my life worth living. I want to worship you. I want to honor you. I want to marry you."

All her life Sophie longed to be loved like this, to be desired so desperately that pain and adoration shifted seamlessly into one another, but it didn't feel the way she expected. It was steel wool in her chest with little flares of warmth. It was affection with so many wounds. It was family with so much fear. It was being loaded down by the gods and demons riding her bones, even as they carried her into the sky.

But when it came down to it, she had nowhere else to go, and the Choir would take care of her. She'd have passion and music and heritage . . . and Liam.

It was crazy, maybe even stupid, but what else was her life up to that point? And now that she knew she'd been living under the same roof as a notorious killer, how could she be anything but grateful for Liam and the Choir for taking her in? That's what she told herself anyway, over and over, brushing aside the day's events as necessary evils in the name of progress.

Avery Norton couldn't make such a claim. She killed to escape punishment. She killed because she was sick in the head, and she put that madness in her niece's brain too. She, Avery Norton, child murderess, was the writhing thing that tilled the sour earth of Sophie's soul. She did this to her. She denied her treatment because of the years at Taunton Hospital. She erased her life on Martha's Vineyard, along with Sophie's real mother, Natalie. She broke their family, and it was time for Sophie to find a new one.

"Yes," she whispered.

Liam's eyebrows lifted. "Yes?"

"Yes, I'll marry you."

Liam whooped and pulled her into his arms. The

Lights clapped and cheered as he spun his future wife and joyous tears ran down his face. They dotted Sophie's as he lowered her, kissing her cheeks until she erupted into giggles.

"Tonight," he said. "Right now. Let's get married right now."

"Whoa! Slow down, cowboy!"

"Why? We're already going a mile a minute. Let's keep on going. It's a big day tomorrow. Why not charge into it together, as a married couple, and show the world what it means to sing our praises to St. Agnes?"

"Don't you mean to *me*?" she asked, winking.

He got down on his knees again, and the parents followed. "Yes," they said in unison. "To you, St. Agnes."

"Whoa! I was joking."

"But we're not," he replied. "Sophie Dillon, daughter of Mary Mother of God, will you rise with me to a new dawn as my spiritual guide and my beloved wife?"

Everything he said was art. His words, like viscera-dripped sculptures, made her feel giddy and helpless at the same time, dangling on the mercy of his tongue.

She nodded, and he embraced her. Burying his face in her belly, he pressed all ten fingertips into her lower back. He'd never held her like that before, like he was trying to find a new way to be inside her, to squeeze her secrets instead of her body.

She supposed she understood. Sophie Francis, whoever she'd been, didn't matter anymore. She was just a shell, a gilded wrapper on something ancient and sacred and far more important than a lonely girl who enjoyed causing pain.

Running her fingers through Liam's hair, she said, "I need a dress."

134

CHAPTER THIRTEEN

PALEO LIGHT HELD the thin white silk against Sophie's body and grinned. "See? I knew we were the same size. Well," she added, tapping her belly, "we used to be."

"I think you're beautiful," Sophie replied, and Paleo blushed, gesturing for the girl to follow her into the master bedroom.

The house was abuzz with activity as the Choir prepared for the impromptu wedding that evening and the holiday feast the next day. Reporters and congresspeople were due to arrive by one o'clock on Thanksgiving, so every member not essential to the marriage ceremony worked hard cleaning the house and prepping the many peace offerings for their boisterous critics. They scrubbed the rooms from top to bottom and polished every surface to reflective perfection. They moved the extra cots and chairs to the labyrinthine basement and organized the chaotic corners of shared living space into neat stacks, like monuments to the merits of Choir life.

The master bedroom, however, was off-limits. Always locked, the room where the Lights slept had the only private bath. The only real bed too. Paleo unlocked and threw open the door, and Sophie entered brimming with awe. They had dressers full of clothes they didn't wear and jewelry boxes like overflowing oysters spilling pearl-encrusted seaweed. In this home of amateur artwork, black curtains, and floor drains, the piles of pretty things struck Sophie odd.

"I hope it'll do as a bridal suite," she said, catching her wandering eyes. "Not that I think such frivolous things are important to someone like you."

Swelling with pride, the woman led her to the plush pink bathroom. She closed the door but stayed close by, her voice coming through so loud and clear Sophie imagined her lips pressed to one of the door's brass-hinged cracks as she swung her gaze around the bathroom.

While the rest of the farmhouse displayed lambs and crosses and countless depictions of their patron saint, the master bed and bath looked more like a museum to the things they'd left behind: former sacred icons, like doilies and crystal figurines, and one gilded picture of Elvis Presley. It didn't occur to Sophie to wonder how the Choir of the Lamb acquired such a perfect spot for their ever-expanding community or who'd lived there before, but the Lights' room looked less like a religious house and more like Dionne's.

Dionne.

Sophie's stomach ached, and she lowered to the tub's edge.

Dionne didn't know where Sophie was. Or that everyone in this house thought she was some kind of reincarnated saint. Christ, Dionne didn't even know Sophie was getting married.

It didn't feel right. It didn't feel real.

"How does it look?" Paleo chirped.

Sophie stripped off her clothes and pulled the dress over her head. She stood on the toilet to get a better look at herself in the mirror over the sink, and smiled as she slid her hands up and down her body. It was little more than a slip, but Sophie looked every bit a heavenly bride. Delight bubbled up in her, and she stepped down from the toilet as if descending an actual throne.

She opened the bathroom door, and Paleo gasped, her hands flying to her face. They clasped in prayer at her lips, then dropped to her chest as she lowered awkwardly to the floor.

"Thank you for this precious gift, oh my Lamb, my mother." She made the sign of the Lamb and pressed her hands to her lips. "If I didn't believe it before, I could never deny it now. You are truly miraculous, my child. Mother Agnes will be so pleased."

"I'll be more pleased if you don't do that ever again," she said, helping the woman to her feet.

"I'll try my best when it's just us, but it would be improper not to show you such respect once Mother Agnes arrives."

"Will she be here for the ceremony?"

"I'm afraid not." Paleo pouted and brushed Sophie's hair back from her shoulders. "But Mother Agnes is always with us. Even now I feel her presence, and she is joyful." She twisted the girl's hair into a ponytail and held it in a messy pile atop her head. "Do you feel her too?"

Sophie didn't feel a damn thing except a new onslaught of cramps and a lingering urge to call Dionne. There was a phone next to the bed—the first Sophie had seen in the entire house—but she dropped her focus when Paleo noticed her staring.

The woman released her hair, took her hands, and led her to the king-sized bed. "I know this is a lot to handle, my dear, but you don't have to be afraid of what's happening to you. I don't flatter myself to say we're the same—I can't imagine the burden of sainthood you've carried around all these years—but I remember the fear of giving in to the Lamb, the fear of acknowledging that I knew nothing, that I'd done nothing of worth my entire life, and of accepting that I had to relinquish everything about myself to something bigger, something I couldn't even touch . . . " She chuckled dryly and wiped a blossoming tear from her eye. "But I *could* touch it, Sophie. Because the Lamb was in Mother Agnes, and when she reached out to me, when she pulled me in and closed me in her embrace, I knew it was in me too. Selflessness. Honor. Chastity. I did not value these things before I joined the Choir because I did not value myself. But the Lamb always did. It told Mother Agnes my name. Just as it told her yours."

Paleo hugged the bride-to-be so tight it felt like her fetus's foot was wedged between Sophie's ribs. Sophie tried to wriggle free, but Paleo locked her wrists behind the girl's back and, pressing her lips to her earlobe, whispered. "When the time comes, you mustn't fight it."

Someone knocked on the door, and Paleo trilled, "Come in!"

Liam swung into the room but recoiled upon seeing Sophie. He covered his eyes with one hand and apologetically turned his back to them. "I'm so sorry! I didn't know you'd be in your dress already." He groaned. "This is just great. A perfectly good marriage and I cursed it."

Paleo snickered as she rocked herself off the bed and pulled Liam's hand from his eyes. Coaxing Sophie to her feet, she passed her into her fiancé's arms. "Oh please. You two are beyond such silly superstitions. The dress is such a tiny part of the ceremony anyway. And we have our own little rituals, don't we."

"Speaking of which . . . " Liam held out a mug with "SOPHIE" emblazoned on the front, grinning sloppily like Nilsson when he bagged a hare. "You're really one of us now."

She traced her name with shaking fingertips, reminded of the day in the black chapel, the nausea and pain of the hallucinations, and the burning girl who lived within. But there was also Liam, handsome and artistic and somehow more angelic after homicide, who offered her the cup like a child whose worth hinged on her acceptance.

She curled her hand over the cup's edge, her nails dipping into the red liquid inside, and flinched.

"It's wine," he said. "Just wine."

"Careful with that. No spilling," Paleo said. "We want our visitors to see our newest member looking her best, don't we?"

Sophie was mid-sip and snorted, covering her mouth as she swallowed. "You want me to wear this tomorrow too?"

"There's nothing more inspirational than a young bride."

"I don't think Agnes of Rome would agree," Sophie muttered.

Paleo's eyes widened in shock. From the minute Sophie met her, the woman's face was an orb of peachy pleasantry, but it looked like pale rock now. Her mouth tightened to a bloodless ring that pitted Sophie's nerves when she said, "I suppose you would know." But it vanished a few seconds later, and her face was flushed with amicable pinkness again. "I just thought it would be kind, you know? Showing those narrow-minded fiends what it means to be part of something real, something clean. They have so little of that in their lives, otherwise they wouldn't be so invested in trying to destroy everything the Lamb has built. Spreading lies about us, acting like this is a loony bin instead of a church—it's enough to make me sick. I'll be lucky if I can hold down my tea when I'm greeting those bloodsuckers."

"But we can't treat them like enemies," Liam said to Sophie, although it was Paleo who'd reddened in anger. "They might be part of the family when the day is through, and we don't want them to carry any ill feelings into their new lives."

Sophie was anxiously gulping down the last of the wine, no longer caring if it contained hallucinogens when Paleo suddenly grabbed her arm.

"A new life!" she exclaimed. "That's what you represent, Sophie. Young and pure . . . "

Sophie winced at Liam, who giggled as Paleo continued dramatically.

" . . . bright and magical. They must know we are not monsters; we are the future. We must help our critics to see it when they come tomorrow."

"And if they only see a child bride married into a cult?"

Sophie expected the rough rocky look from Paleo again, but the woman expelled a hearty belly laugh.

"Oh, I think you know what will happen then, my dear."

She looked to Liam, whose face shone with the many satisfactions of the day, then past him to the rosy bathroom where her reflection glared back in shaky uncertainty. Her face was pale as milk in the glass, and her mouth resembled a ravine hastily carved into a tub of ice cream. Her white lips parted but not enough to accommodate the heavy words that spilled out in a voice unlike her own. She wasn't even certain what the phrase meant, but it charmed Liam and Paleo when she whispered, "A Great Castigation."

Her fiancé wrapped her up in an embrace that lifted her toes from the floor, whooping as he spun her. She couldn't keep a straight face when he did that, no matter how many times she wanted to be scared or angry or a numb drowned thing in a sea of speculations. When Liam broke her connection to the earth, she felt like a new girl . . . a new woman . . . with a new life.

CHAPTER FOURTEEN

THE GARDEN HAD been reaped and replanted to feature the best flowers and vegetation and arranged in grids and pretty little rows for the Choir's critics. But another alteration had been made as well. Adjoined to Liam's space, the Choir had marked off a plot of freshly tilled earth. Sophie now had her own little garden to tend.

Liam was showing it to her from the back steps when he suddenly shouted, "Dammit!" and bolted into the backyard. Dirt sprayed, flowers toppled, and a white tail flashed as a hare dashed across Sophie's plot and out a new hole in the hedgerow.

She hoped for every jackrabbit's escape when Nilsson was on the hunt, but a part of her rooted for him too. Maybe because he was a stray and he needed to eat, but also because of the thing inside her. She briefly lost herself to imagining the first dead hare she found, how interested she was in its anatomy, how happily she shredded it like a chicken wing.

Overcome with nausea, she crouched on the back step. Staring at the frantic paw prints in her garden, she was glad it got away, even if it soured Liam's mood, even if it betrayed the beastly thoughts within her.

"I'm so sorry," he said. "It was supposed to be perfect."

"It is," she said, breathing heavily. "It's just cramps. Probably not the best time to be wearing white."

He shrugged. "If an accident happens, it happens. It's natural."

It didn't feel natural as Liam helped her to her feet. She couldn't stop staring at the paw prints in the soil. She wanted to see them up close and dig her fingers into the dirt, searching for something she couldn't define, but there wasn't time now. She would have to wait until she was married.

As Liam led her to the basement, fear tumbled through Sophie's brain like a shard of glass in a bag of jellybeans. It pierced what confidence she had, leaving soft, dented sweets caught on rigid thoughts that piled up sticky in the back of her mind. She didn't want to feel so troubled in her last unmarried hours. She wished her heart were as light as the silk on her skin, but the black gunk of doubt clogged up her veins, slowed her blood flow, and made her heart heavy and sluggish as the steel door opening to the basement.

Music climbed the stairwell like the Diablo winds: sand and swelter and ghostly voices playing hide-and-go-seek as she descended. She entered the flickering torch light encircling the basement pool ahead of Liam as if he were offering her to the flames. Gray mist and black smoke cavorted like spastic spirits over the cauldron the pool had become, and the longer Sophie watched, the more it danced in time with the voices of the Choir all around her.

Paleo stepped forward and called for quiet as Sophie and Liam stood beside her at the water's edge. "This is an auspicious day for the Lamb," she said, voice booming in the underground grotto. "Today we welcome a new member to our flock. This always pleases the great mothers, but this is no ordinary recruit. She's the one we've been waiting for. After all these years, with all the houses searching for her, she found *us*. The one and only Lamb made flesh, the one foretold to Mother Agnes by the spirit of our patron saint when she was just a child. She has come to save us all."

Doubt like a nest of worms coiled around her organs, writhing and bulging so intensely she thought they had to be visible under her diaphanous dress. Glancing down to check, she stumbled, her head swimming with visions of her inevitable failure to live up to expectations.

Liam pulled her close and allowed her to wilt against his side. "Don't let Paleo scare you. This is *your* moment. This is your *song*."

She tilted her gaze to him, and he wiped the falling tear from her cheek.

"You will always have inspiration now, Sophie. Because you *are* inspiration. For all our people, in houses across the country. While our critics gather to ridicule the Lamb and everything we value, you are being exulted by every follower of Mother Agnes. You are more loved than any other creature on this earth. If your lying snake of an aunt had any sense, she would've treated you like a saint instead of a prisoner."

"Maybe she was afraid of me."

He snickered and ran his fingers through her hair. "Imagine being afraid of you."

Paleo called Sophie forward, and Liam nudged her. Pensively disconnecting with her fiancé, she joined the woman, shoulders hitched and face as hot as a roasted apple.

Paleo continued. "To honor this miracle and toast our patron's return, we give ourselves to the Lamb, to be absorbed by its essence as its essence absorbs and absolves us."

The pair sent out to clean up the Pamela Mason mess had returned and were helping Petal distribute the Choir's labeled mugs. Jugs circulated the congregation, and a dark red liquid ran thick into the cups of adults and children alike. They smacked their lips, some already kissing the rims in anticipation.

Paleo lifted her mug high, and the Choir followed her example. "By consuming the blood of the Lamb, may the luminescence of God and His Mother Mary guide us toward greater service and grander dominion. May it grant us a more intimate connection to St. Agnes, and to the secrets of our mothers' world. We accept these gifts with humility and gratitude. We use these gifts in pursuit of a better, purer life."

The Choir drank deep with baritone gluts and giggles of refreshment, but Sophie stared at her cup, fearful. It wasn't wine this time. It smelled like the tea from the black chapel but thicker, sweeter, and judging by the way her new brothers and sisters danced to the thrumming music, the concoction was far stronger. Children wiped tea from their Kool-Aid red mouths and held up their mugs to toast her, watching intently as she raised her own.

Drawing close, Liam whispered. "You don't have to. The Lamb's already inside you. You're not like the rest of us."

"But I want to be like you," she said. "I want to belong. I want to love this thing inside me as much as everyone else here. I want to believe it's good, because I've never found a reason to think it's anything but a threat." Her voice was low by the end of the reply, and Liam's face looked like pale-yellow wax in the candlelight, melting with each second she remained dubious of her blessings. It hurt her to see him like that, and she pressed her hand to his chest. "But as long as *you* believe it . . . " She lifted the cup to her lips, and Liam's eyes twinkled in adoration as she tilted it back.

The tea flowed like saccharine sludge that ran clotted and tingling down her throat. The congregation roared in worship, and as members embraced, even exchanged kisses that passed the Lamb's essence from one body to another, Liam pinched Sophie's chin.

"You'll believe it too. Soon."

"I love you, Liam."

"Me too, babe. More than life when it's wonderful and death when it's welcome."

Peter clanged his mug with a spoon. "Sophie Marie Dillon!"

When she snapped around, it felt like the tea was a tide ebbing through her, sloshing back and forth as she focused on the Lights standing at the pool's edge.

"You've come to the Choir of the Lamb of your own free will," Peter said, "but like the rest who stand here in solidarity, this choice was not yours alone. You were called here, united in a common goal: to honor Mary, mother of God, and our patron, the glorious and chaste St. Agnes of Rome. You've come to build a better world by introducing your mothers into the lives of those who need them most, to serve mankind by lifting out all who oppose the Lamb's blessings."

Sophie bristled. She agreed that blasphemers and terrorists like Pamela Mason didn't deserve happiness, but "lifting out" sounded more like stain removal than what they'd done to Pam. A splash of bleach, a little elbow grease, and voila! A more chaste world for all.

"Sophie, do you agree to seek enlightenment through community service and to carry St. Agnes in your heart all the days of your life?"

"Yes."

"Do you vow to follow the ways of the Choir, to sing out and spread our joys, to help heal the sick and needy, especially those who can't heal themselves?"

"I do."

"If threatened, if tortured, if torn limb from limb, do you agree to honor the teachings of the Lamb and defend the faith against all those who seek to discredit it?"

She hesitated but eventually creaked, "I do."

"That's a good girl." Paleo patted her back like a newly housebroken puppy and opened her arms to the crowd. "And now, as one, the benediction . . . "

Sophie was silent as the Choir chanted in whispers that made a rustling field of the chamber. It was hard to make out the words, and the more Sophie strained to hear them, the more garbled they became. She closed her eyes as the music swelled up in her like a balloon, and with the torches still somehow flickering behind her eyes, Peter's earlier words sharpened like a tattoo on her brain.

"You will still hurt them for real."

Liam squeezed her hand, and she opened her eyes with a gasp. He was beside her now, both facing Paleo and Peter Light who spoke in unison to the affianced and their reverent witnesses.

"The Lamb stands for chastity," they said, "which is deeper and more complex than sexuality. Mother Agnes teaches us that chastity is intent, not virginity, and that it changes with us and the developing world. Just as her views changed, so we must to provide shelter to even the most haunted among us. It proves how much she cares about our well-being and our health as the Lamb's children. We grow as she's grown. We drink of the same water. We flourish in the same soil. We celebrate every innocent start. We celebrate every sinful end. We rise together."

The Choir hummed in agreement, but Sophie couldn't make a peep. The tea was in her face, making her tongue sluggish and her eyes feel rimmed in crust.

"These souls who make the holiest of vows will celebrate, explore, and worship each other's flesh and blood. Alone and together. In the name of the Lamb, and in the presence of your brothers, sisters, and parents, do you accept these vows put before you today?"

"I do," Liam said, and Sophie nodded dreamily.

Paleo's voice trickled like a lazy stream over ancient stones. "In the eyes of our holy mothers and heavenly guides, I hereby pronounce your union eternal."

Liam's mouth closed on Sophie's bottom lip. His hand glided over the small of her back, and her body blazed with a sensation like hungry termites, itching pinpricks that tunneled to the bone. He severed the kiss, but they were still connected, breast to breast, gaze to gaze. Liam's face didn't look like his, like every time his mouth moved, his entire face shifted to something angular and alien that chilled Sophie to the core.

A new record was playing. The Choir was singing along, swaying and bleating in harmony, and over Liam's shoulder, Sophie saw undulating veins of music that surged at her like purple and green eels. Snaking past her, the melodies dove into the pool, muffling the beauty and accentuating the discordance of conflicting ideologies. Lyrics and tunes battled all around her, each member wearing a different shade of worship in their songs. From their throats more serpentine colors emerged, but they didn't follow the other music into the pool. They slithered to her, waiting. For what, she wasn't certain. Until the Choir gasped as one.

Sophie wasn't sure who pulled down her wedding dress—for all she knew, it was her—but she was suddenly standing naked before the crowd, unafraid and even a bit proud when eels of music became slick tendrils of hair that encircled and armored the new Agnes of Rome against sinful eyes. They pulled her too, around the room for all to see, and then to the ghostly water.

As she entered the pool, the Choir spoke prayers she would learn, vows she would give others, and bizarre yet beautiful things about her fateful part in the Great Castigation. Time had been a slippery bastard on a good day, and on this, the day of her marriage and baptism into the Choir of the Lamb, it was oiliest of all. One moment she was ankle deep, and the next, she was nearly entirely submerged in the steaming water.

"The clean water will protect us," chanted the Choir. "The good water is life."

Sophie inhaled deep, closed her eyes, and allowed her knees to buckle. She sank slowly, extending her legs at the last second to land softly on the smooth bottom of the basin. She knew without looking she wasn't alone. Warmth radiated toward her, but despite its comforting waves, she was terrified to open her eyes. What creature had she attracted this time? Another corpse? Another killer? Or was she finally clean enough to see St. Agnes for who she really was?

Someone touched her cheek, and her eyes flipped open to the angelic face of a young girl framed by clouds of floating hair that softened to misty scarlet ribbons. Sophie twirled her fingers in the tendrils, which thickened and multiplied until the water was striped red. The girl's mouth was pursed, and bubbles escaped her pale lips, but her voice was loud and clear when she said, "You are the Lamb, Sophie. Embrace it."

"I want to," she said, "but I'm afraid."

"You should be." Agnes of Rome giggled with a straight face, and the water temperature plummeted. "You will hurt so many people. In my name, for their own good, you will destroy this world."

"No, that's not what I want. That's not what I agreed to."

Agnes laughed, propelling bubbles like frigid darts that stung Sophie's skin. "Why would those people admit what they really need from you? They need your love and your violence, just as they needed mine. They will squeeze you dry like all the others. They'll use you up. They always use up women like us."

"No, that's not right. Liam loves me . . . "

"He's lying to you. They all are."

The red tendrils were all around her, smoldering seaweed coiling and closing tight on her throat. She clawed at the crimson billows, dividing but not thinning them as they lashed Agnes and Sophie together. They tightened on their wrists, their waists, in and out of their pores until they were sewed into one writhing lump of waterlogged meat. Darkness clouded Sophie's eyes, her ears rang as water flooded her brain, and when Agnes spoke again, her voice tumbled from Sophie's purpling lips.

"You're not like them. You're not like anyone. You're my gift to mankind, Sophie; my muscle on Earth, as has been fated for decades. I give you this world, my child. This is your garden. Do not let them tend it for you."

Sophie didn't know when water became air, or when

148

heavenly singing became screeching pleas, but she did know she was grinning, and she could feel Agnes squirming in every cell.

Someone tugged on her arm. Someone shouted in her ear and pulled her hair while another kicked her in the ribs. But she and Agnes were still tied together. In fact, Sophie locked her grip, savoring the celestial feeling of the saintly girl's body devouring hers.

"Sophie!"

She turned, and a figure in a red hooded cloak swung a cane at her head. It bashed her right temple and cheekbone, and she fell, moaning and leaking blood as the Choir streamed past. Her vision was a fuzzy mess of duplicates, but through the garbled information it looked like Paleo was on the floor, cradling her belly as she crawled away from her supposed savior. Safe in Peter's arms, she wiped blood from her nose and wept as he inspected the flowering bruises on her throat.

Sophie's bones thundered with pain, and hot tears plucked her eyes. She curled into a ball, her body a shivering fist that grew colder the more the Choir distanced itself, her new husband included.

She wasn't underwater anymore, but every voice was a thick echoing orb of a cry, like warnings trapped in inconstant waves that only delivered snatches of sentences. And none of it seemed real. Liam was pointing at her angrily and his voice sounded like something from an old movie—furious and quickened and possessed by a fear that had never grazed his cadence before.

"Did you see that?" Liam demanded of the red stranger. "This isn't what you promised us. She attacked Paleo."

"Yes, I saw," the stranger said.

"Well? What are you going to do about it?" Peter asked.

Grabbing a wool blanket from the corner, the cloaked stranger floated past the Choir and covered the naked girl. It was warm on her back, like she was absorbing Agnes of

JESSICA MCHUGH

Rome all over again, and its benefactor ran tireless through her bones.

It made her feel angry. It made her feel alive. And she could do nothing but weep for her still-beating heart.

"Stay away from her, Mother Agnes," Peter said. "We were wrong. She's not the one."

The woman crouched beside Sophie and hushed her softly. "Don't cry, my child. There's so much to rejoice."

"Rejoice? She could've killed me," Paleo squealed. "She could've killed my baby!"

"You didn't tell us where she came from," Peter said. "When we told you we found her, you didn't say anything about who her mother was. Mother Agnes, you didn't tell us about Avery Norton."

"Because it's not your business," she hissed. "It's mine. And God's."

The woman in red pushed back her hood, and the scar tissue distorting her face gleamed in the candlelight. Melted flesh twisted her lips and bubbled over her left eye, stretching across her patchy scalp, and her fingers resembled twigs hastily dipped in candle wax as she unfolded them to caress Sophie's swollen cheek.

"She can't be the Lamb," Paleo whimpered. "She's too dangerous."

With a grotesque grin that dislodged her false teeth, Mother Agnes whispered, "I know. She's perfect."

150

PART TWO
FIFTEEN YEARS EARLIER
1960

CHAPTER ONE

ANTONIA ARCHER CAME highly recommended.

At the therapist's office in the half-shuttered city of Richmond, California, an eighteen-year-old woman calling herself Ava Francis hushed the baby in her arms and tried not to cry.

The receptionist, a smiley woman with rosy brown skin, leaned over the desk and cooed at the pair. "What a sweetheart. Her eyes are stunning. Such a pretty shade of blue. What's her name?"

"Sophie," Ava whispered, and the baby blinked in response.

"Such a cutie. The doctors will be with you soon, Ms. Francis."

"*Doctors*? More than one?"

She nodded, using her pen to push an oiled curl out of her eyes. "Dr. Julian Archer joins Dr. Antonia's sessions sometimes."

"Her husband?"

"Son."

Sophie burped up frothy formula, and Ava wiped it away with a towel she stole from a motel in Ohio. She kicked her feet with a squeal, and Ava sighed through a pursed smile. There was no denying it: the kid was a damn good distraction when she felt anxious, but when she gazed too long into the little girl's eyes, into the azure pools where Paul Dillon was still drowning, memories like regurgitated citrus dragged her mind of all innocent delight.

Fear grew like a firestorm in her belly, and sweat dotted her brow. She shouldn't be there. She shouldn't have even entertained the idea. They were probably going to turn her in the moment they learned she wasn't Sophie's real mother. Even if they didn't, she didn't know how she'd pay for treatment. Richmond was hardly a hub for the psychological needs of the California elite, but Ava could barely afford her room in the sweltering three-dollar-a-day motel down the street.

She'd made a terrible mistake.

She stood to leave, but like a cruel trick, the office door promptly swung open, and Dr. Antonia Archer gave Ava a slight nod of acknowledgement as she led an older man with black hair, bloodshot eyes, and a photo clutched to his chest into the waiting room.

Summoning an army of smile lines and crow's feet, she patted his back and said, "I'll see you next week, Mr. Mio." When the man shuffled out, she whirled to Ava and clapped her hands. "Ms. Francis, I'm sorry to keep you waiting. This must be Sophie, yes?"

The fire shrank as Dr. Archer extended her slender but tenuous hand. She had nearly a foot on the eighteen-year-old, but it wasn't an intimidating height. Not like Doctors Aslinn or Yingling or like Nurse Meredith in Taunton. Not even like Faye, whose strength Ava admired so when she was young and stupid and blind as a newborn rabbit.

She shook the doctor's hand but didn't follow her into the office. The light was different when Ava stood on the threshold, brightening the autumnal hues that colored the space, but that magic ended the moment she entered. The shadows of her past instantly darkened the room, her presence like ash smeared across the warm walls, stealing the power and comfort in the palette.

Antonia Archer closed the office door, but another closed seconds later, and Ava jumped. From the closet beside the couch, a slim man in a gray suit emerged. Seeing the new patient, he stuck out his hand and beamed with an introduction.

"Ms. Francis, it's a pleasure to meet you. I'm Dr. Julian Archer."

She shook his hand cautiously. "Don't call it a pleasure yet. You don't know anything about me."

Sophie spat up, and Ava dug into her backpack for a towel.

"I'm sorry about bringing the baby," she said, cleaning Sophie's chin. "I didn't have any other choice. I know it's probably not normal procedure."

The mother and son team snatched their notebooks from the coffee table and sat in matching wingback chairs opposite the sofa.

"No apology necessary," Antonia said. "We're here to help, and no good could come from chastising you for being a single mother."

Ava's lips twitched to a half smile. "Thank you."

The large leather sofa felt like a half-toasted marshmallow when she sat down. She sank, surprised by her ability to make an impression in the cushion. It was rare these days. She barely had the money to keep Sophie fed and diapered, let alone afford the gasoline that got them to California, so her needs came dead last. She picked at food here and there, and stole when she felt confident she wouldn't get caught, but she spent most days subsisting on spoonfuls of baby food. She was always thin, but never like this. Her eyes had sunken into bluish-black hollows, and her fingers resembled number two pencils left out to crack and pale in the sun.

"Besides," Antonia said, crossing her left ankle over her right, "who's to say what's normal? You made this appointment with me—just me—and here I am letting my son sit in. Is *that* normal?"

Sophie whined, and Ava bounced her gently. "No, I guess not."

"Precisely. Let's address that before we jump in, shall we?"

Something about the way Antonia Archer moved put

JESSICA MCHUGH

Ava at ease. She had a confident air that bordered on pretension, but even the smallest smile or downward tilt of the chin made her an ally again. Julian Archer hadn't mastered it yet, but the resemblances between mother and son were uncanny. Possessing Antonia's high cheekbones and full lips, Julian was no doubt a beautiful man. The largest difference Ava detected was the constant blush in his cheeks, like he'd busted some blood vessels or recently weathered a bitter snowstorm.

"Ms. Francis—Ava—" Antonia clasped her hands as she leaned forward. "I'm afraid I won't be able to serve as your therapist."

Ava's chest tightened. Dr. Archer knew who she really was. A killer, a kidnapper. This was it, the end of everything.

"It's nothing personal, of course," she continued. "I'm just taking some time off from the practice."

"Oh." Ava exhaled in relief as she feigned fussing over Sophie.

"I understand how upsetting this must be, especially considering how far you traveled for this appointment, but I assure you that Julian is an exceptional therapist. He looks young, but he's very accomplished. You're safe with him, I promise."

She wasn't convinced, and they saw it immediately. Her tension must've affected Sophie because the baby whined, thrashing as she stretched her arms.

Antonia set aside her notepad and crossed to the sofa. "May I?"

Ava bit the inside of her cheek. She didn't mind other people's help, even strangers, but after what happened in New York . . .

Julian sat placid in the wingback, hands folded on his knee, like an ideal example of Antonia's maternal skills. When Ava nodded, the doctor sat beside her, and she passed Sophie into her arms. Despite some wiggling and mild fussing, Antonia's gentle rocking and melodic humming quickly lulled Sophie into a peaceful slumber.

"Amazing, isn't it?" she whispered in admiration. "It's so easy for them. Not that they act like it sometimes. Things like bathing and changing diapers can be the hardest, most torturous things in the world for these little ones, but this . . . " She caressed the child's downy hair, and a sigh rolled out from deep inside. "God, I wish we could keep that simplicity as we age. I wish we could drop out whenever we wanted and know tranquility waits on the other side. But it's impossible, isn't it, Ava? This angel's world is still so small. That's why she has tantrums over insignificant things; they're all she has. And you, of course."

Ava gritted her teeth. "I don't think I'm enough sometimes."

"I thought the same thing with my babies." Looking to Julian, she added, "Sometimes I still do. Our worlds expand as we grow, but when you become a mother, they double, triple, they become galaxies that leak into nearly every thought, every slumber. I doubt I've gotten a good night's sleep since I found out about my first pregnancy over three decades ago. It's a parent's burden."

Ava hummed in agreement. Then again, she *wasn't* a parent, was she?

Julian leaned forward, tapping his chin with his pen. "Do you have trouble sleeping, Ava?"

Calling it "trouble sleeping" was like calling an amputation a "brush burn." She hadn't gotten more than three hours of sleep a day for the past two weeks. The more she thought about it, she realized she probably hadn't had a decent sleep since she was thirteen. Her nights at Taunton weren't exactly restful—tranquilizers brought more darkness than tranquility—and the months in the woods were like a waking dream. So many voices, so many ruined faces and dashed hopes.

But she couldn't tell the Archers about any of that.

"Don't most people have trouble sleeping?" she asked.

"True. But most people don't make appointments with us, Ms. Francis."

"With all due respect, Dr. Archer, I made an appointment with only one of you."

Antonia chuckled, tossing Julian a crinkled grin. "A valid point. Unfortunately, it doesn't change the fact that I won't be here to give you the counseling you requested." She handed Sophie back to Ava and returned to her chair. "For the sake of transparency, and for my own healing process . . . " She sighed heavily, and her voice cracked. "My husband passed away recently, and I've decided to take some time off from the practice."

"Oh." Ava lowered her focus, but the rosy glow of Sophie's carefree slumber inspired an echoing ache in her chest. She wanted to say she understood, that she'd recently lost her fiancé, Sophie's beautiful father, but the words were molasses in the back of her throat. "I'm sorry for your loss" was all she could manage.

"Thank you," Antonia said somberly. "Anyway, I'm not running off just yet. I want very much to discuss what brought you here today. Speaking of which, would you mind if Margie watches Sophie while we speak?"

Ava's skin prickled with icy gooseflesh. The Archers seemed trustworthy, but did her perception of people mean anything anymore? After all the manipulation, all the trauma and death, could anything that *seemed* true ever *be* true when filtered through a killer's spoiled mind.

"I promise no harm will come to her," Antonia added.

It was more than she could say for herself—Sophie was probably least safe in her aunt's arms—but Ava's bottom lip still protruded, and she squinted at the doctor.

"You make lots of promises."

"She also keeps them," Julian said. "Except for the Erector Set she forgot to get for my tenth birthday."

Antonia scrunched her nose at him. "I'll never live that down. Love, support, control over the firm's California branch—they're nothing compared to Erector Sets." She called Margie's name, and the door opened to the secretary's sunny face.

Ava held Sophie tighter, but when Margie outstretched

her arms, she found herself doing the same. As much as it hurt to pass her off again, Ava was so tired. Her arms ached and her throat was raw from the constant stream of lies she told Sophie as she slept. Things like, "no one will hurt you again" and "everything will be okay."

Sophie warbled in her sleep but quieted when Margie snuggled her close. Antonia slung Ava's bag over the woman's shoulder and gave a little wave as she gestured Ava back to the couch.

Even with the door closed, Ava didn't budge. Her hand remained on the door like she could feel Sophie's vibrations through the wood.

"Ava, you can't be much younger than Julian," Antonia said, returning to her chair. "Did your mother ever ruin your life by forgetting to buy you a present?"

Looking over her shoulder, Ava Francis shook her head. "The things she gave me were worse than the things she denied."

The Archers exchanged glances, and Julian primed his pen on the notepad. "Please, go on."

Ava Francis had spent nearly three thousand miles memorizing her new history, but the facts felt like tangled spaghetti in her brain now. Instead of her own story, her mind focused on all the ways her dead mother was still very much alive inside her.

"She was a devout Catholic," Ava said, then swallowed hard. "Devout might be the wrong word. When it came to her faith, my mother was strict ... unreasonable ... scary, sometimes. Her lessons were, anyway."

"Lessons?" Julian asked.

Ava scooted to the end of the sofa, her sweaty hands clenched so hard they trembled. "Cleanliness was a big part of it."

"Cleanliness? As in 'next to Godliness'?" he replied.

"Something like that."

"How about you tell us *exactly* what it was like," Antonia said. "Start with where you grew up."

It was the most nerve-wracking part of the fake backstory. All she knew of Bucyrus, Ohio was what a young hitchhiker named Darren told her about his hometown. She recalled his words as she answered, her chin raised in forced confidence as she recited the words that carried her across the country.

"It felt like the smallest town in the world, but maybe they all feel like that when you're young and trapped."

Growing up on the island of Martha's Vineyard off the coast of Massachusetts, Ava was literally trapped as a child, but she rarely felt that way. Even in winter when the streets were quiet and the sea was a choppy onyx beast, she didn't once consider scraping together what money she could for a ticket off-island. It felt like a betrayal to pave over the glorious place of her birth with the dusty fatigue of Ohio. Then again, she didn't know how accurate Darren's portrayals of Bucyrus were. Maybe it was lovely, maybe it was a carousel of fun he was too traumatized to see as anything but a busted pinwheel.

"Is Bucyrus near Cleveland?" Julian asked. "We have a cousin who runs a practice there."

Ava shrugged. "I never got out that way. There was the farm to tend, stuff to sell at market. My mom wasn't a fan of going into the city anyway. Bad influences, she said."

"And your father?"

Ava wriggled in her seat. "I didn't know him well, and what I did I—" She fidgeted and exhaled the sudden strain from her gut. "I think I remember a lot of things wrong."

"Can you elaborate on that?"

Ava had no reservations about lying to protect Sophie, but she had to slip in some truth to make the therapy worthwhile. For Sophie's sake, she had to get better. She had to find a way to control the fire.

"I get spells," she said. "Blackouts. Seizures. Whatever you want to call them, I get them bad."

"I see," Julian said, scribbling on his pad. "Can you remember what happens during these spells?"

"I didn't used to. I didn't believe it when people told me it was happening. But things are different now. Those memories are coming back. Memories of things I did. People I hurt."

"While you were on the farm," Antonia said.

Ava picked at her cuticles. "Yes. I lost time, but I didn't know it, or I remembered things differently. No one made a big deal about it at first, so I thought it was just one of those things, like it happened to most kids. When my mother finally told me what I'd done, I didn't believe her. I thought—" She tore one cuticle too far, and blood darkened the nail bed. She balled her hand into a fist, covered the wound with her thumb, and averted her eyes. "It doesn't matter what I thought. She was right about almost everything."

"What was she wrong about?" Julian asked, and Ava's throat knotted with grief.

The day the police discovered the bodies in the basement of the Norton's house, Faye told them her daughter killed her father. That was still a lie. Of all the horrible things she remembered from her childhood, that one truth kept her from feeling like she was nothing but a wild animal. She loved her father immeasurably, and the years she spent in Taunton thinking she might've killed him were heart-rending. She endured countless hours of brutality and gory joy when her memories started returning, so vivid she smelled the warm dappled kiss of life spurting from her father's neck after his wife's attack, like cake batter spattering the kitchen when Natalie turned on the mixer too high.

Natalie. The name felt strange now that she had no occasion to use it. Overwhelmed by horror, there remained only a few true memories of the two of them at home, young and happy with a hopeful road at their feet, and unaware it had been carved by a cruel hand long before they were born. So many forks to fool them, so many cracks to catch them. There was never any hope on their road.

When Ava lifted her head, she didn't see the doctors looking back at her. Instead, her mother rose like a mountain behind their chairs, and her father gurgled and sputtered on the carpet behind them all, a shrinking shadow. He twitched and begged for his wife's help, but it was too late. He couldn't even hold his daughter's gaze for more than a second before his eyes rolled up to the heavens, where they stuck eternal.

Flames swelled in Ava's belly and crept like hungry eels into her brain. She clenched her eyes shut and exhaled like the breath might extinguish both the fire and Faye's ghost.

"Ava?"

She held up one hand and asked for a minute.

"But Ms. Francis—"

She clenched her knee and growled, "Just a minute. Please."

"Ava, for God's sake, you're bleeding," Julian said.

She opened her eyes to slippery red fingers and splotches on her pants. Her cuticle was still bleeding slightly, but her jagged nails had done most of the damage, leaving scarlet crescents in her palm. Like a little kid, she didn't feel pain until she saw blood, and now it was everything, screaming through her nerves as Julian handed her a box of tissues.

"Thanks," she whispered, her face aflame.

"Was that a spell?"

She said, "No," then shrugged, "Maybe a mild one."

"Drawing blood is mild?"

The fire was low again, but Ava's words tumbled over her lips like smoldering lumps of charcoal. "When it's my own, yes."

Antonia's eyes snapped from her feverish note taking, and she shifted in her chair. "Is this the first time you've sought medical attention for your blackouts?"

She could almost taste Taunton Asylum's bitter "vitamins" dissolving in the pockets of her cheeks when she said, "Yes."

"What was the first incident you remember?" she asked.

Ava's head sunk into her shoulders. "When I was thirteen, I hurt some rabbits."

The doctors exchanged pensive glances, and Antonia bit her lip. "You did this while you were blacked out?"

Ava had been fully conscious when she beat a drove of unchaste rabbits to flaccid sacks of fur and bone, but she nodded in reply. "Can you help me stop it?"

Antonia laid down her pen. "We'd like to, Ms. Francis, but we can't possibly help you if you insist on lying to us."

Ava's lips quivered, and her voice caught in her throat. "I'm not lying."

"You look like a hot chestnut about to pop. It's obvious you're lying to us about something, and I require complete honesty in this room."

When Ava didn't answer, Antonia frowned and sat her notepad aside. She smoothed her dress as she stood, strode to the door, and opened it with a loaded sigh. "I wish you all the luck in the world, Ms. Francis, but I'm afraid this is where we part. We can't work with someone who won't open up."

Julian joined his mother, twin sentries of hopelessness at the exit, but while Antonia assumed a stern, immovable pose, Julian remained soft and sympathetic. It was Julian who kept Ava clinging to the arm of the sofa.

"Please don't make me leave. I'm being as truthful as I can."

"I don't doubt you think that," he said, "but if you want help, if you want to change whatever you believe prevents you from having a happy, healthy life, you have to let go of the fear that we're going to judge you or hurt you. We won't, I promise you."

He sounded sincere, but she imagined it was easy to be honey-tongued after years of cracking open people's minds and convincing them it was their doing.

Ava's body shivered in conflict. "I can only tell you what I know."

"Okay. Then let me tell you what *I* know," Antonia said, pushing ahead of Julian and leaning over the couch with a sneer. "I know who you really are, Ava Francis."

Ava's heart thudded her breastbone, and smoke snaked up her throat from the fire sparking in her gut. She had no idea how a stranger on the other side of the country recognized her, and she didn't care; she had to get Sophie as far away from the Archers as possible.

She jumped to her feet. "Fine. I'll just go, okay? Forget I was ever here."

"I don't know if I can do that," Antonia said. "This is a big secret you're carrying, and I'm not certain you're capable of lugging it around without hurting others."

"I'm not going to hurt anyone."

"And looking after a baby . . . "

Ava's breath solidified in her chest as Antonia shook her head.

" . . . if I felt like that baby was in danger, I'd have a responsibility to report it."

Ava's body jolted, and she raised her arm—for what, she didn't know, and it didn't matter anyway. The moment Julian Archer perceived a threat, he lunged forward and grabbed her forearm. His fingers were cold against her flushed skin as he forced her hand to her side. He was stronger than he looked.

"Sit down, Ms. Francis."

He released her arm, but her muscles remained tight as a snare drum as she sat on the edge of the sofa.

"Thank you," he said, then looked to his mother. "Would you mind excusing us, Doctor?"

Antonia collected her notepad, and with ferocity disappearing into her formerly regal air, she sashayed from the office.

Tears streaked Ava's face by the time Julian sat again, and her fists trembled in her lap.

"I don't want to hurt anyone," she whispered. "Please don't take her away from me."

"Why do you think I'm going to take your daughter away?"

She wiped her cheek with the back of her arm. "Because you know who I am."

Julian pressed one finger to his lips, hushing her as he pushed over the box of tissues. "My mother doesn't know who you are, or what you're hiding. And neither do I. She said that just to prove that you *are* hiding something."

Ava clamped a tissue to her face and moaned. The room spun, and her stomach lurched as she folded her body over her knees. "God, I'm such an idiot. I'll never pull this off. Someone's going to find out. Someone's going to take her away."

"Pull what off? What have you done that makes you feel like you need to hide, Ms. Francis?"

She sat up slowly, sniffling hard. Her body was a snake pit, her innards twining and striking each other, every bite itchy and hot. The venom shot quick up her throat and settled in her tongue. It flamed, flicking the roof of her mouth like a flint.

"There's a fire inside me," she said. "Maybe it's always been there, maybe my mother put it there. I don't really care where it comes from; I just want it gone. I want it to stop destroying my life, for Sophie's sake."

"And for your own. You deserve peace too."

Tissue stuck to the dried blood on her hand. It didn't pick off easy, the pieces shredding, even spreading it seemed, like rosy snowflakes.

"I'm not sure I do," she said. "I've done so many horrible things. I don't think I've ever been a good person."

"I don't believe that. People aren't born bad, Ava."

Amusement tickled one side of her face as memories of her halcyon youth opened and closed like carnivorous plants in her brain. Even when she didn't remember the pain she and her mother inflicted on the sleepy island, she wasn't innocent. Maybe she wasn't born bad, but it was always in her, waiting like a toxic seed aching to split.

"I wish I never remembered the things I did. I wish I could've kept believing I was innocent."

He uncrossed his legs and leaned forward. "When did you start remembering?"

She licked her lips. "When I killed my mother."

Julian dropped his pen, but he didn't break eye contact. "I can see why you'd want to keep that a secret."

"It's not the only secret." Ava's chin dimpled with grief. "If I tell you everything, I know your mother will turn me in."

"Antonia isn't going to be involved, remember? This is between you and me."

She shook her head. "I'm still scared."

"So am I. But we're going to get through this together, okay, Ava?"

She nodded, and he picked up his pen before leaning back in his chair.

"So tell me. What else have you lied about?"

The flames shrank, and the eighteen-year-old calling herself Ava Francis exhaled a plume of truthful smoke.

"My name is Avery Norton, and I've killed a lot of people."

CHAPTER TWO

OVER THE NEXT few months, Ava Francis spilled her guts to Dr. Julian Archer. But guts weren't everything. There was sin in her bones, violence in her blood, and though Julian comforted her enough to open up about most things, she held on to certain confessions. She told him about her imprisonment in Taunton State Hospital but not the arson that freed her. She spoke of her life-changing and persistent love for Paul Dillon, but not that he still came to her in the night. She told him about her mother's lessons and how she'd unwittingly aided Faye's crimes, but not that she'd derived pleasure from remembering her involvement.

"Did your mother ever mention having blackouts of her own?"

"No. She hurt people consciously. Teenagers mostly. She believed people shouldn't be careless with their bodies, otherwise they'd corrupt their souls and spread the bad water through the rest of humanity." Ava screwed her face to one side. "That's what she called it. We couldn't let *bad water* poison the world."

"How did she teach you to recognize this 'bad water'?"

Ava ran her fingernails over her scalp with a hum. "She showed me. She took me to the garden and showed me the rabbits."

"What were the rabbits doing?'

"They were fucking, Dr. Archer."

His mouth curled. "Isn't that what they're supposed to do?"

"Not if they're being disloyal," she replied. "Switching partners, being brazen. My mom marked pairs of rabbits with colored dots the first time she caught them in the act, and when she saw a mismatched pair, she put a stop to it."

"Put a stop to it? I feel like you're rose-tinting that a bit."

"I learned that from Faye too. She wasn't a direct woman, but she was extremely clear in what she believed was right and good. She wasn't even direct when she took me on her little trips. Bridge games, she called them. Bingo. Quilting. She'd say we were meeting with her friends or my grandmother, but we never did."

"Did Faye speak kindly of her mother?"

"Yes, but she also spent years pretending that my father's secret girlfriend was her sister."

"I'm glad you recognize how manipulative she was. It's an important distinction between the two of you."

Ava's stomach clenched, her mesh of lies darkening. "Being a worse person than me doesn't dig her out of my blood. She's not just some rotten potato in my guts. She's a field of the bastards, sprouting and decaying and scattering a sort of drunken death through my veins. She ruined me, and she thought she was perfecting me. A perfect little partner in crime."

"But you rebelled. You fell in love with Paul."

Ava's chest jerked with stuttered breath. "I was just a kid. I didn't know what love was."

"You knew enough to choose Paul over her."

"But everyone in Taunton was right about him. He couldn't see what I was. I never had spells when he was around."

"It sounds like he *did* help you."

"Maybe. But he couldn't save me."

Julian smiled. "Because you had to save yourself."

"And what a fantastic job I did," she said bitterly. "How many people had to suffer because I had to save myself?"

Flames danced behind Julian, peeling away layer by

serene layer of Flint's smiling face. She couldn't tell him what she saw; mostly because she didn't want to put it into words. There was no glass or smoke between them this time. Ava saw every flake, every fleshy dollop that sloughed to the office carpet. Flint was silent but grateful, the squealing sizzle sounding like her skin was singing in perfect joy. But Flint wasn't the only one in the flames. The others clawed their fingers to bony nubs trying to escape. All around her, children burned, and adults with childish minds bashed themselves against bars until their skulls and shoulders were broken, then melted. The louder the screams, the worse the heat in Julian's office. Ava dabbed her upper lip dry, but also to block the smell. It wouldn't have been so bad if she didn't know the cooking meat was human: people she knew, people with families who might've still loved them.

She squeezed her eyes shut. "I didn't deserve Paul. He came so far for me. He risked so much. When everyone else was positive I killed all those people, he refused to believe it. He only ever saw the good in me."

"He sounds like a good man."

"He was. Though I guess I didn't know him as a man for long," she whispered. "We were going to get married. We were going to . . . " Her voice wavered and she cleared her throat. "It doesn't matter. The point is my mother was a monster, and as hard as I've tried not to be one too, there are claws in me, and fangs."

"And fire," Dr. Archer said.

"Yes. And I never know when any of them will come out."

"You mean when Avery Norton will come out."

"Don't say that name again. That girl's dead."

He set down his pen. "You're not dead, Avery."

"I told you not to call me that." She exhaled a shuddering breath as she rolled onto her feet and strolled to the window. The glass was immaculate, granting the room an unsullied swath of afternoon light crosshatched by the window frame.

"I'm sorry," she said. "It's just—I don't want to be her, Dr. Archer."

"Julian, please." His eyes sparkled behind a veil of raven hair as he twisted in his seat. "And like it or not, you are her. You can't change your name and expect to clean the slate entirely."

"I don't need it clean; I don't care if it's covered with shit as long as it hides the truth." Facing the window again, she gazed out on the remnant of a shipyard. "I thought I'd spend my whole life on the Vineyard, you know. I *wanted* to. I thought my life would be simple. Simple and happy— with him." She felt dumb saying it aloud, but part of her felt lighter afterward. Even believing she didn't deserve any relief from the weight of her crimes, she basked in the relief for a quiet moment.

"I know I'm a bad person," she said, "but I have the same dreams good people do. And I still do, except they're about Sophie now. I need to keep her safe. I need to keep *her* life as simple and happy as possible." Her voice cracked, and tears sprang to her eyes. "But I hate it here, Julian. I hate living on the run, in shitty motels. I hate the noise all around me, the lies, and the stench of it. I can't even smell this ocean sometimes. Everything still smells like scorched isopropyl and the Atlantic." Wiping tears from her cheeks, she dragged herself back to the sofa and sunk deep. "I'm glad when I can actually smell the Pacific. It's different, cleaner. It doesn't smell like death."

"To some it probably does," he said. "Maybe even to people in this city who lost everything when the shipyards closed after the war."

"You're right," she said. "I'm so stupid and selfish. God, if there's anything worse than being a killer, it's being a stupid, selfish one. I guess I am Faye Norton's daughter through and through. The only one left."

"Is that why you didn't change Sophie's name?"

With her hands clasped on her knees, she nervously bounced her legs. "Natalie gave her that name for a reason.

I never got the chance to ask her why, but it must've meant something precious. She's all I have left of my sister, my great and gleaming sister." She gritted her teeth and growled as she pressed her fists against her temples. Her hair hid the faint burn scars from the ECT, but she felt them all the time; the skin was thicker there, rougher, and the scars pulsed like tiny mutilated hearts when she sobbed.

She pounded her legs and growled in furious grief. Catching her breath, she ripped another tissue from the box and blew her nose, while Julian watched calmly.

Sniffling, she met his eyes. "Why are you helping me, Dr. Archer?"

"You're paying me, Ms. Francis."

"Not enough for you to ignore everything I've told you. You know I kidnapped my sister's baby. You know I've killed innocent people, and that I still could. Aren't you worried?"

Julian set down his notepad and stood. "This is what I do, Ms. Francis."

She said, "Ava, please," and Julian's lips twitched to a tiny smile.

"Ava . . . the truth is I don't know what to think at this point. But I know I want to hear more, and I think you need to say more. However," he said somberly, "if I ever suspect that Sophie's in danger, I will not hesitate to report you to the police."

Ava's body tightened, and her insides simmered.

"But I don't think that's going to happen," he continued. "I believe you when you say you want to get better, and I want to help you do that. You said Paul went a long way and risked a lot to find you. Well, you did the same to find my mother and me. And you still have a long way to go, but I think I can help you navigate the road to salvation."

"I'm dangerous," she muttered.

"Everyone's dangerous. Not everyone admits it or seeks a cure."

"It won't change what I've done."

"No, it won't. But it could change *you*," he said, sitting on the arm of the couch. "You hate who you were? You hate pretending to be someone else? Don't pretend, Ava. *Be* who you want and need to be to survive."

His cheeks were redder than normal, but she didn't want to stare, so she dropped her gaze to his ink-stained fingers.

"That's our time for today," he said, standing to open the door. "How do you feel?"

"Terrible," she said. "But better." Smoke curled in her belly, warm and wispy and granting a ghost of happiness to touch her lips.

Sophie was passed out in the secondhand mustard yellow carrier Margie had given her, but woke up the moment Ava entered the room. She squealed, not exactly happy or angry, and Ava's stomach roiled in anxiety. She wondered if Sophie could feel her tension from across the room palpably enough to disturb her sleep, and if she'd always feel it.

As she lifted the carrier, Sophie blinked her sleepy eyes and softly burbled, "Mama." That small sound punched her terror into submission, and caressing Sophie's cheek, she whispered, "Maybe someday, sweetheart."

CHAPTER THREE

"I ALMOST KILLED her in New York."

Julian stared at Ava over his notepad. She was standing at the door, hands splayed as she listened to Sophie's light burbling.

"Were you conscious or blacked out?"

"Conscious, but I couldn't control myself," she said. "When the fire's high like that, it takes over."

Julian lifted his eyebrows. "Interesting."

She spun around and crossed her arms over her chest. "My insanity's interesting to you?"

"Absolutely."

"People are dead, Julian."

"And it's your fault. I don't want you to forget what you did, but at some point you have to stop letting it impede your progress. You have to think of what's best for your daughter."

"That's why I almost left her in New York. I thought she'd be better off growing up with artists and progressives. Safer, at least. Hell, sometimes I still think it."

She hitched her shoulders to her ears and crossed the room to Julian Archer's diplomas and certificates on the wall beside the desk. She'd spent months staring at them, wondering if the frames were cool or warm to the touch, if the glass had fingerprints or the sun had bleached the signatures. The walls were slightly darker where Antonia's many degrees had hung, creating a sort of checkered pattern after her "time off" turned into retirement.

She touched the gold frame around one of Julian's diplomas. She would never have anything like that on her wall; she hardly had a wall, and that one was stained and crumbling in a seedy dockside motel near the Archers' office on 23rd Street. She spoke to as few people as possible—usually just Sophie, Dr. Archer, and Margie—and pushed most strangers into her periphery. That became more difficult when she started working as a snack counter clerk at the Hilltop Drive-In Theater down the street. Even then, what interactions she had were promptly pushed away, no more important than the blurry shadows that shambled past her day after day in Taunton.

Six months living in California, and she didn't feel like she really lived there. Or New York. Or Taunton. Certainly not Bucyrus, Ohio. There was only one place she could ever truly call home.

"How did you get out of Massachusetts?" Julian asked, head tilted to one side as if slowly stretching a tight muscle.

"Faye's car. I didn't know how long it would take for someone to find her body, so I got out as fast as I could. But I did know I couldn't keep that car long. I drove until I felt like I was going to pass out behind the wheel, and I stopped at a Howard Johnson's across the state line. That's where I met a group of teenagers hitchhiking north."

"Runaways?"

"Yes. I told them I was running away too. I said my parents disowned me when they found out I was pregnant, and I was looking for somewhere safe. They told me they'd help me take care of Sophie and maybe even find a place to stay if I gave them a lift to Brooklyn. One of the girls had an aunt there."

"How does it feel knowing you lied to people who helped you in such a big way?"

"Most of it didn't feel like a lie," she said, shrugging.

Julian glanced at his notes. "Except you'd just killed your mother, what, the day before?"

Ava blinked rapidly, and her cheeks filled with

shameful fire as she returned to the couch. "It was two days," she said, then drowned the admission in a gulp of lukewarm water. "I didn't like it, but I fell into deception the same way I fell in love with my sister's child; it all just . . . happened."

"That sounds like passing the buck to me."

"It was survival."

"And you did survive, Ava. You've been sitting right here with me, alive and trying to get well, for the last three months. So let's be real with each other. Where would you have gone if you hadn't met those people?"

Her chin trembled. "I don't know. I was confused and scared and all of the memories were coming back—"

"And you chose to keep them to yourself, thereby possibly endangering those kids' lives. Would you agree?"

Lowering her head, she said, "Yes."

"So, once more, how does it feel knowing you lied to people who helped you in such a big way?" He set pen to paper, and Ava lifted her chin.

"I hate myself for most of the things I've done, Dr. Archer. Believe me, there's almost nothing I want more than to apologize to all the people I've hurt, or to have never hurt them in the first place."

"That's good."

"But," she continued, "had I not done those things, that little girl out there who's toddling around and discovering words and becoming an undeniable living blend of my dear sister and my first love would be learning how to live from a monster."

Julian jotted something in his notes. "Please, continue your story about New York."

"I drove, and the kids paid. And they watched Sophie when I felt ill. When I . . . " She gulped water. " . . . when I needed to be alone."

"You were having blackouts?"

"Like you said, I'd just killed my mom. I was messed up. Fragile."

"You don't strike me as a particularly fragile woman."

Ava straightened her spine. She couldn't recall anyone ever calling her a woman before. Murderer and psychopath, sure, but not something that made her feel bright and mature and capable of controlling her madness. She wanted to believe it, but small flames scraped at her insides and she had to breathe through the rising heat to continue.

"The first few days were fine. One of the girls' aunts lived in an artistic commune thing run by a man named Louis. It was a storefront studio in the East Village, but it actually reminded me of Taunton in a lot of ways. There were kids everywhere, draped over furniture, passing around drugs like candy. But they were good people. Painters, musicians, people I liked right away. People who reminded me of Flint." A smile rose with the name but withered quickly. "So I kept my distance from them as much as I could, and from the drugs. Louis introduced me to someone who'd buy Faye's car for $300 and help me get papers and identification under a new name. But I would have to wait almost a month for them to show up. That's when I offered them my engagement ring. It was worthless, just a trinket Paul gave me to tide us over until he could get a real one, but I thought maybe I could cheat them, or at least claim ignorance if I was caught. But it turns out . . . " She stopped and looked to the ceiling as tears rose. "It was real. Not a goldmine, by any means, but it was more than what he let on. Which was appropriate, I guess, considering the man." She waved away rising sorrow and cleared her throat. "Anyway, the guy showed up much quicker after that. But it was a crazy night. the studio was packed with people. Someone's birthday or a record release. Lots of kids crashed there normally, but this was triple that. I could hardly find a space for Sophie and me to sit where she wouldn't be near speakers or in a room filled with smoke. I hadn't had any violent spells since I took off for New York, but I had violent thoughts . . . feelings . . . "

"And the fire?"

"I controlled it pretty well until that night. Until I saw them."

"Who?"

"The rabbits in the garden," she replied. "In a back bedroom that night, I walked in on friends and strangers being . . . intimate . . . flipping and switching, back and forth, laughing at each other, laughing at me, like they were nothing, like I was nothing."

Ava massaged her hands together, staring as her fingers flashed pink and white with the pressure.

"They *were* nothing, Dr. Archer. In that moment, they had no morals or self-worth. They needed help, like a lame horse needs release, and I thought I could be the one to release them. So I entered the room aiming to do just that: fix them up, clean them out, unburden them of sin like divine bleach." She exhaled a shuddering breath and wiped her sweaty palms on her pants. "At the time, it felt like the right thing to do."

His face was slack, yet eyes probing. "But you don't feel like that anymore."

Her pulse raced. Her brow beaded. She rubbed her aching neck as Julian stared at her. "You want to know if I killed them."

"It's not about me. You should want to tell the truth."

She rolled her shoulders down her back and moaned. "No, I didn't kill them. But that was just circumstance. I might have, if things were different. I thought I'd have to; there were so many of them. They overpowered me, pushed me out of the room. But they made me angrier. I kicked and punched my way through the place and eventually collided with the girl who was watching Sophie. I knocked her over, knocked them both over, and Sophie hit the floor . . . hard."

A whimper stuck in her throat, and she pressed her hand to her lips, weeping. "Dr. Archer, what's wrong with me?"

"Ava, we haven't been talking long enough for me to make a diagnosis."

"Just give me something. Anything."

With a grunt, he moved from the chair to his desk, where he sat and drummed his pen on the desktop. "You have symptoms commonly associated with seizures, but you're not epileptic from what I can tell. I don't know what triggers this bloodlust of yours, or the blackouts, but this isn't unfamiliar territory for me. I've worked with people like you before."

"I know," she said.

He set down his pen and leaned back. "You do?"

"That's why I came here. That night in New York, after they pulled me away from Sophie, after they kicked me and beat me bloody, I ran. I ran until my legs gave out and I collapsed in a disgusting little alley a dozen blocks away. There were people everywhere, in the street and in the alleys, but there was one man in particular . . . " She reached into her pocket, removed a scrap of paper, and set it on Julian's desk. " . . . He gave me this."

Julian ran his thumb over the name "Antonia Archer" scrawled on the scrap of paper.

"He was a soldier," she continued. "A survivor of Omaha Beach. He would've hated me calling him a survivor, though. There was dishonor in it, and so much regret that boiled into anger. I didn't know him long, but I knew him well. In the short time we spent together, I thought I understood him. But there were times when he thought he was still there, nowhere near New York, still *hoping* to survive. He was confused and angry."

"Combat Stress Reaction," Julian said. "It's sadly common."

"It was more than that. When I told him what happened with Sophie, he admitted he'd had issues like mine before he shipped out. When he was younger. When he lived in California."

Julian's eyes widened. "My mother treated him?"

"Your father too, I think."

Julian swallowed hard and his gaze danced across the photos propped on the edge of his desk. "You say he was living on the streets, twelve blocks from the East Village?"

She nodded, and Julian scrawled down the information. "My great uncle runs the New York branch. I'll ask him to do a sweep of the area. If we helped him once, maybe we can help him again."

The kindness brought an unexpectedly large smile to Ava's face, and the tension in the back of her head loosened.

"Julian, can I be honest with you about something?"

"I hope you've been honest about everything."

"Of course. The thing is, I feel better since we've been talking. I know I'm not cured or anything, but whatever my illness is, I feel like it's fading."

Julian's nostrils flared as he exhaled. He pushed up from his desk and sat on the opposite end of the sofa, hands folded in his lap. He was less than ten years older than her, but he looked so mature at that moment. Maybe it was the lighting on the other side of the table, or how he held his body: straight and tight, like a switchblade. When they were side by side, he was on alert, and why shouldn't he be? She was a killer.

"I'm glad you feel better," he said gently. "And I'm grateful you have faith in our work together. But we've only been meeting for a few months. I've had patients who felt the same way, so they stopped coming because they thought they could manage it on their own. Most fail, I'm afraid, so I'm telling you now, before you get to that point. It's not a slight. It's not a judgment. Ava, you can't manage this on your own."

Her brow furrowed. "I thought you said I wasn't fragile."

"I don't think you are."

"But you think I'm incurable."

"I didn't say that." He glanced at his watch. "Ava,

you've made excellent progress so far, but we have a long way to go. On the bright side, you're an excellent candidate for exertion therapy."

"What's exertion therapy?"

"It's complicated . . . and our time is up."

"Your watch is fast. What's exertion therapy?"

He sighed. "It involves finding a way to channel the emotions that fuel your violence into something else, something more constructive."

Ava sprang to her feet. "I want that. Whatever it is, I'll do it. I want to get rid of this feeling as soon as possible."

"You're not ready. Don't take it as an insult; it's just a fact. You need time to heal properly, and I don't even consider exertion therapy until I've been seeing a patient for at least a year."

"This isn't about me. It's about Sophie. The longer I'm sick, the more danger she's in."

Julian sat on the arm of his chair and pushed back his sleeves. "See, that kind of talk worries me, Ms. Francis. For one, I don't like hearing a patient say her child is in danger, especially a patient whose past transgressions have been dealt with fairly leniently in this office. Two, pushing your therapy could impede your progress, and I think you know that."

"Progress," she said harshly. "It was always about progress in Taunton too."

"Except I won't punish you if you lag or get frustrated. But I also won't let you determine what work you need to do. That's *my* job. Your job is to accept, heal, and grow into the person you're meant to be."

She stepped up to him, her hands clenched at her chest. "I want to be that person now. We can meet more if you want, for longer."

"No," he said plainly. "Now, if you don't mind, I have more appointments."

When Ava stepped backward, the odd texture of the carpet jarred her. It was scorched and sticky, and behind her, sun poured through cracks like claw marks in the wall, but the dark figure floating toward her avoided every stripe.

"You're too sick to save," it hissed.

Dr. Archer's office strangled itself to the charred skeleton of Taunton Asylum and its last ghost, wearing Ava's final inferno like a fine cloak.

"Mom? What are you doing here?"

Faye Norton's face flaked and drifted around the room when she laughed. "If you think I'm actually here you're crazier than I thought. You're certainly more pathetic than I thought you'd be. All your gifts, all your prospects, frittered away because of some silly boy who screwed your sister. And here you are again, giving your heart and mind to another silly boy." Her smile peeled a flap of skin from her scabbed lips and snapped a timber of flesh along her chin.

"It's not the same. He's helping me. Hell, he could be married with kids for all I know."

"Then he'd be two ahead of you, my dear." Faye wheezed out a chuckle. "But it doesn't change the fact that you still want him. You might as well admit it. And while you're at it, admit you regret falling for it time and time again. You spent so much time fighting me, making it worse for yourself, and why? Because a juvenile delinquent tricked you into thinking a cock could fill that chasm in your soul."

Ava clapped her hands over her ears. "You're not her. She doesn't talk like that."

"You'd be surprised how electrocution rewires a person's brain, sweetheart."

Faye peeled the ebony scale from her chin, revealing a pink patch that flared, grayed, and blackened within moments. She held it to her craggy lips and blew it like a dandelion, scattering ash to the incinerated corners of the asylum office.

"At least this one can't spurn you for Natalie," she

continued. "Not unless he's got a plane ticket, a shovel, and an iron stomach."

"You're a monster."

Faye shoved her scorched crepe of a face at Ava. "And Mommy's a mirror, *Avery*. Take a good look. Heck, you've come this far. Why not go deeper?"

She grasped her daughter's hand, slapped it to the loose continents of charred flesh, and forced Ava's fingers beneath the sloppy panels of her face. Skin and muscle plopped to the floor, percussing Ava's fingernails screeching on her mother's skull. Faye cackled wildly, even after Ava wrenched off her mushy mandible. She'd just thrown it to the floor when something slammed against her head, and she went down too.

The world was black, then red, then orange and white. Her eyes felt like they were glued shut, but when a stern voice said, "Look at me," she forced them open.

Dr. Archer stood over her, his left cheek aflame with scratches.

"Julian—"

She clenched her fist and wondered if it throbbed in rhythm with his cheek. Her head swam with blissful fear as she crawled up onto the couch like a whipped mutt.

"Julian, Dr. Archer, I'm so sorry. Please forgive me. Please don't send me away."

His nostrils pulsed as he stared at her for a few moments, then strode past her to the closet. He disappeared inside, clattering about until he exited with a washcloth filled with ice pressed to his face.

"Did you even see me?" he asked her.

"No. No, I'm sorry, I didn't."

Lowering the ice, he looked down on her and said, "Stand up, Ms. Francis."

"Julian, please, don't throw me out."

His top lip quivered. "I said stand up."

Ava's eyes filled with tears as she obeyed, but she held them back. Julian Archer was the only person who could help her, and now he knew she was a wild animal after all. Maybe it was time to accept herself for the devil she was and leave the soft trappings of humanity behind.

"I will continue treating you on one condition," Julian said, and Ava's heart stopped. "If you can't comply, our relationship ends here. Do you understand?"

Her heart resumed beating, but every other muscle remained tense. She forced a nod.

"Good." He drew closer and looked deep into her watery eyes. "I need you to think about how you feel right now. How you felt when you attacked me. How you felt right before. As you contemplate those feelings, I want you to be honest with yourself about your fears and your desires and whether you truly believe you deserve to be happy."

"What good will that do?" she whimpered.

"I guess we'll see."

When she averted her eyes, he said her fake name like a song.

"I will not abandon you, Ava Francis. If you do what I ask, I will do everything in my power to help you. Do you believe me?"

"Yes."

"Excellent. Now, I have an assignment for you. I want you to talk to Paul."

Ava lifted her gaze. To a normal person the request might've been odd, but Ava wasn't even a shadow of normal. She'd spoken to Paul many times after his death, but she didn't think a therapist would encourage it. In fact, she hadn't even told Julian she'd seen him since she left Massachusetts.

But he knew. He didn't say it directly, but as he looked into her misty eyes, he exposed one of her greatest secrets. He didn't call her on it; he simply took her hands in his and said, "Speak to him. Write him letters. Letters about your childhood together, and what your life is like now. Everything you wanted to say from the day you met him to today. Especially the things you're most afraid to say. Can you do that, Ava?"

"Yes," she said, then repeated it in a stronger voice. "Yes. I can do that, Dr. Archer."

CHAPTER FOUR

Dear Paul,

Late at night like this I wonder if you ever saw me at my worst. Did you know what I was and ignore it because you loved me? Or were we both sick in our own ways? Me with blood, you with love: dueling illnesses pumped by the same sad heart.

I could be romanticizing it, I suppose. When I imagine you suffered with me, it's easier to believe what we had was real. If we could survive our pain enough to find each other again and again, there must've been some power or fate inside us.

Or above us? Below?

Not that I believe in Heaven or Hell. God and the Devil are shadow play on the walls of the world, and we'll never know who owns the gnarled claws behind it all. But if I could guess—I will, just in case this is all some Rumpelstiltskin kind of game and naming the imp makes it fade—I'd guess the gnarled claw belongs to Faye.

Faye Norton. Faye Hayworth. Mom.

And since it didn't appear to work, I have to assume she isn't an imp. Just a human. Somehow, that's worse.

These letters help, but they seem so silly sometimes. Death has no address, no shipping cost, but there is a weight to these words, and I do pay for them. It's been almost a year I've been writing you, and I do feel a *certain burden lifted, but sometimes, like tonight, the more I write, the more reminders I have that I couldn't save you.*

. . . and how much Julian loves to torture me.

—◣◥—

Dr. Archer sneered from his spot on the other end of the couch. He'd always kept the table between them before, but he'd been closing their distance with each session. The nearer he was, the more comfort he gave her, and while Ava's stomach and throat still knotted often in his presence, she hadn't shed a tear in his office since she struck him over a year ago.

"Torturing you is the last thing on my mind, Ava. But I understand why you feel that way. This is an extremely invasive task I've asked of you, and it would be cruel of me to assume it gets easier over time."

Easier wasn't the right word, but the process had changed. When she first started writing letters to Paul, he was there all the time, whispering, *"Don't let me go, Avery."* But she was alone during this letter. Not a whisper of love or hate, and it hurt her heart so intensely, her spine ached.

The paper trembled and crumpled in her grip, but she didn't lower it.

"Is that all?"

"Yes."

Julian narrowed his eyes, his voice edged with suspicion. "So set the paper down."

With a growl, she lay the letter on the table and winced as she tongued her swollen lip. It was the least noticeable of her injuries, but combined with the black eye she revealed when she removed her sunglasses, and bruises on her neck, it looked like she'd been in a full out brawl.

"My God, Ava—"

"It looks worse than it is," she said deadpan. "It already feels better. And don't worry, I didn't hurt anyone who didn't deserve it."

"But you did hurt someone?"

She'd reopened the wound on her lip during the recitation and pressed the back of her hand to her mouth. Inspecting the splotch of blood, she said, "I did."

"Okay. Then let's talk about it. What happened?"

Ava stared at Paul's name in the letter on the table. It looked strange, almost textured between the other, duller words. Staring at it as she relayed the events of the day made her belly swamp with nausea.

"I did something I've never done before."

"Something violent?"

She shook her head, then added thoughtfully, "Maybe a little." Swallowing a brassy droplet of blood, she stared at the carpet and began. "I met a soldier. He reminded me of a young Marlon Brando . . . minus the attitude . . . and one arm."

"He who?"

"Wilbur," she said. "The boy I had sex with last night."

Julian blinked in shock, and Ava's skin burned with memory.

Wilbur wasn't at all what she envisioned for her first time with a flesh and blood man, but he smelled sweet, like a chocolate cigar, and she relished the break from the overwhelming popcorn stink of the El Rancho drive-in. After the manic day so far, she was one teenage middle finger away from throwing searing oil at the brats lined up at the snack bar.

"He was all by himself. He wasn't even watching the movie." She folded the letter and shoved it in her bag, her upper lip dotted with sweat. "I don't know how it began, to be honest. I was in the stockroom, looking out, while he was looking in, and . . . "

She shivered the way she did when she removed her bra in the stockroom. The soldier had averted his eyes until she gave him the okay, and then, trembling, he touched her. Ava's heart thudded like a drum as he awkwardly moved his fingers over her bristled skin and fumbled with her nipples. For all she knew, it was his first time batting as a southpaw since the Bay of Pigs.

"That's how I remembered his name," Ava said with a tiny smile. "Wilbur, like the pig from *Charlotte's Web*."

"There's also an 'Avery' in that book," Julian said.

She snorted. "That Avery was a rotten egg too. It must be the name."

"Maybe." He paused before speaking next, his lips tight as he seemingly searched for the words. After clearing his throat, he looked straight at Ava, expressionless. "Did you enjoy it?"

Her lips popped apart and her cheeks burned like she had two lit matches under her eyes. Those odd and intimate minutes in the soldier's arms had made her realize what a fantastic actress she'd become, and because of Sophie, she'd also learned to read people, to anticipate what they wanted from her. So she stroked Wilbur's hair and kissed his forehead, and his tears pooled in the notch of her collarbone. Dull pain burned in her tailbone and between her thighs, but her heart stung most of all when her rolling gaze found Paul, weeping in the corner of the El Rancho stockroom.

"Parts of it," she whispered. "It didn't last very long, which I was pretty happy about since my break was almost over, and my spine was pressing into the cooler lid, but it was nice being wanted like that. And I guess it was nice for him too, because he cried after. Do men do that a lot?"

Julian's eyebrow twitched. "Can't say. I've never slept with a man." He crinkled his nose and tapped his pen on his notepad. "Perhaps he was crying because he was afraid war had stolen his humanity. Maybe you were his first since he came home. Or maybe you were his first altogether. You did call him a boy."

"And war made him a killer."

"Like you."

"No, not like me. That boy had a human heart. It's broken now and it probably will be for years, but when it heals he'll have a scar where I have only gangrene and emptiness. And Paul," she added. "I saw him, Julian, when Wilbur and I were together. I was breaking his heart too." She sniffled and wiped the tears from her cheeks. "I know how crazy that sounds."

"I'll determine your craziness level when you tell me how you reacted to seeing him."

Shame bubbled up in her voice when she said, "I went back to work."

"No blackouts?"

"No."

"No feelings of hostility?"

She shook her head. "I was just . . . sad. Paul was sad. Wilbur was sad. And *Splendor in the Grass* was just about to start, so I needed to get back."

Julian's brow crinkled, and his bottom lip protruded in puzzlement. "At what point did he hit you?"

"He didn't." She tongued her lip again. "This happened before work, when a man broke into our motel room."

"Oh my god, Ava—"

"Everything's fine. A gang's been terrorizing the whole neighborhood for a few weeks now, broke into some motel rooms, robbed people, smacked them around. My door was locked and chained, but when your door's made of plywood, I guess locks and chains don't do much. I was getting ready for work when this big guy kicked it in and came straight at me." She squeezed her fists as the memory simmered. "I was in shock. I didn't react fast enough. He knocked me to the floor and headed for the bedroom where Sophie was sleeping. He must've been high or drunk because he didn't see her, and he didn't see me either. I snuck up behind him with a lamp and hit him as hard as I could. I didn't knock him out, but he fell to the floor, and I didn't need the lamp once he was there. I jumped on top of him and . . . " She was pressing her fists into her thighs so hard her biceps trembled with fatigue. " . . . that's when I blacked out, Dr. Archer. At least to what I was actually doing. My brain went somewhere else."

"What did it feel like you were doing?"

She closed her eyes, and flames climbed like ambitious children up her throat. "It was hotter than it's ever been," she whispered. "I couldn't breathe. I couldn't get cool. I thought maybe I was dreaming. Or that me being there, being here, was a complete hallucination. Maybe I've imagined everything that's happened this past year in California. That's when things got clear and I was where I was meant to be. I was at home with Sophie, in my mother's house on the Vineyard. Our real home. That's when it got cold. Freezing. The island was asleep, but Sophie and I were wide awake, at the window, helpless as the snow buried us alive."

"And what were you actually doing?"

"I don't know exactly. When I snapped back to reality, I looked like this. But the guy looked a lot worse. He was barely conscious when the police dragged him away."

"And Sophie?"

A knot of fire scorched Ava's throat, and she doused it with a sip of water. Smoke tickled her tongue as she whispered, "She's what brought me back to reality. She stopped me from killing him." Her lips quavered, and she pressed her fingers to them as she sniffled. "She was watching me, pleading with me. She said, 'What's wrong with you, Mommy?' She begged me to stop."

He pushed the tissue box closer. In their time together, Ava had come to see this offering as the embrace he legally couldn't give.

Ripping a tissue from the box, she grunted through a tortured exhalation. "Goddammit, Julian. I was strangling him when I came to. His face was purple, his eyes were bulged out like a dead fish. I did that to him, and she saw it. I've tried so hard to keep her away from this thing inside me. Do you think I ruin everything?"

"You stopped, Ava. You kept Sophie safe, and yes, you might've gone overboard, but you did what anyone else would've done in that situation. You fought back and defended your home."

"Home," she scoffed. "A three dollar a week shithole."

"Your daughter then."

"Whom I kidnapped."

Julian scowled as he pointed his pen at her. "Stop that. We don't know how any of this will affect Sophie yet. And considering everything she's been through so far, I'm guessing the explosion on the boat when she was a baby was more harmful than you beating the shit out of a thug."

Ava raised her eyebrows, and coy amusement curled her lips. "What's gotten into you?"

"I apologize. I'm a little out of sorts. Antonia left town late last night—transferring the last of the house to Colorado. We usually do a postmortem report on the patients at night, so it was a little strange not speaking to her until this morning." He clicked his pen a few times before setting it down. "This isn't about me. I don't want to spend your time talking about my mother."

"Why not? My mother could probably use the break."

He shuffled to the water pitcher and filled his mug. He didn't look at her as he gulped, but it was clear the wheels were turning in his brain. Setting down the mug, he sighed. "Ava, I understand why you're upset about Sophie seeing you hurt this man, and we'll deal with that if problems arise, but I'm curious about something. You hurt this man, nearly killed him by your description, and then what? You left for work, bloody and bruised, and soon after, you had sex with a stranger?"

Her jaw hung loose, and her mouth instantly went dry. She hadn't thought about it like that, but there was no point in dispute. Her hands went cold, and her belly sparked with nauseating cinders.

"Ava?"

"Yes, that's what happened," she said, mortified. "God, why did I do that?"

"You tell me," he said, sitting opposite.

Her breath came out in wet chunks that made her feel faint as she replayed the scene. "His blood was on my fists, my shirt, my neck. I needed to get to my shift, and I needed to wash off the blood, so I dropped Sophie off at the sitter's and I took a shower." Embarrassment singed her cheeks as she looked away from Julian. All the talk of murder and ghosts, and describing a shower ritual to her therapist discomforted her. She shifted in her seat and fidgeted with her sleeves. "Showers have helped before," she continued. "When the fire's high, I turn up the water so hot my guts feel like ice. Sometimes I imagine I'm inside the flames instead of them being inside me. Sometimes I imagine there's blood."

"But you didn't have to imagine it this time," Julian said.

She rubbed her hands over her arms, remembering how the spots came alive in the water and tied her up in scarlet ribbons.

"It's a beautiful thing, you know, when a stranger's history drips down your body. All the horrors and bad decisions that led him there, the people who hurt him, the people who wanted him to be more, and all the dead dreams he pretends he doesn't mourn, reduced to intimate spatters and smears on my skin. I didn't want to be clean. I wanted to drown in it." She dropped her hands to her lap and sighed. "I couldn't stop thinking about it, and the fire wouldn't shrink, Julian. It really got to me."

"It turned you on?"

Her hands twitched in her lap. "Yes."

"So why Wilbur?"

"Why anyone?" She shrugged and looked to the ceiling with its various stains and age spots. "He seemed nice—as sad as me, maybe sadder. Maybe I thought all those tears could wash away the heat. Maybe I just wanted to lean on someone and know I couldn't fall through. I don't know why he chose me, but I do know he made me feel human. I needed it after the horrible things I did in front of Sophie."

"Sometimes horrible things like that are warranted,"

he replied, moving to his desk. "But you did get lucky. And not just with 'radiant' and 'humble' Wilbur. When it came to that intruder, the wrong bone, the wrong amount of pressure, to the wrong person, and you could be back behind bars, somewhere much worse than Taunton Asylum. It wouldn't be a hospital room this time. It would be a cell. And Sophie would go into the system."

Her stomach squeezed into an acidic geyser. "That's not going to happen."

"Not if I can help it," Julian said. He withdrew a folder from his desk drawer and fanned some papers on the coffee table.

Her hand floated over the descriptions and floor plans of a three-story condominium an hour away in Costa Contra County.

"My father dabbled in real estate before he passed and he left me the lease to this building. There are two empty apartments. One's in the attic, but I was thinking you could move into the one on the second floor," he said, pointing at the blueprint. "It has two bedrooms, one bath, a good sized kitchen and living room, and a shared laundry room. It's not an affluent neighborhood, I admit, but it's a better place than here for Sophie to grow up. For you too."

Ava was certain anxiety wrinkled and reddened her face as she examined the documents. The condo was clearly too rich for her budget, but Julian's kindness was even more lavish. Tears rose to her eyes, and her voice was strained when she spoke.

"Why are you doing this, Dr. Archer?"

In the time it took him to reply, her heart spun a story for which no "happily ever after" could exist. It was a fairy tale unprettied, setting her up for princess tests she was fated to fail. Her feet were too big for glass slippers, her hair was too short to climb. She could snore up a storm sleeping on a pea, and when it came to witches and candy houses, she'd probably be the first one stomping into the death trap. Desertion, darkness, toxicity: those were her offerings to anyone who might love her. And Julian Archer would not be the man to break that spell.

But when he said, "You know why, Ava," even the fire of her disease couldn't consume the slips of hope dancing through her mind.

"Because you care about me?" she asked.

"Of course. I care about your safety and well-being. And the safety of everyone who crosses your path."

Ava's head suddenly weighed a hundred pounds. It drooped, and her breath caught in her throat.

"What's wrong?"

"Have you done this before?"

"I don't understand what you're asking."

"Well, I'm a killer, and you charge me less than half of what you charge normal people for therapy. You say you're going to look for the bum who helped me in New York so you can give him treatment. And now you're offering me an apartment in a building you own?"

All at once, a conspiracy theory formed like a cloud of black smoke in her brain and consumed the fairy tale.

"You want to keep tabs on me, don't you?" she demanded. "You want to lock me up and monitor me like some kind of experiment. Like Dr. Aslinn."

"That's not what this is," he said, moving to the couch. "Yes, I've found housing for my patients before, but I have no intention of watching you, Ava. This isn't Taunton. This is a chance for you and Sophie to start over, somewhere safer than the city, with fewer temptations. And before you ask 'why' again, it has more to do with me than it does with you. I can't sleep at night knowing what could happen to you two in that place. Neither can Antonia. Before she left, she asked me to make you this offer."

"Even though it puts everyone else in that building at risk?"

Julian smacked the couch as he stood, his nostrils flared. "I won't go on playing this game with you. You either believe you deserve peace, or you don't. You either believe you can be a competent mother, or you don't. If you truly think people living around you aren't safe, then neither is Sophie, and in that case, we have to reevaluate the nature of our relationship."

She stood, her gaze slowly climbing the curves and crests of his gray suit until she forced herself to meet his eyes. As much as she hated to admit it, her response *was* part of a game—one that allowed her to keep sparring with Julian, to stay not-quite-healthy so she could pretend it wasn't more than her illness that interested him. Julian was a good and fair man, and his love was equally divvied across the whole of humanity. There was nothing special in his offer to her. *She* was not special to him.

"Sophie's not in danger, Dr. Archer. And I promise no one else will be either."

His eyes widened and lips twitched upward. "Is that a yes? You'll move to Concord?"

"I'll have to get a new job."

"So you get a new job. The schools are better there, anyway. There's a young girl in the building already. She's older than Sophie, but it's something."

"Yes, it's something."

A lump rose in Ava's throat. She had to turn away to swallow it for fear it looked the way it felt: like a fist stopping her from telling Julian Archer all the ways she wanted him.

Faye was right the last time she saw her. Ava was replaying the same doomed affection she'd had for Paul Dillon, and it would be her undoing.

And she didn't care.

Fanning her face, she swallowed the lump and said, "Does it have air conditioning?"

❦

Large, somewhat boastful, air conditioning units protruded from the living room window of each apartment in the condominium on Mohr Lane in Costa Contra

County. Although the unit in the Francis's home was almost constantly on the fritz, the occasional gust of cold air, extra living space, and small-town feel of Concord granted Ava a contentment she hadn't felt in ages.

Despite the building's resemblance to a drab box with cubist tumors, Ava could finally breathe there. She could drop some of the guards she'd had up since she was thirteen and try to enjoy life—even if "enjoying life" actually meant ensuring Sophie enjoyed hers. New happiness aside, there was no diverting the specters of her past. Late at night, she crept to the empty apartment in the attic and wrote her many letters in the hope that one day she wouldn't feel Paul's tears as he read over her shoulder. Though they pained her, rolling frigid down her back, she had so little of their relationship, his sorrow felt like memorabilia. She saved each crinkled, faded, ink-run note, and she soon discovered she wasn't the only one. There were other boxes in the attic, some labeled, some not, some that looked frequently rifled through and others jacketed in years of dust. She never touched them, never even drew close enough to inhale their motes, but she never stopped wondering about their contents. She wasn't permitted to ask Julian about other tenants, but she had her suspicions. She recalled seeing Mr. Akio Mio, who lived in the apartment occupying the lower level, on her first visit to the Archers' office, but he'd given her no reason to suspect he was still a patient, or that his issues were akin to hers.

The same went for Jackie Hamilton across the hall. Ava was certain Jackie owned some of the boxes in the attic—a few probably contained her six-year-old daughter's baby clothes and tinker toys—but the woman never mentioned therapy, a troubled past, or appeared to regard Julian Archer as anything but a landlord.

Maybe one day Ava would view him the same way. Just a landlord, just a man to whom she sent the rent and contacted about the inconsistent AC.

But how, knowing everything he did?

HARES IN THE HEDGEROW

And how, knowing everything she felt?

Sitting in the attic, writing feverishly in the dark, Ava hated all the everythings that entombed her—and how Paul's lips felt like ice against her cheek.

CHAPTER FIVE

Dear Paul,

Your daughter is three years old, and she doesn't know the word 'daddy.' I realized that today when I was teaching her the names of all the things in the kitchen. But thanks to that gross motel, she does know the word 'cockroach.' It sounds like a curse word when she says it though.

I guess your name's a curse word too. She'll pick it up somewhere. She'll say it under her breath. And when she's angry, she'll hurl it at me, I'm sure of it. Just like I hurled it at my mother before me.

But she knows 'love' and 'beautiful' and 'please.' And she cries for her brass ring every morning when she wakes. And I give you to her. That's where you belong. Where it's safe. Where it's real.

Realer than we ever were.

I think about that a lot now. We didn't actually have much, did we? We had hormones. We had the summers. And both of those things lie . . . and fade. But we never got the chance to fade. We were pale from the get-go. I guess we still are.

I wish I could brighten you for Sophie's sake, but every time I try to tell her about who you were to me, I find myself sinking in lies. The truth is too dangerous. I'm afraid she won't be able to understand. I can't understand it myself.

Why was it so easy for you? How were you able to look me in the eye, hand me your beautiful daughter, and say you wanted a life with me? I still stunk of dead bodies. The fire I started. The children I killed.

How could you love me? What was wrong with you?

❧

Ava creased the letter and huffed. "I didn't finish it," she said. "I was too angry."

"At Paul?"

She shook her head. "Sometimes when I'm writing these letters, I say things I don't really believe. Or, I hope I don't believe them. I don't blame him, Julian. And I don't think he was sick. He was just a stupid kid."

Julian hummed as he dotted the end of a sentence and looked up. "Stupid for loving you?"

She fiddled with the paper's edge, shredding it as she shrugged.

"What about Natalie? You don't mention her much in your letters to Paul, but they are undeniably linked. You all are."

"What do you want to know?"

"Do you think your sister was sick? Like you and your mother?"

Ava had considered it many times. If Faye was able to hide her youngest daughter's blackouts from Natalie, she could've hid Natalie's too. But she figured Faye would've been eager to share that information with her. She hated the thought, but if her mother had told her Natalie experienced the same spells, it might've changed her whole perspective. She might've been her mother's little gardener without question. Avery, Natalie, and Faye: a happy band of mercy killers.

But Natalie failed her initiation—she said as much herself on Avery's twelfth birthday—and Faye sent her off-island. Looking back on it, banishment was a mild reaction compared to how Faye usually dealt with bad rabbits like Natalie.

"My mother would've considered her ill, but not like her. Natalie was brimming with bad water."

"She was a sexual person," Julian said.

"Yes. She was normal," Ava said. "Faye sent her to Dana Hall after she caught her fooling around with her boyfriend—the same one they pulled out of our basement."

"He was one of Faye's victims?"

"Yes."

"But some of them were yours."

She averted her eyes. "Yes."

"Which ones?"

"Why is that important?"

"Why do you feel it's unimportant?"

This was a typical response for Julian, and it never failed to twist up Ava's face in annoyance. He mimicked her expression, set aside his notebook, and joined her on the couch.

"I know you don't want to talk about this, which is why I haven't pushed you, but we've spent nearly two years dancing around this topic. You've come a long way. You told me about seeing Paul's ghost, about the arson at Taunton, but there's one huge thing we haven't discussed." Leaning forward, he stared deep into her eyes. "Ava, there were seventeen bodies in that basement, and you put some of them there. According to Faye's testimony, your body count began as early as four years old."

The letter softened in her sweaty hands. She crinkled it and stared at the ink, which appeared to blur and bleed. "That was a lie."

"At one point, you thought everything Faye told the police was a lie. Then you electrocuted her and . . . " He snapped his fingers. " . . . so much was suddenly true."

"I didn't know what I was doing. She forced me."

"It's time for you to tell me how. The first time. Your first kill."

A piece of paper ripped free and stuck to Ava's fingertip. She shook her hand, but it wouldn't budge. The small red spot that glued it to her skin spread, blossoming like the fire in her gut. Paul's letter was the perfect kindling, and the memory of that life-changing night was like a leaky canister of gasoline. The wet scrap disconnected from her finger and fell to her shoe, where it leaked impossible streams of crimson that snaked across the carpet.

"I was twelve," she started. "There was a house up island that belonged to some rich idiots, mainlanders who let their kids sail to the Vineyard with their friends in the summer for parties. I was blacked out when Faye took me there, so I didn't recognize it a month later when Paul and I followed her. But that's where it happened. After she taught me about the garden and the rabbits, she took me to that house for an in-depth lesson—to show me the rabbits in action, out of costume."

Crimson tributaries branched from the carpet into the rocky beach, where fresh-faced teenagers engaged in a romantic wrestling match in front of Doctor Archer's sideboard. Little Avery Norton was crouched next to her mother behind a cluster of rosa rugosa, her heartbeat more rapid than ever before. It was a rhythmic rake in her chest, slamming and hooking into her soul before scraping it away in troubled tracks.

She squinted at the disrobing teens, puzzled. "Where are their dots?"

"There are no dots here, sweetheart." Faye set down her gardening bag and lovingly pushed the hair out of her daughter's eyes. "This kind of work relies on instinct. You have to watch and listen."

"For how long?"

Faye smiled and pinched her daughter's chin. "It shouldn't take long. Sin is easier to spot than virtue. But sometimes, the longer the better. It's a prettier pay off, a deeper castigation."

Avery's face scrunched in puzzlement. "Cazzawhat?"

"Castigation. It means to chastise someone, and to

purify them through punishment." She smiled, her entire face alight. "It's a beautiful word, don't you think? And nearly everyone could do with a little castigation from time to time. Especially that boy of yours."

Ava scooted to the precipice of the cushion, and as she whispered, so did the younger version of herself. "But Mom," they said, "he's my best friend."

Faye oiled closer, her lips hovering at her daughter's ear as she hissed. "He's only your friend because he wants to steal your chastity and strip you of your blessings. He wants to turn you into a Jezebel like your sister, and I won't let that happen. Not you. You have too many God-given talents. I won't see them wasted."

"I won't waste them, Mom. I promise."

Moonlight danced over Faye's teeth when she grinned, and she planted a wet kiss on Avery's forehead. "I'm so happy to hear you say that, darling, because our blessings are going to do good work tonight. Right now." She pointed at the couple tossing their clothes around Julian's office and sneered. "Look at them. They have no idea they're poisoning themselves, and no clue how they spread it to the rest of the world. It's up to you and me to change that."

"How?"

Faye withdrew a pair of gardening shears from her paisley bag and passed them over with a grin. "Pull their insides out, Avery. Show them the rot."

The shears were too heavy and unwieldy in her tiny hands and fell blade-first to the pebbled beach. The noise startled the couple, and the girl craned to scan the surrounding brush.

She called out, "Henry?" and Faye poked her daughter's arm.

"You see, sweetie? Henry. Another boy, another poison."

"Everything's fine," her boyfriend assured her, plucking another beer from the sand. He handed it over, and while one arm remained draped across her chest as she drank and the boy kissed her neck, she quickly dropped the coyness and lay back on the towel. They were again blissfully ignorant to the rising sea and the party on the hill—and the shadows of Faye Norton and her sweet daughter creeping out from the hedgerow of sea tomatoes.

Ava licked her lips and rolled her head back and forth on her shoulders. She'd described the scene as best she could, but there were no words for how those children looked when Avery attacked. For one, she doubted such brutal but beautiful words had yet been created, but more importantly, Avery hadn't seen their faces. Her eyes were closed during the slaughter, and they were closed now too.

She could, however, relay the sounds and smells of that evening . . . and revel secretly in them. Like inhaling a deathly ocean breeze, she lifted her face as the squeals and hisses of dying teenagers washed over her. They were warm and wet and magical, the music of immense spirit trapped in fragile frames, but lovely as it felt when their flesh submitted, it was the resistance that kept her stabbing and swinging the shears like a blindfolded kid bashing a pinata. Blades skidded on bone and caught on ruched cartilage, and they sang—oh what dulcet exultations—until Faye pried the slippery blades from her little hands.

Ava couldn't cry—the feeling was too pleasant to sully with tears—but regret made its inevitable impression, tightening her throat and thinning her voice.

"I don't know what kind of violence my mother expected, but it wasn't that," she said. "I looked right into her eyes when it was done, and I swear to you, Julian, I saw fear like never before. She was afraid of me." Gulping hard, she added, "But she was proud too."

"She finally had proof she could use you," said Dr. Archer. "You showed malleability that night. You showed how well you took direction."

"Except I didn't remember it. Not the murder or hiding the bodies in the brush. Not the ride home or how she bathed me in the tub like I was a baby again. I don't think she saw that coming. She played my tendencies like a symphony, and with no one to tell the tale of her triumph, it was like she hadn't played a single note, let alone a song as glorious as her Great Castigation. Paul and me telling the police she killed the kids in her trunk was the last straw. And it wasn't even true. She didn't kill them. She was cleaning up after me."

Ava's hand jittered against her thigh. She dug her fingernails into her slacks and gritted her teeth as she tried to think of anything but the cloying stench of blood filling the room. The murders were over and Avery Norton was gone, but Julian's office didn't return. Blood clumped like valentines on the beach, and as dead, red-eyed rabbits emerged from the brush and tracked paw prints across the ground, Faye Norton emerged from the sea.

Ava's heart summoned her mother's lessons like a maniac gathering a mob, each mad townsperson igniting a torch that quickened a different shade of dark delight. But there was another light in the horde. Faintly, like a dying firefly, Julian Archer pulsed like a lantern in the fog. She lost him quickly, however, when Faye crawled to her, her face aging and chapping and burning before her eyes.

Blinking her remaining eyelid, Faye tugged an annoying tag of black skin from her forehead and tossed it aside for the rabbits to fight over. Baring dark shards of teeth, she stretched and cracked her neck, allowing her voice to sound from every burnt-out chasm in her throat.

"You know this won't solve anything, Avery," she said, calm and commanding as ever.

"Avery's dead," she replied, and Faye cackled like a hyena in a tornado—a consuming sort of mockery that made her adult daughter cringe like a child.

"You think you can change your name and lie to everyone you meet and you erase what you are? Never. You'll never be free, my darling. You'll never be happy. And as for Sophie . . . " Smoke curled from between Faye's lips when she snickered. "Well, I think you know what will happen to her. You can't protect that girl from her blood. No matter what you do, she will never escape what's innate in her. And God willing, she won't deny her blessings as you have."

Ava's entire body shook in refusal. "No. I promised Natalie and Paul. I'll never stop fighting to give her the life she deserves."

"The fight will drive you mad," said Faye. "And it will drive Sophie away."

The charred woman was in her head, in her soul, in her face, and Ava couldn't take it anymore. She screamed as she jumped from the seat and lunged at her wheezing mother.

Ava Francis had bowled over a lot of unsuspecting people in her life, but Dr. Julian Archer wasn't most people. When she threw herself at Faye but actually smashed into Julian, he immediately shoved her over one side of his chair.

She landed flat on her face, splitting her bottom lip and sending agonizing static through her skull. Flipping onto her back, Ava groaned and struggled to focus on Julian standing above her.

He extended his hand, and she took it, but gravity pummeled her brain when he pulled her into the air. After lowering her into his wingback, he sat on the coffee table and held her hands to retain her focus.

But her attention was a kid on Christmas morning: nearly impossible to restrain. As the rabbits tore a fiery streak around the room, her gaze followed and her belly became a bellows pushing the flames into her grey matter. When she spotted Julian in the sweltering bedlam, it was through Faye's eyes. She feared him like her mother, certain he'd try to tame her talents then snuff them out, like every other man since time began. Every cell in her body ached to punish him, to shred the false concern from his face until he was the raw meat of truth, without sin, without desire, without threat.

And he knew it.

"Do you want to hurt me?" Julian asked her.

The question was nauseating. She tried to retreat, but he caught her by the arms and pulled her closer.

"Do you want to hurt me?" he repeated.

Spraying saliva, she snarled like a starving wolf as she growled, "More than anything."

He sat her back in the chair and released her hands. "You're strong, Ava. You've made a lot of progress over the past few years, but this sickness will kill you. You've gotten too lucky for too long. What happens when that luck runs out? You'll lose Sophie."

"No . . ."

"Yes, you will. Sophie: your last piece of Paul and Natalie. She needs you to be well, Ava. She needs your love."

"Love's not enough to save either of us."

"It is. It can be. But you have to let the fire out. You can't let it consume you." Julian stood and looked down at her, his eyes glittering with ferocity. "Let it consume me."

Her stomach twisted in dark delight. "What do you mean?"

"You want to hurt me? Come on then and do it. Hurt me."

Ava breathed heavily as she stood face-to-face with Dr. Archer, their muscles seemingly already at war with one another. She raised a fist.

"Don't do it, Avery."

Ava looked over her shoulder at the window, where Natalie Norton shook her head in disappointment. A clump of charred scalp sloughed to the floor, but she didn't flinch or break her eye contact.

"You know this isn't right. Indulging this kind of behavior will only make you sicker. I gave into mine when I chose Noah, and look what happened to me." Displaying her ravaged physique, Natalie said, "I don't think I'd get very lucky at the Freshman mixers these days."

"Look at me," Julian said firmly. "Look *only* at me, and squeeze my hand."

Ava obeyed, and though his bones shifted in her crushing grip, his expression didn't. He was a stone in her fist, bloodless, impenetrable.

"You can't ignore me," Natalie said. "It didn't work when we were kids, and it won't work now." She stood behind Julian, stealing moments of Ava's focus. "Remember the first time we met Aunt Lily? She gave me a butterfly barrette."

"Dragonfly," Ava whispered, and Natalie chuckled.

"Of course you remember better. You were only two, barely had any hair, and you were so jealous. She didn't give you anything, and it didn't make sense. Why didn't she bring gifts for both of her nieces?"

"Because she wasn't our aunt. Because Dad hadn't told her I existed yet."

Her grip loosened and Julian whispered her name.

"Ava, who are you talking to?"

"He doesn't know you," Natalie said. "No one ever will but us."

"Us?"

Two men replied. The doctor called her "Ava," and the ghost called her "Avery," but she only listened to one, whose hands smoldered like hot coals on either side of her face.

"This isn't you," Paul Dillon said. "What happened to the girl who scaled gingerbread rooftops without fear? What happened to the innocent woman I loved? The one who wore all my rings?"

"I was never innocent."

"Whatever you did, you never lost my love for one moment. Not even knowing the truth now. That's who you were, who you are. The perfect girl. The perfect friend. The perfect lover."

She clapped her hands to her ears and wailed. "No! I can't fight them anymore!"

Julian wrenched her hands from her ears and stared into her watery eyes as she whispered, "You have to help me. They're going to drive me insane!"

Holding her by the shoulders, he spoke calmly. "I'm not going to let that happen. You will fight them, and I'll help you." He peeled off his jacket and tossed his tie on the couch, and rolling up his sleeves, he said, "Here's how this will work. I want you to hurt me again. But more this time. Fists only, no scratching, and if I tell you to stop, you stop. Say you understand me."

She looked to Paul and Natalie beside her, their molten bodies pulsing like fiery hearts and scattering piteous ash around the room. Shifting her gaze back to Julian, she whispered, "I understand."

"Good. Now hit me."

The strike was sloppy, a limp sort of punch, but delicious pain rang through Ava's bones. She hadn't drawn blood from Julian, but in that moment, she felt she'd drawn something more important from herself. Hitting him drained the rage from her blood like a poultice drawing infection from a wound.

Unflinching, he said, "Do it again."

She hit the same cheek, squarer this time, and his eyebrow twitched.

The fire liked him twitching. It ballooned in Ava with elegant flares that flickered in time with her ghosts. The more pain on Julian's face, the more Natalie faded, and the lovelier the fire became, like a house ablaze shrinking to a campfire's comforting glow. Though Paul remained behind Julian, Natalie strode to the window again and looked out as if devastated to have witnessed such weakness in her afterlife. Giving Ava one more devastated scowl, she thinned to smoke that disappeared into the ceiling.

She punched Julian again, and his abdomen contracted against her knuckles. When a strained grunt burst from his lips, he held up his hand.

"Are you okay?"

He was laughing when he lifted his head. He stretched his jaw and cracked his neck. "You have a hell of a right hook, kid. Who taught you to fight?"

"Every nurse in Taunton," Ava said. "I hated taking my 'vitamins.' Sometimes I gave in quickly because it was easier to sleep through the days, but I fought back too. It never really worked—they got me sooner or later—but at least I felt like I was in control, if only for a minute."

Straightening his back, he said, "Show me how you fought them."

With a cheek-tickling smirk, she grasped Julian's hair and tugged his head down. He moved with her as she pushed him past her chest, past her waist, and down to the floor where she pressed his face to the carpet. Out of the corner of her eye, she spotted the cinder-hot visage of Nurse Meredith Day, but the woman vanished in smoke when Julian groaned in pain.

Holding him by the back of the neck, she said, "I never got this far. Nurse Day was feistier than you, Doc."

"No one's perfect," he said through a strained chuckle.

She chuckled too, but stopped quickly.

Paul, still crouched in the shadowy corner of the therapist's office, wept into his hands, just as he had the day Ava slept with Wilbur. She released Julian's hair and retreated as the doctor rolled onto his back.

His face was flushed and his hair mussed when he sat up. "What's wrong?"

"He's still here. He hates that we're doing this."

"It's not really him. You know that."

"But I don't. Whatever this is . . . it's hurting him, Julian."

He crawled to Ava, his left cheek swollen and lips glazed with saliva, and though she tried to scoot away, he wrapped his arms around her and held her in place.

"Where is he?"

"Let me go, Julian."

"Tell me where he is." He sang out then in a mocking

209

falsetto: "Paul oh Paul! Look who I have. Your true love! What are you going to do about it?"

"I said let go!" Ava slipped an arm free and landed two swift backhand punches that opened Julian's nose like a scarlet faucet. He fell back and pinched the bridge as he scrambled to reach the tissues.

"Oh my God, Dr. Archer! I'm sorry!"

His voice was nasally as he held the tissue to his bloody nose but just as stern as ever. "Where is Paul, Ava?"

Her breath caught in her throat when she looked around the room. She and Julian were alone, no ghosts or gardens, no beaches peppered with red clumps. The office was as cool as a desert night, and though Ava's heart still ached in fear, the organ-twisting rage was gone.

She fell back on the sofa, her jaw loose and wet eyes peeled. "He's gone. The fire too."

"I thought as much." Julian snorted back blood and disappeared into the closet. After opening and closing what sounded like a refrigerator door, he returned with two ice packs. He gave one to Ava and held the other to his face.

"Are you okay?" he asked.

She wiped her eyes. Although her hand echoed anguish, her heart raced in a wonderful way. She didn't initially identify the rapid pulse as happiness, but she couldn't deny the hard-edged smile that suddenly dominated her face.

"You look like you're feeling better."

"Yes."

"I thought as much. It might not last long, but I'm glad to hear it."

"I'm not sure I understand what just happened," she said, rolling the ice over her knuckles. "Why did you want me to hurt you?"

The ice pack muffled his chuckle. "Oh I *don't*, believe me. But I do want you to be healthy, and if this is what it takes, this is what I'll do."

"Is that—" She bit her lip as Julian lowered the ice. "Is that normal?"

He sat on the couch, this time at the end, the way he did during their first month of sessions. His nose was bright red and his cheek bruised, but he looked handsome as ever, his square jaw raised in a confidence Ava was certain she'd never possess. Even after beating the hell out of him, she felt small and unworthy.

"I need you to know that I've never lied to you, Ms. Francis."

Julian hadn't called her "Ms. Francis" in ages. Nor had his voice been so soft and cautious.

Ava's body tightened and she reeled up her feet, prepared to kick at him if necessary. "You're scaring me, Julian. What are you saying?"

"I'm saying I think you're ready. I think *I'm* ready to introduce you to the other side of Archer Family Therapeutics. In fact, I already have."

Her body relaxed, but her heart raced. "Are you talking about exertion therapy?"

His eyes twinkled as he nodded, and then he moved close—tenth session close—near enough to reach out and touch her hand. He didn't, but she wanted him to.

"You remember I told you I've counseled people with issues similar to yours? I can't discuss those patients with you, but in the sake of transparency, I need you to know some things before we continue."

She moved her hand to touch his. Her knuckles were still throbbing, blazing in pain, and his skin looked so cool, soothing. But he folded his hands in his lap before she could touch him, and she dropped her head in a sudden burst of shame.

"Ava, please look at me."

She did, and though it felt like another fire might begin, four beautiful words doused it in an instant.

"You are not alone." Julian smiled, wincing slightly when his nose crinkled. "There are people out there just like you. All ages, genders, colors, and creeds. This sickness of yours is unique to you but not to humanity. And neither is the service I provide. My family members have been dampers for over a century."

"Dampers?"

"My great-great grandfather's name for our profession. Although, if my mother's to be believed, which she usually is, he wasn't the first by a long shot. His wife Tessa had many of the same symptoms as you. After a few incidents he discovered that if he absorbed the shock of her violence privately, she didn't have so many impulses or outbursts. It took a while, but she finally learned to control it. Because they trusted each other completely, Tessa never went overboard. He took all that pain so she didn't have to live with it. That's what a damper does, Ava. That's what I do."

She waited for a punchline that never came. "You're kidding."

He moved closer—twentieth session close—and laid his hand beside hers on the cushion. "If you're serious about getting this illness under control, I can help you."

She stared at the cheek she'd bruised. It was beautiful, like a faded violet she wanted to pluck and pummel until it was a deep royal paste.

He returned the ice pack to his face and said, "It's not a joke. And it's not a trick. I have three other patients currently undergoing exertion therapy."

"And you let them all smack you around?"

"That's simplifying things quite a lot, but yes, there is physical violence involved in our sessions."

Julian moved more gingerly than usual buttoning his shirt, looping his tie, donning his jacket, but except for a few subtle winces, it appeared the pain had fled his body. It was magical, really, how this bizarre heritage had conditioned him to suffer strangers' fists.

Ava's racing heart suddenly tripped on a hurdle, and her eyebrows trembled as the other damper patients again floated into her mind. "How many live in the same building as me?"

He stopped. "I'm sorry?"

"When you got us the apartment, you said you'd found patients housing before. How am I supposed to trust my daughter's not under the same roof as a bunch of crazy people?"

She felt like a complete ass the moment it fell out of her mouth, and the look that seized control of Julian's face suggested he thought the same thing.

He didn't say it though. He sat behind his desk and jotted down some notes while Ava mumbled an apology.

"I don't blame you for being curious; I would be too. But trust, Ava, is the backbone of exertion therapy, and we can't possibly continue without it. If you can't trust that I would never put you in harm's way, I might as well be any other victim to you."

She floated over to his desk and lightly rested her fingertips on the wood. "I trust you. And I want to continue. Please, Julian."

A whisper of relief bloomed in the corners of his mouth and he pushed a stack of papers across the desk. "You'll have to sign some things."

"I'll sign whatever you want. I trust you, I promise. I'll put it in blood if I have to."

Dr. Archer smiled and tongued a split lump on his bottom lip. "From now on, the only blood you spill is mine."

CHAPTER SIX

IFE'S MUSIC HAD returned. The stories, the songs, the laughter like jingling coin-filled pockets in Tivoli's Arcade. Ava had carried each of those sounds from Martha's Vineyard to Taunton, hoping they'd protect her in the vacuous hospital, but the melodies and rhythms became demons of their own in that place. They made her believe she was innocent and deserving of the four most important words in the world, but the words "I believe in you" turned out to be the most cancerous ghost of all. It left her infected and clenched like a tumorous fist, doomed for all time.

Then she found damping.

Ava took to exertion therapy like a duck to water, and after three months of what equated to a one-sided bare knuckle boxing match, Dr. Archer unveiled the next step.

When he opened the mysterious office closet to her, at last she understood. She bristled in exhilaration as he revealed the other damping tools at his disposal. A large selection of riding crops, whips, and canes adorned the closet walls, each decorated with myriad configurations of knotted cord and leather. They fascinated Ava, but twinges of discomfort and envy fired through her body when he introduced the new implements. She knew she wasn't supposed to think about other patients, but questions entered her mind nonetheless. Which were their favorite tools? Which of Julian's bruises belonged to them? Did his flesh submit as easily as it did with her? Did he look as beautiful when he bled for them?

She selected devices she thought others wouldn't pick, but deciding often proved too difficult, and she optioned for bare skin and bone instead.

There were also nylon cords, bungees, and other bizarre restraints, but Ava preferred using Julian's necktie. Through ligature and lash, he opened himself, and though his vulnerability initially frightened her, she allowed him to open her as well. He took her pain. With each scream he swallowed, he excised a slab of carcinogenic flesh from her heart. With each welt, it felt not so cold or dead an organ. With each mutual smack of ice against their wounds, Ava believed more and more that she could be a real person one day. The fire wouldn't just fade; it would die, and Julian would scatter the kindling so far it would never build a pyre inside her again.

Not long after moving to the condo on Mohr Lane, Ava took a job at the JCPenneys lunch counter in the newly opened Sunvalley Shopping Center. She continued exertion therapy without incident outside Julian's office and spent her days off work in the company of her joyful daughter.

But steady contentment eventually caused a sickening sort of anxiety in Ava's chest. It echoed through her arms and made them feel oddly hollow when she wrapped them around Sophie. She found herself getting choked up at odd times, but only after a litany of normal times, like when she mentioned her daughter to strangers who then asked, "How long have you been married?"

Except for Sophie, who needed her to survive, and Dr. Julian Archer, whom she paid to take her bullshit, Ava Francis didn't have any friends. She was friendly with her Penney's coworkers, but they weren't friends, and despite spending time with Jackie Hamilton during their daughter's playdates, an unspoken tension broiled between the women. If their respective childhoods entered the conversation, they quickly changed the subject. Respect between killers, Ava surmised, not between friends.

She longed for a closeness she hadn't felt since her days at Taunton. How sad it was, all those years with not even a sliver of the love she shared with a child arsonist. As it turned out, Flint was far more palatable than the other mothers of Glenbrook students. Rumors about Ava Francis were as wild as the stories coming back from Vietnam, spoken in the same hushed way they spoke of draft dodgers and the marches in Selma. The whispers and stares were fodder in her belly as she sat at meetings and plays and graduations among parents who hadn't dared to fib on their taxes let alone slaughter innocent people.

The rumors didn't come close to nailing what the other parents deemed "off" about Ava Francis and her little girl. They guessed she was on the run from some horrible man or parents who'd tossed her out when she got pregnant. There were even assertions she'd gotten herself into a Marion Crane-type pickle, but she'd gotten away with her employer's cash instead of running afoul of a mother-loving murderer.

It was the most ridiculous theory, yet the nearest to her actual situation, and the only rumor that didn't start her insides sizzling. The attempts at finding friendship quickly became tiresome, and once Sophie hit fifth grade, Ava started letting fifteen-year-old Dionne Hamilton escort her to school functions.

The girls were out at the movies when Julian Archer stopped in to fix the broken air conditioning unit for the second time that summer in 1968.

She gave the contraption an open-palmed slap. "You see? Nothing."

Julian crouched in front of the unit and Ava handed him a glass of water.

"I appreciate you coming by again. I did some work on it myself, but I think I turned it into some kind of alien communicator. It's making even weirder clicks and buzzes now."

"I'm sorry it's giving you so much trouble," Julian said. "Not that I mind seeing you in your natural habitat."

Ava slicked back her damp bangs with a headband and chuckled. "I don't know how natural it is, but it's nice to see you too." When she fanned him with a newspaper, he tilted his face to the breeze.

"Where's Miss Sophie today?"

Ava gulped water and wiped her mouth. "Dionne took her to see *Yellow Submarine* at the mall. That's what she said anyway. God knows what movie they're actually seeing."

"What's that tone about?" he asked, smirking.

She stretched her neck. "It's nothing. Dionne's a great girl—" She stopped and screwed up her face. "Wait, when did this go from handyman work to a therapy session?"

Julian raised his hands in surrender. "You're right, I'm sorry."

"Don't be sorry. Just make it feel like my skin's not melting off, okay?"

He resumed working on the unit, muttering, "One problem at a time, Ms. Francis."

She feigned laughter and slumped down in a chair. As she fanned herself with the newspaper, Julian removed the face of the unit and stuck his nose inside with a deep sniff.

"What are you doing?"

"Trying to figure out where that smell's coming from. I thought maybe a mouse crawled into the unit and died, and it was causing a malfunction, but no dice."

Ava scrunched her nose. "Smell?"

"Uh oh, you're used to it," he laughed. "God knows how long it's been going on then."

"Maybe my skanky sweat is overpowering it," she said, flapping her arms. "Fix the AC, and then I'll be able to pinpoint the smell."

Julian stood and walked to the refrigerator nose-first. Dissatisfied, he opened the cabinet under the sink and inhaled deeply.

"Hey, stop that! If you're smelling something weird, it's probably you."

They popped up at the same time, both of their faces tight with opposition until the AC gurgled and growled, and a blast of stale cold air pelted the pair.

"Oh my gosh! You did it!" She threw her arms around him, inadvertently brushing her lips against his sweaty collarbone. Backing away quickly, she ducked her head into the fridge and said, "Do you want some lemonade?"

"In a minute. I want to find that smell."

"Suit yourself." She poured herself a glass of pulpy juice, sat at the table, and stared at the front page of the week-old newspaper, as she'd done many times since its arrival. Robert Kennedy had been assassinated a month ago, and death still gripped the headlines. Ava tried not to read about things that might whet her destructive appetite, but with Martin Luther King Jr's own assassination not even three months old, it was impossible to avoid bloody thoughts in 1968. But this was in her own backyard, and it set her teeth on edge. Tapping the headline, she inhaled deeply through her nose.

Now that Julian mentioned it, maybe she *could* smell something weird . . .

She shouted toward the bedrooms. "Maybe it's coming from another apartment. Or the attic. All that old stuff up there, you know?"

He didn't answer.

"Julian?"

With a huff, she pushed up from the chair. She lingered in the blast of cold air for a moment before shuffling to Sophie's empty bedroom and then to hers, where Julian stood at the open closet.

"What is it? Stinky shoes or something?"

"Or something." With a wire hanger, he lifted a floral blouse off a mutilated jackrabbit, stiff with rigor mortis, on her closet floor.

It transported her to the day that changed her life forever. The hidden room in the floor of the root cellar, the darkness, and the terrifying clanging of her brass ring that tugged her into that rancid oblivion.

The smell was staggering now, but even as her eyes filled with tears, she reached out to touch it. Julian tossed the blouse over the corpse and pulled her back, out of the bedroom and back to the kitchen, where he grabbed a trash bag and one of her dishwashing gloves. He didn't look at her as he pulled it on, or when he said, "What do you know about this?"

"Nothing, I swear."

"Did you do it?"

Her face tightened. "No. I just told you—"

"You could've done it without knowing. It's happened before."

"Well, it didn't happen this time."

"It's a rabbit, Ava."

"And?"

He exhaled and marched past her to the bedroom to bag the corpse.

"Julian, I didn't do this."

He cinched the bag and faced her, his expression like dry, scored clay. "I believe you."

"It doesn't sound like you do."

"I'm sorry, but it's . . . well . . . " His nostrils flared as he thought.

"Hard?" she suggested.

"Troubling," he said. "Because if *you* didn't do it—"

"Don't say it. There has to be another reason."

"I'm sure there is."

"This can't be what it looks like."

He furrowed his brow. "It *can't* be? Ava, be sensible."

"Julian, be compassionate. Please."

Setting the bag in the sink, he expelled a single chuckle and spun to her. "Of all people, you know my compassion. I would do anything to see you happy and healthy."

"But not just me," she grumbled.

"Well, of course not. What does that even mean?"

She gulped hard. "Nothing." She grabbed the bag and held it at arm's length on her way out the door.

"Don't say 'nothing.' Talk to me. What is it?"

"I don't need to talk to you. I need to talk to Sophie. I'm sure this is all a misunderstanding."

"A misunderstanding?"

"Or there's a reasonable explanation," she said, exasperated. "There's more to this than meets the eye."

"That's what I'm afraid of."

She tossed the bag in the dumpster and averted her eyes as she pushed past Julian into the house. "If you're all done with the AC, I have to make dinner for Sophie."

She washed and dried her hands, pulled out a knife, carrots, and the cutting board, but Julian didn't leave. He watched how she held the knife, tighter than usual because of her sweaty palms.

"You're terrified," he said.

"Of course I'm fucking terrified." She nicked her thumb slicing a carrot and popped it into her mouth. Her teeth sunk into the flesh on either side of the cut, squeezing out both blood and pain.

He touched her wounded hand gently, but she flinched, even fought a bit, when he moved it from her lips to the faucet. He ran the cold water and held both of their hands under the freezing stream as he dabbed the cut with a bar of soap. Washing away the foam, he pulled her hand from the water and dried it with a towel.

"Are you okay?"

"I have to make dinner."

"Fine. Are you're going to talk to Sophie?"

"I said I would."

"I can stay to help if you want."

Ava slapped a head of lettuce on the cutting board, then pointed Julian to the door. "Go help someone else."

He frowned as he glanced at his watch. "I do have an appointment in a few hours," he said. "Will you get in touch if there's trouble with Sophie?"

"I will. Enjoy getting your ass kicked at your appointment."

His mouth was so tight his lips lost all color, but he forced a small, if not pitying, smile before turning on his heel.

Once he'd closed the door behind him, Ava set down the knife and sank to the floor. The lettuce rolled off the cutting board and landed beside her, but she ignored it just as she'd done with the dead rabbit in her closet.

How long had it been there? How long had she cooked and cleaned and ventured into hopeful dreams in that stench?

How long ago had her young daughter taken an animal's life?

Dionne and Sophie rarely came straight home after a movie, which usually annoyed Ava, But she hoped they'd take an extra long route home that night. The last thing she needed was for her young daughter to come home while she was in the dumpster examining the corpse, trying to remember, and hoping it was her handiwork.

CHAPTER SEVEN

S HE TWISTED AND TUGGED, and his lips flowered royal blue.
He pinched her thigh, and she released the necktie,
causing him to wilt onto the couch. He gasped, his eyes
fixed on the ceiling as oxygen flooded his lungs, and Ava
watched in delight as his body recovered from knowing
her.

It was her favorite thing about using his tie. As color
returned to Julian's face and his jugular throbbed, as
pinpoint bruises blossomed between scarlet crisscrosses,
she noted how each ring was a level of her own suffering
. . . and desire.

The first indentation was deepest but nearly hidden by
the angle of his chin. That ring was the fire, the churning
madness in her soul she was learning to control in therapy.

The second ring crossed his adam's apple, rising and
falling like her love for Paul Dillon. She suspected it would
be a difficult habit to break once Julian said she didn't need
to write letters to her dead boyfriend anymore, but it was
surprisingly easy to close the memory inside an attic box
and stop looking over her shoulder for the boy she once
loved.

And with his phantom went the others. She occasionally
caught a whiff of Natalie's perfume or felt fingers crossing
hers and knew at once they were Paul's, but they didn't
plague her anymore. She didn't hunger for them. She had
something else to hunger for now.

Ava licked her lips as she stared at the third scarlet ring

around Julian's neck. It followed the path of the second, but it declined sharply after his adam's apple and sliced the meat between his neck and clavicle. At the twist beneath the bump in his throat, Ava's fingers discovered a knot in her own. That knot in her, that lash on him, that phantom twist in both of their bodies was Sophie Francis.

Ava had full access to the closet now. She fetched the ice packs and gauze. She slathered ointment on his scratches and plugged in heating pads in case either wrenched a muscle during their exertions, but she didn't make a move to tend his wounds that day. Nor her own.

Instead, she folded her body over her knees and sobbed.

"What is it?" Julian asked. "Who's here?"

She shook her head and tried to catch her breath. A million thoughts had been running through her brain since she last saw him; most of them as foul as the gas that distended the gut of the dead animal they pulled from her closet the week before.

She'd spoken to Sophie, though it took longer to work up the courage than she'd ever admit. She wasn't sure which answer would frighten her more—a confession or a denial—but later that night when she asked Sophie to turn down her music so they could talk, her hands were shaking so bad she had to clamp them between her knees.

❧

"Sweetheart," she started dryly, "have you caught any bunnies lately?"

Sophie's face scrunched up like she might sneeze. "Bunnies?"

"A little one with long ears? Maybe to keep as a pet?"

Her eyes widened with a smile. "I'm allowed to have a pet bunny?"

"No, no . . . Did you *hurt* one? Maybe by accident, and you felt like you had to hide it?"

"Why would I do that?"

223

Ava rubbed her forehead and moaned. "I don't know, sweetie."

Sophie crawled across the bed and wrapped her arms around her mother's neck. "You believe me, don't you?"

Holding her daughter tight, she whispered, "I will always believe you, baby."

The girl kissed her cheek, and Ava squeezed her eyes to stop the tears from falling. "You can turn on your music. But not so loud, okay?"

Sophie disconnected from her mother and rolled off the bed. "But the ghost likes it loud."

Ava croaked. "Ghost?"

"In the attic," she said. "The one that stomps around at night." She started the music again and sang in her best Richard Harris vibrato. "I'll never have that recipe again! Oh noooo!"

The song was stuck in Ava's head the entire ride to Archer Therapeutics, which she spent choking back bile.

She gulped back more of the acidic sludge before answering. "Nobody's here, Doc. Nobody but us chickens." With a spine-rolling huff, she continued. "I talked to Sophie. I asked her point blank if she killed that thing, and she didn't know what I was talking about."

"Or so she claimed," he said, massaging his throat.

"She wasn't lying. I know I punish myself by saying she's not my daughter, but goddammit, I know when she's lying."

"Okay," he said. "So who did it?"

Lifting her chin, Ava said, "I did."

"You remember?"

"No, I—I think I do. I mean, it's possible."

Julian squinted as he sat on the edge of his desk. "You wouldn't be taking the blame for Sophie, would you? Because that'll only make things worse for you both. I understand the impulse; I even admire it. But you can't hide something like this for long. You should know that better than anyone."

Smoke bloomed and curled against her tongue as she clenched every muscle in her body. It felt as though letting go even for a second would release a fiery cyclone from her gut. She'd burn the office, Margie, the whole crumbling block . . . and Julian.

Julian Archer, whose flushed cheeks she'd bruised countless times over the past few years, and who stared at her now as if he stood on the edge of a cliff she could crumble with a word.

"If it was her," he began, "if she's capable of the same violence as you, how much are you willing to lose to keep it a secret from her?"

Ribbons of smoke leaked between her lips as she whispered, "Everything. I'll be miserable and lucky all my days if it means she doesn't have to know what it's like being a Norton."

The surname was a punch to the throat. Her breath became shallow and strained, and she couldn't lift her tear-filled eyes to him.

He stood with a sigh and ducked into the closet. She expected him to return with the usual ice packs, but he instead emerged holding a cat-o-nine tails. Ava had never used one before, and her heart raced with terrifying but enticing questions. How much damage would it inflict? Would he bruise instantly? Would it draw blood?

And why now?

Running it through his fingers, Julian Archer tilted his head. "What are you afraid of, Ava? Tell me." He unbuttoned his light blue dress shirt and broke her trance on the instrument, her focus snapping to his back muscles rolling like a ferocious sea beneath a fleet of bruises and scars.

"Tell me what you've been thinking since we found that rabbit."

"Hare."

"What?"

"Lepus Californicus. The desert hare." Ava's chin

trembled, and she wiped budding tears from her eyes. "Sophie has a book about California animals. It was hard to tell at first since it was a baby, but the ears and tail gave it away." She exhaled twin plumes of smoke from her nostrils like a dragon and gripped the sides of her head. Steam swirled from her flaming skin, and fire licked the back of her teeth, which remained gritted.

"Tell me why that scares you."

Her lips quivered as she spoke through clenched teeth. "I can't. If I open up, the fire will get out."

Julian grabbed the cat-o-nine tails, then offered her his hand. It was hot to the touch, and she felt his pulse in his fingertips as he led her away from the couch. He shoved the implement into her fist, turned his back to her, then looked over his shoulder as he growled, "Let it out."

Her eyes were closed when she brought the straps down hard on Julian's back. He hissed at the searing pain, and his muscles flickered beneath scarred flesh, but inside Ava, bravery unfolded like the petals of a water lily.

"Do you know the difference between a rabbit and a hare?" she asked between strikes. "Rabbits are born blind. They're born hairless, powerless. But hares are born with their eyes open, able to fend for themselves. Hares are born ready to run."

She hit him again, and the room flared with fiery music.

"Rabbits hide when they're threatened," she continued. "They go underground and disappear into burrows, but not hares. They just run. It's their most innate instinct. That's why they're used in coursing. People release dogs after hares and bet on whether the hare will escape or be mauled."

Julian shuddered under the crack of the tails, and pink sweat dripped between his shoulder blades. He braced himself on the wingback, and Ava burned through him again.

"The hare is fast. It's resourceful. But it's also alone.

Sometimes they live in families or pairs, but it's rare. Most hares are solitary."

He looked over his scarlet shoulder, panting. "I guess your girl's not a hare then, because she has you."

It sparked an unreasonable fury in her muscles, and she struck Julian so fast and fierce that he cried out and nearly lost his grip on the chair. Blood rolled down his back, and he held up his hand for her to stop.

"I'm . . . I'm sorry."

He coughed as he caught his breath. "Don't be. I shouldn't have said that. We don't know what Sophie's done."

Ava dropped the cat-o-nine tails and fetched ice and ointment from the closet, popping out with a frown when Julian said, "Maybe you should bring her next time."

"Who? Sophie?"

"Just for a chat."

"I don't think so."

"If you're afraid she hurt that animal—"

"I'm not."

"Ava . . ."

"For all we know, it came in by itself. We keep the door open when the AC's broken. And you know how often it's broken."

"That I do."

She ducked back into the closet and returned with antiseptic and thin adhesive strips. They didn't speak again until he was bandaged up and buttoning his shirt, and even then Ava's voice was less than cordial.

"Listen," she said flatly, "I appreciate everything you do for me, Dr. Archer, but I'm not bringing Sophie here. I don't want this life for her."

"Nobody wants this life, Ava. I doubt a single patient wouldn't prefer to be anywhere else when they're in therapy. And frankly, I wish I didn't have to be here either. Why are you afraid to let me talk to her?"

"I'm not."

"Is it because you wanted to hide certain things from me—Paul, the arson, your first kill—and they still came out?"

She flexed her hands, the truth swelling in her like infection in a boil, until finally she blurted, "I don't want you to ruin her."

His forehead scrunched in an amalgamation of puzzlement and pain, and Ava exhaled an apology.

"I'm sorry, Julian. I know what you do helps, but when I imagine Sophie opening up to you here, in the same room where a hundred broken strangers' ghosts have run wild, I can't help thinking it'll make her worse. All this disease. All this pain. It's like rust beneath the skin, hard and itchy and flaking into the bloodstream. There's bad water everywhere."

The color drained from his face, accenting the bruises, scars, and broken blood vessels. In all the years they'd spent together it was the ugliest and angriest he'd ever looked.

"Bad water?"

"You know what I mean," she said quickly, and he nodded like his head was double the weight.

"Yes, I think I do. You don't trust me."

"No, I do."

"You think there's bad water here."

"No! I didn't mean it like that. It's just . . . like Natalie said . . . exertion indulges the worst parts of me. I enjoy hurting you. Maybe the same way Faye enjoyed hurting people."

His nostrils flared, and his lips closed so tight they turned white. "Like Natalie said," he repeated bitterly. "You'd believe a figment over me."

"I don't want to," she said, "but you have to admit that most people wouldn't consider what we do here to be all that healthy."

With a snarl, Julian latched onto her arms and squeezed hard. He'd never held her that way before, and she liked it. Despite the shock, she wanted him to hold her like that, for his perfect slivers of fingernails to leave waxing moons in her skin.

"What I do is sacred," he said. "It's a legacy, and it's saved countless lives. Innocent lives. From people like you."

Her heart sank. She didn't want him to hold her anymore. He was disgusted by her disease, and she by his cure. Dr. Archer trafficked in pain, and Ava—a killer, a liar, an addict—was his bread and butter. Horror and dysfunction got him hard. He was still breathing heavy, the smell of blood wafting off him in hot waves.

She shivered as she pulled away, possessed by the morality of a woman she killed years ago.

"Sophie's fine," she insisted, grabbing her coat. "She got invited to a big party next weekend. A girl from school. One of the most popular families in town."

"I'm glad."

"So you don't have to worry."

"You pay me to worry," he said. "And you still have ten minutes."

Her reply sounded distant and strange as it pinballed off the office walls. She regretted a lot of things in her life, but as she fled Julian's office, telling him to use the extra time to clean himself up shot straight to the top.

CHAPTER EIGHT

A VA CANCELED HER next appointment out of humiliation, but she eventually convinced herself canceling was the most sensible thing to do for everyone involved. She'd been feeling healthier lately anyway, and the more she thought of Julian, bare-chested, blood-slicked, and devastated in the doorway of his office, the unhealthier *he* seemed. Maybe dampers didn't just take someone's violence; maybe they took their sickness as well, and if so, what kind of man was he? So many monsters had spilled Julian's blood, and he'd asked them for it. Ava didn't care what he claimed about it serving a greater purpose. And it didn't matter how strong he believed he was. No one could endure that kind of evil without sustaining injuries deeper than bruises.

The explanation came as easily as her dismissal of the dead hare. She'd left the door open, that's all. The stray dog she'd seen wandering around lately had probably gotten to it, and the poor animal found its way into the Francis's house to die. Yes, she realized a lot of random things had to happen just right for that scenario to occur, but she admitted that to herself alone when she couldn't sleep.

It came down to the simple fact that Ava Francis wasn't sick enough to be seeing a therapist like Julian. Or any therapist. She appreciated how Julian had helped her, but she couldn't keep throwing time and money at something so selfish. She came to California to get better, and she'd done that. It was far past time for Sophie to have her full attention.

With Jenna Galloway's upcoming birthday party, the Francises had the chance to change their fortune. If Sophie made a good impression on Jenna, they might become friends, and maybe that closeness would lead to Ava finding a better job, a better apartment, and the charmed life the daughter of Natalie Norton and Paul Dillon deserved.

The Galloways told her as much while inviting them, and Ava didn't want to screw it up . . . which was why she took a shift at Penney's instead of attending Jenna's party. Just because she felt healthier mentally didn't mean she felt more confident in social situations. She told herself she'd work on it, and until then, she'd do everything she could to make sure Sophie looked like the nice, normal daughter of a nice, normal woman.

Sacrificing a sizable chunk of the money she'd been socking away, she bought Sophie a new party dress. The powder blue taffeta gave the ten-year-old's eyes a chilling glow, especially when Dionne combed a light layer of mascara onto Sophie's eyelashes.

Ava's chin dimpled. She said, "You look so grown up," and she meant it, but she really wanted to say, "You look so much like Natalie."

She took a picture, and the girls groaned.

"I wasn't ready!" Sophie whined. She wrapped her arm around Dionne, who flashed a peace sign and grinned for the picture.

"1 . . . 2 . . . " Ava snapped the photo and teared up as she smiled. "That was a good one."

Dionne fixed a dimple in Sophie's dress. "You sure you don't want to take her, Ms. Francis?"

"I wish I could, but I have a shift." Pinching her daughter's cheek, she smiled. "You'll tell them I'm sorry I'm not there?"

Nodding, Sophie clutched Jenna's birthday present to her chest and bounced on the balls of her feet with increasing excitement.

"Careful. Don't wrinkle your dress. You want it crisp and clean when you show up, okay?"

Sophie warbled in accord, took Dionne's hand, and danced out the door.

According to Dionne, Sophie's dress did remain crisp and clean for their arrival.

But it did not come home that way.

Sophie's face was streaked with paint, and the myriad colors covering her hands made it look like she was wearing gray gloves sporadically accented with vibrant threads. Her dress was mostly clean but oddly rumpled, as if it had been balled up in God's own fist, and there were significant rips along the sleeves and back.

"Sophie, what happened?" Ava screeched as she toddled through the door.

When a woman with long silver hair appeared in the doorway of the Francis home, Ava flinched and shoved Sophie behind her.

"Who are you?"

The woman waved, apologizing as she cautiously stepped inside. "Oh dear. I didn't mean to frighten you, Mrs. Francis. I'm so sorry about that."

"*Ms*. Francis."

"I apologize again," she said. "And I believe I can explain what happened to your daughter's dress."

She patted Sophie's back. "Go get changed, sweetie. I'll call you when dinner's ready."

When Sophie disappeared into her room, the woman extended her hand with a tight-lipped smile. "I'm pleased to meet you, Ms. Francis. My name is Moira Shunn. I was at the Galloways' party today."

"Where's Dionne?"

"Across the hall. I thought it would be best if you and I spoke alone."

"About what?"

"Maybe we should sit down?" The woman raised her eyebrows, and Ava gestured for her to sit at the kitchen table.

"Can I get you some coffee? Tea?"

"Water, please. Is it filtered?"

Ava's heart thudded, and she stopped filling the glass. "No. Sorry."

"That's okay. I'll drink it all the same."

Ava filled two glasses and sat at the table across from the woman with cracked hands and tired eyes. "What's this all about, Mrs. Shunn?"

She wondered if Moira could smell the dead hare. Even with the carcass gone, the smell plugged up Ava's nostrils like cotton. The fetid odor was almost accusatory, like something so horrendous couldn't possibly be natural, or forgivable.

Moira sipped and swallowed, cringing as she set down the water. "I'm afraid there was an incident at the Galloways today. No one was harmed, thank goodness, but the confrontation between your daughter and Jenna Galloway wasn't exactly a peaceful one."

"Confrontation?" Ava's heart became a lump of ice. She guzzled her entire glass and refilled it hurriedly.

"Calm down, dear. The Galloway girl's not hurt. Unless you count her hundred-dollar hairdo, which I certainly don't. But Mrs. Galloway might think differently. She didn't look too pleased when she saw little Sophie had hacked off a bunch of her daughter's hair." She pantomimed an elegant scissor slice. "I didn't see the entire encounter. The girls were listening to records in Jenna's room and I happened to be down the hall waiting for the lavatory. The deed was done by the time I reached them, but your daughter still had the scissors in her hand."

"Sophie, get in here please," Ava yelled over her shoulder. "Now!"

When the girl jogged in, Moira stood with a sigh. "I should be getting home, but—" She jotted her number on a napkin and pushed it across the table. "If you need anything, even just to talk, I'm a retired nurse and school teacher—widowed to boot—so I'm always at home."

"Thank you, Mrs. Shunn."

Ava saw her to the door as calmly as possible, but her sweaty hands shook and slipped on the knob. She wished the woman a good day and closed the door, but it was louder than intended, and Sophie jumped.

Ava's glass was empty again. With a growl, she flipped on the kitchen faucet, and stuck her face underneath. She slurped, apathetic about the volume or mess as she focused on maintaining the steady rhythm of her gulping. Images flashed in her mind between gulps—the dead animal, the scissors, pretty blond hair like strands of golden spider silk strewn about a red and blue art deco playroom—and flipped the water to hot. The water steamed, but it felt cool against her face.

The fire had started, and a sweltering dizziness struck her behind the eyes.

She couldn't let herself black out, and she couldn't call Julian. As much as she needed him, he couldn't find out about this. She had to manage it on her own. She had to protect Natalie and Paul's baby.

Ava jerked her hands from the scalding water and clutched them to her breast.

"What's wrong, Mom? What did I do?" Sophie asked fearfully.

Her voice was soft, but it pierced Ava's head like a jagged syringe. It hit her in a way that made the back of her throat itch. She popped her ears and stretched her jaw as she ran the cold faucet but splashed lukewarm water on her face.

"Just sit down," she said, patting herself with a towel. "I'll get us some milk."

Each with a glass, sitting opposite each other, Ava drank in the girl's ragged appearance. Her hair was tangled, and her ribbons looked like squashed butterflies in the messy coif.

234

"Honey, I need you to tell me what happened at Jenna's party."

Sophie's face lit up, and the thick coating of milk on her upper lip made her bouncily joyful demeanor more comedic as she described the various decorations and party games scattered through the Galloway house. She spoke of music and prizes and sweets around every corner. Not one word seemed disingenuous or forced.

"Mrs. Shunn said a bunch of you girls were listening to records."

Sophie's sunny face didn't fracture. "Yup! Jenna got a bunch of records, and we all wanted to listen." She finally wiped the milk from her lip, then dragged her finger down the glass and cut a stripe through the cool condensation. "But she didn't want to listen to the one I got her."

Ava exhaled heavily, and her fingers found their way to the aching notch in her neck. She tried to dissuade Sophie from buying the David Bowie album for Jenna, but suggesting someone might not like Bowie's music as much as Sophie turned the girl's face into a crumpled mess of offense, and Ava had been too exhausted to argue.

She'd been to the Galloway's house only once at a back-to-school barbecue, where Mr. and Mrs. Galloway greeted the Francises looking picture perfect in their matching polyester plaid. As they led Ava through rooms with bizarre art deco lamp shades and artwork, it was like Barry Manilow was hiding behind every credenza, constantly crooning songs Mr. Galloway kept referring to as "one of the greats." She knew it wasn't right to judge, but she didn't peg the Galloways as a household that kept David Bowie in their regular rotation.

Not that it was any reason to chop off someone's hair.

"Is that why you attacked Jenna?"

"Attacked?" Sophie's eyes didn't look real. They glittered like costume jewelry when she batted her long dark lashes. "I didn't attack her. I was helping her. She said she didn't understand why I'd get her a David Bowie album. She said her mom would get angry if she even saw it in the house."

"That happens sometimes, darling. It's not personal."

Sophie's fingers slid over the cup and her face scrunched. "But it was personal. She made fun of me. At least I think she did."

"What did she say?"

"She said I was weird. And the other girls were saying it too. They said no one wanted me there." Her eyes were darker then, like the Pacific under a veil of stormy tears. "Do *you* think I'm weird?"

Ava patted her hand. "Everyone's weird in their own way, sweetheart. It's not a bad thing, even if people try to make you feel like it is."

"I guess. But then they started talking about my hair. They were going to do all these cool braids Jenna learned at summer camp, but no one would do mine. They said it was too oily. But Dionne does braids in my hair all the time. I tried to tell them that, but they kept saying it was gross." She combed her fingers through her tangled bangs. "It's not, is it?"

"No, honey, it's not gross," she said, tousling Sophie's bangs. "So, who had the scissors?"

Sophie's face was blank as the hair fell through her fingers, staring at her mother with twin pools of azure curiosity, glittering like lakes under a passing warm front. It was a sort of magic having eyes like that. Even under the worst accusations, Sophie had "Who, me?" eyes, just like Paul.

"Jenna had some scissors, I think."

"That woman who walked home with you, Mrs. Shunn, she said she saw you holding a pair of scissors."

"Oh." She twisted her lips and shrugged. "I don't remember that."

The back of Ava's head rang with pain. "Like you don't remember the hare?"

Sophie touched her bangs again and pouted her bottom lip in puzzlement.

"No, honey, the baby hare—the rabbit in the closet I asked you about."

She blinked like the Santa Ana's gusted through their kitchen, then looked back at her room. "I wish I had a pet rabbit. I'd like to know what makes them hop."

Ava crouched in front of Sophie. With her hands on her daughter's knees, she looked up pleadingly. "Honey, I need you to think real hard, okay? Do you remember any part of cutting Jenna's hair?"

She shook her head. "But it looked better after."

Ava couldn't breathe. Her skull flared in throbbing agony, and it felt like lava was leaking out her belly button as she scrambled to her feet.

"Mom?"

"Go to your room."

Sophie stood slowly, head drooped as she shuffled out of the kitchen and closed her bedroom door behind her.

On the floor of the kitchen, Ava covered her face and choked back a sob. The fire was there too, high and hellish and begging to break free, but she swallowed it the best she could by giving her focus to the boy crouched under her table.

He was scrunched up, chin on his knees, arms crossed around his legs, and ice blue eyes smoldering in the dark.

"Tell me it's not true," she mewled at him. "Tell me she's not like me."

Lifting his head, Paul Dillon whispered, "You know I can't lie to you, Avery."

CHAPTER NINE

ARGIE HAD NO chance of stopping Ava from bursting into Dr. Archer's office. By the time the receptionist had escaped the confines of her desk, Ava was inside, staring at a small woman on the couch—in Ava's spot on the couch.

"Ms. Francis? What's the meaning of this?" Julian demanded.

"I'm sorry, Dr. Archer," Margie stammered. "She ran right past me."

"It's not your fault." He gestured to his patient. "I'm sorry about this, Mrs. Black. I'll just be a minute."

He ushered Ava into the waiting room and closed the door. "What the hell do you think you're doing?"

"Is she one of your damper patients?"

"That's none of your business. What are you doing here?"

She glanced at Margie, who was doing her best not to eavesdrop. "We should discuss it in private."

"I agree. You still have an appointment on the books in a few days. Granted you don't cancel, we can talk about it then."

"I can't wait that long. I need your help now."

Julian stuck his hands in his pockets as he strolled around her. "You didn't need it last week. Cured, were you?"

"No, I'm not cured. I'm sorry. I was wrong."

"That's big of you to admit."

"So we can . . . " She cleared her throat. " . . . talk?"

"At your next appointment, absolutely. I'm currently with someone."

"This is more important. And it won't take long. Just a quickie."

Julian's brows fell like visors over his eyes and his mouth shrank to a bloodless knot. Even Margie averted her gaze in shock.

All at once Ava felt like she was sitting on the stone bench in her mother's garden in those quiet moments before Faye revealed her madness. They'd been silent for so long, wreathed in the rustles of the garden and each other's breath, she'd started thinking she was in trouble. Her stomach twisted like something truly wonderful or truly horrible was about to happen. As she stared at Julian, however, she was fairly certain it was the latter.

His cheeks were speckled bright red, and his nostrils pulsed with his rising anger. But when he spoke, it was like the deep whistle of breath over a bottle. It was a distant train whistle, and much as Ava wanted to flee, she was stuck on the tracks.

"That's not how this works, Ms. Francis, and I refuse to stand here and let you reduce and ridicule my family's lifelong work like this. There are no quickies. And your issues, while horrific, are no more important than anyone else's."

"I didn't mean it that way. I'm sorry."

"I don't think you are," he said. "And if you're willing to disrupt another patient's time and demean my work by making wild demands, you obviously don't respect me enough to participate in a therapy built on intimacy and trust."

She shrank back, her mouth agape. Margie was staring at her again, but she tossed her gaze to the ceiling when Ava noticed.

"Can I—" Ava cleared her throat and shifted her voice to a more courteous timbre. "May I wait, Dr. Archer?"

239

He sighed and looked at his watch.

"I do respect you. And I was wrong about everything. I need your help."

Grinding his back teeth, he grunted in surrender. "Forty-five minutes." Opening the office door, he said, "Please forgive me, Mrs. Black," and closed himself inside.

❧

Ava Francis was on her feet the moment Dr. Archer's office door opened. Mrs. Black should've been sour with the rude woman who'd interrupted her therapy, but Ava didn't detect any disdain. The woman chirped a farewell to Margie, and with a whimsical wave, exited on a gust of confidence.

Ava wanted that. She'd gotten it from Julian before, but after the way she'd treated him, she imagined that sort of bliss would be hard-won from here on out. As she did her time in the waiting room, she did all sorts of things to keep the fire low. Because of Margie's watchful eye, she couldn't speak to Paul, but she could subtly hold his hand. She could lean her head ever so slightly and let him kiss her neck.

"I knew you couldn't let me go," he whispered, and Ava's eyes watered.

How the hell did she think she was healthy? How the hell did she think she knew better than Dr. Archer?

Her favorite sofa cushion was still warm. It spiked the oppressive heat in her gut until she moved to the other side of the sofa. Even if Mrs. Black didn't participate in exertion therapy, she didn't like the idea of Julian spreading his talents around, thinning his gifts.

He sat in his wingback, notepad balanced on his knee and pen clicked to readiness, but she didn't speak. She directed her eyes at the floor and wrung her hands. Paul was still there, on the edge of Julian's desk, daring her to say something bad about his only child.

With a huff, she focused on Julian and suddenly

noticed a small purple dot peeking out above his collar. A bruise. Someone else's bruise.

"Ava? What's this all about?"

"She's a Norton," she whispered.

"I'm sorry?"

"Sophie attacked one of her schoolmates earlier today. No one got hurt, thank God, but it could've gone the other way real easy. She had scissors, Julian. She could've killed that girl."

"Did she say why?"

"She . . . she doesn't remember it." She crumpled forward and dug her fingernails into her blistering scalp. "That's it. I thought I could protect her, but I failed. I did this to her. There's something so truly horrible inside me, and the more she's around it, the more she absorbs it."

"If that were true, I would've absorbed it too. Why doesn't your illness have any effect on me?"

She opened her mouth, and though she didn't speak, Paul knew exactly what she was thinking.

"Go on, Avery," he said. "Tell him the bad water was already in him. Tell him what you really think of him doing what he does with all those other freaks."

She said, "No," and when Julian raised an eyebrow, she sniffled hard. "I mean, you're around so many of us. You must be immune. I should've known better about Sophie, but I thought she'd be okay. I really did. She's so sweet, singing all the time, writing little poems and songs on scraps of paper. I had to scrub one off the wall the other day, and I feel like I can still see it."

"What did it say?"

Ava's expression flickered with contemplation. "The sky is in the pond now," she said. "Ducks are going gray. Petals show the path to Heaven, but clouds of stone get in our way."

His forehead creased. "It's lovely."

"Is it? I thought it was kind of sad."

"Some of the loveliest things are."

Ava sighed. "Not for a girl her age. When I was her age, I was running around the island, playing in the woods, fishing off the pier—"

"No, you weren't. You were on a farm. You were in the smallest town in Ohio, bored out of your skull. Sophie's the lucky one of you two. She's a train ride from the Bay, from one of the greatest, most culturally diverse cities in America. And from the caliber of her creativity at her age, it sounds like this is where she's meant to be. You did a good thing bringing her here. Don't feel bad for wanting to give her the childhood you had—or *believed* you had. From what you've told me the island wasn't exactly the idyllic fantasy it seemed."

"Another bit of lovely sadness," she said.

"Like mother, like daughter."

Paul leapt off the desk and strolled the room. "But she's not your daughter, Avery. She's mine, and look what you're doing to her. You're going to listen to this man over her own father? Over the person you claimed to love more than anything in this world?"

"You're not real," she whispered. "Paul would never treat me like this."

"See, that's the funny thing about being murdered. You don't stay the nice, sweet boy you were when you were alive. You think the afterlife is a merry romp for me? All I have is time and you. You—Avery, my everything—and every torturous second of watching you fall in love with another man."

"That's not what's happening!"

Julian dropped his notebook. "Ava, is Paul here?"

She slapped her hands over her ears, growling for her dead boyfriend to stop talking, and Julian began unbuttoning his shirt.

Paul hissed at the doctor. "Oh, this fucking guy."

"Then leave, Paul," she whimpered. "If you can't stand it, go away."

"Oh no, my love. I'm going to stay right here and watch

242

you get sicker and sicker. Because once it's over, once you're little more than one of those limp and broken rabbits you tried to hide as a child, I won't have to worry about my daughter anymore. They'll take her away from you. They *should* take her away from you."

Julian tossed a cane to Ava, turned his back to her, and said, "Get rid of him."

Paul laughed as he stood beside Dr. Archer. "You see? He knows exactly what he's doing. This isn't for you, Avery. It's for him. He gets off on it."

"Do it, Ava."

"Don't do it, Avery."

She screamed and smacked Julian's back, but it was Paul who suffered. He sobbed and flickered and begged her not to do to him what she had done to so many others.

"You're killing me," he cried with each bloody lick. "You're killing my daughter."

Ava was a whirlwind of violence and tears, every joy and sorrow glistening in the wounds she carved into Julian's body, until at last she collapsed onto the sofa and threw the bloody cane at the spot where Paul Dillon's ghost once stood.

Julian's spine straightened, his hips and shoulders flaming with swollen lashes, and his face was scrunched in torment when he looked at her again.

It was an expression she'd not seen on him before. That look and his response to her "quickie" comment made her realize for the first time that, even fortified by legacy or magic, Julian Archer wasn't impenetrable. She could hurt him. She *had* hurt him.

While he caught his breath, she fetched ice from the closet. It felt good in her fist, but not as good as it felt when she held it to his wounds and his body arched into it.

"I'm sorry," she said. "About what I said earlier, about Sophie, about everything. Julian, I'm scared she's turning into me. And I don't even know what I am."

He looked over his shoulder, grunting when she patted

a quartet of welts on his side. "Okay. So what are you going to do about it?"

"I'm going to take her out of school."

He turned and pushed the ice pack down. "Are you sure?"

"She can't hurt other people if she's not around them, right?"

"You do realize that's probably what they thought when they sent you to the hospital?"

"I do."

"And that it didn't work? You still hurt people."

"I'm not locking her up and drugging her. I'm just taking away some of the temptation. Some of the women who work in the mall teach their kids from home. I could do that."

Doubt knitted Julian's brow. "*You're* going to home-school her?"

Ava might've been offended if he didn't have a point. She'd spent her prime education years in Taunton Asylum and didn't have nearly enough qualifications to educate a child. Besides, the last thing Sophie needed was more alone time with her contagious mother.

She slapped the ice onto Julian's palm and guided it to his injured side as she shuffled to the closet. She flicked on the interior light and dove into the medical chest, withdrew a few cotton swabs, and a tube of antibiotic ointment.

He pointed at her. "Light dressings, remember? I don't want to look like I'm lactating through my shirt. I'm sure you understand."

"I don't, actually," Ava said, priming a swab. "Never lactated. Never been pregnant."

"Right. Sorry."

"Maybe Moira Shunn can teach her," she said, swiping on a thin layer of antibiotic. "She's the one who told me about what happened at the party. She saw what Sophie did and brought her home. She's a retired schoolteacher and said she was available to babysit."

The comparison between babysitting and homeschooling was ludicrous, but only Julian's expression said it.

"Let me try at least," she continued. "If it doesn't work out, I promise I'll bring her to see you."

Julian nodded but said nothing. When she finished dabbing on the ointment, he pulled on his shirt. The material waved as he worked, framing the delicate trail of black fuzz that disappeared down the front of his pants.

"Ava?"

She flinched and dropped the ointment. Picking it up, she ducked into the closet, and when she spun around, Julian stood with her cane in hand. Surprised, she stumbled backward, knocking against a tangled forest of steel, leather, and faux-fur handcuffs.

"Are you going to be okay?"

"I'll be fine." She slipped past him to the table, where she gulped lukewarm water. By the time he joined her, the ointment had leaked through his shirt and made him look like he was lactating, but she didn't mention it.

She swiftly threw on her coat and headed for the door. "I'm sorry about earlier. The quickie thing."

His nose crinkled like a bad taste was climbing over his tongue, but he said, "It's fine."

"Oh, before I go, there's something else. If this works out, if I can hire Mrs. Shunn, I'll need to manage my money better. Right now I'm just shoving it in a drawer, and that's not going to work. And the bank wouldn't let me open an account seeing as I'm unmarried. They actually suggested I have my father come in. My *father*."

"I'm sorry. That's not right."

She shrugged. "It's nothing compared to what Jackie Hamilton has to deal with. Either way, I need a better way to save for Sophie's future."

"Let me talk to Antonia and see if there's anything she can do."

He smiled, so did she, and however brief, it was enough to heal the rift between them. He lightly squeezed her arm, only then noticing the ointment seeping through his shirt sleeve. He was chuckling as he cursed, and Ava couldn't help chuckling too.

It felt good to trust each other again. And yet, a part of her still wished he'd throw his arms around her and say, "You've come so far. Let's go the rest of the way together."

But then she remembered the bruise on his neck, someone else's bruise, and a world away, on a blood-stained beach, Faye Norton howled with laughter.

CHAPTER TEN

A S THE YEARS PASSED, Sophie Francis remained a knot in Ava's throat, tightening, bulging, even calcifying as she developed into a rebellious young woman.

When Ava first took Sophie out of school, the girl loved it. She felt special. And in the beginning, she had lots of fun learning from Mrs. Moira Shunn. Ava was ecstatic that they got along, because now dividing her time between therapy, JCPenney, and her new job waitressing at the Robin Hood pub in Sunvalley Mall, Sophie was spending more time with her tutor than anyone else.

Despite pangs of jealousy, Ava was grateful her daughter had a maternal authority figure who wouldn't unconsciously corrupt her. No matter how many times Julian insisted it was ludicrous, it was still one of her greatest fears. And when another year passed without a violent incident from Sophie, she believed more and more it was true.

But even though Sophie hadn't had any incidents like the one at Jenna Galloway's party, there were times her mind felt fuzzier, and time seemed to disappear into itself. It usually happened when she was angry with her mother, which became more frequent as Sophie aged. Ava did her best trying to ignore the problem, but when Sophie attacked her with a broken mirror shard during a spell, it was impossible to deny the madness was with her for the long haul.

She tried to explain to Sophie that she wasn't bad, or

247

damaged; she just had something different in her, and it made her special. But how was Ava supposed to convince her daughter it was true when she didn't believe it herself? She'd made progress with Julian, but parts of her still felt not-quite-right . . . not-quite-human . . . and she was sure Sophie could see it. In Ava's eyes, the little girl saw an unwavering truth that, for her, "special" meant "damaged."

Some days it hurt to be around Sophie. She wanted to be with her daughter, but she wasn't confident during those times she could keep the pain to herself. So she abandoned her daughter to be with someone designed to take it.

The rising stress of two jobs and a crabby preteen increased the frequency of Ava's damping sessions; so much, in fact, that Julian was sometimes already stripping off his shirt when she entered his office. Julian's body had thickened with muscle, and flecks of silver sprouted along his temples. Though his face still possessed angelic Roman features, small scars and divots appeared in certain shades of light, and Ava found her fingers lingering on those beautiful flaws as she applied ointment. Sticky feelings turned over in her like the cotton candy machine at the Flying Horses. His scars felt like hers. She wanted to be the cause of them all. After Sophie's second year of homeschooling, Ava was convinced most of his contusions did belong to her. She cataloged them in her mind, mused about them when she was bored at work, pondered whether he thought of her when he washed off the blood later that night. A yellow aura ringed his right eye from the blow Ava dealt him earlier in the week, but it probably wouldn't have been noticeable to anyone who hadn't buried their knuckles in his eye socket.

She stared at it, unwittingly twisting knots into her sweater sleeves as she wondered how hard she'd need to press on the healing contusion for him to cry out.

"You look agitated," he said, clicking his pen.

She shrugged. "Rough day at the Robin Hood."

"What happened?"

"Nothing special. It's just—I told you how it's decorated like Sherwood Forest in there, right? Everywhere I look there are trees and meadows, like the ones on the Vineyard where I used to camp out. Sometimes when I get in the weeds and can't keep customers straight, I disappear into that forest. Or want to, at least."

"Where you camped out with Paul."

"Yes. I've never seen him there, but sometimes I feel like I'm right on the edge of it, that he's waiting for me just out of view. I do all right easing myself down from that feeling, though."

He smiled. "I hope you know how proud I am of you, Ava."

She did know. She also figured he took pride in most of his patients. But a frail star of hope still glowed in her that he regarded her above all others. Because he believed in her. Because he cared for her.

Because he secretly loved her as much as she loved him.

She chuckled to herself. It made more sense to say, " . . . as she believed she loved him," because Ava Francis absolutely could not love Dr. Archer. She admired him for his selflessness, his courage, his dedication to his family and profession, and she'd never deny that he was an attractive man, but he was also an impossible man. Almost fictional in his passion, beauty, and good sense.

An uncommonly sneaky smile crossed his face then, and Ava giggled nervously.

"What's that look about?" she asked.

"I have something for you." He didn't disappear into the closet like he usually did. He held eye contact the entire time as he reached in, plucked her gift from the wall, and offered it to her on open palms.

The black leather riding crop compelled Ava to glide closer. Not just because she hadn't seen it before, but because it was studded with brass rings.

"It's yours," he said, and she gazed into his emerald eyes. "Only yours."

Ava's soul crackled like a bouquet of sparklers as she tested the crop's flexibility and snap. She danced her fingers over the soft leather and cool brass rings. She'd never used anything like this before. How much damage would it inflict? Would it bruise him instantly? Would it draw blood?

For a moment, as clouds played with the rays of orange light streaming through the window, Ava thought Julian might tell her everything she wanted to hear. It was a moment of pure tranquility, and as such, it was destined to die hard.

"Is this like the house?" she whispered as she examined the crop. "Or the bank account?"

"What do you mean?"

"How many others have their own damping tools?"

"That's not important."

She exhaled a feeble laugh. "Of course it isn't."

Julian was smart, open-minded, and forgiving, and he gave her hope like no other, but she didn't want to be one in a long line of placated patients. She didn't want to be told she was good and sane and capable of living a full life when she knew she wasn't.

But she also didn't want absolute truth. Her actual desire was a tricky planet to reach in a universe clogged with shame and craving, especially when a traveler needed to sidestep the many debris fields and black holes belonging to a shadow galaxy named Avery Norton.

As she lifted the brass-studded crop, the pieces of her that prayed he would fix her heart instead of her mind expanded like a balloon that filled her so completely the fire had no room to grow.

It was surprisingly unpleasant.

Romantic thoughts about Julian often permeated her mind and wriggled their way into her dreams, but she'd refused to believe they had any place in reality.

Until he placed the crop in her hand and said, "It's yours. Only yours."

The contradictions infuriated her. She'd been seeing him long enough to know she was probably acting irrationally, but this gesture was nothing if not a declaration of intimacy.

With her fingers wrapped tight around the instrument, she exhaled her doubts and inhaled the possibility that she could also be his, only his.

"You have no idea what this means to me, Julian."

"Oh, I think I do."

His arched eyebrow regaled her with a fairy tale she'd spun to herself many times at night, but as usual, it ended before she got to the good stuff.

"I want my patients to be comfortable," he continued. "I wouldn't be a very good therapist otherwise."

Her fingers loosened, and the crop fell to the floor.

She was wrong. She was always wrong. Just when she thought the battle might be nearing its end, her fantasies had once again led her astray.

"What a foolish little rabbit."

The voice was the eye of a hurricane, a calm wet rasp, with whipping wind on its edges, threatening to toss her around like a robin's egg in a rock tumbler.

Ava's focus shifted, and the balloon burst, propelling self-hatred and insanity through her bloodstream as she stared at the scorched woman behind Dr. Archer's desk.

Faye grinned blackened shards of teeth, and the gash in her left cheek lengthened to a yawning ravine. "All these years you've learned nothing," she said. "You're the same silly girl slobbering after a sinful boy like a brain-dead puppy. He wanted you to channel your madness into him, sweetie, and you've done exactly that. You've given him the only thing that made you special."

"I don't want to be special if it means being like you."

As she stared at Faye's wheezing grimace, Julian called to her from afar, begging her to come back to him.

"Yes," Faye hissed. "Run, little rabbit. Back to your master. Back to your whore."

"He's not a whore," Ava growled.

"You pay him," she said. "You love him, you hurt him, and you pay him. If that's not a whore, I don't know what is."

"You don't know anything. You thrive on assumption, and maybe you were right sometimes, maybe even about me, but you're not right about Julian. And you were never right to hurt all those people."

"All those people?" Faye chortled. "Oh Avery darling, your body count blows mine out of the water. I admired you, really. I was never so rotten." She lifted a charred, broken fingertip. "And you know I mean that as a compliment."

Julian dug his nails into her flesh, but they were feathers compared to the bolt of heat radiating from her mother's corpse.

"I haven't been that person for a long time, Mom."

"Oh, that's quite clear, dear. It used to upset me, but not anymore. It's Sophie's time to shine, and she's going to make her grandma so proud."

"No!" Ava grabbed the riding crop and dove at the ghost, but Julian latched onto her arm. He spun her from the desk, but it didn't remove Faye from Ava's vision. The more he swung her around, the more mothers sprouted around her. All grinning, all patient, all confident phantoms of Faye Norton determined to destroy the last shred of good in their youngest daughter's soul.

"You're not going to touch her! You're not ruining her like you ruined me!"

"Of course not, dear. You've done it quite well already."

Ava swung the crop with increasing fury. Even when the tool slipped bloody from her fingers, she didn't stop. Someone was yelling at her, pleading with her, but the desperate screams were garbled, and confusion further enraged her. With fingers crooked into claws, she swiped and scratched until a fist like a spiked flail struck the side of her head with a blinding crack.

The blow launched her backward onto the coffee table, and she fell moaning to the carpet as Julian stood over her, red and trembling.

The door flew open and Margie gasped. "Dr. Archer, are you okay?" Squinting at Ava, her hand moved behind her back, and she drew a small silver pistol out of her waistband.

Blood pooled in Ava's mouth when she sat up. She swallowed, and her skull ached, as did her abdomen where the table struck her between the ribs. Holding her side, she leaned against the couch and wished she faced a dozen murderous mothers instead of the person she trusted most in the world glaring at her like a slimy clump of seaweed.

Julian requested Margie put the gun away. "I'm fine. Ms. Francis is fine. She did, however, break one of the most important rules. When I say 'stop,' you stop."

"I didn't hear you," she squeaked.

"Yes, I know." He sniffed back blood and whispered for Margie to wait outside. She hesitated, squinting at Ava, then shuffled out, closing the door behind her.

Julian marched past his patient, her body still in a quivering lump against the couch, and into the closet, where he wiped most of the blood from his face. The scratches swelled instantly, though, and his lacerated scalp bled so heavily it took four bandages to patch. Blood still gummed up one nostril, and red streaks ran down his throat onto his chest when he emerged to find Ava hadn't moved, couldn't move, for all the body-clenching shame.

"This is my fault," he said, summoning her tearful gaze. "And I need to put a stop to it before one of us does something we can't take back." He crouched beside her and lifted the crop from the floor. Swallowing hard, he closed his fingers between the bloody brass rings, and his chin quivered. "You broke the rules, Ava. But so did I. I opened the door for this."

"Julian, it was an accident."

"I know."

"It won't happen again."

"I know that too."

She was on her feet then, but the muscles were still tense and throbbing, and her voice creaked out in pleading run-on sentences.

"It hasn't happened in so long, Julian, and you said yourself you were proud of me, because I truly haven't seen my mother like that in years, and I really thought I could handle her, so please, give me another chance, just one more chance."

"I can't, Ava."

"That's not fair. I refuse to believe your other exertion patients don't slip up."

"Not in a long time."

"Oh great! So I'm just the sickest person there is? No wonder you're kicking me out!"

He stood with a huff, wincing when his nostrils flared. Crossing his arms over his chest, he leaned against his desk and stretched his jaw. "Ava, none of my other patients have slipped up lately because I haven't done exertion therapy for anyone but you in two years."

Her face scrunched. "What? I don't understand. I thought this was your legacy."

He pushed off the desk and swung around to the window where he peered through his reflection to the waning orange day. At last he said, "Not anymore." There was pain the size of a grave in those four syllables, and it seemed he was suddenly so far away on the other side of the office.

"Why not?"

He replied slowly, his voice soft and shaking in anguish. "Because I can't stop thinking about you."

She'd never seen fear affect him so powerfully. He'd never been so young and fragile. He almost seemed an impostor in those moments of vulnerability. Maybe it wasn't him at all. Maybe Faye was just the first of many liars come to torture her today. That's what she wanted, after all: for Ava to once again fall into love's inexorable ruination and emerge the killer she was meant to be.

"I don't believe you," she said. "Julian wouldn't say this. He's disappointed in me. He's afraid of me. This is a lie."

"God, I wish it were," he said, looking over his shoulder. "Not because you don't deserve love, but because I don't know why this is happening to me. I don't know how to reconcile what I'm supposed to be now, how I'm supposed to act, or how I feel about you."

His fingertips glided over the glass as he turned around, like it was his last connection to a world that made sense to him. The one he was having so much trouble facing was a world of chaos and death. Of course he'd be hesitant. Of course he'd be disgusted with himself for being attracted to such a horrible place and such a toxic person.

He broke from the window, and she headed for the door.

"Ava, stop. Please."

There was no exhaling the tension in her stomach as she turned to Julian Archer. She'd nearly forgotten the scratches she'd dealt him, but it was impossible now. They were bright scarlet, shiny with fresh blood; she thought she could even see them pulsing as he strode to her.

He lifted his hand slowly, as if contemplating whether she would feel any different than a sane woman, then rested it gently against her bloody cheek.

"How *do* you feel about me?" she whispered.

"I don't know what it is, but . . . " He shook his head. "It's strong enough that I knew it was wrong to continue treating patients like I was. It wasn't fair to them."

"If you really are Julian Archer," she started, "and this is how you really feel, it means my mother was right about me. It means I'm right about myself. I'm a disease, and you're riddled with me." She broke free and searched for her coat. "I need to go. I need to get out of here before this sickness kills you too."

"Don't you want something more? Ever?"

She stopped at the door and shot him a mournful glower.

"After all these years, all this progress," he continued. "Don't you want something deeper. Not with me, I mean, but with someone? Someone who won't hurt you?"

"Of course I do. God, Julian, my own daughter doesn't even know me. I work myself ragged for someone who doesn't know how much I loved her father, or how beautiful Natalie was, or that I killed her grandmother for trying to kidnap and corrupt her. All I want is someone who can know me and look past all the shit to see the woman I could've been. Do you think I want to be this absolute black hole of a human being? Do you think I want to be ice cold on the outside and a raging fire inside with no way to let it out, no way to blend or normalize or even pretend I was built for something besides pain? When most people talk about having a fire inside them, it's a good thing; it's passion. Well, my passion ruins lives. God knows it's ruined mine. It's probably ruined Sophie's too, and I refuse to let it happen to you."

"But I do see that woman, Ava. Antonia and I saw it from the very beginning; we wouldn't have kept meeting with you otherwise."

"And how does *she* feel about this?"

He dropped his gaze, and Ava nodded.

"You haven't told her. That makes sense. That's smart. I need to be sensible and smart too, for your sake at the very least."

A pearl of blood was rolling down his temple, but it wasn't as captivating as his bruised cheeks or swollen lips or the pulse throbbing hard on the right side of his throat. She wanted so badly to taste his heartbeat, to carry it around on her tongue like a communion wafer, the sacred flavor melting into her until she was the worthy woman he always believed her to be.

HARES IN THE HEDGEROW

But for that to happen, Julian Archer would have to relinquish everything that made him an admirable man. He'd have to set aside both heritage and integrity. Maybe even humanity. Loving a killer had to cause a kind of erosion for which Julian couldn't be prepared.

His emerald eyes burned, somehow brighter with the surrounding inflammation. He was, without question, the most beautiful man she'd ever seen, and it broke her heart.

She desperately wanted to tell him how often he possessed her thoughts. She desperately wanted to pull him close and kiss him. Instead, she walked out of Julian's office without a word.

257

CHAPTER ELEVEN

OVER THE NEXT two months, not a day passed that Ava's disease didn't present itself. Thoughts that hadn't troubled her for years rose from the earth, clawing and turning over the soil of her past until she found herself crouched in the JCPenney dressing room, feet tucked up and fingers crisscrossing her mouth to hold the fire inside while shoppers paced and knocked and asked, "Miss, do you have this in a size two?" until the end of her shift. Then it was time to strip off her pastel Penney's uniform, wrap a Robin Hood apron around her waist, and do it all again. She spent a lot of time in back rooms and bathrooms trying not to drown in her fire, and because of it, her relationship with Sophie deteriorated even faster.

But not tonight. Tonight she'd make up for it. Tonight she'd leave her problems in the attic and focus on making Sophie's fourteenth birthday the best it could be. Because Ava was searching for a new apartment, she had to keep the party small and cheap, which led Sophie to assume there'd be no party at all. But Ava had enough left over in Robin Hood tips to surprise her daughter with a few gifts and a dark chocolate cherry cordial cake.

In the attic, she wrapped a stack of records in newspaper and sprinkled way too much glitter on top. Blowing off the excess coated the attic floor in gold, but she figured the empty apartment could use a little sparkle anyway. She hadn't been up there in nearly a year, and it had accumulated a thick rug of dust that swallowed any trace of her visits to the past.

She was curling the last ribbon when the door to the attic apartment creaked, and she froze in the glittery dust.

Julian's face popped in, pale and apologetic before he ever uttered a word.

Ava was relieved it wasn't Sophie, but the tension between her and her former therapist quickly devoured any comfort. "If this is about the rent, I'm signing over my next Penney's check to you. Once I find a place in my price range, I'll be out of your hair."

He stepped in, silent, and the purple gift box in his hands shimmered in the sunlight. "For Sophie."

"Oh." Ava stood and knocked the glitter off her hands. "You didn't have to do that, but thank you. I'm sure Sophie will appreciate it."

"You don't think she'll wonder why the landlord's giving her a present?"

"I guess it depends what it is."

"It's a harmonica," he said. "I figured it would be a torturous gift for most parents, but you said she picks up instruments really easy, so maybe the learning process won't be so bad for you."

He was wearing a charcoal suit and black tie—she recognized both—but they looked different now, like they belonged to his father instead of him.

"Have you lost weight?" she asked.

He smiled and lowered his focus to his loafers. "Maybe a bit. Or the swelling's finally gone down."

With one friendly allusion, she was back in his office, his body bare and blood-glazed in the streaking moon. Ava bit her lip and told herself she hated him for drawing her in so easily.

She cleared her throat and carried the presents past him to the kitchen. Stacking them with the cake, she leaned on the counter with her shoulders hitched to her ears. "Are you back doing exertion therapy?"

"No. You?"

She frowned. "I haven't hurt anyone, if that's what you mean."

"It's not what I mean."

"Then what, Dr. Archer? Why are you acting like we're just two ordinary people exchanging pleasantries? Why are you pretending I'm not a murderer and you're not a—"

Faye's ghost had burned the word "whore" into Ava's mind. It echoed there now as Julian narrowed his eyes. He could see the word inside her, she was sure of it, so she pushed it back, down her throat, and swallowed hard. The word hurt all the way down, hitting her belly like a jagged eggshell, but she was able to force a small smile through the pain.

"You're dangerous, Dr. Archer."

His entire body flickered with surprise. "I've been called a lot of things in my life, but that's a new one."

"What about what you told me?" she asked. "Was telling one of your patients you can't stop thinking about them new? Or have you tried to date others?"

Surprise crumpled to nothing, and a dark cloud passed over his face. "No, I haven't." He turned his back on her, his shoulders hunched and hands rising slowly as if to catch the sorrow that slipped out of him so suddenly.

His pose sent shameful shivers through Ava's skin, and she apologized.

"I didn't mean that. I was just thinking . . . well, the condo and the bank account—"

"All these years, Ava. You must not think very much of me to still be so suspicious of my kindness."

"Because you have no reason to be kind to me. I can't even find a reason to be kind to myself. And whatever else you were feeling, it's wrong. It has to be."

"Do you think I don't know that? This is my life. I could lose everything. And for what? A woman who's still holding onto a world that doesn't want her anymore." He faced her, exhaling heavily. "You are not Avery Norton. You believed it once, that your mother killed that girl as well, but here you are more than a decade later still sheltering her in your soul. Faye and Paul are the least dangerous of your ghosts.

260

Avery's the most vicious of them all, and if you can't let her go, I doubt you will ever feel happiness again. Or safety. Or love."

"What about you? You're quick to judge my life, but how have *you* embraced love all these years?"

"I've been working," he replied, adding softly, "And since you asked, I was dating a woman when Antonia and I started treating you."

The confession struck Ava's stomach with unexpected nausea. "I . . . I didn't know. You never talk about yourself."

"That's not what a therapist does. But I'm not your therapist anymore. According to you, I won't even be your landlord soon. But I thought maybe we could be friends. I wanted that once."

Her stomach was still whirling, but the nausea had morphed into something else. She raked her top lip with her teeth. "I wanted it too. I guess I still do. It's hard to be friends with someone when they can't actually know you, but you do know me. You're the only one."

"And do you want to know *me*?"

She smiled. "I always have." Clearing her throat, she fiddled with the curly ribbons on Sophie's present. "Who was the woman you were dating?"

He sat on the windowsill, the sunset framing his lean but athletic build in a rosy glow. "Her name was Victoria. I met her just out of medical school, when I was starting in my parents' practice. I loved her right away, more than I thought humanly possible. Sometimes during sessions I found myself thinking about her instead." He laughed. "Antonia put a stop to that right away. She didn't suffer unprofessional behavior of any kind. God, if she saw me now . . . " His cheeks burned, and his focus fell to his hands as he sniffled. "Anyway, I thought that was it: me and Victoria, together forever. But things didn't turn out that way. She loved all my little quirks, my family, my dedication to the practice, but she didn't know about the Archer legacy. I wanted to marry her and start a family of our own, but I couldn't in good conscience propose without telling her the whole truth. I tried to explain that although I wasn't a damper yet, it was expected of me. And more than that, I *wanted* to be a damper. I wanted to be an Archer, in blood and bone and service, and I thought—I hoped—she'd understand."

"She didn't?"

"No, she didn't."

"I don't blame her," Ava said. "It's not the easiest sell for someone without . . . " Her gaze rolled up to the crossbeams laced with vacant spiderwebs. Where were their masters? Were they working together elsewhere, building intricate condos of their own in the attic cracks? Were they watching the killer called Ava fumbling for the right word? Although she hadn't hurt anyone but Julian in over a decade, she was still very much a killer. She'd changed a lot over the years but not enough, she believed, to call herself sane. But neither was she insane. She had troubling thoughts, that's all, and a few strange urges. But didn't everyone? What were those people called? What word was she looking for? Ghosts?

Or bad water . . .

She sucked on her cheeks and tugged on the ribbon.

"I know what you mean," he said. "I tried explaining it to her, but she couldn't understand. She wanted to see it for herself. She begged me."

"You let her watch?"

He swallowed hard, and his jaw trembled as he looked away.

She'd seen him in pain before. Whether a whisper or a whiplash, it had reconfigured his face in ways that comforted Ava in her worst moments. But this was not one of those faces; it gave her no comfort. In fact, it tugged the same string Sophie did when she was sick or lonely, or all those hours she wailed on the drive to California.

She tried not to feel it, and it looked like Julian was trying too, but both failed miserably. Ava squatted beside him at the window, and when she took his hand, he squeezed his eyes shut and exhaled through pursed lips.

"It was a mild session," he continued. "No tools involved, no blood, but she didn't—she couldn't—"

"She couldn't accept the fact that people were paying to smack around her perfect doctor boyfriend?"

Julian nodded. "Something like that." He slipped his hand from hers and combed it through his hair. "I did all I could to convince her to stay, but there was no point. The moment the patient's fist hit my jaw, my fiancé fell out of love with me. There was no going back to what we were. That's when I realized how much my family really sacrifices for this work—and how lucky my mother was to find someone who loved and accepted her." Grief strangled his voice, and he exhaled an airy chuckle. "I buried myself in work after that. I thought even if I found someone I liked half as much as Victoria, I'd lose her when I told her the truth about my family. No one was worth feeling that kind of pain again. And no one was worth giving up what I love."

"Until me," Ava said. "You stopped seeing the others because of me."

"You broke my concentration," he said, smiling slightly. "Focus is essential to being a damper. I spent my life working to achieve it. Training, strengthening myself—mind, body, and soul—to absorb whatever energy someone throws my way without losing myself in it. And I did. I took eons of pain in just a few moments and all the while felt safe in the calming light of my ancestors."

When he noticed how intently she was listening, he smiled shyly as if he'd turned to an embarrassing picture in a childhood photo album.

"When I gave my body to my patients and my mind to the light, nothing could break my focus. In all my years running exertion therapy, through ache and injury, I kept my thoughts blank and soul protected. But something happened to me when we were together. Thoughts penetrated the wall I'd spent my life building. And once they were in, emotion followed. Then fantasy, romantic and sexual, and not only when we were together. You pulled me. You needed me. You terrified me."

Ava's stomach fluttered with exhilaration and disgrace, and her pulse thumped in her throat and chest and between her legs as she stared into his eyes. "I terrified you? That's horrible. I'm sorry."

Amusement sprouted up one side of his face. "Show me someone who isn't slightly terrified of their lover's hold over them, and I'll show you a lying snake."

The word "lover" vibrated in her ears and rollercoastered through her body, all the way to the tips of her fingers, which went frigid as she fidgeted with her shirt hem.

"I don't mean to make you uncomfortable," he said.

She pushed away from the window and paced the attic, her hands drumming her sides, tugging and clawing and punching her legs to distract her from the man silhouetted by a diving sun.

"It's all right if you don't feel the same way about me, Ava. Truly. I'm not offended. That's why I've given you plenty of space."

Her laughter was part disbelief and part sorrow, the tail end of the chuckle sticking in her throat as he stood up from the windowsill.

"Yes, it would be all right," she said. "Better, actually. But I do feel the same way. That's the trouble. You had a perfect life before me, and I destroyed everything. It doesn't matter how I feel. I'll never be able to get over what I've done to you. You're the first person I didn't have to kill to turn into a ghost. Just like Sophie, I've robbed you of your history. I've ruined your livelihood."

"Yet here I am. I still care about you. I still want you."

"A man like you, someone who enjoys pain, I'm not surprised."

"I *take* it. I don't enjoy it."

"No?"

She slapped him across the face before he could respond, and for the first time, his expression juddered into one of devastating shock. Not a hint of pleasure, nor the clinical blankness that possessed him during exertion sessions. His face reddened and crumpled. He looked like a little boy on the verge of a breakdown, but he didn't explode from the building intensity. He just stood there, watched Ava raise her fist, then closed his eyes in anticipation of the mighty whack. It was in every muscle, clenched and fearful of the next strike. He really was afraid of her. He wasn't a damper now, just a man; a lonely and heartsick man who closed his eyes to absorb her aggression.

She didn't strike again. She hated herself enough for the first one. Her hand fell softly, and with her thumb gliding over the broken blood vessels in his cheek, Ava stamped Julian Archer's lips with a kiss.

His eyelids flipped open, locking on Ava's gaze. Her mouth lingered a moment longer, then disconnected as she lowered off her tiptoes, her calves burning from the charm of reaching for him. Stepping back, her fingers moved to her lips as if trying to hold onto the phantom sensation of the kiss, but he didn't allow her to retreat. He decimated the distance between them when his hand unfolded against her face: fingertips, heel, palm, like a series of tandem kisses from the apple of her cheek to her jawbone.

Though connected, an inexorable universe teemed between their bodies, a paradise of possibility to be explored and worshiped if they only had the courage to swim into the starry depths.

Ava searched Julian's face for a shred of belief that if she kissed him again, she could forgive herself for loving and inevitably destroying him. Her belly churned, but not with rage or flame. It turned over and over like hot caramel in the window of Hilliard's on the Vineyard: a disturbing sensation that could satisfy life's greatest cravings if she could just let it cool.

The universe shrank when she stepped closer, but its energy grew, crackling and keening like colliding fireworks. His fingers slid over her ear and around the back of her neck.

"How are you feeling?" he whispered.

"Just peachy, Doc." She wet her lips, and Julian's gaze fell there.

"Are we alone?"

"It's just us. No ghosts," she said, looking around. "No fire."

"Oh no," Julian said with a lusty chuckle. "There's definitely fire."

He kissed her hungrily, and his heat consumed their constellations. Each glowing point, each imaginary border compacted into a singular shaft of crystalline light. Not the blood-sick roots of the garden or the inferno she'd made of Taunton. Not even the scorched love of Paul in the woods. With Julian, the fire was a refractory beam glowing sharp and aching throughout her body.

She started unbuttoning his shirt, but he stopped her.

"We've done this part," he said. "I want to see *you*."

Ava shivered. She hadn't undressed for sex before, not like this. After being closely monitored during baths in Taunton, Ava didn't spend time fretting over other people's opinion of her nudity, but she suddenly felt strange about it. Just because she didn't mind being naked didn't mean she thought any part of her body was alluring. She wasn't nearly as gaunt as when Julian had met her, but she was still thin and flat-chested, and her legs were more muscular than most women her age. As much as she protested caring about whether men thought such things were alluring, she did now. It didn't matter, though. As quickly as disparaging thoughts coasted into her mind, they were faint spots that fluttered through her so quickly she couldn't tell if they were moths or butterflies, there to chew on her or change her. His hands were too quickly on her buttons, slipping them from their sheaths, and coaxing the cloth from her shoulders, which fell to the crooks of her elbows like a mink stole.

She dropped the top to the floor, and Julian dotted her collarbone with kisses as he unlatched her bra. Her stomach briefly knotted with anxiety as his hands parted the mouth of her jeans, but he nuzzled the fear away, and her fingers clawed through his silky silvered hair as he knelt to kiss her deeper.

CHAPTER TWELVE

HEY FELL, but not into sleep. It was a lovely sort of trance that entangled them on the attic floor, their bodies patched with sweat and grime, and faces blazing in placidity. While Ava and Julian were alone, the fire was low. But the higher the moon climbed, the more agitated she became. Realizing she needed to relieve Moira before Sophie's surprise party, she scrambled for her clothes, repeating hushed obscenities that increased in volume when she noticed her bra strap was twisted. She struggled to remove her shirt again, sending one of the buttons flying.

"Calm down," Julian said, kissing her shoulder. "You're already late. What's another minute or two?"

She whipped off her bra and snarled as she straightened the strap. "Maybe everything," she said. "Moira's *this close* to leaving as is."

Julian plucked the runaway button from the floor and dropped it on her palm. "Maybe I should wait for you to get inside, just in case you need backup."

Ava touched his bare chest with drumming fingers. "You don't have to do that."

"Yes, I know." Julian pinched her chin and gave her a peck on the nose. "You don't regret this, do you? This could be really good, Ava."

"*This* has barely begun."

He chuckled. "I've known you over a decade."

"Not this me."

"To be fair, you don't know this you either. And I don't know this me, not how I am with you."

"Not with a killer, you mean."

Julian's forehead furrowed and his eyes darted across her face. "That's *not* what I mean."

"Maybe it should be. It should matter that you've fallen in love with a murderer. You're a good person, Julian. Inside and out, without trying. Do you really want to jeopardize that? You say this could be good, but it could be terrible too. I could be mean. I could be distant. I don't know how to do relationships, maybe even love. I've loved more ghosts than men, and I can't even be certain you're not one of them. I can touch you," she said, stroking his face. "I can feel you and hear you. I can hurt you, but in the end, I might fall right through you."

Julian kissed her hand and clamped it to his chest. "I'm here. I'm real."

"They were all real once."

He embraced her and kissed the top of her head. "We don't have to figure this out tonight. Come on. Let's go give the old girl some relief."

❧

The apartment was quiet, and the smell of burnt toast hung like a specter in the hall. Ava pushed open the door but didn't enter. She stood on the threshold, staring in as a thin canopy of smoke oozed out. There were dark red spots on the kitchen floor that eventually grew to streaks looking like flaring red arrows pointing to Sophie's bedroom.

Julian rushed in first, but Ava leapt over a chair and pushed past him into the bedroom, a scream blaring as she crashed against her daughter's limp body on the bed. She planted her ear to Sophie's chest, and Julian pressed his fingers to her neck. They sighed in unison, but relief caught in Ava's throat when she noticed the red stains on Sophie's hands.

"Mom?" Sophie woke as Ava inspected her daughter's

dirty fingernails, and upon seeing Julian, she scooted away with a whimper.

"Who are you? What's going on?"

"Is she bleeding?" Julian asked.

Ava examined Sophie's head, her sides, her legs, then lifted the stained and dirty fingernails to her eyes.

Sophie pulled back her hand with a snarl. "It's just paint! God, what do you think I did? And who is this guy?" She suddenly winced and pressed her thumb to the middle of her forehead. "Owww. Stupid fumes."

"Lie on down, sweetheart. I'll get you some aspirin."

Ushering Julian from the room, Ava closed the door and started rifling through the cabinets. A few empty aspirin bottles tumbled onto the floor, but Julian collected them and lined them up on the counter.

"I didn't realize you went through so many painkillers."

Ava shook a pill bottle, happy for the rattle. She tipped one out and thanked Julian for his help before pointing him to the door.

"Are you sure you don't want me to stay?"

"I appreciate the concern, but I'm sure everything's fine."

He looked around at the kitchen in disarray, at the smeared red paint on the floor, and started to protest, but she didn't let him finish the first sentence.

"Please, Julian. I don't want to have to explain you today."

"*Explain me?*"

"Who you are, what *we* are."

Close-lipped, he ran his tongue over his teeth and nodded at the floor. "I understand. But you'll tell me how this turns out, right?"

"In therapy?"

"I was thinking more of a date. A real one."

She didn't want to smile. She was still too scared, maybe even dubious that something this good could happen to her. Her lips shook, but also lifted slightly, and the expression instantly brightened Julian's face.

"We'll speak soon."

He nodded again, this time with his chin lifted, and exited on that gust of charm that Julian seemed to slip into so easily.

Once he closed the door, she flipped the lock, exhaled a steadying breath, and returned to Sophie's room. Her daughter jumped when she entered and dropped a baggie on the floor. She ducked to retrieve it, but Ava caught a glimpse of the marijuana before Sophie could tuck it in her pocket. She opened her hand, and Sophie grunted as she passed her the baggie.

"I can't believe this. You've been smoking pot?"

The girl flushed. "Only a little."

"You're fourteen. A little is a lot. Paint fumes, my butt."

"We *were* painting! Me and Dionne and Trey, down by the stream."

"Where's Moira?"

"She left."

"Left? What do you mean she left?"

Collapsing onto her bed, Sophie gripped her head and growled in frustration. "She. Dot. Left. Dot. She was in a foul mood."

"Did you do something? Say something?"

"I didn't say anything. I wanted to paint with my friends and Moira said I couldn't. But it's my birthday—"

"So you *did* do something."

When Sophie growled again and covered her face, Ava's brain boiled with rising anger. She smacked the edge of the bed, prompting her daughter to spring up in shock. They stared at each other, red-cheeked, panting, neither wanting to be the next to speak. The exasperation weighing down Sophie's expression made Ava think her daughter would explode with high-pitched defenses, but the reply, "It's my birthday," tumbled out small and fearful.

"That's no excuse to act out."

"*She* was acting out. She said if I passed the quiz I could hang out with my friends, but she didn't say she was going to come along. She wouldn't leave us alone. I didn't do anything to her, and she tried to pull me away from them." Sophie lifted her sleeve and showed her mother a small bruise on the inside of her wrist. "She grabbed me hard. She tried to drag me away."

"Moira? I've never seen her lay a hand on you before."

"How could you? You're never here."

Ava's mouth went dry. "Fine. Then what happened?"

The top half of Sophie's face remained creased, the remaining anger gradually morphing into confusion, but the bottom went slack. Her lip dragged as if the words were new swimmers on the edge of a diving board. "I . . . don't know," she replied slowly. "Like I said, she left, and I came home, and . . . " She sniffed the air, then gasped. "My toast! I was making toast because I felt sick. But then I smoked some pot, and I must've fallen asleep."

"You could've set the house on fire."

"I'm sorry. It was an accident. Maybe if you'd been here like you said . . . "

"Don't tell me where I should or shouldn't be, young lady. I'm the adult here."

"Don't I know it," Sophie muttered, crossing her arms over her chest. "And you better believe I'm going to do everything I can to not grow up to be an adult like you."

Ava's face crumpled, and she rose from the bed. "I'm doing the best I can. I'm sorry it's not good enough for you."

"You really think it would be good enough for anyone? I never see you, Mom. I never see anyone."

"You see Dionne. And Trey, apparently."

"I want to go to public school."

Ava sighed as she stood from the bed. "Not this again, honey. You know why we can't do that."

"But I haven't had a spell or anything in a long time."

"What about today?" she said, heading for the kitchen. "You got paint all over the floor, and you passed out making toast."

"I felt sick. I was stoned. It wasn't a spell."

Ava squirted soap onto a sponge and thrust it into Sophie's hand. "If you don't remember doing this much damage, how can you be sure it won't happen in the middle of class, or in the hallway? And what about Moira? I'm supposed to fire her after all these years of loyalty?"

"Yes please," Sophie said, as she scrubbed the stained tiles. "She's been a pain in my ass since I was ten."

"Sophie, for the love of—" Ava slumped at the table and rubbed her temples. "She's been good to us." When Sophie showed her the bruise again, she exhaled heavily. "Before today, anyway. You said yourself she inspired a few of your songs."

"You can only write so many songs about killing the babysitter." Sophie snickered as she wrung the sponge in the sink, but Ava abruptly cut her off and whipped her around with a bellow.

"That's not funny. Do you hear me?"

"It was a joke, Mom."

"Killing is not a joke. These spells aren't jokes. This is serious."

Sophie pushed herself free of her mother, and tears sprang to her eyes. "If it's so serious, why don't you just lock me up in a nuthouse. I know that's what you want to do. It's basically what you've been doing since you took me out of elementary school. You want to lock me up and throw away the key so you never have to see me again."

"You couldn't be more wrong about that."

Sophie rolled her eyes. "Right. Well, it looks like you have this pretty much figured out. I'll be sure to submit your name for the Mother of the Year award." She sauntered down the hall to her room, but she swiveled in her doorway, her focus narrowing on the presents under the kitchen table.

"Are those mine?"

Her brow still furrowed, Ava retrieved the sparkly records.

"Happy birthday, sweetheart."

Sophie grumbled a thanks as she tore off the newspaper and squinted at the album on top.

"What's wrong?"

"I already have Joni Mitchell's *Court and Spark*. I listen to it all the time."

Ava's face flushed and her mouth tightened. "Oh. Maybe Dionne would like it then."

She rolled her eyes and tucked the records under her arm, spilling glitter across the carpet. As she turned toward her bedroom, Ava cleared her throat, stopping her.

"I'm not forgetting what you said. Moira shouldn't touch you. No one should."

"Maybe she was defending herself," Sophie said over her shoulder, slowly meeting her mother's gaze. "According to you, I was having a spell. Maybe I *was* trying to hurt her."

"Sophie, if you truly believe that—"

She roared and threw the records to the floor, kicking up a cloud of sparkles. "I don't! I was kidding! And you know what, Mom? If I did have another spell, it's probably because I feel like a fucking prisoner here. I'm all bottled up and all the songs in the world can't change that. Inspiration is useless without results, and no song I ever write will be good because singing is a celebration and, even on my birthday, I have nothing to celebrate. And no one to celebrate with."

"You have me," Ava said.

As Sophie's face crinkled in incredulity, she said, "I don't even know who you are," and slammed the bedroom door in her mother's face.

CHAPTER THIRTEEN

" **I KNEW SHE** didn't love me, but I didn't think she hated me."

Julian set down his mug, and Ava filled it with the watery swill the Robin Hood Pub considered coffee.

"She just doesn't know all the ways you've protected her," he said. "And protected others. It's ignorance, Ava, not hate. She'll grow out of it."

"Well, it feels enough like hate to torture me. And it's worse every day. Some days she won't even look at me, let alone talk to me. Sometimes I start fights about her music just so I can hear her voice."

He folded his hand over hers and sighed. "No word from Moira?"

She shook her head. "I've called a bunch of times, but there's nothing. She just disappeared. I don't know what to do, Julian. Except for her birthday, she hasn't had any spells, and she still claims she didn't have one that day, but I keep having this horrible feeling . . . " She sloshed the dregs at the bottom of the coffee pot and sighed. "Maybe she's right. Maybe Moira just got fed up and left. Maybe I'm punishing Sophie for nothing and she should be in public school with kids her age."

"Maybe."

"And maybe it's the right time to . . . " Her cheeks flushed and she scanned the bar to see if her other customers needed anything.

"To what?"

She gnawed on the inside of her cheek. "To tell her . . . about us."

"Us? This is the first time we've seen each other since Sophie's birthday."

"I know, and I'm sorry. It's just been crazy."

He tapped the table anxiously. "So you do want there to be an *us*? The last we spoke I wasn't sure what you were feeling."

"Mostly fear, to be honest. But beneath that, I do want this. Us." She drew closer, her voice barely audible. "I want you, Julian."

Splotches of scarlet appeared at Julian's temples as he grinned, but white stripes interrupted his blush. Stripes she'd given him. It was all so wrong, and so exhilarating.

The Robin Hood manager Peggy approached Julian's table in the corner so suddenly that her gruff greeting nearly caused Ava to drop the coffee pot. All teased hair and overstretched polyester, Peggy screwed up her mustached lip.

"Is there a problem here?"

"No, everything's wonderful. Thank you," Julian said.

"Excellent." Squinting at Ava, she muttered, "I think other people need coffee, dear, and Denise just sat table eight."

Ava glanced over at the trio of slovenly, swaying men, their menus flapping the table with a repetitive click. They already had drinks, and by the look of the meaty claws around the glasses, constantly lifting and tilting, they were in for the long haul.

"Shit," Ava hissed. "Buzzy and his bozos."

Patty widened her eyes. "Well?"

"I thought I was getting cut soon. I'm having lunch with my daughter, remember? She still doesn't have anyone at home in the afternoons."

"They asked for your section specifically."

"I got it," Dionne said, pinning her tray under her arm. "Go on and meet Sophie. Tell her I said hi."

The staff change appeared to annoy Peggy, but it was enough to consider the problem solved so she could bark at the next issue cropping up in the kitchen.

With a wink, Ava laid the check on Julian's table. "If there's nothing else I can get for you, sir . . . "

"I'm perfect, thank you." He set down a five-dollar bill, and she giggled.

"What?"

"I just realized this is the first time *you've* paid *me*."

He crinkled his nose in amusement. "I like it this way. This might be our best session yet. For me, at least."

"How's that?"

He shrugged. "What can I say? Watching you is highly therapeutic."

She bit her lip and pretended it was him, slightly resentful that she had to so swiftly redirect her thoughts to the teenage girl who hated her.

Julian was gone by the time Ava finished up her side work and left the bar, but she found him not far from the World's Fare food court, standing in front of Radio Shack and staring at a pyramid of televisions playing two simultaneous news programs. On one channel, veteran reporter Michael Wooden was covering President Nixon's escalating Watergate scandal, but Ginger Borowitz's report hit closer to home. With a somber voice pouring from bright pink lips, she relayed a report about the body of an unidentified female recently discovered in Len Hester Park, less than two miles from Mohr Lane.

"The police have not released the name of the deceased," she said, "and despite some rumored signs of struggle, they would not comment on whether there was foul play involved."

Julian couldn't have known the name "Moira Shunn" was striking like lightning bolts in Ava's mind, but he extended his hand to her as if to say, "Hang on to me. Dig in."

She did just that. Her fingernails sank into his callused

skin until it was over. The reporter's tone abruptly changed to a peppy singsong as she dove into the results of a local football game, but Ava couldn't let go so easily. Nor could the newscaster despite her outward appearance. Ava felt like she was underwater, and Ginger Borowitz was holding her there.

Terror compressed her thoughts until she felt cracks forming in her skull, slowly spreading to ravines, then opening spaces where the thoughts could slip loose, leaking into the rest of her like poison. When someone screeched "Mom!" from the food court, it felt like the fissures widened, and the heavy slosh of fear filled her body. The voice was a skeletal tree branch scraping a bedroom window. It was an overturned bucket of ice into cold bath water. It was sizzling engine oil on the Atlantic. It was Avery Norton, shrieking as orderlies dragged her from Natalie's funeral. The palindromic holler echoed in her brain with nauseating clangs that bashed the will to stand out of her as she gazed across the expanse at the girl with ice blue eyes.

She didn't want to think the corpse was Moira, or that Sophie had any part in it, but she had, many times since the tutor's disappearance. What started as a toxic thought sprouted angry roots that tunneled through the soil of her mind. The more Sophie yelled "Mom," the more they colonized her, and the more Ava considered clawing off her skin so no one would recognize her as the monstrous girl's mother.

"Mom, what's wrong with you?" Sophie had jogged over, giving Julian a curious squint as he floated away from Ava's side. "I've been calling you for a million years."

"Sorry. I got a little lightheaded."

"Oh. Are you okay?"

"I'm hungry, that's all."

Sophie's face puckered, and she glared at her mother like she was the most embarrassing person in the entire world. "Okay, well . . . " She gestured to the food court, and Ava nodded.

"Go on. I'm right behind you."

She followed Sophie at a distance, and Julian followed from even further. He sat two tables away while the Francis women ate, and though he and Ava made frequent eye contact, they didn't share looks of secretive longing as they had in the Robin Hood. Every glance was a plea for help followed by a plea for forgiveness that continued through lunch and on to the skating rink, where Ava tearfully watched Sophie sail the ice.

"Don't jump to conclusions," Julian whispered as he sidled up to her.

"You're thinking the same thing," she said. "Maybe not exactly, but it crossed your mind that she—" She arched her fingers against the railing. "No. I can't say it out loud."

"Because you don't know she did anything wrong."

"And because if she did, it's my fault," Ava replied. "I took her out of school because I was afraid of her being around so many kids. I thought all the pressure and competition, maybe even teasing, might trigger her spells, and she didn't have any way to cope with them once they began. But she hasn't been in school for almost a decade and look what happened. You were right. I did the same thing to Sophie that those doctors did to me. I locked her up so tight the loneliness and resentment had nowhere to go. It just built and built until Sophie exploded . . . right into poor Moira Shunn."

"You don't know any of that for certain."

"Nothing is certain. It never has been for us. Not for me," she said, "and least of all when it comes to her."

Sophie waved to her mother and did a clumsy spin, which Ava applauded until Sophie lost her balance. She teetered then toppled into a pair of boys, who crashed against a girl, who latched onto, then dragged her two friends to the ice.

Ava dashed to the rink entrance, but the kids were laughing and helping each other up by the time she reached them. One of the boys braced Sophie as she righted her blades, and one of the girls complimented her on her sweater before squealing at the Doors song oozing from the stereo.

"I love this song!"

"Me too!" the boy said, and unfolded his hand to Sophie. "Wanna skate?"

She crinkled her nose in deliberation, then smacked her palm onto his while opening her hand to one of the girls. One by one they linked into a human chain that coasted the rink like an ambitious minute hand on a frozen clock face.

Julian approached Ava from behind, his breath on her neck conquering the chill rolling off the ice. "She doesn't look like a killer."

"No, she doesn't," Ava said. "Do I?"

Closing his hand on her hip, he kissed her neck.

She hummed. "That's not an answer."

"You don't think so? I thought it was a pretty good one," he said, kissing her again. "And what does it matter when she looks so happy?"

The human chain had broken, and a long-haired boy was spinning Sophie around the ice. She laughed heartily, her head thrown back in delight.

"That's not a girl who hates or hurts innocent people," Julian said. "She's one of them. She's a normal happy kid."

Ava sighed as she watched her daughter laughing and smacking one of the boys with her mittens.

"And if that dead woman turns out to be Moira?"

He glided out from behind her and leaned against the railing, his eyes directed at the teeming Saturday crowd. "Then you turn her in."

"I can't do that."

"Then you better pray that dead woman isn't Moira."

Ava's breath clouded in front of her. She waved at Sophie but couldn't get her attention. "What the fuck are you telling me, Julian? What am I supposed to do?"

"Are you asking your therapist or your . . . " He bobbed his head.

"My boyfriend?"

"I was going to say 'landlord,' but we can use 'boyfriend' if you want." She kicked him playfully, and he faced the ice again.

"Ava, you know what's best for your child. An hour ago, you thought putting her back in school might be the best thing."

She exhaled heavily, watching her daughter blow hot air into her mittens before putting them on.

"What about me? Who am I supposed to be now?"

Standing beside her at the railing, he sighed. "You're not the woman you were at eighteen, but there's always room to grow, and exertion therapy works for you." His expression curled slyly. "And I'll do that for you, only you, if that's what you want."

"No." She covered his hand in pulsing warmth and shook her head. "You're magical, Julian, and what you do is important. Don't make me the reason you deprive the world of that gift. I already have enough strikes against me. I want you to be happy. I want *her* to be happy." Ava gazed out at her apple-cheeked daughter spinning and laughing with the other kids, but as much as she wanted to feel joy, she couldn't. Her chest tightened as if an invisible fist crushed her heart and flooded her withered organs with poison. "But she's not one of them. She's like me. She's a Norton, and she's dangerous."

"Subjective on both counts," he said. "I'm not denying what you've done, or even what *she* might've done, but everyone's dangerous in some way. Hell, I'm dangerous; you said so yourself. I know your secrets, and I don't have to keep them if I believe there are lives at risk."

"But you don't believe that."

"Not at present," he said. "But it's been a while since our last session. I'd need a new evaluation to be sure." He pinched her thigh, and she giggled but abruptly swallowed it as Sophie zoomed past.

It struck her sadly funny that the smile she gave him

was real and the one she gave her daughter was a cover for the better one.

"I'm not sure this relationship is good for your practice. Have you told Antonia about us?"

"I talk to her every night. About every patient, about you, and, yes, about how I feel when I'm with you."

Her eyes widened, and her fingers became rigid beneath his. "And she's okay with it?"

"I'm an adult. I don't need my mother's approval."

"Which means you didn't get it," she said, retracting her hand.

His mouth tightened and his head drooped as he buried his hands in his pockets. "That's not what it meant, but I understand if you're looking for an exit strategy. It would be easier for you to run away, to ignore whatever this is between us. It would be easier for me too, honestly. I won't stop you. But if you do run, you'll have to accept that your abandonment has nothing to do with me. Because I want to know you, Ava. I want to know everything. And I want to know her," he said, tossing a glance at the rink. "I don't want to hide anymore. But I don't want to rush things either, especially if you're re-enrolling her in school. One step at a time."

With a grateful smile, she scooted closer and leaned in to kiss him, but noticing Sophie's swift approach with the other kids, Julian spun away, one eye on Ava as he crossed the mall.

Sophie threw herself against the railing and howled. "Hey Mom, these kids were saying there's a spooky haunted house thing at Ygnacio. It sounds fun."

Nothing about a haunted house sounded fun to the woman who used to be Avery Norton, but she found herself nodding when Sophie asked if she could go. Maybe her heart was too weak or her mind too tired, or maybe she just wanted to spend more time with Julian, but neither appeared to believe it when she agreed to let Sophie go with them.

"Really?" Sophie squealed.

"Yes, really."

"You're going to love it," said one of the girls, linking her arm with Sophie's. "There's apple-bobbing and dunk tanks, and people wear the craziest costumes. You're gonna flip, I promise." As their voices disappeared in the singing swish of their blades across the ice, Julian Archer slid to his place beside Ava again.

"You're going to let her go off with friends? Without knowing about Moira?"

She stared ahead, frozen. "I guess so."

"I'm proud of you. It's a big step overcoming your fear like that."

"I didn't overcome it. I just realized I'll always be afraid, and I'm not going to drive myself crazier looking for it or burying myself in worry. I'm going to do one thing my mother never could," she said. "I'm going to let go. I'm going to let her live the life she wants. And I'm going to live the one I want."

"I hope I get to see that," Julian said.

"You will. And once everything's settled, when she's in school and I'm back in therapy, I promise you, Julian, you will know us."

CHAPTER FOURTEEN

AKIO MIO WAS hunched in the doorway of his basement apartment, barely visible between a pair of stout police officers, when Ava entered with groceries. Only one officer looked over his shoulder as she shuffled to the stairs, but after he whispered to his partner, both swiveled to stare at her.

She readjusted her sweaty grip on the shopping bags and tried to finagle her key out of her pocket, but the officers were on her before she could hook her pinky into the key ring.

"Excuse me, Miss. Do you live here?"

She swung out her keys with a huff. "Yes sir, and I'm dying to get inside, so if you wouldn't mind—"

The older of the men slid two grocery bags out of her fist, allowing her to unlock the door. It wasn't what she was looking for, but she thanked them anyway, dropped the rest of the groceries on the table, and prayed this wouldn't be the day she discovered another hare in the house.

The policeman set the other bags on the table and fished a notepad out of his pocket. He had a lot of notes already, names mostly, one of which was circled several times.

"Is your name . . . "

Not Avery Norton, not Avery Norton . . .

" . . . Ava Francis? Mother of Sophie Francis?"

"Yes, that's me. I mean, that's us."

"I'm Officer Harker, and this is Officer Dehaney," he

said, gesturing to the white-haired policeman. "Your neighbor told us you often had an older woman visit the house. A family member?"

Ava could see Mio's apartment from her kitchen, the door anyway, which he quietly shut when they met eyes.

"No, not a family member," she said. "I'm sorry, can I offer you gentlemen some water?"

"No, thank you," Harker replied. He removed his hat and wiped his forehead with his sleeve. "So she was a friend?"

"An in-home tutor," Ava said, putting the frozen items away. "She homeschooled my daughter for several years, but she up and left earlier this year, and Sophie's over at Ygnacio High now anyway. Why?"

She sat at the table, not trying to focus on the clock counting down to Sophie's usual post-school arrival time.

"We discovered a body in Len Hester Park some months back," Dehaney said. "Perhaps you read about it?"

"Now that you mention it."

"And you said this tutor of yours left earlier in the year?"

She inhaled sharply, then ever so carefully raised her hand to her lips. "Wait a minute. You're not telling me it was Moira, are you?"

The officers flinched, and the one with the notepad scribbled something beside the circled name. "Moira? That's what she called herself?"

Ava scrunched her face, expelling a dry chuckle. "Well, that's her name. Moira Shunn."

The officers looked to each other and Ava sat back, the chair pressing into her shoulder blades.

"That *is* her name, right?"

"One of many it seems," the younger officer said. "And you said she tutored your daughter? Is your daughter here?"

"She's still at school."

"Letting out soon though, isn't it?" he asked, glancing at his watch.

"She takes the long way home with her friends sometimes. You know how kids are."

The way they looked at each other made Ava's stomach clench. But so did the way they glanced into Sophie's bedroom and took stock of the kitchen, the way they watched her fingertips flex against cheap plastic tablecloth. She was afraid to open her mouth again for fear the tight fist her gut had become would squeeze the contents, a greasy Robin Hood Reuben, all over the groceries.

"Ms. Francis, I'm going to be straight with you. This 'Moira Shunn' was a con artist. And if our suspicions are correct, she's also responsible for the disappearance and possible murder of five young girls across the Bay Area over the last thirty years."

She crossed both hands over her mouth and shook her head. "What? I'm sorry, I don't understand. You think Moira's some kind of killer? She was harmless. I mean, she and Sophie had problems, but—"

Shut up, dummy.

Ava's focus shifted to the charred woman sitting opposite her at the table. The plastic grocery bags were melting from Natalie's blistered body heat as she stared at her sister with pleading rage.

Ava's body quaked with terror and self-loathing. She'd been doing so well. She thought she'd actually escaped them, even freed them, but there Natalie Norton sat, every tense and crackling ember urging her sister not to betray their blood.

"We're struggling to understand it ourselves," the policeman continued. "It appears this woman had an affinity for taking young girls under her wing. Meeting them, befriending them, and then—" He cleared his throat. "I'll just say it takes a real viper to make yourself part of someone's home, earn their trust, and all the while plot unspeakable horrors against them. A snake in the grass. A fox in the hen house."

"A rabbit in the garden," Ava whispered.

The men's faces shrank to puckered Os, and Natalie Norton sighed in cinderous disappointment.

"You're going to ruin this," she said. "You're free, Sophie's free, and you're going to rouse their suspicions for no reason."

Ava snapped her lips shut and looked at her feet.

The older officer jumped in. "But your daughter's fine, yes?"

"Yes, of course."

"Then I don't see any cause for concern. Did Moira ever mention other places she worked, other places she lived, other children?"

She hadn't. But Ava had let the woman teach her child god knows what without a single reference or proof of experience. Because it was easier. Because it was safer. Because Sophie Francis nearly killed a little girl with scissors, and what better way to educate her than put her in another killer's hands?

"She said she knew the Galloways," Ava replied. "She was at their daughter's birthday party years back."

The officer jotted down the name and said he'd look into it, but he didn't seem overly concerned. But maybe this was all a ruse to distract her from the fact that Sophie was their actual number one suspect. She straightened her spine and tried to look innocent, whatever that was.

"And this is the woman who worked for you?" he asked, removing a photo from a clipboard. "It's an old photo, so look carefully."

Ava squinted at the picture, but her eyes widened quickly. The woman in the photo was plump with cropped hair and she had a large mole above her left eyebrow. There were similarities between her and Moira, but even if the photo was taken decades before, there was no mistaking it.

"It's not her," she whispered.

"Are you sure?"

She tried not to show her relief, but the giddiness of a narrow escape bubbled up in her belly and doused the crackling inferno. "Yes. I'm sure."

"Well, that's a mercy for your girl's sake," Harker said, snapping the picture back onto the clipboard while the other cop scratched out Moira's name in his notes. "Now, this tutor who went missing . . ."

"I guess she just left," she said, shrugging, her muscles tighter than expected.

"Because of problems with your daughter?"

She shrugged again and pinched a muscle in her neck. With a wince, she rubbed the sore spot and tried to calm herself. She should've been relieved that the corpse in the park wasn't Moira, but a persistent thought wouldn't allow her body to unclench and enjoy the discovery. Something about Sophie had upset Moira so much that she vanished from their lives. Had she seen something? Had Sophie told her something? When they clashed in the park that day, what was the final straw that sent her tutor running?

Ava cracked her neck and savored the rushing endorphins. "That probably had a little something to do with it. But like I said, she's in public school now and doing very well."

"Did you file a missing persons report?" Officer Dehaney asked.

She stretched her neck, trying for another satisfying pop, but there was only pain, in her skull, and pressing on the backs of her eyes.

"I didn't think she was missing. I just figured she'd had enough and didn't want the stress of quitting in person. I didn't want the stress either, frankly."

The officers looked to each other—a sort of dubious telepathy that made Ava's organs cold and twitchy—and then both issued tight-lipped smiles.

"We're sorry to have bothered you," the younger cop said, "and to have stirred up your feelings about this Moira person. But based on her unprofessional behavior, it seems like your daughter is probably better off without her." He flapped the photo of the woman who'd killed so many before it caught up with her in Len Hester Park. "You can never tell about a person, Ms. Francis. What's inside some of these people's heads . . . it would scare the skin right off you."

"Yes, I imagine it would," she said. "Thank you, gentlemen. If I think of anything that might help with your investigation, I'll be sure to let you know."

The men thanked her for her time, wished her a good day, and Ava closed the door.

She emptied her lungs in one long breath through her nose, fearful the police remained in the hall, ears pressed to the door and listening for sighs of relief. Though silent, the exhalation was strong enough to scatter Natalie's ghost like smoke, and Ava felt ten tons lighter.

Safe, alleviated, bordering on exhilarated, Ava resumed putting away the groceries, but the sharp jiggle of the doorknob kicked her heart into overdrive again. She flew from the door, hand to her chest, and whirled around to Sophie's crumpled expression—nearly as bewildered as the cops she passed in the hall.

She had a pencil in one fist, a notebook in the other, like a junior detective.

"What the hell, Mom? Are you okay?"

"Fine, just fine," she said, turning her attention to the groceries on the table. "Good day at school?"

Sophie shrugged and focused on her notebook. She also had circled names and starred words, but Ava couldn't imagine it was anything as ghoulish as the scribbles that departed with the officers.

"Is that a new poem?"

Sophie flinched. "Song."

"Would you sing me some?"

"Don't you have to go to work soon?"

Ava glanced at the clock. She actually had a date with Julian, which would probably turn into a damping session, and as much as she wanted to be honest, she nodded like she always did, putting the blame on work.

"Maybe you could sing me some later?" she asked.

"Why were the cops here?"

"Soliciting," she said as she closed the last loaf in the bread box and stuffed the grocery bags under the sink. "I think they got everyone in the building."

"The person upstairs too?"

Ava grumbled. "Sophie, there's no one upstairs. I don't understand why I have to keep telling you that."

"Then I doubt you'd understand my songs either."

Ava sucked on her top lip as Sophie closed herself in her bedroom and turned her music on high. It was The Grateful Dead, she thought, or maybe the Jerry Garcia Band—probably as a reminder of her mother's recent decision to give Sophie permission to attend her first concert if she brought home a perfect report card, which Sophie absolutely intended to do. Ava thought the deal would win her points with the surly teen, but Sophie's determination to attend the concert manifested as contempt for her mother, who she assumed rooted for her failure.

Maybe the kid was right. Maybe she wouldn't understand her songs any more than Sophie would understand the letters to Paul she kept in the attic.

She made two chicken salad sandwiches, ate one in silence, and put the other in the fridge. "I'll be home by ten," she said through the bedroom door to no reply, standing outside the room longer than she cared to admit.

Julian was parking his car when she hurried out of the building, directing him to stay in the driver's seat.

"Not the attic this time," she said. "I need to make noise."

⬥⬥⬥

She was dripping sweat when the flail hit the floor. As she told Julian about her conversation with the police, a chaotic mix of terror and triumph ran her body like a gauntlet. Fear still trickled through her mind, but the room flexed with waves of relief as she untied Julian's wrists. His shoulders wept hot rubies that ran between the blades, and pressing her chest to his back, Ava kissed his soft, sweaty neck, smothering the fear, the fire, and everything grim.

"Come to dinner," she exhaled against his skin.

Julian looked back at her with a half-smile that bloomed large when she sunk her teeth into his shoulder. "Tonight?"

"For Thanksgiving. Well, the day before. I have to work on the actual holiday, so Sophie's going to be annoyed either way. We might as well tick her all the way off."

"Why now?"

She felt his heart quicken beneath her lips, and she kissed his rosy shoulder. "I don't want to wait anymore to tell her about this. I'm ready for it to be real. I'm ready for us."

He faced her, his fingers grazing her flushed cheek and skating over her wet hair. His lip was bleeding and a small welt swelled on his chin, but he didn't appear to be in pain. He looked peaceful, and his voice was devoid of judgment when he spoke. "You saw a ghost today. You saw Natalie."

"Yes, but it was good, if that's possible."

"I imagine it is, if you felt safe."

"If I hadn't, those cops might've been in a heap of trouble."

Julian retracted his hand, his nostrils flared. "Do you really think you're capable of that anymore?"

A fat drop of blood slid down his chin, and she caught it with a kiss. As she lifted her crimson lips to his, he squinted.

"Ava . . . "

"I know, I'm stalling," she said, licking her lips. "But I don't know how to answer that, Julian. I'm not sure I know what anyone's capable of anymore. I do know I'm better with you in my life. You quiet me, and you awaken me. You are the first person I've ever met who knew my madness and offered me mercy. And I would never intentionally do anything to jeopardize your love or friendship." She dropped her gaze and nervously rubbed her hands on her thighs. "But the real question is, do you think *you'll* be better with me in your life? With Sophie and all her degrees of hate for me? God," she whispered. "And she doesn't even know the truth about who I am. Who she is. I need to tell her all of it. And she's going to hate me so much more! Do you really want to get involved in all this insanity? Do you really want to take such a perilous leap?"

He laughed, apologizing immediately. "The word 'perilous' appears twice in the damper's oath."

"I'm not asking as a patient. I'm asking as your . . . " She crinkled her nose. " . . . your Ava. Do you want to do this for real?"

Curling his fingertips around the back of her neck, he glided her face closer. "Your Julian would love to do this for real, in spite of the peril."

When her lips neared, his gaze suddenly dropped, and his pulse raced between her palms.

"But . . . " He exhaled through quivering lips, and his voice still cracked. "Ava, I need to tell you something."

"What?"

He sighed heavily. "I'm the last Archer in the Bay Area. I'm the only one of two in California. My mother thinks exertion therapy will dwindle to nothing over the next few years, and I believe her. All over the country people are shrinking away from shrinks, even the good ones. Especially practices like ours that cater to the poor. People these days want glitz, even if it's fake, even if it's unhealthy. They want their doctors rich and mean and their therapy quick as cure-alls."

"Okay . . . So what are you saying?"

"I'm saying Archer Therapeutics can't sustain itself here much longer. If I want to keep practicing, I'll need to move on."

Ava's face went slate gray as she pulled out of his grip. She suddenly felt so naked, so weak. Her fists went red and aching and it felt like her heart was pinballing her ribs.

"Move on? You mean from me?"

He crinkled his brow. He said, "Of course not," but she barely heard him. The ocean waves were too loud, and the laughter—oh how long it had been since she heard that raspy laughter, coming from the rosa rugosa bushes behind Julian's desk.

The moment her hands flew to her ears, he knew. He pulled them down to her sides and pressed his cheek to hers, whispering desperately. "It's just us, Ava. It'll always be us. I'm not going anywhere without you."

His fingers tightened around her wrists and her lips parted with a shocking flush of pain. He didn't use force on her, didn't need to, but when he unwrapped his hands, and her flesh shone with stripes of white then pink then red, she found herself strangely comforted by his strength.

He kissed her softly, like warm rain rolling down rose petals, and knelt to lean his head against her bare belly. Her wrists felt wreathed in flame, but her stomach was cool, and where he nuzzled it, Ava could swear she felt like a kid again, innocent and free, in a dew-kissed garden.

"So," he started, "what should I bring for Thanksgiving?"

CHAPTER FIFTEEN

JONI MITCHELL BEGGED for help. She lamented that she was falling in love too fast, that she was hoping about the future and worrying about the past. Ava was doing the same, on the verge of tears when Joni spoke about the hot, hot blazes that came down to smoke and ash.

Sitting on the floor of Sophie's room, Ava held the still glittery album to her chest and tried to visualize her daughter walking into the apartment. She hadn't spoken to her since the morning at Sunvalley Mall when Sophie was applying for jobs, and it felt like her skin was dissolving on her quaking bones in the many hours since.

Sophie could be angry; she could be spiteful or sarcastic or not say a damn word, as long as she walked in. Now. Please, now.

A car door slammed, and Ava popped up. She ran to the front room window and stared down at Julian holding a crock pot the color of burnt pumpkin pie. He waved, but she was already halfway to his car before he finished the greeting.

"I'm not late, am I?"

"She didn't come home last night," Ava said, panting, her eyes bloodshot. "I haven't seen Sophie in almost two days."

"Okay, calm down." He sat the crock pot on his car hood and hugged her tight. "What happened the last time you saw her?"

"We were at the mall. She was applying for a job. I

mean, I've *heard* her since then—we've been home together, but she's been avoiding me like the plague. It's that Liam kid, I just know it," she muttered against his chest. "He's older than her, you know. And I know she's been smoking pot with him, and drinking. And God knows what else—except I think I know what else and—"

He grasped her face and stared deep into her eyes. "Ava, you have every right to be worried, but you need to calm down. Breathe slow, squeeze my hand, dig in—"

"That's not going to work! If he has her, he *has* her, Julian. Him and that crazy family of his in Petaluma. She and I had a big fight the last time I saw her and—"

The sound of singing and barking caught Ava's attention, and she narrowed in on Dionne sashaying up the street with Nilsson on her heels. She yelled the girl's name as she clambered down the sidewalk, frightening the ratty retriever into a vicious growl.

"Dionne! Have you seen Sophie?"

The girl winced. "Shit. Is this about Unit A? I swear I didn't see anything about you." Noticing Julian's approach, she stepped back. "Who's this guy?"

"Dionne, please. Sophie is missing. If you know anything about where she might be, we need to know." Ava had only just squeezed out the last word when she saw it. Nilsson lifted his head, his tongue flopping over his speckled gums, and in his matted caramel fur, sat Sophie's brass ring—Avery Norton's brass ring—dull as a cicada husk.

The dog snapped when Ava grabbed for it, but Dionne was able to settle him enough for Ava to slip off the necklace.

"Is it Sophie's?" Julian asked.

Ava tearfully held it to her chest. "She left it on purpose. She left *me*."

Julian pulled her close and Dionne shuffled her feet.

"I'm so sorry," Dionne said. "I didn't think she'd actually go through with it."

Ava gasped and grabbed the girl by the shoulders. "Go through with what?" She shook her. "For the love of God, Dionne, you need to tell me."

"Hey!" Jackie Hamilton hollered from her living room, her kerchiefed head hanging out the window and arms crossed on the sill. "What's the problem here, Ava? Why'd you call the landlord?"

"Everything's fine, Mama," Dionne yelled back. "No one called the landlord."

Jackie pointed straight at Julian, one eye squinted. "Then I must be seeing things, cuz that looks just like him."

"They're just looking for Sophie, Ma." Scratching Nilsson's head, Dionne pouted. "I'm sorry, but I haven't seen Sophie since we busted into the attic."

Three adult voices came at her at once, and the reply, "You did what?!" caused the twenty-year-old waitress to cower beside the stray dog.

"I didn't see anything! Just some boxes with pictures and letters."

Ava covered her face. "Oh my God."

Jackie had left her apartment and was striding toward her daughter with more zeal than Ava had ever seen out of the woman. Her glare was a four-alarm fire with a tight grimace like a jammed window. Smoke was building behind her eyes, eating away at her composure, nearing combustion by the time she reached her daughter.

"I can't believe what I'm hearing," she growled. "You broke into that apartment and nosed around in my things?"

Dionne's face scrunched. "*Your* things? No, it was Mr. Mio's. Stuff about internment camps—"

"That's enough," Julian said, standing between the women.

It was then Ava knew for certain, as Julian and Jackie exchanged loaded looks, that he'd led her through exertion therapy too. And Jackie knew the same about her. All the passing pleasantries in the hall, the stilted conversation over coffee the morning after Sophie and Dionne's sleepovers, all the years of playing "nice, normal, single mother," to one another, and this was how the charade ended: three women and their therapist-landlord arguing over dusty boxes while a stray dog watched in panting bewilderment.

"Inside," Julian said. "All of you."

"You can't tell me what to do," Dionne said, followed by a pained squeal when her mother latched onto her arm and towed her to the door.

Jackie Hamilton's kitchen was decorated orange and red with crepe paper turkeys accordioned at the center of every surface. The apartment smelled heavily of spices and savory sauces, but after she poured three glasses of gin, the alcohol was all Ava could smell, clean but dirty, like a secret. Delicious as a freshly opened bottle of isopropyl and a lit Zippo.

"No, thank you," she said, pushing the glass away. "Please, Dionne, tell us what's going on."

Dionne downed Ava's gin before anyone could object. She gulped it down hard, then folded her hands on the quilted vinyl tablecloth.

"You know she's dating some religious guy, right? A guy my age?"

"Unfortunately, yes," she said, and Jackie raised her eyebrows.

"Well, she's been obsessed with him ever since the concert last month. Not to say I blame her. He's a cute one. Charming. But I didn't think she'd buy into it so hard that she'd run off. The thing is, though, it's not entirely because of him she ran," she said, sweeping her focus to Ava. "Liam had her convinced you were hiding something. And he was right. Those boxes in the attic—I didn't see any of yours, but Sophie must have. You're hiding something huge. Mr. Mio too. And . . . " Her large brown eyes drifted to her mom, whose hands were tented over her mouth. "Whatever it is, Mama, I don't care. But the things you're hiding, Ava, Sophie cared about those a lot. And if she ran off because of it, I'm not sure me, or Liam, or his crackpot Choir of the Lamb family are to blame."

Jackie dropped her hands to the table. "Choir of the Lamb?"

"I appreciate your honesty, Dionne, but there's a lot you don't know about this situation," Ava said, her palms sweating on the quilted tablecloth.

"I know she was unhappy."

"Thank you for your opinion," Jackie snapped. "You can go to your room now."

"But Ma . . ."

"Finish that sentence and so help me, Jesus . . ."

The girl jumped up with a huff and marched away, but she stopped before her bedroom. Turning slowly, she whispered. "Sophie's going to be okay, isn't she?"

"She'll be fine," Jackie said. "Now get."

The second Dionne's door closed, Jackie ducked her head and lowered her voice. Gleaming like a feasting cougar caught in a beam of light, her eyes darted back and forth between Ava and Julian.

"I don't know what's going on between you two and I don't want to, but Lord knows I owe Dr. Archer a lot, and the last thing I want is Sophie getting tangled up with those blasphemous Choir characters."

"You've heard of them?"

"More than I'd like." She lit a cigarette, creating a cyclone of unfiltered smoke. "Preacher Green's talked about their church a bunch. Unorthodox methods, strange rituals, and loyalty bordering on idolatry. A cult, Preacher Green says. But I can't imagine Sophie getting mixed up with a lot like that."

"Are they dangerous?" Julian asked.

"Can't say for sure, but I've heard rumors about drugs, orgies, even human sacrifices." She exhaled and dissected

298

the smoke with rough but manicured fingers. "But people say the same things about my faith, and if there are drug-fueled orgies going on down at St. Andrew's, they sure as heckfire aren't inviting me. They got Preacher Green convinced, though. He was even planning on paying them a visit up in Petaluma soon, though I can't imagine why he'd waste his time. Senator Shell's tangled with them on several occasions too, on account of them blackmailing members to keep them in. He's made a big stink about it, but it seems like they just keep on recruiting."

"Like Sophie," Ava whispered. "Jesus Christ."

"Oh, they're far from Christlike," Jackie said, grinding her cigarette in the ashtray. "They dress themselves up nice, but they're wolves in sheep's clothing, I'm telling you. Satan's handmaidens through and through. Sophie will be in my prayers, I promise you that."

"Thank you, Jackie."

Reaching across the table, she held Ava's hand, then squeezed it. Their bones crossed and ligaments stretched, and somewhere between all that biological material, secrets like shrapnel twisted their way to the surface. At long last, they understood each other.

Dionne's bedroom door swung open, and she marched out with tight lips and a scrap of paper of her own. With an apology, she thrust it at Ava, turned on her heel, and returned to her room.

Ava gasped. It was Sophie's handwriting, but it was Liam LaSalle's phone number.

"Hello?"

Ava couldn't control her voice. It wavered and cracked and stuck in her throat as she replied to the Choir of the Lamb devotee on the other end of the line.

"Hi, hello, is Sophie Francis there?"

Silence, then hushed voices.

"This is her mother," Ava added.

More hushed voices, then a man cleared his throat.

"Hello, Ava. This is Liam LaSalle. How are you doing today?"

"I've been better. Is Sophie there?"

"She is."

"May I speak with her?"

The lengthy pause suggested it was a matter that needed keen consideration, followed by bustling noises in the background, as if he was in a cafe.

"No," he finally said. "She doesn't want to talk to you."

Her belly boiled and she gritted her teeth. "Well, I don't really care what she wants right now. I need to talk to her."

He covered the receiver so hard it thudded in Ava's ear. He whispered hurriedly, maybe even laughed, then replied to her as if performing a stand-up routine. "She says you can pick her up tomorrow, on the *real* Thanksgiving."

"I'm afraid that won't work for me, so if you could put her on—"

"We're having a big feast at two o'clock. You should join us. Come see how well Sophie fits in."

"I'd rather hear all of this from her."

"Tomorrow," he said. "Have a blessed evening, Ms. Norton."

The line went dead, and the boiling fire changed to a cold cesspool so fast Ava nearly sank to the floor. Slamming the phone into the cradle kept her hooked to the wall, and Julian did the rest.

"Is she there?" he asked.

"He said she is, but he wouldn't let me talk to her." He softened her collapse at the kitchen table, wrapping everything he had around her as she released an angry sob. Burying her face in her hands, she wept. "Julian, what are we going to do?"

Sitting beside her, holding her hand, he said, "I don't know," but his face told a different story. He knew as well as she that if the Choir could blackmail people with secret information, they could've found out who Ava really was, maybe even used it to convince Sophie she was better off with them.

"Do you want to go now?" he asked.

Her head vibrated on her neck, not a yes, not a no, not anything anyone would consider an understandable reply.

"He said she wanted me to pick her up tomorrow. So I guess that's what I do."

"What we do," he said, taking her hands. "Whatever happens, I'll be right there next to you. You won't be alone."

"For how long? You'll have to move eventually, right?"

She looked at him in trembling terror, and he sighed.

That sigh, she believed, signaled their demise. She was a complicated woman on her own, and Sophie's similar complexities made the pair a hard sell, but Julian's affection endured. Now with the cult's involvement, even someone as sensitive and understanding as Julian couldn't be expected to stick it out, especially when he already had designs on leaving California.

But he held her hand as he walked her to her room, and he rubbed her back as she wept on the bed. He curled up beside her, and she squeezed his hands until he had to ask her to stop. She kissed them, and she kissed him, and he held her so tight she couldn't tell whose heartbeat was whose. It was comforting at first, but the longer he was kind to her, the more it felt like a parting gift. And though she tried to ignore the voices telling her it would be her last night with Julian Archer, by the time exhaustion swallowed her mind, it was fixed on the likelihood of losing yet another person she loved to the Norton ghosts.

CHAPTER SIXTEEN

A HALF-DOZEN VEHICLES were parked in the driveway of the Choir of the Lamb's headquarters, with more branching down Gossage Street, when Ava and Julian arrived the next day. But the stately farmhouse was silent. Holiday traffic had delayed them more than an hour, but it didn't make sense that the house would appear abandoned.

No one answered when Ava knocked on the door. No one called out when she jiggled the knob, or demanded to know who she was when she and Julian discovered it unlocked and let themselves inside. The savory smell of Thanksgiving struck instantly, but the typical sounds of conversation and clinking utensils were absent. The deeper Ava and Julian walked into the house, the more the scents soured.

"Hello? Sophie?" Ava's voice resounded in the palatial tomb; someone must've heard her, but no one rushed in to greet them at the door. When Ava and Julian crossed to the dining room where sixteen people sat around a lavish table, they realized why.

The guests were slack in their chairs like a hefty dose of tryptophan had gotten the better of them, except while some diners' heads were tilted back or slumped to the side, two people were collapsed forward, another cold lump in their mashed potatoes. Blood and vomit were splashed and spattered across the festive tablecloth, and cups of loamy liquid sat overturned in front of nearly every guest. The two women whose cups were still full, unblemished by lipstick, looked to be wearing red shift dresses from the blood that had poured unchecked from the gaping wounds in their throats.

Julian shrank back, fighting the rising bile as Ava ran around the table, checking for Sophie. Her daughter wasn't among the press badges and pantsuits, but relief didn't wash over her like it would for other mothers. Because Sophie was still alive, she might've been the reason these people were dead.

"Michael Wooden," Julian said, coughing. "Oh my God, this is the guy from the channel six news. And over there, that's Senator Shell." He held his hand over his nose and mouth as he rounded the table to a man with his head hanging limp over the back of the chair and his lips marbled purple and yellow like two slabs of bruised flesh. "And I think this is . . . "

Ava gasped, and her hand flew to her face as she crouched beside the man. His vacant eyes were rolled back in his head, fixed on the matte black ceiling, and while one wrinkled mahogany hand was still cradling a fork, the other was under the table with a rosary limply coiled around his fingers. It seemed a fantastic coincidence that it would be Preacher Green, especially with the other dead clergy they discovered at the table, but it stuck like an icicle in Ava's heart either way.

One of the bodies juddered, and the pair jumped. A small woman with her cheek in a pool of blood cried as she coughed up large chunks of coagulated blood and gristle. Her body convulsed, her back hunched and feet curled so tight they were half out of her tan flats. Her throat was a clogged whistle as she struggled for breath. Julian pulled her to the floor and tried to administer CPR, but she thrashed and choked and eventually yielded to suffocation, going limp in his arms.

He laid her down, and tilting his blood-spattered face to Ava, he whispered shakily, "We need to get out of here."

"We need to find Sophie first."

"We'll have to trust that the police can find her. You and I need to leave."

He grabbed her hand and started towing her to the door, but she pulled free and backed into the dining room again.

"Whatever happened to these people could be happening to Sophie right now. I can't leave her." She retreated to the kitchen and pressed her ear to the steel security door. "They're down here, Julian, I just know it."

"I don't doubt it. But we can't take them on alone."

"We can't just leave."

"Ava, look at me. Listen to me. You can't be here when the cops show up, and you know why."

"Julian, the cops already know who I am and where I live. If they find Sophie here, they will come for me either way."

She tested the door's handle, sure it wouldn't open, so when the door swung toward her it seemed like more than luck.

"Ava, please don't do this."

"It's over, Julian. If Sophie's running, it means my running's done. I won't leave her."

Peering down the dark stairwell, she saw another steel door, slightly open, through which amber light strobed with entrancing irregularity. And it might have drawn her down at that very moment if not for the muffled scream that barreled up the stairs.

Ava didn't see herself as a real mother, and she didn't know if it was Sophie's voice, but the possibility made a hollowing pain spread through her abdomen as if she'd been split open and emptied of life. The one that counted, anyway. The one that cried all those nights between Taunton and San Francisco when her belly ached from hunger. Ava often thought Sophie's cries might obliterate the last of her sanity on that drive. When the crying got so bad she nearly passed out, she had to stop the car and kill some poor frog or fish or rabbit—if she could catch one—

then resume the long journey across the country. She didn't think of it much anymore. It was too painful remembering how many times she thought about leaving Sophie behind, even if it meant death for the baby. She kept count. She still knew that number. It was smoldering hatred in her brain like a scorch mark that spread further the longer she contemplated.

She had the same disorienting desire now, and Julian saw it.

He stuffed his sticky hands in hers and pleaded her name again, low and scratchy but almost musical in its desperation. It was like a dream. Julian's voice was as comforting as the calliope of the Flying Horses and just as dizzying when she gazed into his ice blue eyes.

Ice blue eyes . . .

"Avery . . ."

Paul was all at once within and around her, like sea spray and the woodland whispers of the island night. *"Do you remember when I used to chase you?"* he said, his voice rolling from Julian's lips as well as his own, smiling from the bottom of the stairwell.

It felt like a snakebite when Julian dug his thumbnail into the fleshy part of her hand, snapping Ava out of the dark.

Holding her by the shoulders, forcing her eyes to him, Julian said, "I won't make you leave, but we need to find a phone. We need to call the police."

"You go look. I'll stay here."

He squeezed his eyes shut and bared his teeth, and the snarl that rattled out between them deflated him entirely. Loosening his grip, he dropped his head and pressed it to Ava's chest.

It reminded her of the way she slept in Taunton, her fists curled against her breastbone. Even though her hands ached in the morning, the pressure against her chest made her feel like she wasn't just some lonely monster. Julian loved her, really loved her. He was the fists at her heart.

Even though she ached constantly from loving him, it reminded her that she could be better and deserved better than living in the madness of her past. But right now, with her baby's life in danger, she needed the monster to come out.

"I'm going to look upstairs," he said. "I'll be right back. Please don't do anything stupid."

It would've been stupid to stand there while a cult tortured her baby, but she said, "I promise," and kissed him before he bounded away.

The girl wailed again, her voice raw and cracking, followed by two distinct snaps like someone breaking dry kindling. The moment Ava heard what she believed were Sophie's bones breaking, she flew, involuntary as swallowing, down the dark throat of the house.

The noises were unnaturally discordant, but they embraced and blended into an exquisite melody before she reached the bottom. Her skin bristling, Ava crept on tiptoes to the opening, and her jaw dropped at the sight of more than a dozen people, children and adults, in diaphanous gowns surrounded by firelight and spiritual fury. Ava didn't see Sophie, but the Choir was chanting her name, swearing vows, even shouting through heavy sobs.

None so heavy, however, as the man and woman quivering on the lip of a large steaming pool encircled by curtained walls. By the American flag pins, Ava assumed they were politicians. But now they were just meat for the Choir, their faces splotchy and blood-streaked and their eyes like blue-black pits of whirling terror. The woman was especially horrified as she stared at the two broken fingers on her left hand like none of it could possibly be real.

A door thudded closed, and someone boomed from the back hall. "It's done!"

The Choir swiveled and buzzed with excitement as the man lifted his hands to the crowd, then pulled open his robe. They cheered with blessings as Liam LaSalle strode through them, displaying the fresh tattoo on his chest.

Blood pearled from the image of the martyr's palm, and the red aura of irritation made it look like it was burning.

Ava's gaze felt the same, two fiery lanterns searching the faces of the crowd for her little girl, so she had no one to blame but herself when Liam LaSalle found her quickly in the dark.

He grinned. "There you are, Ms. Francis. You missed dinner."

The Choir turned as one entity to the intruder on the stairs. Their mouths shone blood red in the firelight, like open wounds too jagged to heal properly, and despite Ava's swift retreat, three Choir members were on her before she reached the top of the stairs. They grabbed her waist, her sweater, her hair. They wrenched her fingers from the railing and pulled her so hard from the stairs she lost her footing and smacked her face on the edge of a step. They dragged her the rest of the way, locking the steel doors behind them. So as much as Ava and the other Thanksgiving guests screamed, Julian couldn't hear a note.

"I'm so glad you decided to come," Liam said, as a bearded man bound her wrists with twine. "Sophie said you wouldn't. I guess it's good for us you're dumber than she thinks."

"Where is she?" Ava growled.

"She'll be along shortly. She needs her rest before the Great Castigation."

Ava's stomach dropped, and she pulled herself to her knees. "What did you say?"

The bearded man suddenly grabbed her hair and held her at attention while Liam strolled closer, blood and black ink running into his belly button.

"Thank you, Peter." He winked at the man, then drew close, his voice menacing in its softness. "You tried to cage her, Ms. Francis. You tried to stifle her gifts. We want to celebrate her for the magical creature she is. What's wrong with that?"

"You killed my wife," said the man with the blood-spattered flag pin. "You poisoned her."

Liam closed his eyes as if nearing his wit's end with such ignorance. "Because of us, your wife is in Heaven, Congressman. Because of the Lamb, she is now worthy to sit in the presence of St. Agnes and the holy mothers. They are as we all shall be: purified and beloved in the gardens of the world."

Bile filled Ava's mouth. She tried to choke it back, but up it came, splashing her morning coffee over Liam's bare feet.

"No!" mewled the woman with the broken fingers. "I can't watch another person die!"

Only slightly perturbed, Liam crouched in front of Ava and cocked his head. "She's not poisoned. She's just starting to realize what's happening. Aren't you, Ms. Francis?" He sneered. "Or do you prefer *Norton?*"

She met his smiling eyes in devastation, and he hooted in jubilation.

"Look at you. Sophie doesn't see it, but there's a distinct resemblance between you two. That same glazy look of bloodlust, that beautiful magic St. Agnes adores." He leaned in, his voice a threatening rasp. "I adore it too, you know. Her power . . . it's intoxicating. I imagine it would be the same with you."

The man pushed Ava's face closer to Liam's, and he exhaled a melodic breath against her neck. "Show me what you've got, Avery."

There was no fire to inspire her. No ghosts to cheer her on. There was only the whipcrack swivel of Ava's neck, and the merciless clenching of her teeth on the boy's salty earlobe.

The bearded man pulled her hair, which worsened the situation drastically. Ava's teeth tore through Liam's ear like it was biscuit dough, and blood spurted onto the floor. She spat the chunk of flesh at him and kicked at his shins until Choir members piled on top of her and pulled her away, far away. As Liam screamed that he'd "take good care of Natalie Dillon's daughter," they pushed Ava to the back corridor, through the heavy sound-proof door, past rooms filled with vats and misty-eyed worshipers mixing steaming concoctions, and into a room flickering with ghostly light. They pushed her to the floor, then gently fell into kneeling prayer as she patted blood from her scuffed chin.

On either side of a large wooden throne, bronze lamb statues looked like they were laughing in the dancing flames. But it was the cloaked figure sitting atop the throne that made rage boil in every cell as Ava lifted her head.

Her face still shrouded by the hood, the red-cloaked woman's burnt hands shook in eagerness as she revealed the extent of her disfigurement . . . and the depth of her love. Scars bubbled over the bottoms of her eyes, and her once pert nose was little more than a used pencil eraser with malformed nostrils. Her jaw was a different shape due to tooth loss, and most of her hair had been burned away, but Ava didn't question what she saw for a second.

It wasn't a ghost. It wasn't a corpse. It was Faye Norton.

Liam stood at Ava's side, a rag clamped to what remained of his ear. "You should be on your knees. You're addressing Mother Agnes, our blessed guide through this swamp of sin." He kicked her in the side, and she fell over, teeth gritted in pain.

"You people have no idea what you've done," she said. "This woman is no one's guide. She's a sociopath. She's a killer."

The Choir laughed, and Ava screamed.

"Please, you have to believe me! This woman is evil! Her name is Faye Norton!"

The woman descended her throne, her false teeth slightly off-center when she said, "Oh Avery, please call me Mom."

CHAPTER SEVENTEEN

"**T**HIS IS IMPOSSIBLE. I saw you die."

"Did you?" Mother Agnes tsk-tsked as she pulled the hood over her scarred scalp. "I'm not surprised you thought that. A few sparks, the smell of Mommy's burning flesh, and you figured you'd gotten away with murder. But the wiring was weak after the fire—sorry, *your* fire," she added, smirking. "And I guess you didn't count on me calling the police before I walked into the hospital that day."

Ava gritted her teeth. She should've known Faye was too cowardly to meet her without back-up. But devastating as it was realizing her mom survived, it was worse knowing the ghost that haunted her all these years must have come from her own diseased mind.

Mother Agnes raised her hands and begged the crowd's attention. "My children, I'm over the moon that we're all gathered here today to witness this miraculous moment. This creature before you, whom I haven't seen in fifteen years, is my daughter Avery Norton, also known as the Murderess of Martha's Vineyard and the perpetrator of the arson of Taunton State Hospital, which killed dozens of innocent people. Children mostly." She pouted as much as physically possible as her followers glared at the disgusting daughter of their prophet. "And now she has come to deliver you all from my wicked reign. Isn't that right, sweetheart?"

"I came for my daughter," she grunted.

Paleo stepped forward, her voice a snide sing-song. "Don't you mean your *niece*, Avery?"

It no longer mattered how many years Ava spent punishing herself for not being Sophie's real mother, or how far she'd come in accepting it; hearing someone else say it, along with her old name, instantly filled her with fire that consumed her breath and crumpled her into a quivering knot of rage. She clenched her jaw and closed her eyes, and all the whispers around her became white noise that swallowed the anger, dampened the fire. She imagined Julian's fingers pressing hard into the flesh below her knuckles, the meat of their palms flush and tendons taut. And for a shining moment, she could even see him: the most beautiful ghost.

She hoped he was far away by now, and that the police were coming. She hoped he ran into Sophie upstairs, dragged her from the house, and drove her back to Concord. She hoped they were on the road, because, after this day, Ava didn't believe she'd ever see another highway.

Faye looked at her wistfully. "Don't take it so hard, my darling. You were never good with follow-through. And I think you know that. You may have wanted me dead, but you didn't have the stomach to kill me. Or to forget me." She snickered. "I suppose that's lucky for me."

"Lucky for all of us," Liam proclaimed, and the Choir cheered in agreement.

"Thank you, my children. But I suppose we have to admit it wasn't all luck. It was Agnes." She looked to the ceiling and made the sign of the Lamb, and the Choir copied her. "She's protected women of our blood for decades, Avery. She's the reason you, me, and Sophie are finally under the same roof today. She's the reason all of us are here today. And so we drink to her. Paleo, the cups . . . "

A pregnant woman distributed labeled mugs among the members while her husband filled each with a dark liquid. The Choir drank enthusiastically, praising Mother Agnes and their patron saint, but one mug remained on

Paleo's tray when she returned to her spot in the mob. A mug labeled "Sophie."

"Where is she?" Ava asked as the woman passed with the cup, but Paleo veered away like Ava was covered in contagious boils.

They all looked at her like that. And maybe she deserved it. Bowing her head, Ava apologized. "Really, Mom. For all of it."

Agnes squinted, and jagged lines of confusion puckered around her scars. "Go on . . . "

"I'm sorry I tried to kill you, and I'm *really* sorry I failed. But most of all, I'm sorry you haven't found peace. All these years, and you're still just as scared and angry as you were on the island. So I'm sorry. And yes," she continued steadily, "I did come for my daughter. But now that I'm here, now that I see what you've done to these people, I've come for them all. I'm getting them all out of here, Faye."

Her eyes traveled over Ava's face. She wasn't a shadow of the woman Ava had known, but something about her mother's expression reminded her of bedtime on the Vineyard. When Faye doubted her daughters had properly brushed their teeth, she inspected them with a surgeon's precision, her lips peeled back in a grimace as she said, "Okay, if you think you'll be happy about that job when your teeth rot out of your head, go on to bed."

She sneered, looking down on her estranged daughter in contempt. "You really think you're something, don't you?"

"No," Ava said with a sad chuckle. "That's part of why I'm so sorry. I didn't think I had the power to do this to you. In my wildest, most terrifying dreams, I never imagined this sort of poison would grow from Avery Norton's grave."

Agnes shook her head. "That's where you're wrong, darling. This has nothing to do with you." With a snort, she brushed a hand over her scars. "The makeover you can take credit for, but St. Agnes has been with me since I was a child. The Lamb is in my blood, as it's in Sophie's. And in yours." She raised her hands. "Blessed be the gifts of the Lamb!"

The Choir howled. "Praise St. Agnes! Blessed be the Lamb!"

"Listen to me," Ava barked at the crowd. "I know you can't see it now, but what you're doing here isn't what any god or saint would want. Every member of every legitimate religion would agree what you're doing is wrong."

"We don't build our lives around the choices of the masses," the pregnant woman said. "We build our lives on the word of the Lamb. We are not other religions. We are the chosen."

"Oh, I don't doubt she made you believe that." Ava sneered at Faye, who grimaced with the same contempt she gave her daughter the day she was arrested on the Vineyard.

"Why are you still fighting me, Avery?"

"My name is Ava."

She snorted. "I created you, I named you. You wouldn't exist without me, so I think I and my choices deserve a tad more respect, Avery."

"Sometimes I wish I didn't exist," Ava whimpered.

"You selfish bitch." Liam stepped from the crowd, his expression a helix of disgust and pain as he circled Sophie's mother. "All my life I've been told I'm nothing. Ridiculed, beaten down, left behind, and this woman . . . " he said, pointing to Mother Agnes, " . . . this woman, and these people, saved me from being a victim. She took me off the street, fed me, clothed me, talked to me more than anyone had in years. And you actually have people who *want* to love you. You and Sophie, you have people who *want* to know all your secrets and worship the fact that you can speak to the Lamb without chemicals. But you don't care. No, worse than that. You refuse it. Why?"

His anger dissolved like Rolaids in warm water, and

with it went the splotched wrinkled face of a man trapped in a lifelong tantrum. The wrinkles were cracks now, and his teeth became a cage trying to hold in the hell the Choir was supposed to have obliterated. He was a little boy again, red with envy, white-knuckled and weeping like she'd taken away his favorite toy. But this was a little boy who could cause a lot of damage. And he knew it.

"I understand why you're angry with Mother Agnes," he continued. "And I understand why you're afraid. Sophie was afraid too."

"Where is she, Liam?" she begged.

"But you don't understand *us*," he continued, "or the majesty of what we do. You will though, Ms. Norton. You will see the greatness of our service and pledge your loyalty to the Lamb as Sophie has. You will vow to live in chastity, love your brothers and sisters, and help lead the world to the Great Castigation it sorely needs."

Liam remained in front of her while Mother Agnes reclaimed her place on the throne, but Ava looked right through him. "Faye, please don't do this. Sophie still has a chance for a normal life. She can be better than we were."

"Oh I know," she said. "That's why I've been searching for her for so long. By the Lamb's will, she will take root in these sour plots and bloom into her power, the likes of which the world has never seen."

"Root. Bloom. Goddammit, Faye. This isn't a game. It isn't a garden."

"Have I taught you nothing, Avery? The world is a garden, and it must be tended."

"The world is a garden," the Choir chanted. "It must be tended."

Mother Agnes opened her hands to soak it in, and she exhaled through a beaming smile. "You see? They understand something you never could. They understand the beauty in rebirth, even if that means digging out the bad seeds. But they also believe in forgiveness. As Agnes of Rome forgave those who tried to violate her, we shall try to forgive you. We shall try to make you our daughter again."

"So I take it these people have forgiven you for what you did to your other daughter?"

Faye squirmed in her seat and lifted her chin.

"They do know what you did to Natalie, right?" Ava looked to Liam, whose face was screwed up in revulsion. "Do you know what your dear Mother Agnes did to her firstborn child?"

"We know how Natalie Norton died," Paleo said, her hands resting on her belly. "We know how she paid the price for betraying her husband's fidelity."

"The price? So you told them that you planted a bomb in Noah Hanson's apartment?"

Faye didn't answer.

"Just like on Paul's boat."

She scoffed. "I wish I could take responsibility, Avery, if only to give you some satisfaction in this fantasy you've created. But I'm not a gas leak. And I'm not Anna Mulberry, driven by false faith."

"What the hell are you talking about?"

"I will admit I've made some hard choices in the service of St. Agnes," Faye continued. "I've done things I'm certain many people wouldn't approve of. But many people are blind and don't know it. If they did, they'd be down on their knees begging for a cure—*our* cure. The Lamb saves. Every person here has a story to prove it. And now so will you."

"You killed my sister," Ava hissed. "You tried to kill me and Paul and Sophie. I don't care what you told them. You murdered Natalie because you couldn't control her."

"Mother Agnes didn't tell us," Liam said, and Ava refocused on him. "It was your friend Pam."

"Pam? I don't know a Pam."

"Now who's the liar? You lived with her in Taunton Hospital. She told us all about you. You set the place on fire and watched your friends burn."

Ava went limp. "Pam . . . Pamela Mason?" Self-loathing

sprung up like mushrooms in her gut. Though sporadic at first, the spots of soft fungal hate merged to fill her with a hundred varieties of nausea that made her wilt to the floor.

Liam and Peter used the opportunity to latch onto her and shove her into a chair, to which they quickly tied her wrists and ankles. She fought, but every time she met a child's eyes, the weakness prickled through her again. She looked to a skinny freckled girl with fat pupil dancing with firelight and knew something was horribly wrong with her, with everyone. They were so viciously blissful, hissing and spitting as they mocked Ava with strange prayers.

Liam cinched the twine on her left wrist and whispered in her ear. "Pam told Sophie everything, Avery. All about those people you killed in Taunton so you could run away, fuck your dead sister's husband, and steal her baby. But Pam also told us that she ran too, and we didn't like that. *Sophie* didn't like that. She earned her first CI for community service that day. Needless to say, Pamela Mason won't be flapping her gums about anything anymore."

"Community service? Is that a fancy way of telling me you convinced my daughter to murder some crazy woman I lived with in the 1950s?"

"It didn't take much convincing. And she did well enough killing that tutor of hers before I came along."

"Moira?"

"She sees her, you know. Ever since the cops found her body in the park, Sophie's guilt has been a twenty-ton weight around her neck, and she's been seeing the woman ever since, probably more often than she's admitted to me. But she's free of that guilt now. She's accepted what she is, what she's always been."

Ava growled. "Sophie didn't kill her. That woman in the park wasn't Moira Shunn."

Liam froze. "Bullshit."

"Listen to me. Sophie is innocent. I don't know what happened between them, but she didn't hurt Moira. She didn't hurt anyone until you forced her."

"It doesn't matter."

"No? How much CI did murdering Pam give *you*, Liam?"

His smirk spread into a grin, and he crinkled his nose. "Not as much as I got for marrying Sophie."

Mother Agnes stood, and the Choir members snapped to attention. Even the skinny, freckled girl now wearing was resembled a Kool-Aid mustache. Her hands looked so tiny wrapped around her "Bella" mug, but her pupils were wide as saucers and darting over their leader like the woman was spangled in Christmas lights.

"The castigation is near," Mother Agnes announced to the sea of swaying smiles. "My chaste and devoted children, when the Lamb rises again, you will see a different world at your feet. You will hear the miraculous voice of God, and you will feel, for the rest of your lives, the love of St. Agnes in your hearts."

"We are her hair . . ." they chanted, " . . . her flesh, her womb."

"And when the time comes . . . " Mother Agnes declared.

" . . . we will feed at the altar of shame."

She made the sign of the Lamb, and her followers responded in kind. But the children didn't bow in unison with the adults. They broke from the group and bounded to the door, whooping and shrieking about "swim time."

Mother Agnes clapped. "What exuberance! We should all take a lesson from the children. This is a joyous occasion! A celebration!"

The Choir cheered, mystified by their own hands in the air and the shadows on each other's faces.

Mother Agnes signaled for their attention again. "I leave the remaining preparations to you, my blessed ones. Leave me with this sad creature, and pray that I can save her from herself."

They jubilantly funneled out of the room, closing the door behind them. Shouts and clangs and bizarre wet splashes sounded in the hall as Faye descended her throne, but Ava refused to look at her.

"Don't act this way, Avery. This is the opportunity of a lifetime. It's your chance to make everything right, and it's the last one you'll ever get."

She didn't respond, and Faye grabbed her by the chin. Her fingertips dug into her daughter's bruised flesh and forced Ava to look upon the monster she'd made. She didn't care what Faye said; Ava had taken a run-of-the-mill madwoman and inspired her to tend bigger gardens, to collect broken people and use them to destroy what remained of her family.

"Say something," Faye hissed, her breath like fetid dirt. "I bet there are all kinds of hideous things you've dreamed of saying to me." When Ava didn't answer, Faye curled her fingers under her collar and revealed the chain on which Sophie's brass ring hung like the girl's heart itself, tight in her grandmother's fist. "How about now?"

Faye had taken so many things while Ava wasn't looking—even when she was—but she wasn't going to let this one affect her. To do so would've allowed her to corrupt it, and Ava'd had quite enough of that already.

"Speak, you ungrateful harlot."

"I've said plenty, more times than I can count, to the ghost I thought you were," Ava spat. "And even though I know none of it was real now, I have no desire to repeat myself."

"What wasn't real, dear?"

"Every ghost was a figment of my guilt and self-loathing. I created them, and I've destroyed them as well."

Faye's false teeth juddered in her mouth when she laughed. "Oh you silly girl. You haven't learned a damn thing since you were thirteen, have you?"

"Maybe not, but at least I'm still pretty," she said, and Faye forcibly released Ava's chin. "How did you find us, anyway?" she asked, stretching her jaw.

Spite flashed over her mother's face. "I didn't. For a long time I thought you were hiding somewhere in New York, but I must've gotten false information. Thank the great mothers for Liam. Though I suppose I should thank myself for bringing him to the church in the first place."

"Humble as always, Mom."

"And you get my thanks too, Avery. If you hadn't bungled up Sophie so bad, I might've never found her." She tilted her head to the ceiling. "Not that I ever doubted you, St. Agnes. You knew this would happen from the beginning, when I was just a child."

"What happened to you, Faye?" Avery whispered, and her mother's gaze snapped back to her. "You were pious when I was little, but not like this. You were softer, kinder."

"No, sweetheart. You just didn't know me."

Avery's nostrils flared and she twisted her wrists in the twine. "But I did, better than anyone else on that island. I was the only person you let see that part of yourself. You never took Natalie out to hunt."

"Hunt?" She spat out the word like gristle and had to readjust her teeth. "I was doing God's work, you horrible girl, and you made me believe I could share it with you. But then you told that boy and brought the police into our secret. You ruined everything." She patted sweat from her forehead as she caught her breath. "It's no wonder Sophie was eager to get away from you," she continued softly. "You're far too self-centered to be a mother. And so dramatic. I used to think you were lucky not to have any of Amelia in you, but I was wrong. The way you hate me is so obstinate, so prejudiced, it's my brazen mother through and through."

"If being like Grandma Amelia is an insult to you, then I'm happy to be like her."

"Oh please. You never even met your grandmother. Not your *real* grandmother, anyway. Amelia was bedridden your entire life."

"What are you talking about? She was sick, sure, but I met her when I was little. She gave me a diary for my twelfth birthday."

Mother Agnes snorted as she shuffled back to her seat,

then deflated into it as if preparing to disappear into sleep. "Oh sweetheart, that woman you met was a nurse your father was screwing. And *I* gave you that diary, I just put 'Love Grandma' on it."

"What?! Why?"

She fanned her face as she laughed. "You poor dear, what you don't know could fill a Bible. I suppose I'm thankful you aren't as adept at burying your past as I was—Amelia's part in it, most of all."

"I don't understand. Was your mother like us?"

"Sadly, no. She had other . . . issues."

"Like what?"

Faye's face twisted like a bad tooth rang anguish through her jaw, and unfolding her hand on the bronze lamb statue beside her, she wheezed a chuckle.

"Bad water."

PART THREE
THIRTY-SEVEN YEARS EARLIER
1938

CHAPTER ONE

N O ONE WAS more surprised than Amelia Hayworth when she gave birth in the hallway of her charming inn on Martha's Vineyard. But the six guests staying at Stirling Cottage in the summer of 1922 certainly hadn't expected to find her on the floor either, writhing in an appalling amount of bodily fluids and wailing out prayers to whatever gods or devils listened. None did, it seemed, but at least she wasn't alone when the guests began to gather.

A Portuguese-Catholic priest named Marcelo Melo was delivering a sermon in Wesleyan Grove that morning when Amelia cried out from her kitchen. No one else appeared to hear her, but Father Marcelo, who so often listened with his heart, heard Amelia's screams and abandoned the pulpit in front of his would-be parishioners.

For her.

He flew into the house, sidestepping puddles to the kitchen, where Satan himself might've lost his lunch at the sight. But Father Marcelo didn't waver. He pushed up his sleeves, knelt beside Amelia, and spoke to her calmly, as if trying to subdue a wild mare.

"I'm here, child. You're safe."

She responded with mewling gibberish and wide eyes that spilled tears down her cheeks.

"What's your name?"

She panted. "Amelia."

"And the baby, how far along?"

"I don't know. I didn't know—"

323

Marcelo pressed his hand to her forehead and smiled. "*Esta bem*. Let's just get your baby out into the world."

"Wait, who are you?" she squealed between gasps.

Marcelo answered, but Amelia's pulse thumped like a bass drum in her ears and garbled his words. She couldn't have heard his answer right. Still, it comforted her when the Catholic priest who'd left his flock of sheep to herd a lost lamb from the devil's wood squeezed her hand and said, "I am God."

—➤◄—

Faye Hayworth leaned against the garden gate with a huff that blew the dirty blond hair from her eyes. "Did I get the story right, Father?"

Marcelo clapped then fanned a fresh veil of sweat from his face. "*Perfeito, cordeirinha!* But I wish you would leave out that 'I am God' business. It was a miraculous day, but that's one thing I'd be happy to forget."

"But she heard it, didn't she?" Faye rested her chin on her sunburnt forearms and winced. Her scalp was burnt too: a pink stripe down the center of her parted hair that she was desperately trying not to fuss with. It itched terribly, but her mother would be crosser than usual if it peeled like last year. The constant itching and flaking upset more than a few people at the inn, so she fought the urge to claw at it. She smacked it instead, and Father Marcelo giggled when relief poured out of her in a baritone sigh.

She made him laugh all the time, but unlike her mother, Faye never felt like Marcelo was laughing *at* her. On the contrary, he treated Faye with a sort of reverence and adoration that made her feel like they'd lived lifetimes together before this one. He was her best friend and greatest teacher, and until that summer they'd seen each other every day since she was born.

But Marcelo was getting older, and he couldn't tell stories with the same fervor as before. He missed scheduled prayer sessions. He canceled last minute walks

324

in the park. Faye did her best to take up the mantle, but she never quite captured Marcelo's spirit. And especially not his stories. They weren't hers, after all, and would never roll off her tongue with as much beauty or authenticity.

Maybe that was why, on her seventeenth birthday, she couldn't shake the feeling that he still saw her as a little girl toddling around Stirling Cottage.

With more than five decades between them, Faye and Marcelo were an unlikely duo, but few others, her age or otherwise, sought out the little girl's friendship. It didn't bother her, though. She loved being alone. When she wasn't with Marcelo, she preferred long quiet stretches in her bedroom or curling up in the inn's makeshift library. Reading, praying, even practicing stories from Father Marcelo's home on the Azores, also called "The Islands of Magic." Numbering among his favorites were stories about the sunken kingdom of Atlantis, which still lived in the modern world as the nine islands of the Azores. But he spoke also of the *Alvéloa* bird who covered the tracks of the Holy Virgin fleeing from wicked King Herod with the Christ Child, and the *Codorniz* bird who earned an eternal curse for beckoning the army to the Holy Mother's location.

But Faye preferred tales of the *Culto do Divino Espírito Santo*. Though Marcelo hadn't been a priest for many years, he spoke of the faith spawned by millenarian mystics and enriched by Azorean culture with such passionate and cinematic extravagance that it was easy for Faye to imagine herself into his stories: as an observer, a worshiper, and frequently, in the pivotal role of an unlikely hero chosen to rescue a world gone mad.

Was it really so strange for her mind to wander down that path? Marcelo had told her dozens of tales of put-upon girls who rose above adversity to change the world. As long as she was good and devout, nurtured her faith and encouraged others to do the same, kept her heart open to possibilities like Marcelo had done for Amelia, maybe Faye would be the next Lúcia, to whom the Virgin Mary appeared six times in 1917. It was Mary who compelled the young girl to learn how to read and write so she could, in time, communicate to the world three secrets the luminous deity revealed to Lúcia and her siblings. But in return, Lúcia would suffer greatly for her divine knowledge, from her mother in particular.

"Your mother probably heard a number of strange things while she was in labor. She was in great pain. The greatest physical pain a human can experience," Marcelo said, dabbing sweat with a vibrant embroidered handkerchief. "She was confused also. You were quite the surprise, *cordeirinha*."

"I know, I know. She didn't want me."

"She didn't *expect* you, child. There's a difference."

Faye rolled her eyes and rocked against the fence. Maybe there *was* a difference when she was little, before she'd analyzed her birth story to death, and the rumors about her mother hadn't become so pervasive, but it had evaporated into a soupy haze of unanswered questions. She used to see a giantess of power and industry when her mother dashed around the Stirling, but now, watching her flit about the Boatman Inn, Faye felt sorry for the woman.

Most Vineyarders did their best not to gossip—or at least enjoyed declaring so—but on an island of fewer than five thousand, even the most mundane rumors spread like cancer. And when a neighbor with too much time on her hands noticed more and more single men booking rooms at her inn, the whispers that so often surrounded adolescent Amelia began again.

Faye knew that story too.

The old money Hayworths of Cape Cod had gotten fed up with their daughter's loose morals and unhinged antics, but they didn't feel like they could chuck her into the gutter.

"Not because they cared," Amelia drunkenly told her

326

six-year-old child. "Because they didn't want their friends and associates to think they'd dropped me in bedlam. That would've been as scandalous as any of the positions I got into with the governor's boy." She cackled, and moonshine spilled down her chin. "So they gave me a house on Martha's Vineyard as a graduation present. *A graduation present?* More like a bribe to get out of their hair so I didn't ruin their social standing. But seeing as I couldn't stand the ogres, I took it. I got the house, and they got to put an ocean between us."

Her daughter sniffled and asked for a hug, which she gave, one-armed, so she could take another drag off her cigarette.

The gift of distance was the clearest indication of love Amelia's parents had ever given her. With their financial assistance, she thrived on the Vineyard, and when she got up the guff to open the Stirling Inn, she embarked upon the happiest days of her life.

Even now, everything returned to the Stirling. It was her Garden of Eden, a source of great pride and a haven of hope, perpetually filled with laughter and song. As the largest of the gingerbread houses, the Stirling boasted eleven elegant rooms, two tiered porches, and all the majesty of the Tabernacle, but it was never meant to be an inn. Nor was it advertised as such, and therefore catered to a diverse and sometimes suspicious clientele.

But that was before the serpent ruined paradise.

Guests were still booking after the little serpent's birth, but the added expense of a child and mounting rumors of Amelia's night life piled an impossible amount of stress on the young mother. When little Faye was learning to walk, Marcelo began spending time at the inn to protect the toddler from tumbles and bumps while Amelia was working . . . or drinking . . . or out on the porch flirting with the passersby.

She spent a great deal of time pretending she didn't have a child, which Faye assumed came naturally, but

Amelia was also actively hiding Faye's existence from her parents. As it turned out, the contract that put the Stirling into Amelia's hands had something of a morality clause, which the Hayworth's daughter had violated on the regular, most of all by conceiving a child out of wedlock.

It took a few years, but when news reached the mainland that Amelia Hayworth had birthed a bastard on the floor of the highly sought-after home in Wesleyan Grove, her parents cut her off completely.

But Amelia didn't bat an eye. She was resolved to make up the financial deficit of her parents' withdrawal and keep the inn afloat. The year was extremely lean—it would've been impossible if not for Father Marcelo's help—but she worked her tail off covering most of the inn's expenses on her own.

Tourism in general was way down, though, and because of persistent rumors, god-fearing women traveling with their husbands avoided the Jezebel innkeeper at the Stirling at all costs. Less than two years later, Amelia had to give up the ghost and move out of Wesleyan Grove. She resented Faye for the change of scenery, and her daughter suspected as much for years, but Amelia confirmed it when she got drunk on moonshine on Faye's tenth birthday. It had become a sad little tradition of its very own, a chewed-up tail on the doe-eyed rabbit that was Father Marcelo's recitation of Faye's birth story. It was no wonder she recalled it perfectly.

"Help me, my dear." Marcelo threw back his long coat, and Faye helped him lower shakily to the back steps. "My sweet Faye, my little lamb, even if she didn't want you, it would not change the truth."

"What's that, Father?"

"You are my touchstone, *cordeirinha*, and my truest friend. I thank Our Lady of Fátima every day for bringing us together." He crinkled his large sun-speckled nose, and strands of gray hair like spider silk fell into his eyes. Smoothing back the renegades with thick fingers allowed the sun to hit his chocolate irises directly and summon the sparkle that had been such a comfort to young Faye Hayworth over the last seventeen years.

Amelia sometimes accused her daughter of purposefully deflecting other offers of friendship, waving her oddness like a flag to frighten away prospective playmates. She'd done so that very morning, in fact, scolding the girl for not having enough close companions to warrant a party. Although she'd let her daughter sleep in, she awoke her at 10am shouting about how if she wasn't going to celebrate her birthday properly, she better harvest the tomatoes before they rotted off the vine.

She was getting drunk earlier every year. And angrier. Amelia had never laid a hand on her daughter, but Faye wasn't sure she would've minded. When it came to her mother, she thought an icy palm would be better than a cold shoulder. Aggression would feel far sweeter than erasure. At times like those, she fondly recalled her fourteenth birthday, when Amelia hurled a sack of geranium bulbs at her and it nearly felt like love.

Father Marcelo's affections were different. Obvious without being stifling, unconditional without being lazy. His love for Faye was crystal clear warmth, like the ocean swallowing her feet when she stood on the lowest shelf of jetties in the July sun. Marcelo was always stopping by to make sure she was eating right, that her mind was being stimulated by both knowledge and spirituality, and, most important, that she wasn't alone in her garden that morning.

He fanned his face and gazed into the distance like he was watching a creature gallop away, then focused on Faye with a red-faced chuckle. "Where is your darling mother, anyway?"

She poked at the wet soil with the rake and huffed. "Bedroom probably. I don't know whose."

When he patted the spot beside him, she wiped her hands on her skirt, knocked the dirt off her boots, and joined him on the step. With a heavy sigh, she clasped her hands and bowed her head in prayer.

"Why are you praying?" he asked.

"Because I want to be patient and kind like you. Because I want to be strong. Every day I pray. No, I beg: 'Please, in the name of Mary, your Holy Mother, make me as strong as Father Marcelo.'"

He sat up a little taller, then deflated when his back twinged with pain. "What makes you think I'm so strong, *cordeirinha*?"

She pressed her folded hands to her lips and exhaled into the shaking lumps of flesh and bone. "Because you love her, and I can't even bring myself to like her. I pray for the strength to change. I pray someday I'll be as good as you."

He sighed her name like he was hoisting a fifty-pound weight off his chest. "You *are* good, Faye. Even if you weren't, there's no use breaking your heart to pieces on the off-chance she'll see the sacrifice. Don't lose your footing pulling a sinking basket from a cranberry bog. It will pull you down too."

Faye screwed her face to one side. "So much for 'Honor thy mother . . .'"

"When she does something honorable, by all means, give her your respect," he said, smirking. "Mateus 5:5 also says, 'blessed are the meek, for they will inherit the earth.'" He gestured to the rich soil and vegetation before them. "This garden is just the first plot of earth you're destined to inherit. Whether your mother knows it or not, she has already fulfilled a great prophecy in passing it to you. Perhaps I can now do my part." From his pocket, Marcelo withdrew a small box wrapped in purple paper, and joy instantly illuminated Faye's face.

She tore off the wrapping, flipped open the lid, and gasped. The necklace twinkled as she lifted it from the box, the small silver links leading to an oval pendant wreathed in delicate filigree. And upon the pendant, finely detailed, was a depiction of St. Agnes of Rome cradling a lamb in one arm and a martyr's palm in the other.

Faye knew all about martyrs, and St. Agnes had been her favorite since she was a little girl. Marcelo used to snipe a bit when she spoke of Agnes like she was Princess Azulverde from the Atlantis stories and not the selfless young woman who dedicated her life to God, but he leaned into her childlike adoration now, even celebrated how much unfettered love she bore for the martyred girl.

"She was a great beauty like you," Marcelo said, as he looped the chain around her neck. "And she was kind. She was honorable, chaste, and resourceful. She cared for the earth, the flowers, and the fruits of all labors. And vigilant though she was about her beliefs, she was regarded as being gentle as a lamb."

"But I could never be that blessed," Faye said. Holding the pendant between two fingers, she looked down upon the small cherubic face unburdened by the weight in her arms and history in her heart and wondered if she could ever feel so light.

He crouched in front of her, his face glittering with silky hair again. "You already are. Do not mistake outside opinions for your inner critic. Listen to your friends and family. Listen to the world around you. But do not believe what they say without reflection or investigation. Do not fall into the trap of thinking there is good in everyone, or that those who are meant to love us always have our best interests at heart."

As if she'd been waiting in the wings for just this moment, Amelia swung open the back door and exhaled a stream of smoke. Her hair was loosely pinned, the curled ends barely touching her shoulders, but it was going limp the longer she stood in the wet heat of September. "Jesus Christ, Marcelo, haven't you filled her head with enough of that nonsense? We're not Catholic. We're not *anything*." She stumbled as she joined them on the porch, her tumbler glass swinging wildly and splashing Faye's arm with mint julep. "So, who's this one?" she asked, as Faye wiped her arm on her mother's blouse.

Marcelo started to speak, but his voice seemed caught in his throat. He looked around, brow furrowed, then up at Amelia with an almost pleading expression.

"It's St. Agnes of Rome," Faye replied, doting and dramatic. "She's the patron saint of chastity, mothers, and gardeners."

Amelia laughed and clinked her ornately jeweled fingers against her glass. "Mothers and gardeners. I remember thinking something like that when I became a mother."

Marcelo's face went slack and he groaned as he stood, shuddering despite Faye's helping hand. "Come now, Amelia. You promised to show me the room you painted."

"It's still green. It's just dark green now," Faye mumbled.

"Dark green is my favorite green." He kissed a fingertip and bopped Faye on the nose as Amelia opened the door for him.

"Go on up, Marc. I'm right behind you." She knew Faye despised when Amelia called him "Marc," especially since it seemed a privilege granted to only her.

Not that Faye cared; she wouldn't dream of reducing his greatness like that.

"Agnes of Rome," Amelia snorted, clumsily descending the stairs. "I wonder if she would be happy with the things she represents. She didn't exactly choose them, right? Some old men in Rome did, right? Think of it, darling. Gardens. Mothers." She dug her toe into the earth and uprooted a geranium. "Chastity," she chuckled. "The poor girl was a virgin when she was killed, wasn't she? I've heard enough of your and Marc's stories about her to remember that. That's not a fair association, don't you think? That's not right."

"She chose to devote her heart, soul, and chastity to God," Faye said. "There's nothing more 'right' in the world."

332

"Because if she didn't, she would've been raped, probably repeatedly, by monstrous men who wouldn't have cared a wit if she died in the process. That's not choosing chastity for God, my love. That's cutting off your leg to escape a bear trap. Some choice."

Faye suddenly regretted telling her mother so many stories of St. Agnes. But how could she have known Amelia was actually listening? Every other story she'd tried to impart had been wasted breath up to that point. When hotel guests didn't touch their breakfast and Faye stressed the importance of charity, Amelia threw the food in the garbage instead of feeding the less fortunate. When she caught her mother flirting with three different men in six hours and lectured her on the majesty of fidelity, Amelia responded by kissing a married man's cheek while his wife was distracted by a Thomas Hart Benton painting.

The fact that Amelia was using St. Agnes's tortured life to undermine Faye's faith made her head hurt. The pounding was erratic, but it soon fell into a predictable rhythm that followed her mother's inebriated swaying in the garden. Amelia tried to toe the unearthed geranium back in place, but the roots were ruined, the petals smashed and broken. "Sorry about that."

Shrugging stung a spot on the back of Faye's head. It felt like a warzone back there: a knot of simmering rage and flaring sorrow that tightened the more she worked to loosen it. "It's your house," Faye said, massaging her scalp. "It's your garden."

"Oh, that's not true," Amelia said, tossing the watery dregs of her drink over her shoulder as she headed for the steps. "The Stirling garden was mine. Do you remember? I loved it so much. The guests would help me out there sometimes. You too."

"I remember."

"That's what's so funny about gardens and mothers," she started. Though she drummed her fingers on the railing, her gaze was faraway, her voice longing. "Did I ever tell you that story? How you felt in my arms the day you were born?"

Faye's sweaty fingers loosened on the handle and dropped to her side, where they gathered up the hem of her blouse. Like most truths her mother spilled on birthdays, Faye didn't want to hear it.

And she *desperately* wanted to hear it.

She said, "No," as in "No, please don't tell me," but she was helpless to stop what God had commanded her to endure every September, so she let it wash over her like an abrasive wave.

"You were like a seed," Amelia said to the horizon. "A slippery little seed, smooth and soft, even a bit green, always threatening to crack open and spill your complications across my life. Not like a flower. So many parents compare their children to flowers, but not me. You had no petals, no pollen. You weren't going to open up and show me something miraculous. No. When Marc put you in my arms, all I could see were roots, thick, strangling things that excavated and coiled and suffocated what I loved most: parties, sunshine, men and women who told me I was lovely and smart and didn't expect me to say it back, people who couldn't hold me to any one place." She plucked the petal and dropped it to the wet earth. "But that tiny creature with its ruddy wrinkled face could. You were born with that malicious talent, my darling. All babies are. You cried a lot, but not for me. You'd clutch air but never my hand. You just stared at me with these massive wet eyes, speaking long before you learned the words. I knew it. I heard you. 'Let's drown together, Mommy. You and me forever.'" She looked into her empty glass, adding, "'But you go first.'"

Amelia's eyelids fluttered as she focused on her daughter. She reached out, caressed her cheek, and tears welled in her eyes when she smiled. "But I don't feel that way anymore. I just . . . don't know what to do with you, sweetheart. I never liked playing with dolls."

"Me neither," Faye whispered.

Her hand dropped from her daughter's face, to the pendant around the girl's neck. Pinching it, she muttered, "You don't say." She sniffled. "It does suit you, though. Better than any present I got you, I'm afraid. Then again, there was the Holy Ghost Festival, wasn't there?"

Faye winced. Her mother hadn't mentioned the festival for a few months, so she hoped Amelia had forgotten their bargain. It was an idiotic notion in hindsight. As an early birthday present, the woman whose absence had forced her young daughter to attend the two-day celebration with Father Marcelo for the last seven years was finally attending herself. And she hadn't stopped lording it over her since.

As the festivities began, it still seemed a fair trade. The joyful music and colorful costumes appealed to Amelia's frolicsome nature, and she eventually gave in to dancing alongside the parade route and tasting the various platters of decadent food that circulated the crowds. But as the day continued and summer temperatures soared, the festivities melted into one of the strangest in Faye's life. Not even Father Marcelo, from whom she kept nothing, had attempted to discuss what transpired during the festival, though she sometimes thought he wanted to. When his eyes narrowed and he wrung his hands in silent contemplation, she wished he would ask her what she learned that day when the heat got the best of her and she ended up in the forest outside his house.

She thought of it daily since, even hourly, especially when her mother stood across from her with heat and dehydration making her look twenty years older, wearing a scowl like a dare.

"Tell me the crazy things you saw," it demanded. "Go on. Give me a good reason to get rid of you."

She was wearing the same dry mask that morning, and the air had the same briny swelter of festival day, like a bloated corpse on the shore threatening to spill its secrets.

It couldn't just be the storm crawling up the coast. It had to be more.

Gripping the pendant, Faye Hayworth prayed harder than she ever had before.

"Please let it be today. Let me see Agnes again."

CHAPTER TWO

A S SHE WASHED off the dirt from her morning in the garden, Faye's mind whirled with memories from the Holy Ghost Feast. The best parts were frantic and hazy, like the first and only time she drank wine. But unlike the twenty-four-hour hangover that followed that night, Faye had no proof of her glorious encounter at the festival except the overwhelming feeling that it had changed her irrevocably.

The day of celebrating St. Queen Isabel's devotion to feeding the poor came with a stifling heat that made Faye want to skip the event entirely, but she had a sinking suspicion Amelia would count the promise of attendance as a birthday gift even if they stayed home, and she wasn't about to risk it.

Besides, Queen Isabel was the ideal influence for her fickle mother, and Father Marcelo agreed it couldn't hurt for Faye to educate her on the tenets of the *Divinio Espírto Santo*, but as usual, his endorsement came with a grain of salt.

"Enlightenment is a wonderful thing, little lamb, and I'm sure the Almighty appreciates your efforts, but you must realize that it is not your job to save sinners. The Holy Spirit is the fount of all knowledge and order. Only God and Our Lady of Fátima may rescue those who are lost."

Her chin dimpled, and she pressed her pendant to her lips. "But the Holy Spirit is in me, Father, like Agnes of Rome. I know it sounds crazy, but I can feel her. As Christ encouraged purity among his followers, and angels protect us from corruption, there is such love in me that if Lucia can speak for the Virgin Mary, I believe I can speak for the Holy Spirit. And it's telling me that it will be more of a mother to me than Amelia." Wrinkling her nose, she looked to him in blushing sorrow. "Is that sacrilegious, Father?"

Marcelo wrapped an arm around her shoulders and hugged her tight. "No, my dear *cordeirinha*. Family is not bound to the blood, just as faith is not bound to the church. I know you wish to change your mother, but if you can't, I pray you seek out other families. God willing, you may even create a few."

She nodded, but hope remained in her that by the time the Portuguese-American Society crowned this year's manifestation of Mary, Amelia Hayworth would be just as devoted to Our Lady of Fátima as her daughter.

Marcelo found the pair right away that morning. His jubilant laughter parted the crowd as he approached and pinned a red and white corsage in Faye's hair.

"It suits you," Amelia said, dizzying her daughter with the compliment.

Or maybe it was the heat. Even the minimal breezes that day felt like human breath, wet and fiery on the back of Faye's neck. She tugged at her collar and fanned herself, but it only made her hotter.

Light-headed, she shut her eyes and rubbed her aching temples, and all around her the voices of the boisterous crowd became an oppressive cloud of nonsense. She couldn't have been in the dark cacophony long, but when she opened her eyes and blinked back the oppressive sun, both Amelia and Father Marcelo were disappearing into the crowd.

She chased after them, but whenever she was within arm's reach, people closed around Amelia and Marcelo like greedy waves. The crowd carried them into the distance, but not so far that Faye couldn't see her mother smirking over her shoulder as she hung on Marcelo, or pulled him close, or kissed his cheek, his lips, his neck . . .

Faye hollered for them to stop, but the jubilant music swallowed her voice as quickly as Amelia swallowed Marcelo's attention. It didn't make sense. Her mother was supposed to be the third wheel, not Faye. This was her and Marcelo's day—had been for years—and Amelia wasn't going to steal it . . . or him.

She pushed through the crowd, and it pushed back. Tossing and tugging, the flow of the parade carried Faye through the town on waves of exuberance. Prayers and holy song zoomed around her like cinders in a cyclone, and moments slipped out of her grasp like thrashing fish. Her head felt like it was splitting into pieces, and the more she tried to concentrate on the Portuguese songs Marcelo had taught her as a child, the closer another voice came.

"She's poison."

A cool breeze whistled past her ear, and she spun with the swell of traffic. She snapped around, searching for the source, but another voice captured her attention.

"She's already left her mark."

Faye spun again, catching eyes with the girl chosen to embody Queen Isabel. She strolled up to Faye, her hair like opaque oil mixing with the white garlands cascading down her bony shoulders from the crystalline crown. The chosen one's nails were encrusted in dirt, the cuticles shredded and wet, and when she handed Faye a loaf of bread, fat purple worms spilled from the mealy innards.

Faye threw the bread at the girl and pushed through the horde, away from the parade route, where it wasn't so hot and dark. But even alone, collapsed on the grass, she felt hands upon her—so many pinching and groping that her flesh could no longer take it and surrendered to the ghostly fingers.

Lifting her head, Faye beheld her body soaked in blackish blood. But despite the nausea and pain, a cool, prickling euphoria washed over her. Bliss soon overpowered the anguish, and Faye lay her face upon a patch of earth to watch the queen and her court march down the streets of Oak Bluffs.

"It's beautiful," she whispered, eyelids heavy.

"You're beautiful, little lamb."

Closing her eyes, Faye saw a young woman lying beside her in the dark. Despite her youthful complexion, the exhaustion of eternity roiled in the girl's jeweled eyes, and her body curled in on itself like a dead centipede. A crown of light orbed her head, but it was dim and flickering until she reached out and closed her hand on Faye's. Instantly, the light increased, and torturous pain returned to Faye's body.

She writhed on the ground, weeping as the stranger's light snaked in and out of her flesh, scraping her bones and squeezing her organs. But for all the pain, when the young woman released her, Faye felt lighter and clearer than she had in ages. She felt new, unburdened by the sins of unbelievers.

And yet, she couldn't move.

The young woman sat up, aglow, pulsing, but burning fiercest from the Immaculate Heart cradled at her breast. Like the sword piercing the muscle in depictions of the Virgin Mary, looking upon the celestial woman slit open a secret cavern inside Faye. There were stars within it far more complex than any galaxy humans knew, and they spoke to her in soft voices that thanked her for her devotion and welcomed her to the fold.

"Am I dying?" Faye whimpered at the woman. "Am I already dead?"

"Sweet girl, no. You are only just born," she said. "Now that all doubt has been drained from your soul, you are nearly ready to house the holy mothers."

The young woman touched Faye again, and the light burned away her pain. It burned away her fear and shame and showed her a world where Amelia celebrated her daughter's faith; where everyone did.

She liked it. She wanted to stay there. She wanted to rule there.

Able to move again, Faye sat up and looked around her. She was even farther from the festival now. The saints in the streets were gone. The sun had set, and the buildings had shrunken and twisted into a dark nest of claustrophobic trees outside the Heath Hen Reserve more than five miles from the parade route.

Faye panted. "How did we get here?"

The woman smiled and plunged her hand into the soft, wet soil of the forest floor. "I can take you many places," she said, wriggling her fingers. "I can show you many things." Lifting her fist from the bed of earth, she withdrew a leaf unlike anything Faye had ever seen on Martha's Vineyard.

A palm branch, she realized. A *martyr's palm.*

This wasn't just any celestial woman. She was Agnes of Rome.

Faye bowed, apologizing for not recognizing the saint sooner, but Agnes bid her to rise and look into her eyes.

"You have been chosen," Agnes proclaimed. "Like many before you, you were selected to prepare the world for the return of the great mothers, for the blessed virgins, for God, and for me. Do you understand?"

Faye shook her head. "No, I don't. I know I'm good—or at least I try to be—and I'm faithful to God, but I don't deserve whatever this is. I'm no one special. My mother didn't even want me. She hates me."

"But you *are* wanted, Faye Hayworth. You are born of ancient energy as powerful and pure as mine, and you will find your place in our line. Until then, I'm afraid you will face persecution like the rest of us. But . . ." Her voice was a single string playing the truth. " . . . love will find you, my child. In many ways. Throughout the years, come fear and lament, you will be given many opportunities for love."

"I don't see how. I barely have any friends. My own mother—"

"That is not your mother. I am. We are." The saint brushed away the girl's blooming tears and said, "Amelia Hayworth is merely a vessel, a gateway for your magnificence. She can't be a sliver of the mother we can," she said, stroking the girl's face. "You too will be a vessel, but you will be far grander, with more channels and chambers than a small woman like Amelia could ever understand. The magic you cultivate and colonize will save us all. But you are young. That's why we gave you Father Marcelo, to guide you as I have guided so many others. With his help, we are destined to succeed. And . . . " Agnes said, extending a thin finger, " . . . he must be kept safe."

"Why wouldn't he be safe?"

"The Devil knows how important he is to your ascension. He has disciples everywhere, even in your own home. Faye, you must ensure that Father Marcelo remains pure, or our chance to save this world could be lost. As you will be: alone and lost, forever."

Faye's chin trembled, and she threw herself into the open arms of Agnes of Rome.

"I'm lost now," she whimpered. "I've dreamt all my life of seeing you, and now I'm terrified. What's happening to me? I don't want to be chosen. I just want to be normal."

"You will be," Agnes said, patting the girl's hair. "But you will need to work very hard to help people adapt to our version of normal. Teach them our ways. As we impart our lessons to you, impart those lessons to others."

"What if they don't want to listen to me?"

Agnes released Faye, crouched at her eye line, and said sternly, "Do not let them refuse. Oblivion is better than concupiscence."

"I don't understand."

St. Agnes kissed Faye's cheek, and it seemed all the world's hope was contained in her voice when she said, "You will, my lamb. You will."

The trees rustled, and Faye's lungs filled with balmy July air that made her cough. She wilted to the ground, but she wasn't there long before tender arms wrapped around her body and lifted her into the air.

Her head flopped to her guardian angel's shoulder, and her eyes rolled up to his weathered face.

"You're going to be fine, *menina*."

Raising folded fingers to Father Marcelo's cheek, Faye whispered. "I know. I'm going to save you."

CHAPTER THREE

SHE DIDN'T REMEMBER much after that. Marcelo put her in his bed, and she assumed Amelia collected her soon after, because she woke up in her own bedroom the next morning.

On the floor.

In a dirty, rumpled dress.

With her door open for all to see.

The humiliation still fresh in her mind months later, Faye dried and dressed quickly, all the while keeping one toe on the door of the shared bathroom. It probably wouldn't do much to prevent a guest from barging in, but it gave her a sense of safety she'd been lacking since the day of the Holy Ghost Festival.

She got lucky that time and scurried to her room, thanking Agnes all the way. Now came the question of what to do with the rest of her seventeenth birthday. They'd only had four guests at the inn that week, and with the anniversary of her calamitous emergence strangling Amelia's last nerve, Faye was eager to flit through the rest of the day with as little interaction with her mother as possible. She still hoped Agnes would come to her, but she had to accept it might never happen again. Besides, waiting around, praying, and finding serenity were the worst ways to avoid her mother's ire. They summoned Amelia like an offensive smell, towing her around bends and up the stairs, until she rooted out the rot that was her daughter's peace.

No, the best way to avoid her mother was by doing

custodial work. By the end of the day, every sheet was taut, every curtain fluffed and pinned. Not a speck of dust escaped her cleaning frenzy, and though she twice verified the carpets were free of debris and the floors waxed to a stellar sheen, Faye redid them to kill time. She decided the dishes weren't clean enough for her to escape scolding, so she pulled each one out and washed them again.

When something squeaked, she thought it was the sponge against the plate. But it happened again while she was still, louder and from above. It wasn't the first time she'd heard it. It wasn't the fifteenth or even the fiftieth time. But she said her prayers and resumed scrubbing the plate, trying her best to ignore it like always.

Tranquility flooded through her for the seconds her lips moved in prayer, but the "amen" brought ghostly hands to her sides. Fingers skated over her belly, working their way inside of her again, but it wasn't a slow draining this time. This time, they were hollowing her all at once, yanking out her doubt and fear like ropes of rotten offal. When she was empty, she dropped the plate and folded over the sink, her hands shaking on the edge as the water boiled and frothed. Faye gasped as a steaming hand emerged from the bubbles, latched onto her face, and pulled her down into the suds.

Faye beat at the sink and tried to free herself, but the dirty water glutted down her throat and pulled her deeper into the muck. She was drowning, yet she could suddenly see so clearly. She saw Marcelo, his body withered and pale, and his mind a jumbled mess of immorality and fear. The flesh peeled from his body and floated toward her, filling her mouth and lungs until all her breath was gone and her body jerked in futile rebellion.

"Hey, little girl. Are you okay?"

Faye opened her eyes and squinted up at a bearded man with a receding hairline. One of the guests. The one who couldn't keep his shirt buttoned. It was wide open, a nest of black hair glistening with perspiration when he bent over her and said, *"Do you know where you are? Do you know your name?"*

Her name was Faye Hayworth. She was flat on her back in her kitchen with a broken plate beside her.

He helped her up and sat her at the table.

"I must've slipped," she said, as he tumbled a few chunks from the icebox into a dishtowel. Allowing him to hold it to her head, she said, "Mr. Bellamy, right? You're here with your wife?"

"Oh, you're Amelia's kid. Right, I should've known."

His drifting gaze prickled her skin, and she thanked him as she took over icing her head.

"Can I help you, Mr. Bellamy?"

"I don't know if this is a you-job, kid. Fact is, there's a big storm coming in and lots of folks are catching the ferry back to the mainland. I was considering it myself, and I was hoping to cut a deal with the lady of the house, since we only arrived yesterday. That's hardly worth what I'm paying for lodging."

Amelia wouldn't like losing money she'd probably already spent. Plus, disturbing her, wherever she was, probably wouldn't turn out well in the long run. The simple request would likely set her on a warpath that would take hours to fizzle out, and Faye didn't have time to waste. If her vision was true, Father Marcelo was in active danger, and she had to get to him, even if she had to walk there.

Faye dumped the ice into the sink and wrung out the towel. Drying her hands on her pants, she gulped hard and captured the man's wandering eye. "I can refund your money, sir. I'd be happy to."

"That's sweet, kid, but I should really discuss this with the head honcho."

"I do it all the time," she said, with two fingers crossed behind her back. "I promise it's no trouble."

The man snorted, then pinched Faye's cheek. "Thanks, but I came for your mom. I'll just wait till she's done with the other fella." He smacked his wallet on the table and winked.

"I'm sorry?"

The water in the sink gurgled, and the man snickered.

"Aww you know," he said, and pointed at the ceiling. "All that jazz."

A baritone moan rolled through every plank of wood between the kitchen and Amelia's garret room, and Faye's entire body clenched.

Of course she knew. There'd been rumors about Amelia's sidejob since the Stirling days—since she lived in Cape Cod, actually—but no one had spoken the words aloud. Euphemism was an island gossip's best friend, and for a pious young woman who wanted to believe her mother was anything but a whore, she accepted euphemism as fact. Even now, she tried to fall back on innocent explanations for the noises and "other fellas." But when the house moaned in her mother's voice again, Faye doubled over in disgust.

"Are you sure you're all right? Let me grab your mother."

She sprang up and pushed him against the wall, shocked by how easy it was. "Don't you dare. Don't you move a muscle."

He laughed and jerked to push her back, but Faye gracefully slipped out of the way, causing the man to skid forward and crash into the kitchen table. He swiped at her, but she dashed around him and galloped up the steps to her mother's room in the groaning attic.

She'd never stood outside Amelia's bedroom like that, her stomach in knots, listening, knowing, and finally accepting that everyone was right about her. She would never be the kind of mother Faye needed or deserved. There was nothing Faye could do to repair the damage in her mother's soul, and she refused to risk breaking one more piece of her heart in the process.

But she also wouldn't turn a blind eye to her mother's dirty deeds. The woman was steeped in sin, and she had to be exposed for the lying whore she was, at long last.

Faye thrust open the door, casting a triangle of light across the bed that illuminated Amelia's eyes like a feral cat. She exploded with expletives as she jumped off her customer, naked as a jaybird, and tried to push Faye out of the room.

But Faye wouldn't move. She was frozen to her spot, staring in horror at her mother's bedmate.

Marcelo Melo wrapped a sheet around his thick body as he stood, one hand closing at his hairy chest as if trying to keep self-respect from leaking out of his heart. But it was gone, from him and from Faye. And worse, when Faye saw his bare body break from Amelia's, she also lost any hope that she could fulfill the mission bestowed upon her by St. Agnes.

"Why are you doing this?" she whimpered at him. "With *her* of all people?"

Amelia scoffed and lit a cigarette. "So high and mighty. I swear I don't know where you get it from."

"Oh, that's obvious, Mom." She turned her watery eyes back to Marcelo, who took several seconds to meet her gaze. "Did you pay her like the others?"

"Please, Faye, you don't understand."

"Then explain."

He shook his head, and Amelia coughed up a smoky chuckle.

"No, he didn't pay. Not with cash anyway. I cut the Padre a special deal."

"What deal?"

Marcelo's face was beet red and glistening with sweat. "Amelia, don't."

He should've known she wouldn't listen; she'd been given this wonderful opportunity to hurt and humiliate her daughter, and she wasn't going to pass it up.

"It's a fair trade for all his babysitting," Amelia said, eyes narrowed. "All these years you've been friends—he deserved something special."

Faye was a crumpled paper ball by the end, her hand

clenched so tight around her St. Agnes pendant that she thought it might've punctured the bone, and though she was certain Father Marcelo would refute Amelia's claim, he had shrunken too, his body tense and tears veiling his eyes.

"It's not true," she whispered. "It can't be. St. Agnes wouldn't let it be true. It has to be a trick."

Amelia groaned and gestured at Marcelo in frustration. "You see what all that religious mumbo jumbo did to her? She doesn't believe her own eyes anymore. It's all some mystical test." Refocusing on Faye, she shook her finger. "Now listen to me, you pious little shit, Marcelo is a good man, and I won't have you belittling everything he's done for you. He deserves to spend his last days in peace."

Marcelo's face drained to gray, and he turned his back on the women.

Faye gulped. "Last days?"

He didn't answer. He dressed quickly and swiveled to leave the room, but he had to brace himself on the dresser when dizziness overcame him.

"What do you mean 'last days?'" she pushed, and Amelia groaned.

"Oh Christ, Marcelo, you haven't told her you're sick?"

Regaining his balance, Marcelo tried to scoot past them, but Amelia grabbed his hand. She grabbed Faye's next, and in a gesture Faye would remember as the only true kindness her mother offered, she led them both solemnly to the bed, left the room, and closed the door behind her.

"Father, what's going on?"

He licked his lips and hesitantly lifted his bloodshot gaze. "I'm sorry, little lamb. I should have told you much sooner, but I was afraid."

"Whatever it is, I'll help you get through it. *We* will help you," she said, touching his arm. Remembering how she'd found him and her mother, she wanted to recoil, to burn his sins off her skin, but she forced her hand to remain upon him, even cling tighter. "Agnes of Rome came to me, Marcelo."

He sighed heavily. "So you said the night of the feast."

"I did?"

"When I found you in the woods, you told me she said you were a vessel for greatness, and that I would help guide you to a holy destiny."

"Yes! Yes, that's what happened, Father!"

"And that you would save me."

"Yes! And I will. If you're sick, if you need me, I'll still try. All I needed was for you to believe me."

She threw her arms around him, crying, laughing, and resigned to forget what she'd seen that evening. It didn't matter anymore. They were together, and together they would rescue the world from sin.

But he was shivering when he pulled out of her embrace, and again, he couldn't meet her eyes. "No, Faye. It's not your responsibility to save me. And even if it was, you couldn't. This illness is incurable, and it is brutal. Especially when it comes to memory. I've been forgetting more and more. I've been losing hours, days even. There are times when we're together and I'm not certain who you are. Or who I am. And I can feel it, just around the corner, God is calling me home." He looked to her again, and his chin quivered. "I'm terrified, my little Faye. I do not want to forget you. But I do not want to remember this version of you either."

Faye's face tightened. "This *version* of me? I'm chosen, Father. Agnes told me."

"No, she didn't."

She backed away from him, her forehead furrowed. "You said you believed me."

"It would be blasphemous to believe such a thing, *cordeirinha*. And to be frank," he said, voice breaking, "continuing to pretend causes me nothing but pain. You are a good person, Faye, and I love you more than anyone else in this world, but you were not chosen by St. Agnes."

350

"You were there in the woods. You saw me have the vision."

"I saw you dizzy and rambling and digging in the dirt. And I've seen it more than a few times."

She shook her head. "You're lying."

"No, no more. Things have gotten much worse since the night of the feast. I've seen you lose consciousness during prayer before, I've seen you walk and talk in your sleep, but what's happening to you now is more extreme."

"Because she took my doubt. Father, please." She held his hands and stared into his watery eyes. "Marcelo, she had her hands in me. She took everything soft and scared and begging for love and gave me the truth about who I am. When you found me, I was filled with Agnes's light. And God's."

His face twitched into a crueler expression than she'd ever seen—even on Amelia—and he said, "Whatever possessed you that night was not godly."

She gritted her teeth and beat the bed before retreating to the wall. "No, this can't be happening. This isn't right. This isn't how she said it would be."

"I'm sorry, my child. I should've stopped the obsession before it got to this point, but the disease, the dementia . . . " His voice caught in his throat. "I'm afraid I did believe it sometimes. If anyone was devout enough to truly hear God in times like these, it would be you. You made it seem so real. And you were so happy."

"Then why don't you believe it now?" she whimpered.

"Because what I saw in you that night terrified me. And I have to accept that my willingness to believe stemmed from my sickness. I was seeing angels everywhere, little lamb." Marcelo approached her, hands open, but she pointed a threatening finger in his direction, and he stopped.

"Stay away from me. I don't want to catch it."

He lowered his hands in surrender. "You can't catch this disease, Faye."

"Not the one that'll kill you. But I don't want your sin on me either. What you and Amelia have been doing is wrong, and you knew it. If anyone's harboring a demon, it's you, Father. And you know what?" She pushed off the wall and backed him against the bed. "Agnes told me this would happen. She told me you were in danger, but not how much, or how sin would rot your mind."

He trembled, his voice thick with sorrow. "No, Faye."

"You did this to yourself. You knew it was wrong, and now God is doling out a divine punishment."

"Please, stop. You need help."

She grasped her St. Agnes medal, tore it from her neck, and cast it at Father Marcelo. "Not from you. Never again."

Lightning flashed like Cheshire teeth in the sky, and thunder rolled so hard it knocked the weeping teenager off-balance as she ran from the room. Slamming the door behind her, she collapsed against the wall and sobbed.

Father Marcelo was going to die, but before that, he was going to forget. All his sins, all his shame and weakness, evaporated like morning dew.

But Faye would never be able to forget what she'd learned that night.

Wiping her eyes and catching her breath, she strode down the stairs intent on giving Marcelo one last memory.

CHAPTER FOUR

MOTHER AGNES EXHALED a shuddering breath, and Ava Francis lifted her aching head. In the shadowy haze, the woman looked like Faye Norton again: proud, but weary of waiting for her spiteful daughter to see it.

"I failed you," she said, running a gnarled hand down the lamb statue's bronze curls. "Just as I failed Marcelo. I don't like admitting it, but I think it's important. After all this time, I still feel responsible for what I let happen to that dear man. I should've never left him alone with your horrible grandmother."

Ava smirked. "It sounds like he preferred it to being alone with you."

Faye's fingers arched to claws. "You haven't been listening."

"Because it all sounds so familiar, Mom."

"Oh, I see," Faye hummed. "You think this is about you."

Shaking her head, Ava whispered. "No. I don't think it's about anyone but you. So please, Faye, I'm asking *you*: Where is Sophie?"

The old woman's fingers relaxed, and she slouched in the chair, her eyes farcast. "I admire your devotion to her, even if it's misplaced—"

"Misplaced? She's my daughter! I love her!"

Leaning forward, Faye pouted her bottom lip. "But your love is made of ashes, Avery. Piled up, it's a great and awing thing, but all it takes is one breath to scatter it, like blowing out a birthday candle. Except your love isn't the kind that grants wishes, is it? It's not the kind of love that helps people. You know that." She leaned back in the chair and drummed her fingers on the statue. "I tried to make up for failing Marcelo that night. Not to him, but to St. Agnes, and to God. There was still time to live up to their dreams for me, and something in the air that day told me I could, that this was my last, best chance to save the Marcelos to come. And I got that chance, later that day, when a Category 3 hurricane washed Menemsha clean off the island."

Ava met her eyes, but the smirk Faye pulled in response made her squeeze them shut. The smirk remained briefly like a scorch mark in her mind, though, until the darkness swallowed it and allowed another face to bloom. Her father's face—not the charred creature that appeared during exertion therapy but the smooth placid man that slithered around corners during games of tag when she was little. He never jumped out to scare or amuse her. Even at play, he was as slow and deliberate as a python. She supposed it wasn't surprising why Faye fell for the slick doctor, but she'd never actually heard the story of how they met. She'd asked a few times, but her mother and father only ever replied, "The night of the hurricane," and quickly changed the subject.

Her eyes were tearing when she opened them to stare down Faye Hayworth still sneering on her throne.

"Do you want to know how I saved us, Avery? How I'm still saving us?"

"I want my daughter."

She tilted her head. "So did I. And that night, when the sea rose to devour us, St. Agnes delivered."

CHAPTER FIVE

THE PEOPLE LIVING and vacationing on Martha's Vineyard were aware of the hurricane cutting a swath of destruction up the New England coast, but no one expected it to devastate the island like it did. After slamming into and unmaking the small fishing village of Menemsha, the storm pummeled North and West Tisbury, and left Chappaquiddick, which had only gotten its first electric lights four years prior, in shambled darkness. With waters swiftly rising in Oak Bluffs, residents and tourists fled their beachfront buildings and took shelter further in-island, with several displaced families taking refuge in Amelia's hotel. It was a good opportunity for her to get some new customers—and if that meant she'd stop prostituting herself, Faye was all for it.

But it also meant Father Marcelo couldn't leave, and he was the last person Faye wanted to be trapped with in a storm. Luckily for her, he stayed out of sight, and taking care of the influx of guests proved a good distraction from his betrayal. But as the storm worsened into a maelstrom of harsh winds and hailstones, she found it impossible to focus on comforting the guests. The streets turned to frothy gray rivers that ripped through gates and beat gardens to muddy graves, but the hotel was warm and unflinching in the long storm.

Eventually Faye stopped refilling teacups and asking if anyone needed an extra blanket. Most of the guests seemed like they'd grown tired of her constant prodding anyway, especially the three whiny daughters of an obviously exhausted couple from Texas. They giggled in Faye's direction so often she was convinced they were making fun of her.

She was used to it. Besides, she was in desperate need of a haircut, and it took her a good four hours to realize she'd dropped a pat of butter on her blouse, so she didn't blame them for some light ribbing. But as the hurricane whipped the windows and the nerves of those on the other side, time and tension escalated the teasing.

Faye had moved into the dark dining room by then, her head on her folded arms as she watched furious races between raindrops, ignorant to the trio who'd snuck up behind her until the oldest screamed in her ear.

She yelped and flapped her arms, nearly tumbling out of her chair as the girls laughed at the top of their lungs. Two boys rushed in, and Faye rubbed her ringing ear as she rose from the table and looped around to the kitchen.

The tallest boy blocked her way. "Are you okay?" he asked, his eyes narrowed like he was trying to read the answer in the pores of her nose.

He seemed nice at that moment, but Faye didn't trust it. She'd heard him telling dirty jokes earlier when she delivered the cream for his tea, and the dark-haired beanpole who now stood smiling behind him had looked up from his book and snickered right along. She looked right at him, though it was the book, not the laughter, that snagged her attention.

She'd heard horrid things about *Brave New World* with its boorish sexual content and immoral themes. It was banned from every school and library on the island as far as she knew, so the novel's presence there, in her house of all places, coupled with brash and wolfish smiles, offended Faye on a personal level.

She usually ignored boys who smiled at her like that; most boys her age, actually. They were dreadfully silly, and she found the vast majority only treated her respectfully until they discovered she wasn't fast.

She said, "Excuse me," and they stepped aside, the girly trio giggling to themselves as they trailed her into the kitchen. Exasperated, she turned and asked if they needed anything.

"Who's the old man in your bed?" the smallest girl asked, her nose crinkled.

"What do you mean?"

"You've got the room without a number, right?"

"Yes."

"Well, there's an old man in there. In your bed," the eldest said, biting her lip and tossing a playful gaze at her sisters. "There have got to be better ways to fight the boredom, sweetie."

Faye sighed. Father Marcelo. He must've gotten confused and laid down in the wrong room. She didn't feel it necessary to explain him to the girls, nor the beanpole boy who stared at her with his head cocked and book pressed to his lips. She simply thanked them and turned on her heel to head upstairs.

It took ten minutes to climb the steps to her bedroom. Her heart raced so fast she felt like she might faint halfway up. It was as if she hadn't run down them just hours before, devastated by the evil that had infected her beloved Marcelo. He called it "dementia," but she knew what it really was. It was a demon sent to distort their love and destroy what remained of Faye's hope. Standing outside her bedroom, she held one hand to her stomach, one hand to her heart, and prayed for God and His great mothers to take away her fear.

It had been hours since they last spoke, but it felt like years since she looked upon the man she knew. That man was lost, and she was the only one who could save him.

The light was on, but Father Marcelo was fast asleep in her small white bed. He should've been too big for it, but the way he was curled tight, his hands knotted up at his mouth, it looked like a child in the bed, younger than Faye, slighter and more fragile. She longed to wrap her arms around him and forgive all the vicious lies he'd thrown at her earlier that day, but she had to stay strong. This, she knew, was the demon's doing.

She entered the room cautiously, like the shadows on either side of the bed were dark leathery wings waiting to snap closed on her. Quietly shutting the door, she tiptoed around the shadows and stood at the foot of her bed. With the storm beating the walls and whipping hail against the roof, she felt like she was trapped inside a drum. It was so loud, she didn't understand how he could sleep through it. That, too, must have been the monster inside.

She didn't want to wake him. She didn't want to touch him. She didn't want to sleep in her own bed after the disease riding her best friend's bones wrapped itself up in her sheets.

Faye cleared her throat, and Marcelo stirred with a groan like an old squeezebox. He sat up slowly, rubbed his eyes, and like a child lost in the forest, he whispered, "*Onde estou?*"

"You're in my room, Marcelo."

"*Cadê minha mamãe?*" His jaw trembled, hanging loose from his skull as if carrying an invisible weight, the stiff white hairs on his chin like slivers of frosted glass. Balling the sheets in his fists, he repeated shakily, "*Cadê minha mamãe?*"

Faye at last stepped into the shadows wreathing the bed and gazed fully at the ancient child before her. His face was wan, his rich caramel skin fallen to chalk, and he peered at her like she was made of gears and puzzle pieces he couldn't figure out. Then his eyes widened, and he pushed himself off the edge of the bed.

"It's you," he said, his hand shaking as he extended it. "*O que você está fazendo aqui?*"

"Of course it's me. It's *my* room."

He sank to his knees, but they wouldn't support him.

Wilting to his side, eyes gleaming in wonder, he whispered, "*Santa Mãe* . . . . you have risen to shine your light upon me."

He was worshiping her again. After everything he'd said, now he believed in her?

Faye couldn't hear the rain anymore, but she could feel it. The hurricane pinged ice off her ribs and flooded her veins with filthy water. The storm quieted and shrank within her, but it didn't vanish, and neither did its damage. It condensed and hardened to one jagged hailstone in her chest that she felt every time she breathed. With a gasp, the coldness filled her entirely, but when she touched Marcelo, he felt warm and alive and capable of defeating the evil thing inside . . . with her help.

"I hoped I would see you," he said, gazing up at her. "Since I was a little boy, I would visit the *Lagoa das Sete Cidades* and pray to see you."

Faye stumbled backward in shock. His words turned over and over in her mind as her brain translated, then reminded her where she'd heard them before. "Are you talking about the lagoon on São Miguel?" Bearing her teeth, she said, "Who do you think I am, Father?"

All signs of worship dropped from his face, and his expression shifted into one of intense terror, colonizing him as he mumbled through a few nonsensical responses before Faye snapped her fingers in his face.

"You know who I am, Marcelo. Look at me. Fight through this."

He shook his head, afraid and stuttering as she grabbed him by the shoulders. She hadn't realized how emaciated he'd become, stiff as the garden fence but not nearly as effective. He crumpled into her arms and wept. He cried out, "*Azulverde!*" and Faye released him violently.

"Maybe you *can't* beat this," she said. "If you can look at me after all these years and see some fairy tale princess from Atlantis instead of the chastity and light of St. Agnes, you really are doomed." With a sigh, she apologized and helped Marcelo stand. He felt like brittle driftwood slowly unfolding to a defective ladder of a man.

But when he was on his feet again, hands open at his

sides and eyes locking firmly on Faye, he looked like Father Marcelo Melo again. Bright, alert, and agonizing over what he'd done.

He cradled Faye's face and touched his forehead to hers. "*Por favor, Vossa Graça,*" he whispered. "*Santa Mãe, abençoe-me com seu perdão. Torne-me limpo novamente.*"

Faye's heart thudded her breastbone, and her gaze dashed across his trembling face as she backed away from him. "Do you see me now, Father?"

"Yes, I see you, *cordeirinha*. The real you." He pulled the necklace from his pocket and held it out, his arm steady as Queen Isabel when she revealed an apron full of roses instead of the bread she'd stolen to feed the poor.

He was fighting back. He was peering through the haze of disease to the holy martyr shining under Faye Hayworth's skin. He was battling to remember their strength.

"Who am I?" she demanded, striding to him with an ache blooming in her belly.

"*Santa Agnes de Roma,*" he said, eyes brimming. "Mother. Guide. Gardener. Lamb."

"*He's lying . . .*"

Thunder pummeled the house, and the sky brightened to an alien yellow hue. It faded with thunder, but a ring of light remained around Agnes's celestial face. The crown was brighter than the last time Faye saw her but still sickly, endangered. And her ancient eyes were dark with worry.

"He wants to see you," Agnes said. "He wants to see more than he wants to live, but sin has stricken him blind. And even if it hadn't, the demon's taken away too much. How long until he thinks you're another ghost from a fairy tale?"

"I don't know."

St. Agnes drew nearer, and her light pulsed with the thunder as she whispered in Faye's ear. "How long until he accuses you of being the sick one?"

She looked into the martyr's eyes, those jewels of fidelity and grief, and swallowed hard. "He already has."

Agnes nodded. "This man is not the Marcelo we love. He is six strangers—children, elders, and demons—trapped on an island, naked and afraid. He's clinging to anything he can to save himself. But you can't allow him to cling to you, Faye. He will drag you down. *Like a sinking basket in a cranberry bog*," Agnes added in Father Marcelo's voice.

Marcelo clasped his hands together and wailed. "Lay your blessings upon me. *Por favor, Vossa Graça.* Free me from this overwhelming guilt."

"It's the sickness, Faye. It's desperate to infect you, the way it tried to infect me," Agnes said. "Marcelo served us well, but this isn't him. This thing wearing his face deserves nothing from us but a quick castigation. We can't let our love for a man who no longer exists compromise our plans."

Agnes backed away, dimming to a sallow shade Faye could swear she felt flowering in her belly. Her cold, pale, marigold guts, drained by the hands of saints and hollowed by her mentor's treachery, ached for restoration, just as the real Marcelo ached for absolution.

He offered the pendant to her again, but she didn't take it. And when the wind slammed the house with hail like an invading army, the electricity flickered and blinked out . . . and St. Agnes with it.

Marcelo whimpered, and though it disgusted Faye to touch the doomed creature, she led him to her bed. She lay him down and sat beside him, and as his head sunk into the pillow, she smoothed his wild gray hair and hummed. He smiled, but she didn't. Her face was as sharp as sea glass, and the icy pain of the hailstone in her chest pushed words from her mouth like a body rejecting new organs.

"We could've changed the world," she said to him. "We could've served God together and helped usher in the age of the Holy Ghost. But it's too late. You let the devil mutilate your beautiful mind, and you've fallen too far for Heaven to see."

He protested, but she shushed the thing begging for her mercy. Marcelo Melo was gone, and no amount of prayer or service would restore him to his former glory.

"I'm sorry, but you don't deserve our blessings," she continued. "You don't deserve forgiveness or admiration or anything that might cleanse your soul before judgment. You deserve to die, Father. You deserve to die sick and weeping."

His face creased with devastation, and his lips slipped around oily words he couldn't lob off his tongue. He sputtered and moaned as he thrust the necklace at her, but she forced his hand to his side and closed his fingers tight around the pendant.

"Keep it, Father." She kissed his cheek, slid the pillow out from under his head, and whispered, "Take it to the grave."

362

CHAPTER SIX

SHE CLOSED THE bedroom door, her body buzzing and mind whirring—not with words, but with colors. With the red and green flags of the Holy Ghost Feast fluttering behind her eyes and the feeling of stars burning beneath her skin, she floated down the dark stairwell.

Amelia hadn't noticed her absence. She was still playing the dutiful host stuffing her guests with biscuits, cookies, and tea while they played bridge and canasta by candlelight. And she wasn't annoying them the way Faye did. Her fawning was somehow endearing, even as she pushed for the displaced families to come back for the holidays.

"I'll give you a good price," she said, frequently accompanied by a wink in the gentleman's direction.

The performance sickened Faye, but she couldn't ignore the joyful glow which orbed her mother as she flitted about the room. Tending to guests lit her up like Christmas Eve, though her attitude had more of a New Year's Eve gleam. Maybe it was just the dark and frenzied storm making her shine by comparison. Or maybe Marcelo's castigation had changed something in Faye, or lifted a veil, allowing her to see the pure joy sparking within her mother, uncorrupted by carnality.

The thought trapped the breath in her throat. She'd long ago stopped believing there was any part of Amelia untouched by sin, and if she *wasn't* a gnarled mass of depravity, maybe Marcelo hadn't been beyond saving either.

Her chest cold and aching, she slipped down the stairs, around the kitchen, and to the glorified closet Amelia advertised as a reading room. It was the least popular part of the inn, so it made a fine refuge for Faye when the house was full.

Flickering light shone under the door, and her breath released in shock. Too loudly it seemed, because the door opened, and the beanpole boy with the brazen book smirked at her. He lowered his Huxley and stepped aside to let her into the tiny study.

There was just enough room for the pair of them, two stools, and a dubious ladder leaning against the recessed shelves of books and religious artifacts. It was a place of comfort and magic for Faye, but she couldn't stop herself from blushing when she imagined it through the eyes of someone who read filthy things like *Brave New World*.

"I hope you don't mind me hiding out in here," he said. "It was getting a bit loud out there."

"Of course not. You're our guest. I guess I was looking for the same thing. But I'll leave you—"

"No," he said curtly, followed by nervous laughter. "Sorry. I like company. Just not *loud* company."

She glared at the book in his hand. The title, and the globe at the center.

"You don't seem very loud," he continued, and she hummed at the stylish blue cover.

Noticing her focus, he chuckled and waggled the book in front of her face. "Have you read it?"

"Goodness, no." Faye turned her attention to a shelf of her favorites, but the boy leaned against it with a toothy smile.

"This oughta be good." He crossed his arms over his chest. "Why not?"

"Not my cup of tea," she said, as cordially as possible without looking at him.

He thrust out his bottom lip as he nodded. "That's fair. So let's see what kind of tea you do like." He edged her out of the way and scanned the books on the shelf she'd been eyeing. His finger glided over the spines, dipping into the ravines as he recited the titles. *"Eucharist Lilies. St. Thomas Aquinas: Summa Theologica. The Little Colonel Stories—"*

"I don't think we have the same tastes," Faye said. "If you'll excuse me, I'll be out of your way in a minute."

She tried to focus on the titles, but she kept hearing them in the boy's voice, and her focus eventually slid back to him.

He lifted his chin as if he'd been expecting her to surrender her gaze. "You're a virgin, aren't you?"

"Excuse me? What kind of question is that?"

He shrugged. "Probably an inappropriate one. I was just curious. You don't have to answer."

She shouldn't have. She should've walked out. She should've ripped the obscene book from his hands and smacked him over the head with it. But the pale marigolds in her stomach made her feel like she was weightless again, and those five words—*you're a virgin, aren't you*—felt like a dried-out seed rolling around in the husks.

"I'm not married," she replied matter-of-factly.

He laid his hand upon the book like it was a holy tome and bowed his head in reverence. "Of course. But you do realize you don't need to be married to do it, right? It's not like your legs only open at a priest's say so."

She immediately turned for the door, and the boy ran ahead of her. He got in her way to apologize like blocking the door didn't negate the apology entirely, and held up his hands in supplication.

"I'm sorry. That was rude of me."

"It's all been rude."

"You're right. I have no excuse." He cocked his head, and his lips twitched in and out of a smile. "Your name is Faye, isn't it?"

She blinked, and his smile returned to stay. He tossed his book onto the floor under a stool and stepped away from the door. Again, she should've fled, or retrieved the book to burn and light her way to the dining room. But when he extended his hand, pale yellow in the candlelight, she took it and said, "Yes, I'm Faye."

"It's nice to meet you," he said. "I'm Jason. Jason Norton."

"Hello."

"Aren't you supposed to say it's nice to meet me too? That's the polite thing to do."

She sat on the stool above *Brave New World,* ankles locked and hands clasped. "Are we being polite now? After you insulted my virtue?"

Thunder struck, and their combined yelps extinguished Jason's candle. Only Faye's remained. They scooted their chairs closer, and she shielded the flame from her frantic breath.

"How long do you think the storm will last?" she asked.

He shrugged. "Forever?"

"I'm not sure I want to be trapped in here forever."

"I've been trapped in worse places."

"Like where?" Her breath troubled the flame, and she covered her mouth as Jason laughed.

"Maybe we should be quiet," he said. "There are better ways to get to know each other, anyway."

"Lots of people in Chilmark use sign language," she said. "I know a little."

"I know something better we could do with our hands." He slid his fingers over her thigh, and seemingly sincere in his passionate designs, but Faye expelled a loud, pointed chuckle.

The heartbreak that crumpled Jason's face was the last thing she saw before her ridicule blew out her candle. With a heavy sigh, she apologized, and he instantly forgave her.

His voice sounded different in the dark. Warmer. And when he scooted his chair close enough to lock knees with her, Faye discovered she was warmer too. The buzzing feeling was back, as was the sensation of blooming in her belly. But she wasn't a wilted flower anymore. She was a field of golden stargrass, open wide and sunshine bright, and Jason Norton could see it. He could see *her*—everything—what she'd experienced at the feast, what she'd done to Marcelo, what she heard in her mind as she threaded her fingers with his.

"You too will be a vessel, little lamb . . . "

Faye smiled. This wasn't how she'd pictured her ascension to a higher purpose. But until recently, she hadn't known for certain she had one. Not until Marcelo closed his eyes could she truly open hers, but they were wide now, so much that they spilled tears down her cheeks. In fear, yes, and in lingering confusion for the choice of partner, but she had to accept that this was what Agnes wanted. This was the reward for Faye's first castigation. She just had to be brave enough to accept it.

Her hands were sweaty, but he didn't mind; he was pulling himself closer to her, his kneecaps grinding against hers until she opened her thighs and his knee slipped between, nearly slamming against her pelvic bone. She gasped, then giggled.

"Sorry about that. I didn't mean to—"

"It's all right. I'm fine. You didn't hurt me."

His fingers slid free and glided up to her cheek like he could see perfectly in the dark. Maybe he really could see the light inside her, like St. Agnes and the holy mothers were guiding him—guiding them both—to a new union, far stronger than her bond with Marcelo.

Cupping her face, Jason whispered, his breath pitching off her lips. "I would never hurt you. You wouldn't hurt me, would you?"

She shook her head but said, "I don't know."

He smiled. "At least you're honest."

Cracking to nervous laughter, she pressed one hand to her racing heart. "I can't believe this is happening. Is it real? Are you real?"

Jason's head shook that time. "I don't know. But it feels real. And you . . . "

His lips pressed against hers, surprising her, making her gasp and yelp before the warmth of the dark made her insides shine like Heaven. Her mouth pressed back, harder, hungrier. Petals did backbends and pistils stood tall, and Faye parted her lips.

Part of her screamed, "This is exactly what the devil wants, Marcelo's disease is inside you, like this boy will soon be inside you, no excuses about blessings and martyrs will save you, no prayers will change what you've become." She wanted to fight the desperate squirmy desires, but the harder she tried the more they divided and spread, until lust had colonized every inch of her humming body.

It wasn't a disease. It was a blessing.

There was a brave new world inside her, islands of fear and magic, and stories of martyrs and mothers that made Faye realize that she had no life of her own. Between Amelia's maternal resentment and Marcelo's intoxicating fairy tales, Faye was never given the opportunity to develop her own ideas about what she wanted out of life.

It was that emptiness which made her so appealing to the powers that be. They could fill her with whatever light they wanted, and now, with Jason Norton, they were following through on the promises St. Agnes made in the woods outside Hen Heath.

"This is crazy," she said, and he kissed her forehead.

"Love is like that."

She didn't believe him until she felt the pain. Nothing but love could hurt so much. Tears filled her eyes, but she didn't blink them away, for in that watery veil when the pain was loudest, a ghostly face looked down at her.

As she tilted her head back and Jason kissed her neck, Faye grinned at Father Marcelo and whispered, "Now *I* am God."

CHAPTER SEVEN

AYE FELT SAFE with her arms and legs wrapped around Jason's body. When the thunder clapped, she couldn't tell if it was applause or condemnation, but Jason's lips silenced every doubt. She could've stayed entwined forever, breathing in time with him, feeling his pulse inside her, but he scooted her off his lap just a few minutes later.

It was at that moment she realized it wasn't her virginity she'd been protecting. It was something nameless and far more sacred.

And it was free now.

Jason pulled a box of matches from his pocket and lit one of the candles without explaining why he hadn't done so in previous times of darkness, and Faye didn't dwell on it once the room illuminated. She hadn't seen his naked body during lovemaking and it shocked her now. Her own body shocked her too, and she covered her exposed breasts.

He snickered. "Little late for that, kid."

The warmth was gone. He sounded more like Mr. Bellamy, his voice clipped and eyes narrowed in an almost judgmental squint. As she rushed to dress, he retrieved his Huxley, flipped to the bookmarked page, and continued reading.

Once buttoned and cinched and her hair as neat as it would get, she stood before him shaking in silence as he read. After what felt like a lifetime, he looked up.

"Are you all right?" he asked.

"I think so. Are you?"

"Of course," he replied, grinning. "I'm with you. Beautiful, perfect, amazing you."

But his eyes dropped back to the prose before he finished speaking, and Faye's skin iced over. Her breath stuck like a hailstorm in her throat, and she snatched the book from his hands.

"What's the big idea, kid?"

He hadn't called her 'kid' before, but now he seemed to think it was her name.

"Maybe this isn't a big deal to you, but it is to me."

Jason's face softened and he exhaled heavily. "Oh. I get it. You want romance."

It wasn't the word she had in mind, but it wasn't far off. She shrugged, and he rocked onto his feet. Holding her by the shoulders, he kissed her forehead.

"What we have surpasses romance. Anyone can have that cookie cutter bull. What we have," he said, almost singing the pronouncement, "is built on a stronger foundation than romance. We have fate on our side."

"So . . . you *do* like me?"

He was looking away, but he said it so sincerely. "Honey, I love you. It's just a shame we live so far apart."

"So you are going to leave me?"

"What other choice do I have? Once summer ends, I'll go back to the mainland. I have a responsibility to myself and my family to finish medical school. I have a job, Faye. I have a life."

Panic rung through her like a fire alarm. The dream of motherhood exhilarated her, but it included a partner who doted on them both, and she assumed that's the kind of mate the saints would provide. If he didn't plan on sticking around, it meant she'd be the same kind of mother as Amelia, though not as easy.

Or was she?

Faye backed away from Jason. She wanted to thrash her marigold insides, rip the feelings out at the root, but it was too late. She wasn't hollow anymore; she felt it as surely as she felt the pain masquerading as love.

"You don't love me." She gripped her stomach. "You don't love *us*."

He pulled her into an embrace and kissed the top of her head. "Calm down, kid. God, if you want to know the truth of it, I feel like *you're* the one who doesn't love *me*."

"What? Why?"

"Because you obviously don't want me to leave. But someone who loved me wouldn't ask me to give up practicing medicine, something I've spent my entire life dreaming about. Unless you're not the woman I thought you were."

The tests never stopped. The opportunities to prove herself worthy of Agnes's belief were archipelagos from which she could never sail away. She would have to shipwreck into them all, walk their beauties and dangers alone, and find her way to the next without losing faith that she wouldn't be alone again.

"Will you come back?" she whispered.

"My family always comes for Christmas. I doubt our plans will change this year."

"Christmas is so far away. Maybe I can visit you next month. My grandparents live in Cape Cod. I've never met them, but—"

A bloodcurdling scream swallowed the conversation, and Jason stared at Faye in puzzled shock. She thought the doctor-to-be had learned everything while he was inside her, but he didn't know why the innkeeper was screeching the name "Marcelo," or why Faye's face turned scarlet as she tried to stop him from opening the door.

She clung to his shirt and repeated herself. "Maybe I can visit you."

He didn't respond, spinning her out of his arms and flinging open the door instead. He took the candle and left her to join the crowd gathering at the bottom of the steps, staring up while Amelia Hayworth's wailing filled the house.

She followed them upstairs because she had to play along. Because she had to wail like her pathetic mother. She had to throw herself upon his corpse and weep like she'd never forgive God for this grievous error. But when it came time to put on a show, she couldn't move. She stood in the doorway of her bedroom like a corpse herself as her mother sobbed over Marcelo Melo.

"He's gone," she cried. "I can't believe it, I thought he had more time, oh my God . . . "

Amelia sought and needed comfort, and as a Catholic—as well as someone who needed to exude innocence—Faye desperately wanted to give it to her, but there were too many emotions swirling through her to snatch out the one she needed. When Amelia looked over her shoulder and reached for her daughter's hand, the tension commandeering Faye's body prevented her from reaching back. She just crossed herself and whispered, "Oh Mother . . . what did you do to him?"

Amelia sprang to her feet. "What? I didn't do anything."

"Why did you put Father Marcelo's body in my room?"

"I didn't!"

"You knew he was sick, but you had to use him one more time, didn't you? Squeeze out one more donation for the poor?"

"I was looking for him all night—"

"You were refilling tea and booking rooms for Christmas."

She turned back to Marcelo. She clutched and kissed his hand. "I was looking for you. I promise."

Faye's stomach turned as she stepped into the room. Assuring the guests everything was fine, she coaxed them back and closed the door.

Even with the myriad madness besieging her heart that night, she hadn't expected so many intense emotions watching her whore mother mourn her favorite customer.

Amelia Hayworth didn't love anyone. She couldn't. So

why was she playing the part better than Faye, someone who'd actually loved Marcelo all her life?

"Maybe it's better," Amelia said, stroking his face. "He was in so much pain."

"He was fine this morning. You must've done something to him."

"What the hell is wrong with you?" she hissed. "I know you just found out Marcelo was sick, but I've known for over a year. A *year*, Faye. We lived through it together, with friendship, with love."

"I don't believe you."

"I don't care if you believe me. I just want you to act like a human and grieve with me."

Something in Faye snapped. It urged her to give in and throw her arms around her devious mother, just as it had urged her to forgive Marcelo. But it was weakness rearing its destructive head—and after she'd been so strong and brave in the reading room. She'd done what the great mothers wanted and taken her first step to becoming one of them.

A bolt of lightning struck the tree outside the window, and the women screamed. But while Amelia draped herself over Marcelo's body like lightning could still hurt him, Faye stood at the glass to watch the tree burn.

It sparked and sizzled, slicing through one of the tree's twisted limbs, and dropping it to the flooded garden below. The fire in the branch went out immediately, but in Faye's mind it raged on. When her gaze floated from the charred wood sinking in the garden mud to the filthy woman holding her dead lover's hand, she realized she was staring into the past. The room didn't look like hers anymore, and the harder Amelia urged her daughter to join her in mourning, the more Faye disconnected from her.

Someone knocked on the door, asking if there was anything they could do. Despite Amelia's protest, Faye stuck her head into the hall.

"Thank you for the concern, but we'll take care of this."

She lifted her chin, gaze circling the onlookers. "We lost a very dear friend today, but it's nothing you need to trouble yourselves with. In fact . . . " She stepped into the corridor and closed the door behind her. "I can take care of anything you need." She zeroed in on Jason then, her voice softer and sweeter as she added, "Do you need me?"

Only Agnes of Rome answered, in a voice from deep inside. She said it was time to walk away. And though shocking pain like a secret splinter struck her chest as she imagined her mother still folded over the corpse, she told herself it wasn't Amelia, it wasn't Marcelo. They were just shadows of the past.

Looking forward, she led the strangers into the dark.

CHAPTER EIGHT

FOUR MONTHS LATER, Faye wrapped her arms around the toilet bowl and suffered her Christmas dinner in reverse. She was still spitting out chunks of green beans and almonds when Amelia flung open the bathroom door.

"That's it. You're going to the doctor. And if the 'man upstairs' cares about you at all, you better pray this isn't what it looks like."

Faye wiped her mouth with a towel, hiding her cheeky smile, then spat again. "I don't know what you're talking about."

Amelia loomed over her, hands on her hips. "Oh please. You have the gall to judge me, to judge poor Marcelo who did nothing but love you, then you go and get yourself knocked up at seventeen. What a respectable God-fearing woman you turned out to be."

Faye stood shakily and tossed the towel in the sink. Amelia was hot on her heels as she left the bathroom, but she didn't feel strong enough to speed up. Nausea swelled over her when she reached the kitchen, the house still heavily perfumed with savory food, and she leaned on the table to steady herself. There were only four guests at the inn over the holidays, but they'd left earlier that morning to walk the quiet streets and visit the few establishments open in the off-season. Business hadn't increased since the hurricane as hoped. A goodly amount of the Vineyard had been reduced to sticks and stones, and even with volunteer crews working around the clock, the island was still a mess come December. It took all of Faye's power working through Jason Norton to convince his family to keep up their Christmas tradition.

They didn't stay at the Boatman though, choosing to stay at another hotel that had weathered the hurricane. Amelia blamed Faye, since she should've been able to sell a room to her purported boyfriend, and Faye placed the blame squarely on her mother's increasingly erratic behavior. It was actually something of a miracle that there were no guests to witness Amelia, inebriated at 2pm, shouting as she stumbled through the inn in pursuit of her pregnant daughter.

"I'm not going to live like this," she said. "You better pray that whoever knocked you up is rolling in it, because we sure as shit aren't."

"Don't worry about it."

"Oh that's easy for you to say. You've got a time bomb in your tummy, darling, and it's going to blow both of our lives to Hell."

Faye stopped in the hall, holding her breath as she turned. "You don't know anything about Hell. You don't believe in God or Satan or St. Agnes. You don't believe in me. I've tried to help you so many times. I wanted us to be better than this. To love each other, care for each other, the way we're supposed to. But you wouldn't listen. You refused to change, and I can't waste any more time trying to help you."

"I didn't ask for your help," she spat. "I loved my life before you came along. Hell, I loved it every day after too, right up until a few months ago . . . " Amelia's voice caught in her throat. "I know I stand for everything you hate, but no matter all the cruel things you said to me, I never tried to change you. I never degraded your religion even when it bordered on zealotry. And I didn't listen to Marcelo when he said your blackouts were a sign of the devil in you."

Faye blinked rapidly. "He never said that."

"No? Would you like to ask him?"

Faye shook her head in pity. "That might be the nastiest thing you've ever said. But you're still mourning the loss of income, so I'll let it slide."

Amelia gasped as Faye pushed past her and returned to the upstairs bathroom. She tried closing the door, but her mother stopped her, pushing it open with a grunt. Faye didn't want to fight, so she let her stay, and directed her attention to running a bath.

"You might not approve of my relationship with Father Marcelo or anyone else," Amelia said, "but he was a good man, probably the best man I've ever known, and when you found out he was dying, you mocked him. You abandoned him. All those years he kept you alive when I was a wreck, all those stories about the Azores and Agnes that shaped the person you are today . . . did they disappear completely the moment you found him doing something a little less than chaste? All his goodness forgotten. How can you believe that's right, Faye?"

At some point in her speech, her voice cleared and leveled, and though she still wobbled in place, her eyes were bright with genuine curiosity.

Faye tested the water, shook off her hand, and sat on the edge of the tub. "Do you really want to know?"

"Please."

"I was warned that he might be sick. And if he was, that I would have to find a different path to my destiny."

Amelia was all at once drunk again. She stumbled and caught the edge of the sink, lowering herself to the toilet. "Warned? By whom?"

Sour fire flicked Faye's esophagus, but she dammed her throat with her tongue and swallowed hard as she swam her fingers through the warm water.

"The day of the Holy Ghost Feast—"

Amelia held up her hands. "I don't want to hear this. Marcelo told me more than enough."

"If he had, you would've been prepared for his death . . . and for the life we were given in exchange," Faye said, laying her hand to her belly. It was only a slight prominence, but it was enough. And unlike Faye was to Amelia, her daughter would also be enough. "St. Agnes told me I'd be a vessel," she said.

"Oh Jesus Christ."

"She told me I'd help rescue this world from the corruption threatening to destroy goodness and peace forever."

"That's it," Amelia said, throwing her hands in the air. "You don't need a doctor. You need a rubber room." She opened the door, but Faye jumped up and slammed it closed.

"I'm not crazy."

"Oh sweetheart, you very clearly are."

"I'm blessed."

"You're a pious little ingrate who can't possibly take care of a baby. But don't worry," Amelia said, pinching her daughter's cheek, "we'll find someone who can."

Faye held her stomach as she backed away. "You wouldn't."

"Honey, this isn't a punishment. It's a fact. You can't raise this child. *I* can't raise this child." Her expression softened, and she sucked on her top lip as she fought to hold her daughter's gaze. "Look. However we feel about each other, I need you to know that I don't want you to be in pain. I don't want you to struggle like I did. And hating *me* because *you* had some bad luck won't solve this problem."

"There's no problem to solve. This is what God wanted. It's what I wanted." She turned off the water and sat on the edge of the tub again, her hands clasped in prayer. "St. Agnes said I would face opposition, and I have—enough for ten people—"

Amelia rolled her eyes, but Faye continued undeterred. "So yes, I know this isn't a punishment. This is a reward. For all the loneliness and judgment, for the lies I mistook as love, I will finally have someone who understands me. Someone who'll love me no matter what."

Amelia's face dripped with spiteful mirth, and she slapped her knee as she laughed. "Oh honey, you're in for a hell of a shock. You think I didn't feel the same way about you?"

"No, I don't."

"I'm not surprised. You were disagreeable from the start and haven't changed one wit. But you'll have to now, darling. And so will whatever unlucky lad you dragged into this madness."

"At least I know who fathered my baby," she hissed.

Amelia lifted her eyebrows and exhaled stiffly through her nostrils, but she wasn't wounded. Her nonchalance made Faye's brain simmer with rage. Even now Amelia couldn't feel the shame of her actions. She still stood with her chest puffed and chin high, like she was wearing an invisible crown.

"Does *he* know?" she asked.

"I'm telling him tonight. So if you don't mind, I'd like to take a bath."

"I'm afraid I do mind, Faye. You have some serious issues that need attention, and we've put it off long enough. If you really want to be a good mother to this child, you need to get your head right."

"You don't understand."

"I know. And I'm sure you think it's because of gods and saints and fairy princesses, but I can't let you bring a child into this world when you have such a skewed view of it."

"What do you think you're going to do to stop me?"

"I'll call the hospital. They'll know what to do with you," she said sadly. "I'm sorry, Faye, I really am, but you'll thank me someday." Whipping open the door, Amelia marched into the hall, and slammed it behind her.

She had a head-start, but Faye caught up quickly. On the precipice of the staircase they'd traversed a hundred times every day to wake guests and change sheets, to deliver room service, to sleep and bathe and sin, the Hayworth women collided.

Amelia appeared to hover in mid-air after the crash, and in the moments before she tumbled backward, she was nearly an angel, her arms open like wings and the fear of God rising rosy in her cheeks. Then, with wet snaps and glottal yelps, she hit the steps, one after another, until the final smack lay a quilted silence over the stairwell.

Faye left on tiptoes, careful of the blood.

CHAPTER NINE

Ava's chin trembled. "You killed her?"

Faye exhaled and gazed at a lamb tapestry on the wall, her focus faraway as if she were looking through it. "No. She smacked her head and smashed her spine and lay there bleeding for hours until the guests returned, but she survived. There was significant brain damage, of course, and she was paralyzed from the neck down, but still . . . alive." Smirking, she swung her focus back to her daughter. "It worked out pretty well, actually. I moved her into my old room, into the bed where Marcelo died, and did my very best to give her the care she deserved. But I also had to make sure the inn didn't go belly up. We needed the money. Your father wasn't a doctor yet."

"And I assume he reacted to the news of your pregnancy with all the excitement a first-time father should."

Faye bared her tilted acrylic teeth. "Of course."

Ava scoffed. "Right. And I'm sure he had no problem with the fact that you believed you were giving birth to the chosen one." She suddenly snorted, jolting with laughter. "Oh my God, I just realized you thought Natalie was going to be some kind of female Jesus. How did Dad react to that?" She jerked her hands and feet as she cackled, quickly realizing she'd loosened the twine on her right wrist. It had also sliced her wrist pretty badly, but she tried not to call Faye's attention to it.

The old woman smacked the lamb statue. It rang so

loud in the room, it must've hurt her hand, but no pain registered on her face. Her scars erased many treacherous emotions, but she couldn't hide the way her expression scrunched when speaking about her dead husband.

"He didn't shirk his responsibilities. He wasn't happy about it, and I don't think he really loved me, but he found a job at the hospital and did what he had to do. It was enough. Unfortunately, he didn't value faith like I did."

"That's an understatement if ever I heard one," Ava said. "And how long was it before he cheated on you? How old was Natalie? Or were you still pregnant with her when he met Aunt Lily?"

Her eyes burning, Faye snarled. "I'll admit it now, if it'll help you understand what I've endured." Gripping the arms of her throne, she leaned forward and stretched her neck to one side. "I knew Jason wouldn't be the partner I needed him to be. I knew he wasn't a good man. But St. Agnes didn't speak to me of partners or good men. She spoke of Marcelo's corruption, my ascension, and the child who'd save the world." She glared at Ava, her wrinkled lips twitching. "I just didn't know which child it would be."

A cacophony exploded in the hall outside, and Ava flinched when a steel door slammed. Faye wriggled off her throne and limped toward her daughter, who twisted her body to the sounds. With a grunt, Faye slapped her withered hands over Ava's ears and yanked her face close.

"I wanted it to be me," she said, her fingers pressing into Ava's scalp. "I wanted to believe an actual child couldn't possibly save this world, and I prayed for the great mothers to be wrong. That's why they saw fit to test me. They gave me anger and envy. They gave me hate and indifference. They were my crosses to bear and mountains to cross, but for all the pain, I found places where I could curl up and remember. Not just my mission, but Marcelo."

Doors closed and voices died, and Faye's hands flew from Ava's ears with a disturbingly crooked smile.

"I resented what he became, but his lessons stayed with

me. They *were* me. But I had to teach myself to accept it, and to evolve my faith. One of the tenets of the Divino Espírito Santo encourages autonomy from the church, especially when clergy aren't available for consultation. So I took the pieces that would serve me and let go of those that wouldn't. I found ways to speak to Agnes, to stay on my path, and to spread her message of chastity and sacrifice to those who needed it most."

"You stole the culture of the man you killed, chose whichever rules suited you, and used it to kill people you deemed insignificant." Ava cocked her head. "Is that about right?"

Faye hummed through a chuckle and tousled Ava's hair. "Well it's closer than whatever Jason thought I was doing. He was a good doctor but not a smart man."

"Smart enough to get away with cheating on you for almost a decade."

Faye inhaled sharply, closed one eye, and waggled a finger. "*There* she is. That's Amelia, clear as day. Cheeky. Viperous. You and Natalie, both. It proved to be a bigger problem than I'd ever anticipated."

Ava squinted. "Did you ever think maybe it's because *you* were the problem?"

"I thought that for a long time, I assure you. I questioned my intentions, my blessings, especially when it became obvious that Natalie didn't have any of the qualities St. Agnes described—and worse, she acted in direct opposition. I thought perhaps I'd failed again. I was depressed, beyond stressed. I experienced blackouts like I hadn't in years, and—" She sucked in her cheeks. "Well, Jason didn't know how to handle it. I think they scared him."

"I don't blame him. They scare the hell out of me," Ava replied.

Julian's face bloomed in her mind, and her heart ached far worse than her ripped-up wrist. Where was he? Where were the police?

"You never even tried to embrace them," Faye said. "How can you ever see the beauty in something if you start out thinking it's ugly and wrong? If you spend all your time hating that part of you, how can it be anything but evil?"

Ava shook her head slowly. It was throbbing all over, like rubber bands were tightening around her skull, but the longer Faye rambled about what a bad hand the gods had dealt her, the longer Sophie was safe.

She hoped.

"So you gave up on her," Ava said. "Natalie, who you conceived the night you killed your mentor, the one you thought might save the world. You abandoned her."

"Not intentionally. Though I did have reservations about her soon after she was born. She bonded with Jason much easier than me. She didn't want to breastfeed. She didn't like being held. I still believed in her, but when I found out I was pregnant again, everything changed. In that moment I knew St. Agnes had moved on from Natalie to this new baby . . . to you . . . " Faye touched Avery's face and hair. She squeezed her shoulder and sniffled, blinking slowly as if tranquilized by the drug of nostalgia. "I don't even know where you came from. I wasn't exactly performing my . . . wifely duties . . . but I wasn't with anyone else. I must've blacked out; it's the only explanation. Agnes must've been inside of me—she must've made it happen. That's how I knew you were going to be something really special."

"Mom, that's insane."

"Yes, that's what Jason said too." Sighing, she moved to the lamb tapestry. It fluttered slightly, swelling against the palm of her hovering hand. "I know Amelia thought it too. But by then we'd sold the inn, and we used the money to move my dear broken mother to her parents' old house in Cape Cod. I hired people to care for her, and the house, of course. It came in handy years later . . . more than Amelia did." She grazed the tapestry and turned with a chilling flourish. "But they were both wrong. You *were* special, Avery, and I wasn't about to let your gifts go to waste. Even if I had to dumb down my spirituality to simple Christian parables and metaphors, I was going to help you grow into your destiny. And you took to it like a duck to water."

"Like a rabbit to a garden," Ava muttered.

"It was beautiful watching you blossom," Faye said, wistful. "All those nights, finding them on beaches, dragging them from back yards and back seats—"

"None of that was my choice."

"No? Because you really seemed to enjoy watching me for years. You laughed. You clapped. You told me you loved me."

"Shut up!"

"I will not," she said stiffly. "Those years were a revelation. Our secret midnights were the only thing that kept me going when your father was running around. We'd just celebrated your fourth birthday. He took the day off work, which he rarely did, and spent every minute with us, with you. He looked truly happy for the first time in years. He *acted* happy. I thought, 'This is it. We're going to be happy.'" She swallowed hard and sucked on the inside of her remaining cheek. "And then he disappeared for almost four days. He didn't miss work; he just didn't come home. And because I had the car, I assumed he didn't intend on returning. So on the third day, I sat outside the hospital and watched him get into another woman's car. I followed them. I parked at her house in Chilmark. I watched them through a window she'd obviously never cleaned."

"Aunt Lily?"

Faye didn't speak, but the tightness in her jaw was answer enough.

"But she wasn't the only one," Ava added.

Faye inhaled sharply and looked to the curtain on the wall. "No. But she was the one he loved. More than he ever loved me, and he said so, many times."

"But you stayed with him."

"For you," she said. "For Natalie."

"No. That was for you, Mom, so you wouldn't look like the only fool on the island who couldn't keep a man."

"I don't care about men!" she screamed, spraying the floor with spittle.

Ava raised her eyebrows, and a slow smile spread across her face. "No, you just needed his money and drugs and the prestige that being a doctor's wife afforded you. Then no one would suspect that you were the cruelest, most sadistic bitch on that island."

Faye's top lip quivered, and between gruesome folds her skin grew beet red. "You don't know anything about what I endured being married to a man who was no better than my disgraceful mother. And, frankly, he got off light. I said I'd let him have his women as long as he didn't throw it in my face, but then he introduced Lily to you girls like she was part of the family, and I couldn't take it. So yes, I let my emotions get the better of me. But do you think it was easy telling people my husband had run off with another woman?"

"No. For you, I know killing them was far easier. And all those years, they were right under our noses. Dead. Rotting. My father, who I loved."

"Don't be so dramatic. You hardly knew him."

"Knowing him four years was better than the lifetime I've known you."

Faye smacked her cane on the floor, and drool spilled down her chin when her teeth dislodged. "You don't even care how hard I worked to save our family. I wanted us to be happy, I really did. For all of Jason's faults, I wanted to be kind to him."

"Kindness isn't exactly your strong suit, Mom."

A stiff chortle shot out Faye's nose, and she leaned forward. "You're joking, right? The people under this roof are alive today because of my kindness. And not just them. Half a dozen houses shelter the poor wretches I've rescued over the years. I nurtured and protected them when no one else would. I listened to them. I supported them. For years after I served my time in Framingham for you—"

Ava's voice was a woken dragon. "*You* killed most of those people! You! Faye Norton! You killed teenagers just for being teenagers!"

But Mother Agnes didn't flinch. She folded her mangled hands and smiled.

"After I served time for you, I was alone and searching just like those lost souls up there. You and Natalie didn't want anything to do with me."

"Because you killed people and blamed me for it!"

"I had no one. I was losing faith. I was suicidal, if you want the truth of it."

Ava rolled her eyes. "Gee, I wonder why your own mother didn't swoop in to comfort you."

"She died while I was in prison, Avery, but thank you for salting the wound."

Ava scoffed. "Oh please. If it were up to you, she would've died a lot sooner."

She shrugged. "But it's not up to me. None of it. I'm just a vessel, like you and Sophie. Like Amelia might've been if she could've cleaned up her act. That's all these people want: to be filled with something other than despair. It's all anyone wants. Don't you, sweetheart?"

Ava didn't reply, and Faye lowered her head as if suddenly overcome with emotion.

"I realized that in Framingham. Lots of time to think and reflect in there. And most importantly, lots of time to plan."

"I'm glad the time was beneficial to you," Ava said spitefully. "I wish I could say the same for *my* prison."

"Whose fault is that?"

The chair shook as Ava roared, "It's yours! You horrible fucking bitch, it's all yours."

Faye fanned away the dirty words like windblown cinders, chuckling softly until a knock on the door pulled her from the tapestry. She shuffled to the entrance and spoke to the person in hurried whispers. Ava could only turn enough to see the person's hair over Faye's patchy scalp, but it was enough to see it wasn't Sophie.

A caustic odor oozed into the room, tickling Ava's nostrils with possible explanations. A few of the odor's notes reminded her of the tinctures and ointments in Julian's closet, but there was a hint of isopropyl too, chlorine, and something sickly sweet, like the tea everyone had been guzzling.

When Faye closed the door, she approached Ava from behind and crossed her arms over her daughter's front. "This doesn't have to end badly," the chapped lips of a ghost whispered against her neck. "This can end with a family: good and truthful, full of acceptance and love. The people I met changed me, and now I know meeting them is exactly what St. Agnes wanted from the beginning. She allowed me to realize I didn't have to strike down sinners; I could *change* them. I could enfold them in safety and introduce them to my faith, and maybe, just maybe, they would see the light in her wisdom." She grinned, tilting her face to the ceiling and inhaling deeply through malformed nostrils. "It was the awakening I was waiting for. The Cape Cod house filled quickly. Runaways, draft dodgers, whores, and addicts: all looking for a better, cleaner life. While you were in Taunton plotting how to kill me and steal your daughter's child, I used what was left of Amelia's money to feed, clothe, and house dozens of lost souls: children I might have condemn just a few years earlier. In return, they taught me compassion and helped me fine-tune my skills." She bowed her head and made the sign of the Lamb. "It was a time of great evolution and productivity for me. I wish you could've seen it for yourself."

"So, instead of killing them, you collected them . . . to be brainwashed into killing others." Ava's chin trembled. "Jesus Christ, Mom. Was it your lost souls that killed Natalie and Noah? Or did you do that yourself?"

Faye lifted her chin, revealing a shiny swath of loose scar tissue, and she tightened what was left of her lips.

"Why did you still condemn *those* children, Mom? Where was your compassion for the daughter you thought would save the world?"

"What I did to Natalie and Noah *was* compassion, Avery. I may have eased up on my rules for castigation, but the core tenets remain strong as ever. Especially 'what God has joined let no man put asunder.' Natalie and Noah knew the consequences of their sin, and they chose to violate that sacred vow anyway. Still," she said, massaging her gnarled pinkie finger, "I put the question to those first members of the Choir of the Lamb. Sophie was an infant, and she needed a mother; on that, we all agreed. We also agreed that Natalie's disloyal actions made her unfit to mother Sophie the way she deserved. So we chose another."

"Gee I wonder who," Ava said, deadpan. "Despite the fact that her father was still very much alive."

It looked like Faye wanted to bray so loud the entire Choir would come down to investigate, but she hid her amusement demurely behind her hand and turned away.

"You had an alibi for the day Paul's boat exploded," Ava whispered, her voice catching in her throat. The memory seeped through her like a slow-acting poison, coloring her thoughts with bloody water and the crisp stench of combustion. Sophie crying. Paul bobbing. The prospect of a happy life both burning and sinking into oblivion.

She exhaled raggedly, and though Faye shivered, she didn't turn. "Did the Choir of the Lamb rig it?"

Faye looked over her shoulder, subtly gleeful. "Along with being a damn good babysitter, Anna Mulberry was one of our first members. She loved Sophie, truly, and she assured me my granddaughter wouldn't be on the boat."

"She failed."

The glee was gone when Faye faced her again. "Not completely. She believed Agnes wanted Sophie to die. She thought she'd been through enough in her short life, and that if Anna could deliver her to heaven, St. Agnes would grant Anna the peace she so desperately wanted." She drummed her cane on the floor as if tapping away a mild anxiety attack. "She was a troubled woman. It was unfortunate."

"Unfortunate?" Ava's wrist rang with pain as she thrashed in her chair. "You've been building a cult of crazies for two decades, and you're calling their crimes 'unfortunate?' God, your brain must be a steaming heap of shit to think like that, and your soul . . . " Ava shook her head. " . . . I can't imagine a single god or devil who'd want a piece of that festering trash."

"Don't you dare talk to me like that."

"What are you going to do, Faye? Lock me up? Kill my sister? How about killing my fiancé? Whoops, you already played those cards. Too bad."

Faye floated over and pressed her cane to her daughter's chest until Ava was silent. "Calm down, or I'll do something to calm you myself."

"You mean drug me?" Ava laughed. "I spent most of my teenage years drugged up, and I still burned down a hospital. What do you think you can do?"

Faye pulled back the cane and bent at the waist, her entire face a wrinkled grimace. "I still have Sophie."

That shut her up. Ava curled her tongue against the roof of her mouth and clenched the arms of the chair as her mother continued.

"I don't even know why you're fighting so hard to get her back. It seems to me she was pretty eager to get away from you."

Ava's expression didn't change, but her eyes glimmered with fresh tears. She whispered, "I tried," and Faye frowned.

"Not hard enough. Again and again, you fought your nature, these precious gifts Agnes bestowed upon us, and what good has it done you? What good has it done *anyone*? Sophie's miserable, and you're an absolute wreck. I hear you don't even see her very often. What could you possibly be off doing instead of spending time with your stolen daughter?"

"I'm off doing whatever I can to improve her life and provide for her future."

Faye sneered. "Well, thank you for the valiant effort, darling, but I'll take it from here. Agnes and I have big plans for Sophie, and I'm certain she won't disappoint me as you did." Her lips trembled suddenly, and her head drooped. "It's crazy, but I have to admit it now. Amelia called Natalie a punishment when I first got pregnant, but she was wrong. You were the punishment. You were so much like me at first. You enjoyed the same stories, you had the same magic, and still, you rebelled against me and the only thing that made you a success. It's simple, Avery. You are destined to fail at whatever you do, including love, as long as you deny your nature."

"Nature." Ava scoffed. "You used me, conditioned me. All of us. You used the threat of disease and damnation to pull our strings, but we should've been so much more afraid. The disease wasn't coming for us; it was already there . . . in you."

"It's in you too, Avery. And you loved every second of it."

"I didn't even remember what you made me do."

Faye groaned. "Believe me, I know. Realizing you hadn't retained my lessons was one of the saddest moments of my life. But I've moved on from it, and so must you. That's why I wanted you here." She patted Avery's hand and looked down on her in wistful adoration. "There's still a chance for you. There's still a chance for our family."

Gritting her teeth, Ava stared so hard at her mother that tears ran down her cheeks. "There's no place for you in my family, Faye. There's no place anywhere; not for you or your disease."

The woman's chin trembled, and Ava tested the twine around her waist as she leaned into a glare.

"I see it now clear as day, Mom. And it sounds like Marcelo saw it too. You host the most deadly and contagious sickness of all: fear."

The sadness dropped from Faye's face, and she jerked back with a robotic chuckle. "You're way off, sweetheart. I haven't been afraid in a long time."

"Because you forced it into me. Into *us*. Everyone you've loved, everyone you've hated, you filled us all with your fear, over and over, until there was nothing left in you. Not even love or hate. You're a January Gingerbread house: dark and empty, but trimmed prettily enough to draw wanderers from their path. The difference is, you don't let them walk away. Your darkness is quicksand. Your emptiness consumes."

"No. St. Agnes chose me to be a vessel."

"Someone so good would never be so stupid."

Faye smacked Ava across the face but lost her balance when she released her cane. She fell to her hands and knees and briefly collapsed under her lopsided weight before pushing herself back up. Bracing herself on Ava's leg, her jagged nails digging into bruised flesh, she planted her cane on the floor and rose to her feet, somehow taller than before. Her eye gleamed white as she hissed at Ava, and though her muscles shuddered and sweat beaded on her forehead, her voice was eerily steady.

"You've made your choice, and I suppose I have to respect it. Yes, the sad and empty woman can respect others. But know now, once the Great Castigation is over and you're choking on your blood, begging me to take you back, the little girl in me, the one Agnes chose first, she won't be empty anymore. She will finally be happy and free, the way God intended. And then, Avery . . . " Amusement crackled like TV static in her throat, and a cloud of grave-dirt breath pelted Ava's face. "Then, I'll make castigation look like a day at the beach. You think I'm a monster now? Just wait. Together, Sophie and I are going to change the course of all life on Earth—death too—and the great mothers will rise once again. You might even rise again, little Avery Norton. Whether you live through this or not."

Faye Norton's survival and subsequent transformation into Mother Agnes had shocked the hell out of her, but not so much as the transformation into whatever stood before Ava now. That creature reminded her more of the ghosts she faced in Julian's office: seemingly real and doing a damn good job of speaking alleged truths, yet there was a certain look or turn of phrase that betrayed them. She'd long ago accepted the ghosts were figments concocted by her broken mind—their little inconsistencies too—but what if Faye wasn't just blowing smoke about the spirit that came to her. St. Agnes, the Lamb, the great mothers, whatever name she assigned it to make herself sound blessed—what if there was something inside her? Something more dangerous than Faye ever could be. What if it was in Ava and Sophie too?

Her head ached, and her belly churned, but the fire wouldn't come. It wouldn't charge her muscles the way she needed to break through the last of the twine. So she sat still, seething in the creature's shadow, powerless except for the sharpness of her tongue.

"I believe you now," she whispered, and the woman cocked her head. "I couldn't have done this to you. All these years I thought I'd killed my mother—I was even proud of it—and it was impossible. I couldn't have killed her, because she never existed. No Faye Hayworth, no Faye Norton, and this Mother Agnes character is the flimsiest incarnation of all. The truth is you've always been a wolf in a henhouse, a devil plucking angels' wings bare for your disguise, and you've gotten so goddamn good at it you've actually convinced yourself you're more than a lonely demon gifted with charisma. But you aren't. You aren't even human."

Faye slithered closer, bones cracking as she hissed, "Oh my dear sweet girl, you have no idea how right you are."

CHAPTER TEN

SOMEONE KNOCKED ON the door, and Faye pulled up her hood. She became genderless, bloodless, and devoid of emotion when she said, "Come in!" But that changed when the pregnant woman waddled over and whispered in her ear. Even shrouded, Faye's face turned sunny, and her voice softened to a musical tone.

"Thank you, Paleo. You may begin the conversion."

The woman bowed her head, flashing Ava a nose-crinkling smirk as she turned on her heel and shuffled out the door.

Drawing close, Faye's gnarled hand caressed Ava's cheek with all the grace of a frostbitten ogre, and her mouth twisted into a twitchy gash of satisfaction.

"You talk about stupidity, but you're the one who came here uninformed, unarmed and faithless, and to top it all off, you thought, 'Hey, why not bring my boyfriend along?'"

Ava's jaw fell loose and her eyes widened in terror as Faye oozed over to the lamb tapestry. Something metallic slid open on the other side, and the tapestry fluttered. Pulling it aside, Faye revealed the hidden pass-through with bars so similar to the ones in Taunton, it felt like Ava was looking into the past. It was the sight *through* the corroded bars, however, that sent panic charging through every muscle in her body.

As Ava screamed and tugged at the ropes, Faye laughed in maniacal delight, drumming the bars in jittery excitement as Peter and Paleo slithered closer to the captive in the neighboring room.

Ava screamed his name, but Julian Archer didn't wake. "Please, Faye. He doesn't know anything about this. He drove me here, that's all."

Faye's fingers fell from the window, and she tilted her head. "Then you shouldn't mind us making him the same offer we make everyone else. If he means nothing to you—"

"I didn't say that."

"So he *is* your boyfriend. And here I thought you'd never get over that nasty little cretin Paul Dillon. Though knowing you, this one can't be much better." Snapping back to the window, she put on her best Mother Agnes snarl and said, "Wake him up."

Peter Light blazed in satisfaction as his fist slammed against Julian's face and drew a fountain of blood from his nose. Julian woke with a sputtering growl, but Peter struck him before his eyes could clear, spattering a polygon of blood across the captive's face.

Paleo stood nearby, rubbing her belly and exhaling long, deep breaths between quiet reassurances to her unborn child. "Daddy's so good. Daddy's so strong. Daddy is filled with holy light. And so are you." She gulped suddenly and leaned against the wall as she expelled an anguished breath.

Julian's head bobbed on his shoulders, and he spat blood before shifting his bleary focus to Paleo.

"Don't look at her," Peter hissed before slamming his knuckles against Julian's cheekbone. "Not that I blame you," he wheezed at the moaning prisoner. With dripping scarlet knuckles, he gazed adoringly at his wife. "She is so bright, so blessed, so beautiful, don't you think?"

Julian grunted as his eyes opened to slits he swung up to Peter. "No, not really. But neither are you, so I'd say you suit each other."

Ava whimpered, "Julian," and as if shocked to life, he straightened his spine and pitched all his attention through the barred window to the prisoner on the other side. Seeing

Ava, he smiled in relief, and tears cut through the blood on his cheeks.

"Now *that woman* . . . " he said, voice wavering, " . . . is really something."

Ava's heart fluttered, then sank. She didn't want this to be the end, but every lick of the flame told her it was. And she had to believe it. It had never spoken so clearly or with such little malice. It wound itself around her heart and squeezed so hard a sob escaped her lips.

"When will it be enough?" she demanded as Faye looked over her shoulder. "How much of my heart do you need to sacrifice for yours to beat again?"

"Oh," she said, turning back to Julian. "One more chunk should do it."

She nodded at Peter, and his fist flew again. But this time when Julian's head wilted, Peter caught him by the hair and forced him to stare into his eyes. Pinning Julian's head against the pole, his voice boomed.

"You wake up on an island, naked and afraid. To your right is a low field at midnight, and to your left, a lush garden in Spring. Just before you are two men and three women clothed in one-piece tunics. Whom do you ask for clothes?"

"No one," Julian replied, blood bubbling off his lips, and Peter released his hair, eyebrows raised.

"Why is that, brother?"

"Because the Lamb wants me to be proud of how it made me, right? It wants me to be secure in my body so I can judge and punish those who *do* question the Lamb's gifts." He crinkled his nose. "How am I doing? Am I part of your sad little club yet?"

Peter's face wrinkled and turned as red as a second-place ribbon. When Julian laughed, the man threw all his weight into his fist and slammed it against his captive's jaw. The impact cut his laughter short, but not his resolve. After spitting a wad of blood at Peter's feet, he shrugged off the blow and looked to Paleo, who'd become gray as dirty laundry in the corner of the room.

"Aren't *you* going to ask me any questions?"

She shook her head, teeth gritted.

"Do you not love your god as much as the others?"

She shook her head again, her shoulders hunched and eyes to the floor as she waddled to the window where Mother Agnes stood, agog at her refusal to answer.

"Forgive me, Mother, I'm not feeling well. I think I need to get some fresh air. This baby feels like a boulder in my stomach."

Mother Agnes hummed in sympathy, then shook her head. "Drink more tea, child. The Lamb wants you right where you are."

Paleo's knees buckled, and with a guttural groan she grabbed the bars to keep herself from sinking to the floor.

"For God's sake, let her get some fresh air," Julian said, and Peter backhanded him so hard his skull rang off the pole.

"Faye, listen to him!" Ava said. "He's a doctor!"

She scoffed. "I thought he just 'drove you here'. How can I believe anything you say, Avery?"

"Mother . . ." Paleo pulled herself closer, opening and closing her grip as if squeezing back a rising swell of pain. "I need to lie down. Just for a minute." Her calm suddenly cracked into a billion pieces, and her scream sliced through her husband's bloodlust enough to let him hear her anguish. He rushed to her side and wrapped his arm around her to lead her from the room, but the firm "No" from Mother Agnes halted them.

She closed a skeletal hand around Paleo's, crushing the woman's fingers against the rusted metal bars. "What you need," she said, "what you *both* need, is the glory of St. Agnes, and there's nothing more glorious than converting a sinner in her name. Do this and your pain will cease, I promise you. Refuse, and . . . well, you do know what happens if our garden isn't completely pure during the Great Castigation, don't you?"

"One drop of bad water is as dangerous as a bog," Peter said, chin lifted.

But Paleo diminished, her body folding over the torturous rock in her stomach.

"You're the best parent of them all, Paleo. You've come so far. You've grown so much from that helpless urchin I found in the gutter in Chicago. But there are miles to go before we're in Agnes's arms. For your child's sake, we need to convert this man. Your child will never know paradise if he remains the filthy thing he is now. It will never know peace. If you refuse this task, you are condemning your child to eternal damnation."

"She's lying to you," Ava said. "She has no access to that kind of information, no divine powers. She's just a sad woman who thrives on deception. She thinks only of herself."

Pain twisted Paleo's face and she gripped her belly, but it was rage, not anguish, that propelled frothy words through her teeth. "She saved me from the street. She made me pure." Narrowing her eyes, she spat strained words that pounded Ava's heart like frozen fists. "She made me more of a mother than you will ever be. And I won't allow anyone to ruin my daughter's ascension."

Faye's eyebrow twitched. "Daughter?"

Paleo shrugged. "I suppose I'll never know, but—" She fell into Ava's intrusive stare, and her face blanched as she backed away from the window. "We will convert him, Mother Agnes. You can count on us."

Faye slipped a thin hand through the bars and cradled Paleo's ashen face. "I know you will, my darling. Now, strip him. Let's see how merry he is once he's been purified."

Julian exhaled raggedly through blood-encrusted nostrils. "You're wasting your time. You won't get what you want from me."

Peter gripped Julian's chin and chuckled. "You say that now, but I can be very persuasive. Everyone has a breaking point."

"You might be surprised," Ava said, and Julian smiled at her through the window.

Faye closed the tapestry with a huff, and the sound of Julian's anguish rose like a hurricane tide as a waltz of pride and doubt carried Mother Agnes past Ava to the door.

With tears falling, Ava said, "You'll never be her, you know."

Faye stopped and turned, her pale eye a slit of curiosity. "St. Agnes? Sweetheart, don't talk about things you don't understand."

"No, not Agnes. You will never be Amelia."

Faye's nostrils flared a warning, but as Julian's screams barreled through the tapestry like a titan's breath, Ava's pulse calmed, and in the sound of his mounting pain, strength like early morning fog awaiting the Island Queen's penetration ballooned inside her.

"It's all you ever wanted, isn't it?" she continued. "You pretended to hate her, but the truth is, you were envious of her. And I understand, because it's impossible for you to be like her. You could never be that free. Or that beloved."

The woman's grimace shook as it spread. "You're a blasphemous little thing. Always were."

"Just like her. And Natalie. And Paul. And your dear Father Marcelo. No one's good enough. Especially not you."

Julian's scream rattled the room, and Faye's face warmed in delight.

"You can still save him. His life is in your hands."

"It usually is," Ava said. "But he doesn't need saving, and neither do I."

A gurgling noise leaked from the room, and Paleo's strained voice came like a whistle through a meat grinder. "You awaken on an island, naked and afraid . . . "

Flesh smacked flesh, bones splintered, and Mother Agnes's eye shone with promise as she opened the door.

"Wait! Where is she?" Ava bellowed. "Where is my daughter?!"

The door slammed, preventing her voice from traveling down the hall, where, behind another steel door, Sophie Francis sat up in bed with a pounding headache.

CHAPTER ELEVEN

A PLATTER OF FOOD had been sitting by the bed so long the butter on the green beans had congealed into a thick yellow paste.

Sophie squeezed her eyes shut and told herself it was all a bad dream. She told herself it was the day before Thanksgiving again and she'd stuffed herself silly with her mother's feast. She was sleeping it off, that's all. She hadn't helped Liam murder someone in a sleazy hotel. She hadn't gotten married to a man she hardly knew, or seen St. Agnes in a baptismal pool. And her mom for sure wasn't an escaped convict from an island off the east coast. When she worked up the courage to look at the ceiling, she would see chunks of stars and appreciate them more than ever.

But the ceiling was blank, and the large orange rug at the center of the room knotted her stomach. She was in the basement of the Choir house, in the room where she'd given her statement about Pamela Mason. Except, there hadn't been a bed in that room. When had they brought in a bed? Who'd put her in it? And just how long had she been shut up in that dark place, alone?

Sophie buried her aching head in her palms and squeezed. Pain burst like a cherry tomato, spraying seeds of torment throughout her body. Waves of nausea forced her to lie down again, but with her eyes closed, the undulations brought hazy flashes of the Thanksgiving feast she'd actually attended—or what little remained of it when Liam roused her from the floor of the black chapel and led

401

her to the table. She'd woken groggy that time too, also unaware of how she'd gotten there.

Sweat glazed her face. The pattern of waking in confusion felt like a frightened fish in her gut, slapping and slashing her insides and sinking razor-sharp scales of doubt into her soft tissue. But between the nauseating pricks of uncertainty, she felt Liam's hands on her body again, exploring the skin exposed by her shredded wedding dress as he whispered, "Everything's going to plan, my love."

She peered into her hazy memory, but she couldn't find anything after the moment Mother Agnes pressed chapped lips to her forehead. Had she and Liam even consummated their marriage? Had the woman in red been real, or was she another version of St. Agnes sent to deceive and dismantle Sophie's mind?

"They've come," he said to her in the black chapel. "And they can't run. You did so well. You're everything I hoped for." He peeled her from the floor, and the pain ringing between her ears thudded all the way down to her toes.

She squeaked dryly. "What did I do?"

"You brought them here."

"I didn't . . . they were already coming . . . "

"For you," he said. "They just didn't know it."

Dizziness crashed over her like a polluted wave. The hangover was much worse than after her first Choir visit, and she nearly lost her balance when she shook her head, so Liam bundled her up in his arms. As he carried her from the black chapel, he reminded her of the part she had to play. She was the main event; the one who would convince the biased reporters and politicians that there was nothing sinister afoot with the Choir of the Lamb. He reiterated that she'd probably find the results of the Thanksgiving ritual unusual, maybe even frightening, but she also had to understand that no one was asking the Thanksgiving visitors to abandon their lifelong religious beliefs to go slaughtering heretics like Pamela Mason. No one was asking them to do anything but have faith, and Sophie, a representation of the Lamb on Earth, would show the skeptics that nothing bad was happening in the house.

But "bad" was the temperature of the room.

Liam had layered Sophie's face with lace veils that pelted hot breath back at her and distorted her vision. She thought the latter was at work when she entered the dining room and saw the turkey already reduced to a cage of glistening bone, but the sounds of a gathering at its start weren't right either. There were no discussions of gratitude or happy recollections of the past year, no compliments to the chef or requests to pass dishes or napkins.

There was singing, though. And intermittent lip-smacking. And frantic, percussive coughing that made Sophie flinch after Liam pushed her into a chair. She tried lifting the veil to see what was happening, but he forced her hands into her lap and whispered like a viper, "Not yet. Not until they're ready."

She wanted to run, if not from the house, then to the nearest record player. Not to listen, but to vanish. She wanted to fall headfirst into the tranquil familiarity of Bowie or Nina or Joni . . . God, just a little Joni . . .

But she couldn't. Despite Liam's claims about the house's music collection, the only records she'd seen were instrumental tracks and the Choir's homespun spirituals. So she allowed the spastic shadows beyond the veil to blend into the lace as she played Joni in her mind.

The singer was right. It did always seem so righteous at the start, with so much laughter and spark. But she was seeing the stain now, beyond the sweetness in the dark, because it was on her too.

The older members of the Choir chanted prayers while the children sang, their soprano warbling as piercing as warped saws, until Paleo Light's voice mounted the spiritual cacophony.

"You've heard our pleas for compassion," she started,

hushing the room. "You've consumed our food and drink and seen the buoyant joy of St. Agnes in our family. You've seen the strength of our love. And still you do not believe in the Lamb."

Someone whimpered—a woman, Sophie thought, but she couldn't parse any detail through the lace. She did, however, see many shadows twist toward her at once when Paleo said, "The Lamb sits among you now. Here, in the flesh, and she is willing to forgive your sins."

Ragged gasps and panting came at Sophie from all sides, and the table juddered, knocking silver and dishware onto the floor. Grabbing Liam's hand, she shrank in her seat and squeaked, "What's going on?"

"Shhh . . . " he said, as if calming an animal spooked by thunder. "You're changing them. You're bringing them home."

The breathing of the shadows increased, and what light shone through Sophie's veil was crowded out by darkness. She swung her head around for more light, but the shadows boxed her in, and their body heat was cooking her alive.

"The Lamb has what you need," boomed Peter Light. "The cure for all your ills."

The table shook violently and Sophie shrieked when strange wet hands closed on her shoulders. Fingertips sunk into her forearms and thighs, and sour breath rolled over the back of her neck as she fought to break free from Liam's iron grip.

"Forgive me," they growled against her skin. "The cure. Please give me the cure. I have a family."

In full dark, she thrashed. She kicked whoever touched her legs, and she swung her head like a club at anyone close enough to breathe in her ear.

Then Liam let go.

Sophie flew off her chair, her equilibrium a sloppy cluster as she crashed into a crowd of sweaty strangers who didn't let her touch the ground. They carried her several feet before she was able to wriggle free of their slippery grasp and rip the veil from her face.

The scene was a suckerpunch that flung Sophie backward against the wall. A dozen men and women in business attire, politicians, priests, and reporters shambled at her with desperate pleas for a cure she didn't have. They reached for her, ripping off scraps of her dress and sucking on the dirty fabric when they couldn't touch her bare skin.

"Stop!" she shrieked. "I don't know what you want! Liam! Paleo!"

But neither were there anymore, and as the remaining Choir of the Lamb filtered out of the dining room, Sophie was left alone with the sweaty strangers either crowding her into a corner or staring at her from the table, hunched and coughing crimson specks across the runner.

She caught eyes with one of them, a priest with a gold wedding band and pink drool spilling heavy from his lips, but a waxy-faced woman with a press badge suddenly grabbed her by the chin and demanded her attention.

Through clamped, blood-tinged teeth, she growled, "Give us the cure."

Their hands were everywhere, their metallic breath and salty bodies sliding against her used tissue of a wedding gown.

Or was it her skin? She felt shrunken and rumpled, and all around her the writhing things clawed to get inside. For a few seconds she thought she should let them. Maybe that was her real purpose. If she was the Lamb, if she was Agnes of Rome, maybe ripping her to ribbons and scattering her far and wide was exactly what the Choir intended . . . and what the world needed.

Floating behind the wilted priest, a young girl with hair like an underwater jungle gave Sophie Francis a smile that leaked smoke across the dining room. The gray wisps smelled of rotten earth and putrid flesh, but the scent triggered the corners of Sophie's mouth to lift.

Then, her fist lifted too.

When her knuckles crashed into the reporter's waxy cheek, something delicious and terrifying exploded within her. Flames of ambition surged throughout her buzzing body, and though her mind whirred with fear, the fire was stronger. It swung her fists again and again—the more damage, the more fireworks to propel her—until the battered visitors slunk away.

They were still screeching pleas, but the tone shifted dramatically. Begging turned to alarm, and staccato coughs became glottal choking that intensified the buzzing in Sophie's body to bone-deep ripples of panic.

It shrank and snuffed the fire so violently that the ashes of her rage felt like jagged glass in the pit of her stomach. She sank to the floor, her vision spinning as she focused on a woman's feet curling out of her shoes. Convulsing in her seat, the woman fell from her chair and expelled frothy yellowed bile swirled with blood, and Sophie had to turn away for fear of vomiting herself, but they were all around her. Thanksgiving guests disgorged their meals and flailed on the floor, the milk of their eyes speckling red and throats bulging from the onslaught of slop pumping out of them.

It was too much, and the glassy residue in Sophie's gut was so heavy.

The visitors were still convulsing when Liam ripped her off the floor. She wanted so badly to sleep, but he wouldn't let her. He pulled her out of the noxious stench of gravy and bile and down the dark stairwell between entombing steel doors to the baptismal pool, where several members of the Choir were praying along the edge.

They looked to Sophie Francis as one, faces brightening as if watching their first sunrise. But she couldn't focus on them, rather the cloudy water at their feet and the acrid stench permeating the basement. She wanted to ask him about the water, and about the large silver vats exhaling ribbons of steam like the underwater girl's grin, but she sunk her teeth into the questions and swallowed them, dubious he'd give her a real answer—or if he ever had.

He pulled her hard and fast down the corridor and threw her into the room like a teenager discarding a childhood doll. She landed on the floor, one knee hitting carpet, the other smacking the cold cement, and spun quickly to see Liam's frame swallow the light in the doorway.

"Liam . . . " She rubbed her knee and curled into a ball, whimpering. "What's going on? I feel like I'm going crazy."

His silence seemed to last an eternity, and his eventual response, a cold whisper of "sleep tight" made her mind spin farther out of grasp. She collapsed in on herself like a dying star, and he closed the door with what sounded like a sigh of frustration.

Sophie sat up in bed again, the sounds of people choking on vomit like a hammer striking the bell of her memory. Dropping her head into blood-stained hands, she mewled.

"What the hell's wrong with you? You were happy last night. You were in love. You were blessed."

The shadows shifted, and someone hissed, "You still are."

CHAPTER TWELVE

ROM THE DARKNESS of the windowless cell, Mother Agnes rose like a vengeful tide. She brought the shadows with her as she limped toward the bed, her face still obscured, but her movements were soft as dandelion fluff as she extended one gnarled hand to the trembling girl, like coaxing a kitten from a tree.

Sophie wasn't about to leave her branch, however, and instead set her sights on the platter beside the bed; should she need to defend herself, it would work nicely.

Mother Agnes's hand crumpled to her chest with a frown. "Oh dear. I know that look. You're afraid of me, aren't you? Yes, of course, why wouldn't you be?" She dropped her hood, and Sophie beheld the breadth of the woman's deformities. "I know it's a lot. It might shock you now, but I was once just as lovely as you."

"What happened?"

Her chin lifted, and wiggling her fingers in the air, she said, "Energy, my girl. Which is also what saved me. It will save us both in the end. But I understand why you're defensive, and why you're frightened."

"Why are you doing this to me. I can't understand. I can't trust anyone here. But," she said, chin trembling, "I'm not frightened of you. You might be the only one here I'm not afraid of."

One side of her mouth curled, and she whispered, "Just between us girls, who *are* you afraid of?"

The dried blood on Sophie's knuckles splintered when she flexed her fingers. "I think it's me."

"You poor girl. I'm sure you've heard a lot lately about who you are and what you're supposed to be . . . and all from people who barely know you. My children mean well, I assure you, but they can't possibly grasp just how important you are to the world. And to me." Sighing, she tapped her cane on the floor. "That won't stop them from acting like they know everything, though. Your new husband especially. He knows how insecure you're feeling about all of this, and I'm afraid he's using it."

Wide-eyed, Sophie ventured from her corner. "He frightened me. He hurt me."

"Yes. And I'm sure he told you it was for your own good."

"No, he's not like that. He's never treated me like anything but a princess. He's always been gentle and considerate. He's a poet—"

Mother Agnes snorted a laugh, for which she apologized. "I don't mean to mock you, dear. It's just that after so many years of hearing the same story from girls like you—heck, after *living* the same story and *being* a girl like you—it's impossible for me to stay silent."

"Liam's different. He has to be. I wouldn't have married him if I thought he was a bad person."

"I'm sure you believe that. Still, you did say he hurt you."

She swallowed hard as the memory of him pinning her hands at the dinner table charged through her bones. "It was so strange. He was treating me like . . . like . . . "

"A weapon." Breath whistled through Mother Agnes's craggy nostrils, and she released the weight of her history onto the bed. "I'm sorry to say that weapons are all we are to them. Even the ones who claim to love us. If we aren't wet with worship, we're witches for the burning. And if we survive the flames, we're weapons to be used in their silly war for power and control. But not for long. The Great Castigation will show them, and it will change them."

"But he was already changed . . . by you," Sophie said

dryly. "He talks about it all the time. You took him in and saved his life. You changed him into a better man."

"Better isn't where evolution ends. There is always more one can do, always sacrifices to be made to the greater good. In his heart Liam knows that. And he knows he isn't exempt from castigation. No one is. But some are luckier than others," she said, stroking the unnatural divots in her cheek. "Liam won't have to wear the evidence of his punishment, day in and day out. He won't have to endure the stares and laughter. He won't have to leave anything of himself behind. He will make his sacrifice today just like everyone else, and he will be remembered for the good man he was, before he sought to use you as a weapon." She touched Sophie's face, her eye glittering with tears. "Do you believe me, child?"

Sophie pulled away. "I need to think about it. About everything."

"Of course. There's still a bit of time before the castigation."

"No, not here. I need to go home."

Mother Agnes straightened her spine and lifted her chin as she looked down at Sophie. "This is your home."

"I want to see my mom."

"She's dead. She has been for quite a long time." Her voice caught in her throat, and she clenched her jaw as her gaze shot away from the wide-eyed girl.

"They told you about my family?"

"They didn't need to," she said, holding the frightened girl's gaze with an intensity that made Sophie's eyes water when the Choir leader's voice poured out in honeyed fortitude. "Dear Agnes," she began, "blessed guide who found me as a child and showed me the future on the day of the Holy Ghost Feast, give your strength to this child now, so that she may become a vessel for your truth. Forgive her doubt. Forgive her fear. Grant this lonely girl the power to open her heart and mind to the transformative magic of the Lamb, which has dwelt in her

410

since birth, as it dwelt in her mother Natalie, her aunt Avery, and her grandmother, who sits before her now."

"Grandmother?" Dizziness struck Sophie like a wrecking ball, but she couldn't stay on the bed; she had to move away from the woman with a mountain of secrets crumbling beneath her. She paced the room, the movement cooling the sweat jeweling her face, and the plush carpet sweating under her toes.

"I'm sorry you had to learn this way. My name is Faye Hayworth, mother to Natalie and Avery Norton, and the person who was meant to raise you."

"How am I supposed to believe any of this?" Sophie's skull throbbed so hard she thought she might pass out. Leaning against the wall, she massaged her temples. "This is too much, it's too insane. My mother is my aunt, my grandmother is a religious leader, and oh, I just happen to be the resurrected saint that inspired that religion. It's impossible."

Mother Agnes chuckled. "You might be right. Except . . . " Her smile fell slightly, and the melancholy that possessed her voice made her sound like a different person: like someone named Faye Hayworth. "I thought *this moment* was impossible too, Sophie. After over so many years searching for you with so much failure, so many mistakes, I admit I gave up hope. I never stopped searching, I need you to know that, but there were times I believed my efforts would remain fruitless forever." She exhaled a shuddering breath with a tinge of joy. "But here you are. Here we are together. I was wrong, and I will gladly take whatever punishment I deserve for losing faith. I'm just so happy to finally see you. To touch you. To comfort you as I haven't since you were a baby. You must have been so afraid."

Sophie peered at the woman from whom scars had ripped any familiarity. Could it really be true? Marriage and deception and murder aside, how could one person seek reconciliation with Sophie so passionately that she tasked dozens of people around the country to be on the lookout? How could Sophie be loved that much and still feel so alone?

Despite her misgivings, something drew her to the woman's unfolding hand. The memory of Mother Agnes's protection the previous night warmed her through, and she realized she wanted, more than anything, for this one thing to be true. Liam's love, her mother's past: it could all be a sopping knot of lies if this woman was her honest to God grandmother. Confused, frightened, and desperate for an embrace like an anchor, she threw herself into Faye Hayworth's arms and sobbed.

The woman rocked Sophie and kissed her head, and she said, "It's okay, darling, Grandma's here," like she'd practiced it a million times to a million shadows. "I swear I did everything I could to find you. Since the day Avery ripped you from my arms—" Her voice caught in her throat, and she apologized. "I should've fought harder for you. I'll never stop being sorry for that. And for everything you've gone through since. I tried to save you that day, but Avery was so strong . . . and what she did to me—" Faye withdrew from Sophie in shame, jaw and fists clenched. "I'm sorry it took so long for me to recover."

"Wait, *she* did this to you?"

Faye nodded. "Payback for what she endured in Taunton. My youngest child—my *only* child by that point— left me near-death in an insane asylum she incinerated so she could kidnap you and fill your head with lies. I was in Mass General for months after. Confused, in and out of surgery, in and out of consciousness. Sometimes I didn't know who I was, and I regret to admit I sometimes didn't remember I was supposed to be looking for you."

"But the police were, right?"

"For a time, yes, but that ended once I left the hospital. Avery ruined my reputation on the island. All the years of kindness and service in the community destroyed because of her accusations. No one would believe me. No one would help me."

412

"Except the Choir of the Lamb."

Faye's face warmed, and she brushed the hair from Sophie's bloodshot eyes. "Yes. And now that we're together, I'm never letting you go. I'm going to keep you safe."

Sophie jolted back. "But I'm not safe. Something horrible happened in the dining room. There were people dying all around me, clawing at me, saying I had some cure."

"I know, and I'm sorry you had to see that. I think bringing you here opened this house to vulnerabilities they didn't have before. New cracks for the bad water to flow free."

"What did I have to do with it?"

"My dear girl, you are filled with magic. That's why those people came after you for a cure. They saw it clear as sun breaking through storm clouds. The beauty and purity of the power inside you is capable of redeeming the most corrupted soul."

"No it's not," she said, retreating. "It's not beautiful. It's terrifying. It always has been, even when I denied it was there. When I accused my mom of making it up so she could keep me a prisoner in our house, I knew deep-down I was the one lying. It's real, and it's wrong. And now I know why. We share the same sickness, Avery and me. It wants me to hurt people the way she did."

Her grandmother grabbed her by the arms. "Don't you dare believe that. Maybe there was some darkness in you, but it's gone now. Just like those people in the dining room. All the ugliness is melting away, and when the Great Castigation is over, you and I will finally get our chance to live as we should have for the last fifteen years." Releasing her, Faye exhaled a breath possessed by both sorrow and hope. "But that's all in the past. What happens next is about us. You and me."

"And the Choir?"

She didn't answer, didn't nod. She slowly closed her

hand around Sophie's and pulled it to her chest. "There's a future for us, little lamb. When the others have gone, we will go too, far away from the foul tea and grim songs, to a place where only St. Agnes can find us."

"But Liam—"

"What about him? After how he treated you today, do you really want to be with him? Knowing he fell in love with who you might be instead of who you are, do you think he's worthy of either?"

She shook her head. It sloshed with muddy pain as she reeled in her hand. "I don't know. I need time to think."

"He's not worthy of you, Sophie. It may be that no one is."

"What?"

"It doesn't matter. Not yet. After the castigation, we can talk about boys as much as you want, but right now we need to focus on the Lamb's plan for us."

"I don't even know the plan! I don't understand what's going on!"

When her grandmother reached out, Sophie screamed and kicked the cane out of her hand. The woman crumpled fast, yelping like a trampled puppy as she hit the floor. She said, "No, don't help me," but quickly realized Sophie wasn't offering her assistance. She glared at the woman, her chin trembling and bloody fist raised.

"Maybe I *am* a weapon," she said.

Faye's lips shifted to one side and slowly curled. "Like grandmother, like granddaughter."

"And like the killer that raised me?"

"Yes." Pushing her cane out of the way and rising with proud independence, she added, "Though I'm pleased to see she's not half the woman she used to be. Except for the boyfriend. Why does Avery always need a boy tagging along?"

"What are you talking about?"

"Oh. I thought Liam would've told you." She swiped her cane from the floor and rested both hands on the handle as she stretched her legs. "Your Aunt Avery is here, right now. Come to save you, apparently, as if you actually needed or wanted it."

Sophie stood up with purpose, but Faye sliced her cane through the air, blocking her granddaughter's path.

"Where are you going, dear?"

"I need to talk to her. To say goodbye at the very least."

"You'll get your chance, don't worry." Faye tapped Sophie's toes with her cane to back her up. Once her granddaughter was situated in a stiff pretzel on the bed, she held one hand to her heart and said, "I promise, I won't let this end without you getting an opportunity to speak your piece to Avery, but I also understand how hard it is for you to trust me, so let me offer you something for your faith."

Sophie's posture softened, and Faye sat beside her, hands shaking as she met her granddaughter's teary eyes. "The Lamb wants us to live. It needs us to. The Choir will need a new voice to act as a vaccine against the disease of hate. Because some of them will hate us, Sophie. When this is all over, people might want us dead. But not forever. Your voice will change them."

She drew her legs to her body and pressed her hands to her quivering mouth. "I'm sorry. I don't understand.'

"You will. When the time comes to drink of the baptismal pool, wait for me, watch me, and as Agnes foretold, we will be together again, forever, and we'll be free. You haven't been to the Vineyard since you were a baby. I'll take you there, where you belong, to the island, where I first saw Agnes, where your real mother lived happily, before the garden died."

"What happened to her? Who was she?"

"There will be time enough for that after the castigation. Until then, you need to play along like nothing's changed. You need to pretend you still love Liam."

Sophie whimpered, "I *do* love him . . . " and her grandmother laughed.

"Yes, say it just like that."

Burying her face in her hands, Sophie felt the cool rich kiss of earth. She tasted dirt like a wedding ring, metallic and binding, but with the occasional brush of earthworm softness that made her feel like she wasn't completely lost yet. If she could still feel life in the graveyard of her spirit, she could still make sense of all this death.

Drawing close, her teeth off-center, Faye whispered, "I'll tell you everything. Things I've never told anyone. I'll tell you what's inside us."

Someone knocked on the door, and Faye Hayworth vanished. Pulling up her hood and hunching her spine, Mother Agnes beckoned them in.

The woman called Garza had black ink on her fingers and a suitcase she sat on the end of the bed with the reverence of a holy relic. Sophie didn't think she'd spoken to her, but by the sheer breadth of artwork decorating the Choir member's skin, she had a fair idea why Garza was there.

Flipping open the latches on the suitcase, she grinned. "Is the Lamb ready to show her devotion?"

"We were just discussing that very thing." Mother Agnes wrapped one arm around Sophie and pulled her tight. "She's been so excited for this. Now the entire world will know that she and Liam are one, now and forever."

Sophie looked to her grandmother in confusion, but when the woman's wrinkled face tilted down at her, nothing grandmotherly remained. She was every bit as frightening as the rest of them now, and when the choking sounds barged into her mind again, and a miasma of acidic blood-gravy floated all around her, Sophie realized that nobody under that roof would let her go free. Even if Mother Agnes followed through on her word and they left the Choir house together, there was no freedom in Sophie's future.

When Garza removed her tattoo machine from the case, Sophie squirmed out of Mother Agnes's grip and off the bed, knocking over the platter of cold food.

HARES IN THE HEDGEROW

"Oh my. What's wrong?" Mother Agnes asked, theatrically oblivious.

"I don't want it. You said—"

"Oh! I nearly forgot! My apologies!" She fanned the heat of embarrassment from her face, and Garza furrowed her brow.

"Is everything all right?"

"Yes, of course. Sophie would just rather think of her tattoo as an equal marriage to Liam *and* the Lamb. Forgive me, my dear. I meant no offense." When she headed for the door, Sophie started after, but Mother Agnes stopped her.

"I wish I could stay, but there's still so much to do. Garza will take wonderful care of you, I promise." She gestured to the woman, who grabbed Sophie by the shoulders and towed her back to the bed. "Try to relax. Think of the Lamb. Think of the new life the Great Castigation will bring, and all the souls you will save."

Garza dipped the needles into a cup of black ink, and Sophie jumped to her feet, but the artist quickly yanked her back down. "It's best you remain still," she said. "The chest can be a tricky spot."

Sophie eyes whispered, "Grandma," and wilted from the buzzing machine as Mother Agnes made the sign of the Lamb and closed the door on her scream.

CHAPTER THIRTEEN

"**S**OMETHING'S WRONG . . ."

It was the first sensible thing Ava Francis heard in hours.

Paleo's voice sounded as if she had wet tufts of cotton damming her throat, and both words were attempts to clear the blockage. She hadn't spoken much since the second run-through of Julian's purity test when he laughed over almost every question she asked. Peter took over after that, and he wasn't nearly as patient as his wife had been. Due to his near-constant pummeling, Julian Archer was much quieter during the third test.

By the fourth time around, however, Julian was right back to laughter, and it continued into the fifth run-through until Peter Light threatened to cut out his tongue.

That was the last thing Ava remembered. She must've passed out some time during the last hour; her neck ached terribly as she lifted her head, and the sound of Julian's voice, calm and comforting, disoriented her.

She felt his lips on her inner thigh, the leather crop sweaty in her fist, and his back, as scarred as the world itself, undulating in lustful anticipation between her legs.

"Relax . . . breathe . . . "

She emptied her lungs.

"Squeeze my hand. Dig in."

Her fingernails sank into her palm, but it was the pain from her ripped wrist that charged up her arm and jolted her back to reality.

"Relax . . . just breathe . . . "

"I *can't* breathe*!*" someone screamed. "Something's wrong! It's too early!"

Ava tried to scoot the chair closer to the window but stopped trying when she almost toppled. "Julian, what's going on in there?"

The tapestry fluttered, and Peter Light growled through the bars. "Shut up, Avery."

"Ooh, you're a tough man," she said, dripping with sarcasm. "Does it usually take this long to convert someone, or are you just really terrible at your job?"

Paleo wailed, and when Peter fled the window, the tapestry flapped high enough to grant Ava a glance of Julian's swollen face. He was more injured than she'd ever seen him, but he wasn't afraid. And as Ava ripped her right arm free of the twine, neither was she.

"The baby can't come yet," Paleo screeched. "Not before the castigation."

"I don't think you have a choice," Julian said. "But I can help. I'm a doctor. You just need to untie me."

Peter scoffed. "Not a chance."

"Wait," Paleo barked.

Her voice fell to a whisper, and as she and Peter conversed, inaudible, Ava took advantage of the extra time. She clawed at the twine around her other arm, but the pain ringing through her right wrist weakened her fingers. When Peter Light yelled, "No!" Ava thought she'd been caught, but no one was looking through the pass-through. The "no" was meant for his wife, and from the sound of it, Paleo didn't appreciate the order.

"I don't care what you say," she grunted. "I'm untying him."

"Do it and your soul is forfeit. If you betray St. Agnes, she won't let us find each other in paradise. Or the baby," he said. "I'm sorry, sweetheart, but you need to accept that this is the path the Lamb has set before us."

"She could die," Julian said. "They both could. Do you want your wife and child to die like this?"

"It doesn't matter what I want. Or what she wants," Peter replied. "Now is a time to think of others. Of the world at large. Of the gardens we won't live to tend."

Ava gasped in horror, and Paleo sighed. "You're right," she said.

Something shattered. Someone squealed while someone else moaned and grunted . . . until something thudded wet against the concrete.

Then there was silence, followed by a whimper and frantic skittering across the floor.

"Julian?" Ava clawed desperately at the twine. "Julian? Are you okay?"

The lamb tapestry waved, and something twisted behind it: a hand, blood-spattered and all the more familiar because of it. Fingers flew through the slats and closed around the cloth, pulling it taut and revealing Julian Archer's beautiful broken face. Relief emptied Ava's lungs with a chuckle that was surprisingly contagious. He laughed softly as he gazed at her and said, "You okay?"

"Yes. You?"

Paleo screamed, and Julian said, "Hold that thought, Ava."

He said her name with such warmth and softness that she almost convinced herself it was all a nightmare, that she'd wake up far away from here, in Julian's arms.

But disoriented as she felt, she knew it was all too real: the blood under her nails, the bars on the window, and the frantic woman wailing for St. Agnes to make her labor stop.

Julian yanked the tapestry off the wall and pulled it through the bars into the other room. Folding it into a pillow, he placed it behind Paleo's head as he helped her lie down. Her husband was nearby, unconscious on the floor, blood running down his temple and the broken mug beside him, but Julian hadn't taken any chances. He used the ropes from which Paleo had freed him to restrain Peter Light and drag him into a corner.

"Is he going to be okay?" Paleo whimpered. "I didn't hurt him too badly?"

"He's fine. Try not to worry about him, okay? You need to focus on your baby."

"You don't understand. I'm not supposed to do this."

He hushed her. "It's okay. I'm here with you. Just breathe."

"I can't!"

"Then think of the Lamb. Think of how proud you're making the great mothers by becoming one of them."

For the first time since her labor began, Paleo Light exhaled a breath so full that Ava felt it in the next room. With all the talk of saints and saviors, no one but she understood the real blessing among them. Julian Archer had seen every kind of madness and forgiven every sin the disorders begat. He was saintlier than any Hayworth, Norton, or Francis could ever be, and no one in this hell house deserved him.

Except maybe Paul and Natalie's little girl.

Ava called Julian's name, and he crashed against the bars. Despite the extensive damage to his face and the pain it must have caused, when Ava waved her free hand at him, Julian smiled and waved back.

"Did you see Sophie?" she asked. "Any sign of her?"

Gaze downturned, he shook his head. "No. But I did see chemicals. Barrels of them. Enough to fill a swimming pool."

"Me too. I think Faye is planning on killing everyone in this house."

"From what I've heard, there are other Choir houses preparing for this Great Castigation thing. If it goes down here, I think it's going down everywhere."

"You don't know anything about it!" Paleo screamed, her voice vanishing into glottal pain. She keened through gritted teeth, spraying foam down her front as her eyes rolled to the ceiling. "Agnes, my guide, my everything, please don't make me see her. I won't be able to do it if I see her." Motley fluid flowed across the floor as she begged the Lamb to take her pain. She cried out to God in Heaven and her husband in the corner, and lastly, to the child inside, whom she'd told no one she dreamed of naming "Rachel." Rocking back and forth, she hugged her knees to her chest and whimpered, "Doctor . . . "

Ava blinked, "It's okay," to Julian, and he hesitantly left the window.

"We have to stop it," she mewled as he knelt beside her.

"It's too late. The baby's coming."

"No! The castigation!" Paleo sobbed. "We have to stop—"

The vibratory slam of a steel door cut her off, and her eyebrows shot up her forehead. When she looked to the door, Julian leapt to his feet and turned the lock— seconds before someone pounded frantically on the other side.

"What's going on in there?" the person called, jiggling the handle. "Paleo, is that you?"

"Back off," Julian barked, "or this woman and her baby are in big trouble."

The handle went still, and sudden panic glazed Julian in sweat. He dashed to the barred window and shouted, "Ava! Get out now!"

But it was too late. Liam LaSalle barreled into the neighboring room, shouting for help from his Choir cohorts as he sailed past Ava and slammed against the bars.

"What do you think you're doing?" he growled at Julian. "Open that door right now."

When Julian didn't respond, he shifted his efforts to Paleo. "Open the door."

"I can't!" she blubbered.

"Yes, you can. Just stand up and unlock it. He won't get in your way. He doesn't have the guts."

"She's not going anywhere," Julian said. Approaching the window slowly, he lifted his hands in an offer of peace. "Please, Liam, you need to let me help her."

His nostrils flared. "How do you know my name?"

"Ava told me about you. You met Sophie at a concert, right? The Jerry Garcia Band?"

"What are you, the murderer's parole officer?"

"No. Just someone who listens. And someone you clearly, in all your wisdom, in all your secret cult research, don't know a damn thing about. Doesn't that worry you? It must. Especially since your people did their best to kick the shit out of me, and I'm still standing, with one of your leaders possibly bleeding to death next to me, and the other one tied up, unconscious. Tell me, Liam. I'm listening. How does that make you feel?"

Liam threw himself at the bars and craned to see Peter tangled in the corner, motionless, while Julian fought to keep his focus from slipping to Ava shredding the twine on her left wrist. Her jagged nails slashed skin as well, but within seconds, the final thread snapped and her wrist flew free. Julian flinched and, noticing hope flash through his expression, Liam spun around. Ava was hard at work on her ankle restraints and had just freed her left foot when Liam charged. She jumped up, dragging the chair as he pursued her across the room. Unable to liberate her right ankle by the time she reached the wall, she swung her leg— and the chair attached to it—at Liam's knees.

He howled as he crumpled to the floor. She kicked out the chair again, smacking him in the shoulder, but despite the pain roiling through his body, he grabbed one of the chair's arms and yanked Ava off her feet.

She smacked her head on the concrete and moaned as nausea flooded her senses. But it wasn't alone. The fire came too, low but hungry as Liam LaSalle towered over her and stepped on her chest.

"I could kill you now and no one would care. Not Sophie, not even your own mother. But you know that, don't you?" He cracked his neck and sighed as he rolled his gaze over her. "How long did you think this charade would last, Avery? How long did you think you could play the role of a loving mother while there are people out there still suffering because of what you did to their children and fathers and wives? God, if it were me, I'd be relieved it's finally over. No more running from your past. No more pretending you know how to love."

She looked to Julian, a man she believed she loved with every fiber of her being, good and bad, healed and festering, and wondered if Liam was right. Was it actually love she felt, or was it a deformed sort of addiction that had her substituting one type of violence for another?

"Don't listen to him." Julian Archer pressed his bruised face to the bars and whispered, "I believe in you. And so will Sophie."

When she smiled, Liam pushed more weight into her breastbone, and she cried out. Wheezing laughter, he arched his body over her like a diseased willow and hissed. "Sophie hates you, and she has for a long time. Before she knew what you are . . . and what you *aren't*. If you think any version of this story ends with you two leaving together, you're sadly mistaken. You might as well let me put you out of your misery right now."

"Try it, and the woman over here is as good as dead," Julian said.

Liam scoffed. "Oh please. If you were going to kill her, you would've done it already."

"I don't have to kill her. I just have to let her bleed out."

Paleo screamed, and Liam turned to see Julian had abandoned the window. Curious, he removed his foot from Ava's chest, but he didn't leave her behind. Grasping the back of the chair, he dragged her across the floor until he could see Paleo through the bars, her skin waxy and bone white. Spotting Liam, her weeping turned to bawling, and she pleaded for him to call an ambulance.

He huffed sadly. "You know I can't do that."

Her eyes rolled in her skull, and her lips moved sluggishly as if they'd been numbed. "But I need a hospital."

Ava tried to crawl away, and Liam winced at her like she was a maggoty corpse before stomping on her left calf. She wailed and pulled her leg to her chest as Liam swiveled back to the window.

424

"Listen to me, Paleo. Everything's fine. This is a minor complication, a bump in the road. The Lamb will see you through it, I promise."

"But the baby's coming . . . " Paleo whined.

"If it comes, it comes. We knew that was a possibility." Tapping his fingers on the bars, he added, "And we knew what might have to be done."

She sobbed and shook her head, flinging sweat and tears as blood trickled between her legs.

"Calm down," he said softly. "You won't have to be the one. I'll castigate the child myself."

Paleo wailed and clawed at Julian's clothes if she were trapped in a pit and trying to climb the walls. She kicked her legs, spreading the blood and slipping out of Julian's arms as she screeched. "He can't! Please, don't let him kill my baby!"

"No one's going to kill your baby," Julian said, and Liam hummed.

"Let her bleed out, huh?"

He exhaled heavily and focused on Paleo. "You're going to be okay, but your baby is coming, and I need you to get ready to push."

"No!"

When she tried to scramble away, Julian forced her spine against the wall and pressed her knees to her chest. "Yes. Now."

As Paleo started to push, Liam hunched his shoulders to his ears and grunted like he was in his own kind of labor, oblivious to Ava nearing freedom. When the last thread snapped from the chair, she rose silently and limped to the open door. But when someone suddenly stepped out from the hallway and blocked the exit, Ava scrambled backward and fell to the floor.

The young woman stared down at her as she entered the room, her sheer white dress shredded, her dark hair tangled, and a scratch of black ink weeping blood down her chest.

"Ah," Liam said, turning. "My wife."

CHAPTER FOURTEEN

I T HAD ONLY been a few days, but Sophie Francis looked nothing like the irritable teenager who suspected her mother of keeping secrets. She *knew* every secret now, and they'd transformed her into something else: a creature that looked cool to the touch but, should she desire it, possessed the ability to burn her enemies to cinders in seconds.

Liam seemed to sense it, because when he reached out, he didn't actually try to touch her. His hand floated inches away from the black mark on her chest, and he furrowed his brow when he saw the porcelain platter hanging at her side.

"My love, you should be resting."

"I've rested enough," Sophie replied flatly. She looked to Ava only briefly, focusing instead on backing Liam into the room, her head bowed like a seething bull.

"What's the plate for, Soph?"

Flipping it up into two hands, she showed him the bloody underside, and he narrowed his eyes in doubt.

"Whose blood is that?"

"Garza's. And two others. I don't know their names," she said. "You wouldn't let me get to know anyone. But I guess it made them easier to hurt, and easier to sacrifice. Just nameless sheep in the flock." Sophie's arms shuddered from the platter's weight, and her focus shot to Ava who'd started to inch out from the wall.

"Sophie sweetheart, you're not thinking straight. And

I'm not surprised. I can't imagine how overwhelming all of this has been for you. Even someone with your magic and strength can't be expected to keep it together all the time. That's why I wanted to give you plenty of time to rest before the castigation." His voice was as lullaby-soft as on any starry evening in his Kombi. Unfolding his arms to her, he sang about watching her hair and clouds and stars as they rocked away on a sleeping car, and she was instantly back in his smoke and sweat and the lustful ache that twisted her tongue with ambition.

She wanted to be wrapped up in him, even the lies, especially the lies, because they made her feel most beautiful, and most human. But what she saw during the Thanksgiving feast wasn't beautiful or human. It was more monstrous than any of her nightmarish visions, because it was real. Because he wanted her to worship him for it.

Pouting, he said, "I thought I was being a good husband," and Sophie's entire body tensed.

"A good husband . . . " She lowered the platter and squinted as she approached him. "You left me to sleep alone on the floor of the Black Chapel on our wedding night."

"As is ritual."

"You blinded me and restrained me and told poisoned people there was a cure inside me."

"There is, Sophie."

"And again, you threw me into a room alone, like a prisoner. Was that part of the ritual too?"

"No." He slithered toward her, and she extended the platter, keeping him at a distance. "Honey, that was to keep you safe . . . from *her*." He glared at Ava, but Sophie forcibly reclaimed his eyeline.

"For all her faults," she spat, "she's never forced me to sit at a table of people choking on blood and vomit."

Liam's mouth twitched in staunched amusement. "Well, that's not really her M.O., is it? She prefers to burn people alive. And kidnap children. She prefers to hide her sins in others like festering seeds."

427

"You told me today was about ascension," Sophie said. "You told me I would show the Choir's critics what a loving and open-minded family we are, but we aren't anything like that. We didn't even give them a choice."

He blinked, then laughed. "Is that what you think? Sophie, each one of them was given plenty of opportunities to repent their sins and welcome Agnes into their lives. We were even willing to let them go without pledging loyalty to the Lamb, as long as they agreed to cease their hateful crusades against us. I regret to say hate won today, and that's not how I wanted your first hours with us to go. I'm so sorry for that. But the Lamb chose you for a reason. It chose you for *me* for a reason."

Sophie was so thirsty it was difficult to swallow. Her throat burned, and her voice crackled like a scratched record when she said, "Do you even really love me? Or is it all about the Lamb?"

He shook his head as if disbelieving she could ask him such a question, but if he intended to answer, the words were lost in Paleo's roaring screams from the next room.

Noises for which only mothers knew the names captured everyone's attention so entirely that Ava thought they might be enough to stop the Choir's madness. If anything could drown out their hostile song, it would be the struggling, terrified, hopeful peals of birth, when the voices of mother and child met for the first time as two sides of the same magic. She, Sophie, and Liam watched in stunned silence as Paleo pushed a child she never expected to draw breath into Julian's waiting hands. But draw breath it did, and the most miraculous sound in all of human history rang through the basement.

Cries of oxygen and fear and the shock of cold air against damp skin burst from the baby girl's lips, and everything in the adjoining rooms softened. Even Liam in his savage virtue momentarily relaxed and stepped back from the window to absorb the breadth of the scene. Sophie's eyes teared as she watched the bruised stranger wipe blood and vernix from the newborn's face and showed its mother just what a beautiful creature she'd made. Unable to cut the umbilical cord, he wrapped up the baby girl, placenta and all, in the lamb tapestry and set the bundle in Paleo's arms. And as Sophie watched mother and child, Ava watched her.

She wanted so badly to touch her daughter, to enfold her in a hug tight enough to erase a lifetime of deception. Maybe there were more lies between them than truths, but it didn't mean they couldn't move forward together.

Ava hadn't heard Sophie's newborn cries. Locked up in Taunton when her sister gave birth to Paul's child, she could only imagine being in the room when the little girl released her first wail into the world. But it didn't negate the fact that she'd heard every other kind of cry. She'd suffered the screams of hunger and exhaustion and fright at the vastness of a dark and empty American sky. She'd also rejoiced in the joyful shrieks residing in her heart as permanently as Natalie's midnight laughter and the musical clanging of the most precious brass ring ever forged.

Her heart ached for the baby gulping air in the room next door, and for the death of whom glittered wild in the eyes of Liam LaSalle as he whispered, "She's beautiful, Paleo. St. Agnes will be pleased."

Paleo didn't hear him. She leaned her head against the wall and whispered Peter's name. "She's here. Wake up and see." She tried to cradle the baby when Julian set it in her arms, but she was too weak. In a spreading pool of blood, she looked down at the baby balanced on her lap and thanked Agnes for giving her that moment, even if it was *only* a moment.

Julian sidled up to the window, voice lowered. "She's bleeding badly. She needs to get to a hospital."

"She's not going anywhere," Liam said.

"Then she's going to die. Do you want that?"

"The Lamb was going to kill her anyway," he said

matter-of-factly, and a sorrowful breath jumped up Sophie's throat.

"So it's true," she said. "From the very beginning, you brought me here to kill them. You know what I did to Moira, and you're using me for it."

"Moira? What did you do to Moira?"

"She . . . " Sophie lowered her gaze, but tears spilled nonetheless. "She disappeared."

"She left town," Ava said.

"Yeah but . . . " she sniffled, her voice strained. "Then they found a body in the park."

"It wasn't her. I promise you it wasn't. The police interviewed me about it."

Sophie's jaw dropped. "What? And you didn't tell me?"

"I didn't know you were even worrying about it," Ava squealed. "I thought I might be projecting my anxiety on you, but I couldn't tell you I was projecting because then you'd know—" Her voice caught and she backed farther away as Sophie's focus returned to her husband. "I'm so sorry, sweetheart."

"But . . . I didn't kill her?" she asked shakily.

Liam cleared his throat. "That's not what she said, babe. She said the body in the park wasn't Moira. It doesn't mean you don't have a gift. It doesn't mean you aren't chosen. You have already done great things, and I'm proud to call you my wife."

She grunted. "That's bullshit. I'm just a weapon to you."

"No," he said fondly. "Not *just* a weapon."

His hand shot out for hers, and she swung the platter at his head, narrowly missing his chin and sending him into a stumbling retreat. When he held up a hand in surrender she made contact, smashing his fingers with a satisfying clang. Tripping over his feet, he fell backward against the window where Julian was waiting to catch him.

He closed his hands around Liam's neck and pinned him to the bars while Ava and Sophie collected the bloody twine scattered around the room.

430

Liam laughed. "I can't believe you're on her side, Soph. After everything she did to you—"

"And what have *you* done to me?"

"I've set you on a path to freedom," he said, gagging when Julian tightened his grip.

"Freedom. It's always about freedom with you people." Sophie wound the twine around his wrists and gritted her teeth as she knotted it as tight as possible. He yelped, and Julian squeezed, cutting off his voice when he tried to reply. "But your idea of freedom is obviously different from mine," she continued. "And Mother Agnes's is different from yours." His eyes widened, and she sighed. "Liam, she's playing you just as much as you played me."

Ava handed her more twine, voice lowered. "I tried to tell him."

"I actually don't want to hear anything from you right now," Sophie said coldly and tied Liam's neck to the bars. "I can only handle one liar at a time."

Julian released him, and the color bled back to the boy's face. He winced, struggling to make the sign of the Lamb as he whispered frantic prayers for St. Agnes to save his new bride from herself.

She exhaled heavily. "If you really love me, Liam, you have to stop the ritual. No one else needs to die."

He wriggled closer to her, and the twine sliced his neck. "Oh, but they do. Once the castigation starts, the entire ritual must be performed. You can't let that kind of energy out into the world and not put it back. It could damage the very fabric of existence, and then, not even the great mothers could save us."

"Fine," Ava said, and Sophie shot her a puzzled glare. "Do what you want with your people. Kill them all if it makes your god happy. But we're not your people," she declared. "Sophie, Julian, and me, that baby and its mom if she wants: we're walking out of here."

"The doors are sealed by now," he replied. "No one's getting into or out of this basement for a long time."

As Ava, Sophie, and Julian exchanged worried glances, Paleo Light giggled softly. She wearily patted the baby on her lap and said, "The pool tunnel."

Liam growled, "Shut up, Paleo!" and without thinking, Ava punched him in the face. He howled, and she groaned as she tried to shake the pain out of her fist.

Sophie raised her eyebrows, impressed until Ava noticed. Standing on tiptoes, she peered at Paleo over Liam's head. "What did you say? There's a tunnel out of the pool?"

She nodded woozily and patted the baby's tapestry cocoon. Her eyelids were drifting closed again when the squeal-thud of a steel door opening heralded a cacophony like a pigpen during feeding time. Paleo's eyes snapped open, and her fingers flexed against her crying child when Mother Agnes warbled, "What a beautiful day for a castigation!"

Bundling the baby to her chest, Paleo crawled out of the mire of bodily fluids and headed for the door. Julian tried to stop her, but she smacked him away, mumbling about how Mother Agnes would understand. Her baby was innocent; it deserved the chance to live and cultivate the Lamb's capacity for forgiveness in the hearts of a new generation. Sophie and Ava screamed for her to stay in the room, but she was so sure Mother Agnes would spare her baby's life, she unlocked the door and crawled into the hall.

She met Mother Agnes with bawling worship. The baby cried too, but its wails were far more tormented, as if it could sense its mother's horrible decision in the way Paleo's arms tensed when Mother Agnes raised her cane.

Paleo Light hit the floor with a thud, and the baby's panicked scream tugged Ava and Julian from their respective rooms to the corridor where Mother Agnes was gathering the sopping bundle in her arms.

Julian knelt beside Paleo, who moaned and wept for the Lamb's forgiveness before fading into a tortured sleep.

"What are you doing, Faye?" Ava stepped toward her,

and Mother Agnes nuzzled her lips against the child's sticky forehead.

The terror, the damp, the look of victory on her mother's face: it was Natalie's funeral all over again. Except she couldn't lunge at Faye this time. The threat of the woman's skeletal fingers curling around the baby's soft skull was enough to make her and Julian back away. She sneered in victory as she left her cane behind and walked them into the room, but triumph turned to confusion when she saw Sophie brandishing the blood-stained platter.

"What's going on here?" she demanded. "What happened to your tattoo, Sophie? I thought we talked about this."

"We did. You told me Liam was using me. And I'm not staying married to someone like that, let alone getting a permanent reminder of it."

Liam squeaked at Mother Agnes. "You did what?"

"A misunderstanding," she said, waving away his concern. "Sophie told me she was worried that her lust for other men would get the better of her, but I explained to her that the sanctity of your love would cure her of those filthy thoughts."

"I never said that!" Sophie shouted.

Mother Agnes shrugged at Liam. "She's her mother's daughter, I'm afraid. Ask Avery. Natalie's appetites were insatiable. It's what drove her to pursue her younger sister's boyfriend, then his best friend."

"That's not how it happened," Ava growled. "Don't believe a word she says."

"Oh, but she's supposed to believe *you*?" Mother Agnes snickered. "Sophie, trust me, I have your best interests at heart, just as I had Natalie's, right up to the end."

"When you killed her," Ava said, and Sophie's face blanched in shock. "Whatever you thought about her 'appetites,' at least Natalie could survive them. But she couldn't survive you, Faye."

Mother Agnes's fingertips tensed against the child's

skull, and her rocking turned reckless. "I suggest you free your husband, Sophie. This behavior is unbecoming for someone as blessed as you."

"Just so we're on the same page," Julian started, cracking his knuckles. "You're going to kill that baby unless we untie the other person who threatened to kill that baby?"

Liam hissed, his neck spilling blood as he leaned forward. "Mother Agnes, allow me to castigate these heathens for you myself. Nothing would give me greater pleasure."

Her lip twitched as it curled. "Not even marrying the Lamb? If I remember correctly, you fought pretty hard for that pleasure, Liam. Is that blessing no longer enough for you?"

"There will never be enough honor or pleasure I can feel for St. Agnes, Mother. I am bound to the pursuit, and I will not apologize for it."

"Yes, my dear, that's what worries me." Mother Agnes released the baby's head and smiled. "I must apologize, Sophie. I shouldn't have compared you to your mother, even as a test." When Liam's face scrunched, Mother Agnes sighed. "Yes, it was a test. I said something horrible about your wife, the representation of the Lamb on Earth, and you didn't even flinch to defend her. The pursuit of honor is all well and good, but what use is it when you'd sit idly by while someone, even me, insults your bride?"

"I'm sorry, Mother."

"I'm certain you are." Turning to Sophie, she chirped, "On second thought, let's leave him to pursue his own escape. If it pleases the Lamb, of course."

Sophie adverted her eyes. "It does."

"Good! Now that that's settled, let's head to the pool. Oh, but first . . . " She tapped a finger on the weeping baby's head and bared her teeth. "I'd like to know which one of you called the police."

CHAPTER FIFTEEN

"**W**AS IT YOU, Mr. Archer?"

Ava's heart raced as she fought the urge to find Julian's fingers beside her—not to squeeze for comfort but so she could weave herself into his armor. They were strongest together, flesh against flesh, bone crossing bone, and she didn't want him to feel alone for even one second while Faye Hayworth spit curses on his name.

"I'm sorry to break it to you," she continued, "but it would've been kinder to leave the police out of it. The castigation ceremony was meant to go slow. My children were supposed to be able to take their time. When you called the police, you stole that right from them. Not to mention the lives of those officers."

Sophie stepped forward. "Wait, what are you saying?"

"I'm saying the Choir stood its ground against people who entered without permission, just as we did with your mother and her bodyguard here. Also like them, the officers were not receptive to our beliefs and had to be cleansed for the sake of the ceremony, just as we all shall be. Unfortunately . . . " She made the sign of the Lamb and pressed her hand to the steel door separating them from the pool. "The threat of more police forced us to move quicker than I would've liked."

"What does that mean?" Julian asked.

Paleo and Peter's baby cried, and in a simpering voice, she jiggled the child and said, "It means someone has a heck of a clean-up job ahead of them." She nodded at the door and said, "Sophie, if you wouldn't mind . . . "

The girl started forward, head bowed, but Ava pushed past and stood between her daughter and the door. She didn't wait for permission or beg an apology, but after opening the portal into the chamber stinking of chemicals and bile, apologizing was all she wanted to do for the rest of her life. The stench seared her sinuses and transformed her stomach into a pit of fiery nausea while the ragged screams and frantic splashing from the pool hung like kettlebells in her knees.

It must have hit the others differently, because both Sophie and Julian scrambled to see through the opening for an explanation for the sensory assault, maybe even a way to stop it. Unfortunately, they caught the Choir's song at its denouement, the carnage of which lay before them like a quilt of gore stretching across the stone and into the water.

Only one Choir member remained standing, and not for long. The mild-mannered guitarist Yanosh glanced at them from the edge of the pool, winked with sickening excitement and dove into the foamy liquid choked with bloated bodies.

The corpses floated lazily like petals on a pond until Yanosh pierced the water. His force sent them bobbing into one another and smacking the sides of the pool. While he remained under the surface, drinking it in like a childhood tea party, his brothers and sisters rode the waves like empty beetle shells. But his body soon rose to meet them, his eyes blankly fixed on the ceiling and his hair like silver seaweed in the toxic froth.

Mother Agnes blazed with pride as she made the sign of the Lamb over the pool and swept her gaze across the rest of the graveyard, her focus settling on her granddaughter as Sophie fell sobbing beside a little girl.

Sunny's face was now as round and blue as a storybook moon, and her eyes were as dull as scratched gemstones. Several of her fingers were broken, like she'd spent her last seconds alive in a brawl, and slivers of ceramic stuck out of her forearm. Mugs lay shattered all around them, their names broken and stained and likely forgotten forever now that the only one left to tell their stories was a woman who rarely spoke the truth.

"What did you do to her?" Sophie asked Mother Agnes, chin trembling. "She fought back. She didn't want to die."

"Oh no, she did. Just not like this, mostly likely. And that would be . . ." She waved a skeletal finger mockingly around the room, then pointed at Julian with a snarl. ". . . your fault, Mr. Archer! These people wanted to die with dignity, and you gave them bedlam: the kind of frantic death Avery delivered all those children in Taunton. This was not St. Agnes's intention, nor mine. But we did what had to be done to fulfill the ritual . . . as we all must."

A high-pitched wail suddenly claimed the room, slowly building to a chorus of police sirens that rollercoastered through the bones of those still living.

"You see?" Mother Agnes said. "We were none too soon. They're coming for the rest of us." She reached out to Sophie, who shrank back. "It will take them time to break through, dear, but eventually they will. Who do you think will take the blame? We have to seize this opportunity. We have to take the next step."

Sophie stood, the back of her head aching and her fingers tingling hot. The acrid odors and grisly images came at her so heavy she felt like she was part of a stew in a witch's cauldron: soft and dissolving into the broth of gullibility flavored by those she was meant to lead.

Looking away from Sunny's small body didn't help. There were always more of them, more empty eyes and broken bones. The other new girl, Bella, whom Peter had forbidden Sophie from knowing, was propped against a wall with her empty mug still in hand and the teenager Irina awkwardly collapsed over her legs. Even Garza, whose nose was still bloody from the wallop Sophie had dealt with the platter, had scraped herself off the floor of the room down the hall to join her family in death: one of the few corpses wearing a triumphant smile.

The policemen certainly weren't. The only of the deceased that hadn't died of baptismal poison were peppered with stab wounds and frantic slashes, and they wore the furious shock of someone who wanted to honor the soul through service and ended up disconnected from it, like so many others in that house.

Footsteps thudded above them, and Mother Agnes looked to the ceiling.

"They're in the garden. We don't have much time." Clearing her throat, she readjusted her grip on the baby, then raised it over her head as she proclaimed: "Gather 'round, my children, for the first of the final sacrifices."

Sophie screamed for her to stop, and Mother Agnes chuckled.

"Calm down, you silly goose. I'm just kidding. I wouldn't toss a newborn baby into the water. This ritual is like a baptism. It takes tenderness." She lowered the shrieking infant, rocked it until the shrill noise turned to soft burbling, and shook off her hood like Farrah Fawcett whipping expertly coiffed hair out of her eyes.

Sophie shivered at the action. Playfulness wasn't characteristic of the stoic Mother Agnes, who had previously removed her hood with all the suavity of a diabolical sorcerer stroking a pet cat. But it disturbed Ava even more, because it wasn't something Faye Norton would've done either. Though the woman's attitude resembled Faye's more after the hood fell, such a coltish shimmy was never part of her repertoire. Faye's hair had almost always been slicked back and pinned at the nape of her neck, granting her the "put together" appearance of a woman who would never murder teenagers a few miles from her doorstep, let alone all the people who'd died for her just minutes before.

Seconds later, the girlish glee was gone, and the woman was Faye Norton through and through. That mysterious creature, regal in her brutality, with hands like gnarled twigs that snagged the drapery but whose limbs gave the child still entangled in its umbilical cord the softest cradle, inched closer to the water and slowly extended her arms.

"Grandma, no!" Sophie cried. "You can't do this. This isn't what Agnes of Rome would've done. She didn't even seek punishment for the men who tried to hurt her. If she really is looking down on us, this isn't what she'd want."

"You're right," Faye replied blankly. "But I am not Agnes of Rome. I've known that for a long time. I am the vessel, the harbinger, the procurer. I am the means to which this mad era of war and depravity will end. Because of my hard work, because of my sacrifices, the great mothers will make a better world for you, Sophie. For your children, and for your children's children, I would reform the world."

"I never asked for that."

"Oh, but you did. You've been crying out for it: family, history, horrible and beautiful things to write songs about. Entombed by your mother's fear, you reached across starry skies to find your purpose, and you found me." She faced the pool again and slowly lowered to the floor. "I gave all of myself to the great mothers, to the guides and the gardeners, so the Lamb could return, reap this world of its sinners, and sow peace and chastity back into the fabric of humanity. And I will do it again." Looking down on the baby, she added blissfully, "But you first."

Julian lunged at Faye, but someone else reached her before him.

Paleo screeched as she threw her blood-drenched body at the woman and put herself between her baby and the water. Julian grabbed Faye around the waist while Paleo tried to wrestle the baby free, her face fishy white and feet slipping like crazy on the slick stone floor. She yelped when her heel slid over the lip of the pool and quickly righted herself, but her command over balance was short-lived.

With a grunt, Faye shoved the child into Paleo's arms, causing the parent of the Petaluma chapter to teeter on the edge of the pool. She didn't have a good grip—didn't *want* a good grip as she tilted backward—and floundered with the slippery child in the tapestry, warring between trying to hold on forever and trying to shove her toward safety. In her panic, the tapestry unwrapped, the placenta fell from the bundle, and the little girl was pulled out of Paleo's arms.

When the baby hit the floor, it was still nameless. But when its mother hit the water, everyone knew the child's name was Rachel. Paleo screamed her daughter's name over and over as she resurfaced, floundering to keep her head above water and paddle back to the edge, where Ava and Sophie crouched with hands extended. While Julian gathered up the wailing child and liberated it from the afterbirth using a cop's car key, Faye stood on the lip of the pool, hands in prayer and head bowed.

"Thank you, sister," she said as Paleo began sputtering blood. "You've done so much for the Lamb, and you, more than anyone, have earned this rest. Let go. Your child will be with you soon."

Rachel's name fell like red and yellow leaves coating the autumnal pond in which her mother drowned. Slipping too far for Sophie or Ava to reach, Paleo Light sank between the bodies of those who trusted her, with only a few bubbles rising as the epilogue to her blessed story.

Ava's hand was still extended over the pool, but Sophie had retreated to the wall, where she cowered in black curtains from the wide-eyed man standing in the back corridor, still ripping twine from his wrists.

"Oh my God . . . " Tears ran down Liam LaSalle's cheeks as his gaze devoured the gruesome scene. "Mother Agnes, it's so beautiful. And you, Sophie . . . " He advanced on her, arms open and face blazing with worship, but Ava intercepted him with a ferocious smack across the cheek.

He froze, aghast, and clutched his face as Ava stood her ground.

"Pay her no mind," Faye said. "Come to me, Liam dear."

Sneering at Ava, he marched to Mother Agnes, head lifted in pride, and she took his face into her hands. She kissed the red mark from Ava's strike and sighed.

"You are my most prized child. Since the day we plucked you from that San Francisco gutter, you have been a true and devout follower. You, more than anyone in any Choir house, have honored this community with your service." Pushing the sweaty hair from his forehead, she said, "You should die next."

As police slammed against the steel door at the top of the stairs, Liam nodded to Faye and extended his hand to Sophie.

He said, "It's time, my love," and Faye chuckled, instantly wiping the smile from his face.

As confusion colonized his expression, she continued. "I'm afraid you misunderstood me, Liam. Sophie isn't joining you in the pool. The Lamb and I must stand apart and bear witness to the castigation."

"But she's my wife."

"She is the Lamb first. Tell him, Sophie."

Sophie shook her head. "I don't know what to say. I don't know what you're talking about."

"The carafes are right there, dear. Behind the curtain."

Sophie pulled the black drape aside, revealing two stone carafes along the wall. She opened one and sniffed the contents: earthy like the palm tea she drank her first day in the house, not a hint of the other acidic stenches infesting her senses for the last few hours.

"That concoction will deliver me and the Lamb to our maker," she said. "Once we've witnessed the last castigation, we shall speak the words that make Agnes flesh and blood again, and powerful enough to remake this ruined world. It's a path I'm afraid you can't walk with us, Liam, beloved as you are."

"You're our holy guide. She's the Lamb. If you can't bend some rules, who can?" he asked. "I was given the Lamb as my partner. By Agnes of Rome herself, I was chosen to join my life with hers. If she can't swim into the next life with me, let me drink with her. And with you. It would be my last and greatest honor to die the way you die."

Faye Norton laughed so heartily that Liam actually stumbled backward in shock. Pushing past Ava, he grasped Sophie's hand and towed her between the bodies to the pool side.

"We are one," he said, twisting her wrist until she cried out. "We should die as one."

Faye cackled. "Did you even consummate your union? If I recall correctly, she spent the evening drugged out of her skull. Most of the morning too."

The battering upstairs increased, and Liam growled as he tugged Sophie into a bone-crunching embrace.

"We were together before we got married," he said. "We became one." Spinning her around, he stared into her watering eyes and spoke so fiercely he spattered her face with spit. "Tell her. Tell her what you felt when we made love."

Sophie looked at the floor, her cheeks aflame and the pounding overhead sounding more and more like a grieving widower banging on the lid of his spouse's coffin. She thought she might throw up; not bile and cold turkey, but rocks and earth and all those pretty, wet petals that opened on the ceiling of his Kombi that night.

"Sophie, tell her what happened," he demanded. "Tell her how you blessed me."

She tried to wriggle free, but his wrists locked around her back. "I'm sorry, Liam," she whispered. "I don't remember blessing you. I don't remember any of it."

His face looked like it might crack in half and spill enough tears to drown the rest of them. But instead of cracking, it seemed to sink into itself, as if gathering to propel a spout of fire. He shoved her so hard she nearly fell, but she regained her balance quickly and retreated to the wall as he roared. "You're lying! Why are you lying? You said you loved me! You gave yourself to me!"

"Liam, calm down," Faye said. "You're acting like St. Agnes doesn't know what's best for all of us. It's quite simple. If the Lamb insists you are nothing, then you are nothing. And frankly, the way you're behaving, I'm inclined to agree."

With teeth clenched, he breathed heavily. "You said I was your most prized child."

"And I meant it. But a servant, even a prized one, is not a saint. All the CI in the world couldn't have made you worthy of dying alongside someone like her."

"But *I* found her! Out of everyone searching for her, *I* was the one. Agnes wouldn't let that happen unless I was special."

Faye cocked her head and narrowed her eye as her sweet smile spread to a menacing grin. "If I recall correctly, you thought you found her twice before. Twice before, you claimed to sense the Lamb in the soul of a sixteen-year-old girl named Sophie, and twice before, you married those girls in the hope they were the one we were looking for."

Sophie's stomach turned. "You did what?"

He stared down his nose at her, more frustrated than embarrassed.

"He married them," Faye said.

"Briefly," he grumbled. "We didn't even get to the tattoo stage before I realized I'd been misled."

Julian asked, "What did you do with those girls when you realized your mistake?" But then he looked to the injured baby in his arms and the corpses at his feet and held up his hand. "Never mind. I can guess."

"It wasn't like that," Liam said, eyes wild and mouth frothing.

"Oh it was exactly like that," Faye said. "The simple fact is those girls weren't chosen, and neither were you."

His nostrils flared as he grabbed the other stone carafe. "You're wrong! I was chosen! I am the Lamb's loyal servant! I've lied and bled and killed to deliver her to you, Mother, and I will receive the reward I'm owed."

"You were bait, you stupid boy. Just like you were on the street, reeling in whatever warm body you could to feed your addiction," she said. "Let's not forget who got you clean. Paleo and Peter, under my direct orders, liberated you from that junk, got you fed and clothed and safe from the man who was hunting you, and this is how you thank me?"

"How can you blame him when he sees how you repaid Peter and Paleo?" Ava said. "Or how you repaid my father for staying by your side after so much hatred and grief? Or how you repaid Natalie and Noah for daring to be human beings in love?"

Faye pointed a splintered fingernail at her and hissed. "Stay out of this, Avery. You've killed more people than everyone here combined."

"I never said I didn't."

Sophie threw a mournful gaze at Ava, who bowed her head and balled her fist at her chest.

"Please, Faye," she said softly, "just let it end. You've ruined the poor boy enough."

"Don't you dare speak for me," Liam barked at Ava. "You spent your entire childhood killing and your entire adulthood lying about it. Yes, I was looking for Sophie, but you drove her into my arms, and now you want to act all high and mighty like you'll be the one to save us all? For what? Redemption?" He slithered to her, the carafe shaking in his hand. "I read all about what you did: how you ran away while sick people burned, how you murdered an innocent woman who picked you up hitchhiking. You killed people who tried to help you. Do you really think anything will atone for such a horrendous crime?"

"Ava regrets what she did," Julian said. "She hates herself for it, and she's spent the last fifteen years in therapy trying to make amends."

Sophie turned to her mother, jaw clenched and brow furrowed, but Ava averted her eyes, cheeks aflame. "Is that true?" she asked.

HARES IN THE HEDGEROW

"It's true," Julian replied. "Nights, weekends, whenever she felt the impulse arise, she was in my office, working through it."

Ava wanted so badly to hold Julian at that moment, but she was afraid to move. She felt small and weak with all eyes upon her, like even the tiniest shuffle toward the man she loved might shatter her. Mostly because it was, in that moment, unmistakable that she truly did love him. Against all odds, with all her ghosts, she loved him more than she ever loved the boy from the island. Her stomach burned—not with fire but with light—and she shone like a beacon of hope as she shifted her focus to Faye.

To Ava, the woman was seething, nearly steaming, but her expression was soft and amiable as she sighed at Liam. "You see? Beloved as you are, my doomed daughter, a traitor, a slave to lust, and a disgrace to the saint who chose her, is more blessed than you'll ever be."

Faye beckoned him to hand over the carafe, but he refused. Howling in rage, he flipped it open, pressed it to his lips, and after drinking deep, he charged at Faye. Grasping her by the shoulder, he poured the contents into her mouth. She fought him with little success, and no one moved a muscle to help her despite her begging. When the carafe was empty, he smashed it on the floor, decorating the corpses with shards, and grinned at Faye with a triumphant exhalation.

"Now we'll die together, and we'll see who Agnes of Rome honors in the afterlife."

Sophie looked away, and Faye laughed, and though the realization hit Ava and Julian before Liam, the truth revealed itself when he felt a flush of euphoria instead of nausea.

"It's palm tea," he said, squeezing his eyes shut. "It's not poisoned. It's dosed." His eyes glistened with sorrow as they opened. "You never intended to die with us, did you, Mother?"

Faye wiped her mouth and flashed her shiny fake teeth.

445

"What a smart boy. Now, if you wouldn't mind staying smart a little longer . . . " She gestured to the pool. " . . . so Sophie and I can get out of here."

"Out?" He stumbled back as if punched in the gut. "There's not supposed to be a way out."

"For *you*," Faye said. "For the chosen, the ways out are innumerable. Out of death, out of homes and prisons, out of dead-end lives surrounded by people you pretend to value. There is no place Sophie and I cannot leave . . . even if we built it."

"But once the castigation begins—"

Faye sighed heavily, her patience thinning the more the tea took hold. "That's just a line, dear. Like a million lines you've spouted to get people on our side."

His chin trembling, Liam plucked a stone shard from the floor, yanked Sophie close, and pressed it to her neck. "And how will the chosen one get out of *this*? If I try to shred the Lamb's throat, will St. Agnes stop me? Will you?"

Sophie whimpered his name, and he pressed the shard harder into her flesh.

"I did everything the Choir asked of me. Every choice I've made for the last five years I made in the service of the Lamb. Things that frightened me. Things I regret."

"Things like me?" Sophie mewled, and his grip loosened slightly. "You didn't answer me before. Please, answer me now. Did you ever love me? Or was I just another stupid girl named Sophie who fell for your pretty words?"

His hand shook, and his breath was cold against the blood trickling down her throat. He backed the shard off a bit, but his arm tightened around her waist as he kissed the back of her neck. "No. You aren't like them at all, Soph. I love you. I knew from the moment I saw you we were destined to be together. Twin souls spinning wildly, even destructively, until that night when we became one."

She closed her eyes. He always knew the right thing to say, and the right way to say it. Powerful yet gentle, with a

446

fathomless voice like Jim Morrison, his poetry led her down a mysterious road she thought less traveled, but it had been trod so many times before, by people just as weak and gullible as she'd been. She was so consumed by his adoration, along with her anger and doubt toward her mother, that she would've given up everything for a new life, far from the cube on Mohr Lane, to live with a man who was still threatening to shred her throat while professing his continued love.

"Malarkey."

Sophie's focus shot to the steel door, where Moira Shunn's rotten neck wound flexed like a bad memory as she scraped herself from the sticky floor.

447

CHAPTER SIXTEEN

"**H**E DOESN'T LOVE YOU,**"** Moira wheezed as she shambled forward. "He's conning you, sweetheart. If you want my opinion on it—"

"I don't," Sophie spat. "What are you doing here, anyway? My mom told me I didn't kill you. She said you're probably not even dead."

Moira Shunn's corpse shuddered in delight, and her head lolled as she hissed, "Your *mom* . . . " With joints crackling like burning straw, she shuffled to Sophie and laughed acerbic breath in her face. "I love how naive you are. A normal girl would've never let her mother imprison her without cause. A normal girl wouldn't have married a near-stranger because he liked the same music . . . or claimed to," she mumbled. "I mean, how hard is it to memorize lyrics and trivia? And you just . . . gave it up."

"Stop it! You're not real!"

"Except I've got you yelling at the top of your lungs, which is pretty good for a ghost and extremely impressive for someone who's not real. A normal girl wouldn't even respond." With her blue lips close to Sophie's ear, she added, "But you're not normal, are you? There aren't enough mourners treading to and fro to help sense penetrate the funeral in your brain. You're doomed, Sophie Marie Francis. Infected. Broken. Or as these wackos prefer to say, *blessed*. You might as well lean into it."

Sophie squinted, and the woman's pale eyes flashed with lightning color. "You're not Moira. Who are you really?"

448

The corpse shrugged. "It's hard to tell these days. Everything's so fragmented, so scattered. But we can piece it back together, you and me. Would you like that? The truth about who I am. Who you are. What's inside us."

As blood dripped down her collarbone, she whispered, "Yes."

"Good. Then we need to get you out of here."

"How?"

Wiggling her sunken nose, she flashed a mouth of rotten gums and wheezed. "Liam is loyal to the Lamb. So *be* the Lamb. You have the power, not Mother Agnes. She's tired and tripping, and if you expect to get out of this alive, you can't depend on her. *We*," she said, batting sporadic eyelashes, "can't depend on her. Not anymore. You are the true vessel. Your gifts, your music, your fire . . . you alone can save us."

"Us?" She started to look to Ava, but Moira grabbed her face and hissed so violently Sophie tasted the woman's putrid saliva on her lips.

"This is bigger than them. Wider. Deeper. You have to let them go. But you need to let go of yourself first. Give in to the lie, and I will give you the truth."

When Moira released her, Sophie swiveled to Liam and spoke with such confidence she hardly recognized her own voice.

"I believe you," she said. "My love, my husband, we are destined to be together."

Ava shouted, "Sophie, you can't!" while Faye cackled like a dying hyena.

Folding her hand over Liam's cold fingers, Sophie leaned against him, and though it drove the ceramic shard deeper into her, it also drove her deeper into his expanding mind.

His heart raced. His panicked breath gusted her hair. But the more she caressed his hand at her neck, the more he calmed.

In that foul coffin packed with corpses and danger on

all sides, Sophie Francis wriggled her fingers into the wet earth of her soul and plucked out a surprising tranquility she allowed to run through her like a hapless weed. But it was a weed with heavenly blooms and thorns like pitons, and it grew in time with the song rising and rolling off her lips with more skill and courage than any that came before. And though she made Liam sway with the music of her words, her gaze fell upon the woman who'd done her best to raise her.

"Listen to me," she said softly. "You knew what I was before I did and loved me harder because of it. You loved me like something ancient and rare, like a pyramid—you worshipped the surface beauty but also the secrets, the hidden dead and all their treasures. And even though the secrets have hurt me, I don't blame you for any of this, because I see now the kind of life I would've had without you." Tears rolled down her cheeks as she stared into Ava's eyes. "You saved me. You could've just run away, many times, but you always came back for me. You refused to live without me. And I've done nothing but hurt you." Lowering her gaze, she whispered, "I'm sorry for what I said about our first night together, Liam. It's true, I don't remember it, but I wish I did."

He dropped the shard and twirled her to face him. She tried to look deep into his eyes, but his pupils were fat and shaking, and the harder he stared the more he perspired. His gaze jumped to the blood trickling down her chest, and his dry lips parted. He was hard. He was hungry. He was begging to be blessed, some way, any way.

As the police rammed the steel kitchen door, Sophie Francis touched his face and lifted her voice to the heavens.

"I am the Lamb," she declared. "I am Agnes of Rome reborn, chosen to deliver us into an age of kindness and joy, of chastity and light, where we shall worship at the altar of pride, for shame shall sink as hard and fast as sin."

Faye laughed, her eye rolling so violently in her skull she appeared to have popped a blood vessel. "Do you see?!" she squealed at Ava. "Do you see the greatness you nearly stole from the world when you ripped her from my arms? You will see more, I guarantee you that, Avery. The glory of Agnes on Earth. The ending, the remaking. All will be tested. All will be tended." Giggling like a brainless child, she reached out to her granddaughter in camaraderie. "This is just the beginning, *cordeirinha*."

But Sophie did not return her excitement. Turning from Liam, she said, "Keep your distance, Faye Norton," and all joy vanished from the woman's expression.

"How dare you . . . "

Sophie faced her, chin lifted, and eyes wide with warning. "Do not speak again. Do not move. Do not pretend I'm causing you pain when you can't even feel it. You wanted me to watch you, to leave this place with you, leave everything I dreamt of to *become* you, but I can't. I can only follow Agnes of Rome, and you said yourself, you are not Agnes of Rome."

Faye tried to answer, but her teeth floated around her mouth, garbling her words. She tried to approach Sophie, but balance was a tenuous thing, and she nearly fell when she stepped forward.

"You're a liar, and everyone here knows it. It was the last thing a lot of these people learned," she said, her sad gaze dropping to the bodies. "And I won't let you inflict your lies on anyone else." She scanned her the woman's trembling face, every gnarled scar given to her by little Avery Norton, every wrinkle bestowed by age, and every smile she'd worn too easily on a day filled with death. "You're finished, Faye. You're not our guide, not our mother. And remember, if the Lamb says you're nothing, you're nothing. It's quite simple."

Faye growled. "St. Agnes came to *me*." She beat her chest. "This all started with *me*."

"And it will end with you, Grandmother."

The expression that seized control of Faye's face was one Ava knew well. She looked the same the day the police questioned her about the bodies in the cellar. Through the lingering haze of the spell that sent her into the crypt that day, Ava saw the bloody satisfaction that fit her mother's face so well, clear as mismatched dots on bad rabbits. The look was offense and anger, but it was also the unwavering faith that she, Faye Hayworth, whom Agnes of Rome marked for glory, would walk away from this a free woman.

Sophie read the same story in her grandmother's appearance. Without a lifetime of learning how dangerous Faye's smile could be, she advanced on the old woman with a look that blazed its own courageous malice.

"I was afraid of myself," she started. "Of what I saw and felt when the Lamb woke inside me. I was afraid of what I was missing, what I'd lost without ever knowing I'd lost it, but I'm not afraid anymore. Agnes of Rome told me her secret."

Faye snorted. "And what's that?"

Sophie dragged her fingers through her blood, and when she lifted her scarlet hands, the voices of her favorite poets rolled like salvation off her lips. "There are better ways to control people than death. That's why Agnes spared those men's lives—because something deeper in them was not spared. For the rest of their lives, they were beset by failure and betrayal and lost love. For what they did to her, they suffered until the end of their days. As will you."

"What are you going to do? Kill your own grandmother?"

"No. Agnes says you're not blessed enough to die for her. She says you should die alone, weeping in a dark cell, knowing that God and the great mothers have forgotten your name." She turned to Liam. "My love. My partner and my child. Drink from me. Taste, for the rest of time, the Lamb on your lips, and be my champion."

He rushed to her, dutifully licking the blood from her fingers, and as he sank to his knees, Faye watched in blanching horror.

"The garden is dead," Sophie decreed, "and it's time to uproot the cause." When she whispered in Liam's ear, he arose like a sentinel, strong as the steel door slowly bending under the officers' force.

Faye screamed for him to stop as he advanced. She fell to the floor, her hands moving wild across the tiles as she retreated, but under the spell of the palm tea and Sophie's musical voice, Liam persisted. He grabbed hold of Faye's wrist, tugged her to her feet, and pinned her arms behind her back.

"You horrible traitor!" she shrieked. "I gave you everything! There's not a drop of love or knowledge in you that doesn't originate with me."

"Nor hate," Ava said, and Faye's teeth chattered in rage.

"If it weren't for my hate, you'd have nothing, Avery. If it weren't for all the *me* in *you*, you wouldn't have Sophie, wouldn't have the Lamb, and you sure as shit wouldn't have your little doctor friend."

"Her name is Ava," Sophie said, and the breath left Ava's lungs in the most delicious way: a moment of serenity before the door at the top of the stairs smashed in, and police barreled down to tackle the next.

"You idiots. Do you really think you'll be better off in the hands of the law? Even if they believe you weren't part of all this, once they find out who 'Ava Francis' really is, she's going to jail for the rest of her life. They might even send her to the chair. And then what? What becomes of a baby lamb without flock or shepherd?"

"She's not a baby lamb," Ava said, and standing face to face with her mother, she hooked her fingers on the chain around Faye's neck and pulled so hard she felt the links tear her mother's papery flesh. Pocketing the brass ring, she said, "She's a hare. And she'll run like one. Eyes open and unafraid."

"And I'll be by her side every step of the way," Liam said, his pupils like swollen cherries.

453

"Just as you were by mine?" Faye asked, and he deflated with a whimper. "Look at me, Liam, as you once did, before she tricked you into this madness."

With a grunt, he turned her around and stared down at the gnarled creature he once revered with all his heart. He couldn't understand how swiftly his admiration had changed, or why this new age of kindness and chastity was so dark and loud and stunk of death. And so many slack faces. Children's faces. Children who called him "Lee-Lee" and opened their tender minds to him.

He was already crying when Faye Norton slipped her hand free and plunged a ceramic shard into his neck. With a guttural gasp, he stumbled backward, pulling out the fragment and releasing a geyser of blood. He apologized as he wilted to the floor, and Sophie ran to him, weeping in spite of everything he'd done. As he closed his eyes, the wound said, "I love you," and when Sophie kissed the wilted wet blossom Liam LaSalle had become, she once again tasted blood and the boy.

"He deserved it," Faye hissed at her. "You know he did."

Sophie nodded, then looked to her mother. With all the force of the police battering the door, Ava suddenly charged at Faye. Knocking her to the ground, she grabbed what little hair remained and slammed her skull on the tile.

Voices built like thunder behind the door, and the scrapes and squeals of the police's breaching tools prying through the steel sounded like ravenous vultures picking apart a skull. They were using fire too; Ava felt it boring through the steel as she stood from her mother's slack body and beheld the crossroads between a life she'd dreamt of in Taunton and a life that would never let her breathe free air again.

It wasn't a hard decision, but it was one she never foresaw making. Even with all the times Julian made her say she deserved peace and forgiveness, she didn't believe it until that moment. Surrounded by the dead, with fire at her back, Ava was seventeen again, and she had the opportunity to make a different choice. One of the door hinges popped off and the metal folded inward, allowing a glimpse of the police battering the blockade.

"Sophie, the tunnel Paleo mentioned. Do you know where it is?"

"Yes, behind that tapestry," she said, pointing across the pool.

"Good. Give me the baby, Julian."

Puzzled, he handed it over, and she tenderly curled her hand around the back of its head. "Get Sophie out of here. Get her somewhere safe. Out of California if you have to. You were planning on moving, anyway."

"Ava—"

"I love you," she said tearfully. "Julian Archer, I love you more than I thought possible. I didn't think there was even room enough for love with all the pain, but you proved me wrong . . . about so many things. Thank you for that. And thank you for this, your final lesson."

Realization darkened his face, and he shook his head desperately. "No, Ava. Throwing yourself to the wolves isn't my lesson."

"But it is," she said, stroking his cheek. "If I hadn't fallen in love with you, I never would've understood what it'll take for me to finally feel human again. Until I've paid my debt to the many people whose lives I extinguished, I will never be anything but a torch for ghosts. They'll find me wherever I go, just as they find her." Glancing at Faye panting on the floor, she said, "I need to do this."

He clutched her hair and kissed her forehead, and tears ran unchecked down his cheeks as he sobbed. "I'm not leaving without you."

"I know," she said, her hand upon his chest.

He bowed his head and choked back a sob as Ava ran her fingers through his hair. "But we were so close," he whispered.

"Yes, we were. That's why I believe it'll happen again." Gazing into his trembling eyes, she said, "Do you?"

He kissed her and wiped fresh tears from her face. "I believe in you, Ava."

"Me too. At long last. Because of you."

His voice faltered and he gritted his teeth. "Goddammit. I'm going to miss you so much."

She chuckled. "You'll miss bruises and bloody lips?"

"You bet your ass I will."

They embraced, and he kissed her again, holding on, both of their lips fearful of release until the steel-shuddering blast of the battering ram knocked the door off its hinges and wedged it in its track.

Ava followed Sophie and Julian away from the door, around the pool to the tapestry hiding the secret hatch in the wall. Julian pried it open and beckoned Sophie in, but she didn't move.

She stared at Ava Francis as if seeing her for the first time. This liar, this killer, this tormented woman who hadn't known how to raise a teenage girl because she didn't get to be one: she was nothing Sophie thought she was.

With a pained howl, she threw herself into Ava's arms, which closed tighter than ever around her back. Their twin heartbeats found each other in the chaos, the same blood pumping in rhythm with a new future mere seconds before it pounded down the door.

"Your parents trusted me to protect you," Ava whispered. "I'm sorry I failed, and I'm sorry I kept them from you. I promise you, when I'm able, I'll tell you everything. I'll tell you how much your father loved me, how much I loved your mother, and how much they both loved you."

When they broke apart, all that remained between the Francis women was the truth and a brass ring. Ava dangled it before Sophie's eyes just as she'd done the day they fled Massachusetts, and hanging it around her neck, Sophie clamped the ring to her heart.

"I already know how much my mom loves me," she said. "And I love you too."

456

Faye gurgled as she lifted her bloody broken head. Spotting them across the pool, she wailed and pulled herself over the tiles like a beached mermaid.

"Take them, Agnes!" she screamed. "Reach inside and pull out all the sin. Before the end, purify them with blessed fire!"

The water rippled, and from the toxic depths, a hand emerged, slender and slick fingers that beckoned to Faye. But it did not belong to Agnes of Rome. When the woman's face surfaced, Faye recoiled and tried to scurry away but found she couldn't gather enough strength to stand.

Amelia Hayworth couldn't stand anymore either, but she floated perfectly well between the bodies in the pool. As did Father Marcelo Melo, whose hands ventured over Amelia's body, acutely visible beneath her soaked white Choir gown. And while he kissed her neck, she wrapped her wrinkled fingers around her daughter's twisted ankle and pulled her toward the pool.

"No! Don't touch me!" she squealed. "You're filthy! You're poison!"

"You're the poison, *cordeirinha*," Marcelo said, "and we've come to draw you from this world like a holy poultice."

Kicking and flailing, she screamed. "You never understood what was in me, and you hated me for it!"

"No, child," Marcelo said. "We hated you because we knew exactly what was in you. There is no glory in your heart, Faye, no harbinger for salvation. There is only death, and it runs too deep for you to ever neutralize. You're weak, little lamb, and you always have been. It's as clear as the scars on your face."

"Weak?!" Faye roared. "Does this look weak?!" Hooking her fingers into the marred roll of skin along her forehead, she dragged her nails down her temples, her cheeks, her neck. With each ribbon of shredded flesh, another face brightened in the water. With each lump of tissue that hit her lap, another child sat up to behold her strength.

"Nothing's too deep to root out," she shouted as the dead crawled toward her. "No garden dies forever. The *world* is a garden!" The blood loss hit her like a hammer, and she pitched forward. Her lolling gaze drifted to Ava across the teeming water of corpses, and as she wilted to her side, still faintly clutching her mangled face, Ava whispered to herself: "It must be tended."

The sound of splitting steel made the trio by the hatch jump, and with a final embrace, Sophie Francis dove, weeping, into the tunnel. Ava squeezed Julian's hand once more, something that usually made her ghosts vanish, but when he closed himself inside the passage and she faced the buckling basement door, every ghost she'd ever seen appeared before her.

For the first time in ages, Paul Dillon was a young boy, clean and bright as any sunrise climb over a gingerbread roof. And Natalie, cool Natalie, with waves of blond hair, gave her a sweet but devious wink, the way she did during games of hide-and-seek when they were kids. Then there was Flint, with eyes like firecrackers, and Frankie who taught her how to foxtrot. And her father, a man she barely knew, a man *Faye* barely knew, who seemed just as much a pawn in this dangerous game as any of his daughters.

She wasn't afraid as she walked back to them, the baby burbling in her arms as they crowded around her. They touched her back and kissed her cheeks, and there was so much warmth in them that a new fire began within her, and she stood beside her mother like a pillar of light.

The door collapsed in with a clang, and officers swarmed in with pistols drawn. A few choked back vomit and others turned from the scene completely, but the policewoman who trained her gun on Ava didn't hesitate.

"Hand over the baby."

Ava slowly extended her arms, and another cop collected the infant while the policewoman cuffed Ava's hands behind her back. She was forced to the floor, her cheek pressed to the bloody concrete as an officer shoved

Faye into the same position, his knee planted in the small of her back.

She awoke with a start. "Don't touch me, Marcelo! I'm not your whore! I'll never be your whore! I'm clean now! I dug out the bad water, and I'm clean!"

She growled as the man smashed her ravaged face against the tile, but she eventually quieted and found Ava's gaze in the madness.

"You filthy girl," she hissed. "You did this to us."

"Yes," she said. "I did this to us."

"You'll regret it. One day soon, you'll see what a stupid choice this was. It won't stop what's coming."

As the officer yanked Faye from the floor and pushed her to the door, she shouted, "Do you hear me, Avery? You will burn for this!"

It was the first time in nearly three decades that she believed her mother completely. As the police escorted them from the Choir of the Lamb's baptismal pool, the fire raged so bright within her that sparks jumped off her skin. Like little rabbits, they bounded and tracked firelight across the crypt, each their own little blaze but still part of the original. She'd tried all her life to snuff those flames, and now she saw how foolish it was. They were part of another fire, something bigger and brighter than she'd ever be. For better or worse, the flames inside her would never diminish, and for that, for the first time, little Ava Francis was grateful.

459

CHAPTER SEVENTEEN

HE TUNNEL ENDED at an abandoned farm where a few goats still gnawed at dead grass. Sophie and Julian didn't speak until they were outside, gulping fresh air and squinting back at the Choir house crawling with police.

As Sophie stared teary-eyed at the officers pushing the Martha's Vineyard murderesses to their cars, Julian tore a blanket from a clothesline and wrapped it around her. The blanket was thin and threadbare, but the moment it hit her back she collapsed to the hard dry earth.

"She did the right thing," Julian said, his voice wavering as if even he didn't believe it.

"But will it matter?" Sophie asked. "After all this, will any of our lives be better? What will they do with her? What will happen to me?" Her breath became rapid, and Julian crouched in front of her, his soothing voice slowing her panic.

"I'm going to take you away from here," he said. "I'm going to keep you safe, just like she wanted. It's all she ever wanted."

Peering toward the house, she whispered. "Will you tell me about her?"

"I think Ava's the better one to tell you about her childhood."

"I already know about her childhood. I want to know who she was with you." She looked up at him, this man who loved her mother despite everything he'd seen, and he exhaled, one side of his mouth twitching into a tiny smile.

"To be honest, she mostly talked about you."

It was an icicle to the heart, spreading brutal cold throughout her body. It paralyzed her so completely that, as much as she wanted to, she couldn't mourn everything she'd lost that day. She couldn't beat the ground or rip out her hair or weep herself into a barren husk of a girl.

A girl. What a compact word for someone with so many unwieldy pieces, especially ones that became flintstones when mismatched. But "woman" wasn't right either, and "human" felt as foreign as "the Lamb" the first time they pinned it to her heart.

She gritted her teeth and clenched her belly, and the grief that cycloned inside her tumbled all those unwieldy pieces until they glinted and set her skin aflame. The soil beneath her palms was soft then, warm and teeming with whispering life. It told her she could end the pain if she wished, maybe even the lives of the people taking her mother away. The power was within her, swimming in every cell that was and would be. And she knew it didn't come from Agnes of Rome or any Christian saint. It was something else entirely, and now she was too.

Dangerous ambition billowed with the fire, lifting her from the ground and starting her back toward the farmhouse, but when Julian grabbed her hand, she stopped. When he squeezed it, she turned. And when pain flooded through her like a river through a slipshod dam, her fiery thoughts melted into music.

Maybe she'd never feel like a girl again, or even like a woman, but she had to find her way back to humanity. And she would do it through fire and song.

None of them could rekindle the lives they'd extinguished, but those lives also wouldn't be forgotten. Each was a petal of the flowering inferno that grew rampant in them all. Norton, Francis, Hayworth, and Dillon: Sickness, spell, saint, and death.

Like her mother, grandmother, and aunt before her, Sophie possessed an internal tinderbox capable of delivering either destruction or illumination. What she'd seen in the pool wasn't a hallucination. It was real and hungry and inevitable, and she refused to fear it anymore.

Each spark courted her like a new lover and sang of a heritage glowing just under the surface of a secret garden. And somehow, as she held the doctor's hand, she heard the songs of her mother and grandmother. There were stories in those melodies, as much light as ash, and though the flames still frightened her, she relished the sound of them crackling and crooning inside.

To heal, she had to listen.

To be free, she had to sing along.

To be human, she had to burn.

ACKNOWLEDGEMENTS

What a long strange (sometimes painful) trip it's been. First off, I need to thank my husband Dave for his patience and grace over the last seven years of working to get this book out into the world. The way he showered me with sunny thoughts and support throughout rewrites, publication changes, and my nonstop jabbering about characters he doesn't know nearly as well as I do means everything to me, especially as we mourned our cat Tyler during and after the first draft of this book. He is everything an artist could ask for in a partner, and I'm eternally grateful I have his love and encouragement.

Thank you also to Pedro Proença for his invaluable help with the Portuguese portions of this book. It was extremely important to me to honor the Portuguese Americans who've been an integral part of Martha's Vineyard's culture for so long, and I couldn't have done it without the time and energy he dedicated to this crucial section of the island's story.

Thank you to Max and Lori at Perpetual Motion Machine Publishing / Ghoulish Books for taking a chance on these books. I had no illusions about how difficult it might be to find a publisher willing to re-release Rabbits in the Garden and finally put out Hares in the Hedgerow, and since they were my first choice, I feel so incredibly lucky and appreciative to be working with them again on these bonkers books.

And lastly, but most importantly, thank you to the readers who've been following Avery Norton's story since

its first publication in 2011. I probably wouldn't have
written the sequel if folks hadn't asked me over and over
to do so, and I'm so glad I did. Despite many hiccups,
Hares is one of my favorites to this day, and I have
everyone who's supported me over the years to thank for
that. And who knows what the future holds? There are lots
of tunnels left to explore in this warren . . .

ABOUT THE AUTHOR

Jessica McHugh is a novelist, a 2x Bram Stoker Award®-nominated poet, & an internationally-produced playwright running amok in the fields of horror, sci-fi, young adult, and wherever else her peculiar mind leads. She's had twenty-nine books published in fourteen years, including her bizarro romp, *The Green Kangaroos,* her YA series, *The Darla Decker Diaries*, and her Elgin Award nominated blackout poetry collections, *A Complex Accident of Life* and *Strange Nests*. For more info about publications and blackout poetry commissions, please visit McHughniverse.com.

SPOOKY TALES FROM GHOULISH BOOKS

☐**BELOW | Laurel Hightower**
ISBN: 978-1-943720-69-9 $12.95
A creature feature about a recently divorced woman trying to survive a road trip through the mountains of West Virginia.

☐**MAGGOTS SCREAMING! | Max Booth III**
ISBN: 978-1-943720-68-2 $18.95
On a hot summer weekend in San Antonio, Texas, a father and son bond after discovering three impossible corpses buried in their back yard.

☐**LEECH | John C. Foster**
ISBN: 978-1-943720-70-5 $14.95
Horror / noir mashup about a top secret government agency's most dangerous employee. Doppelgangers, demigods, and revenants, oh my!

☐**RABBITS IN THE GARDEN | Jessica McHugh**
ISBN: 978-1-943720-73-6 $16.95
13-year-old Avery Norton is a crazed killer—according to the staff at Taunton Asylum, anyway. But as she struggles to prove her innocence in the aftermath of gruesome murders spanning the 1950s, Avery discovers there's a darker force keeping her locked away . . . which she calls "Mom."

☐**PERFECT UNION | Cody Goodfellow**
ISBN: 978-1-943720-74-3 $18.95
Three brothers searching the wilderness for their mother instead find a utopian cult that seeks to reinvent society, family . . . humanity

☐**SOFT PLACES | Betty Rocksteady**
ISBN: 978-1-943720-75-0 $14.95
A novella/graphic novel hybrid about a seemingly psychotic woman who suffers a mysterious head injury.

☐ **HARES IN THE HEDGEROW | Jessica McHugh**

ISBN: 978-1-943720-76-7 $21.95

15 years after the events in *Rabbits in the Garden*, Avery Norton is a ghost. 16-year-old Sophie Dillon doesn't know anything about the alleged murderer, yet she's haunted nightly by the same dark urges, which send her on a journey to uncover her past with the Norton family and to embrace the future with her spiritual family, the Choir of the Lamb. But Sophie's devotions can't protect her from the ghosts waiting in the wings. After all, she's the one they've been waiting for.

Not all titles available for immediate shipping. All credit card purchases must be made online at GhoulishBooks.com. Shipping is 5.80 for one book and an additional dollar for each additional book. Contact us for international shipping prices. All checks and money orders should be made payable to Perpetual Motion Machine Publishing.

Ghoulish Books
PO Box 1104
Cibolo, TX 78108

Ship to:

Name _____

Address _____

City_____State_____Zip _____

Phone Number _____

Book Total: $_____

Shipping Total: $_____

Grand Total: $_____

Patreon:
www.patreon.com/pmmpublishing

Website:
www.PerpetualPublishing.com

Facebook:
www.facebook.com/PerpetualPublishing

Twitter:
@PMMPublishing

Newsletter:
www.PMMPNews.com

Email Us:
Contact@PerpetualPublishing.com

CPSIA information can be obtained
at www.ICGtesting.com
Printed in the USA
BVHW080103160223
658636BV00022B/411

9 781943 720767